Anne Marsh writes sex[...] romances—because the[...] more alpha male. She s[...] getting laid off from her [...] quickly decided happily-ever-afters trumped software manuals. She lives in North Carolina with her two kids and five cats.

USA TODAY bestselling author **Jamie K. Schmidt** is known for her erotically charged romances. As a number one Amazon bestseller and a 2018 Romance Writers of America RITA® finalist in erotica, Jamie writes daily, drinks lots of tea and sneaks away to play World of Warcraft whenever she makes her deadlines. Along with her husband and twelve-year-old son, Jamie lives in Connecticut with her rescue pup Romeo. You can find Jamie on Twitter at @jamiekswriter and on Facebook at jamie.k.schmidt.1.

If you liked
Hot Boss and *Wild Wedding Hookup*
why not try

At Your Service by A.C. Arthur
Guilty Pleasure by Taryn Leigh Taylor

Also by Anne Marsh

Her Intern
Hookup

Discover more at millsandboon.co.uk

HOT BOSS

ANNE MARSH

WILD WEDDING HOOKUP

JAMIE K. SCHMIDT

MILLS & BOON

First Published in Great Britain 2020
by Mills & Boon, an imprint of HarperCollins*Publishers*
1 London Bridge Street, London, SE1 9GF

Hot Boss © 2020 Anne Marsh

Wild Wedding Hookup © 2020 Jamie K. Schmidt

ISBN: 978-0-263-27759-3

Printed and bound in Spain
by CPI, Barcelona

HOT BOSS

ANNE MARSH

MILLS & BOON

PROLOGUE

SOME WOMEN DREAM of marrying Prince Charming. They fantasize about the slow, stately march up the aisle of a medieval cathedral, the big white dress and a rock the size of Gibraltar on their ring finger. Molly, my ex-wife, once admitted under the influence of tequila shooters that she phoned Westminster Abbey—a transatlantic call—at the age of twelve because she wanted to save the date. Ten years in advance. And her parents did *not* have an international calling plan. It took her years to pay off that adventure.

Princes don't do it for me. More to the point, when I was twenty-one and naked on a Santa Cruz beach, I was just glad I'd dodged a royal bullet, because if Molly had truly wanted an English peer and a glass-carriage wedding, I would have moved to London and made it happen. That's what you do when you love someone. You keep that someone safe and deliver her dreams to her, gift-wrapped with a big-ass bow. I'm not sure how I feel about ribbons on my dick, but I was definitely willing to find out back then.

"I don't suppose you'd marry me?" I whispered against her ear. "So we could stay like this forever?"

"You're asking me now?" She grinned up at me, heels digging into my ass as her hips moved in a way guaranteed to make me forget both graduation the next day and my big financial plans for our future. "Pretty sure we can't stay *exactly* like this forever."

Counteroffering is an art form. "Mostly forever."

I let my mouth—and my tongue—underscore my point. She groaned something. My name, a few cute curses—Molly was opposed to swearing—and then that one word. *Yes.*

I remember that night on the beach, the beginning of forever. What I didn't know then was that forever would last nine years… 108 months… 3285 days. More than five million minutes. All that time and I didn't see the end coming. Imagine you're reading a book and there's another half inch of paper, or twenty percent left in your e-reader, so you're settling in, getting comfortable because this is clearly going to be the best ending ever, and then *bam*. The end. The story's done and you're left wondering just how much damage hurling the e-reader at your drywall will cause. That was our story, Molly and me. Boy meets girl in college and falls in love. He proposes on a beach and they get married. Then they're supposed to spend the next sixty years having hot sex, watching each other's back and popping out a few Mini-Mes along the way. I wasn't stupid. I knew it wouldn't always be easy or fun. Marriage is like a roller coaster. You buy your ticket and then, once you're on, you're *on*. You don't hop off at the top or in the dips. You ride for as long as it takes and you're grateful for each exhilarating, wonderful, scary-as-hell second.

We got married in an outdoor chapel surrounded by California redwoods and our friends and families, and then we got on with the business of living. I started a venture capital firm with a college friend and made money; Molly earned a PhD in English. While I was busy settling down, my friends were playing the field. You've met them. Devlin King is scary smart, a brilliant programmer with a Machiavellian streak. He'd never hooked up with the same woman more than once until he fell for a fellow start-up entrepreneur and accidentally-on-purpose spent the summer working as her intern.

Dev's dick was so popular it had its own Instagram…until he met Lola and suddenly he got the appeal of monogamy. It's not that you *can't* bang other women—it's that you don't want to because those other women aren't *her*. Your one and only. The woman who makes you look up and drool like Pavlov's dog when she waltzes through the door and for whom you'd do anything—hot sex on the beach, excruciating family dinners, half-assed home repairs, or volunteer to go and kick the ass of anyone and everyone dumb enough to hurt her feelings.

The third in our triumvirate fell hard, too. Like Dev, Max O'Reilly wasn't in the business of relationships. In fact, he was so averse that he created Billionaire Bachelors, a dating app to connect to the many tech billionaires of Silicon Valley, including himself. He'd also launched Kinkster, mostly so he could order kinky-sex hookups the same way he ordered in Chinese food and pizza. A ballet dancer and influencer named Maple had changed his mind and he claimed to be a happy, happy man about that course reversal.

Take a note and remember that app name.

It'll come up again.

Most days I was too busy working and plotting to take over the world, one disruptive start-up at a time, to think about Molly and me. We loved each other. We talked. Even at the end, we still had amazing sex, because practice does make perfect. Or maybe it's just that I was willfully blind and not ready to admit that something wasn't quite right. The realization isn't like a dam-bursting hurricane that sweeps in and wipes out your town, while you huddle on the roof and hope to God you haven't pissed off the local search-and-rescue team lately because you need saving. It's slower, a steady chipping away at some essential piece of Molly and me.

I never saw it coming.

When Molly and I ended, my friends were there for me, Hazel leading the pack. Of course, Hazel being Hazel, she wasn't rubbing my back or listing the million ways Molly would regret ending our marriage. She just insisted that I look forward, not back. Keep moving toward the future because, she said, not even I could fund a company that would successfully invent a time machine so I could go back and fix where things had gone wrong. She kicked my ass and I liked it, and that led to kissing—

And that was where I made my big mistake. I thought there could only be one The One. I thought her name was Molly and that I'd met her and loved her and it was game over, but sometimes the universe is generous and offers second chances. I was just too dumb to see it, so I took her first offer when I should have held out for more. Because it didn't take too many months for me to realize that Hazel was a unicorn.

No, she's not a mythical animal. Not even close. She's gorgeous and bold and totally sure of herself, but she's thankfully no virgin lover, because I was already on my second chance even if I didn't know it. A unicorn is the ultimate fantasy of the VC world—like banging triplet gymnasts with DDD boobs. When a start-up company goes public and is valued at more than a billion dollars, you've found your unicorn. There aren't many of them and they're rare, but if you back one, you're a guaranteed legend and a filthy rich bastard.

When you find a potential unicorn, you thank your lucky stars and you put in the work to make it happen.

You do whatever it takes.

You *make* it happen.

You hold on.

CHAPTER ONE

Ten months ago...

"HARD AND FAST. Come on, big guy." Hazel sucks in a breath. "Almost there."

I brace my arms on either side of her. My nose crinkles as her hair tickles me. "If it rises too fast, it's just gonna run out of steam and collapse. I'm in this for the long term."

Hazel makes a mock-shocked face, her eyes meeting mine. "Mr. Reed, do I hear an innuendo?"

I highly doubt I need to answer that question, but I wink at her because that's how we play the game. Hazel's good people and we've known each other since college, after all. "Ms. Coleman, you most definitely do."

Yesterday I was a filthy rich bastard. Today? I, Jack Reed, am the filthiest, richest bastard of them all. People dream of hitting it big—winning the lottery, cashing in at the racetrack, maybe inheriting a secret stock fortune from good old Aunt Betty. Those aren't bad ways to fill your bank account, but trust me, doing it by using your head, by earning every penny, nickel and dime, is the best. You're in control, you call the shots. The lucky ticket or racetrack bet? Just dumb luck—and luck is for losers.

The New York Stock Exchange is minutes away from recording the final trade of the day and everyone at the venture capital firm of Coleman and Reed is glued to their laptops and CNBC, watching what our latest start-up to IPO trades for. Our firm has spent the last three years mentoring the start-up and pouring cash into it. We found them a kick-ass CEO, refined their business plan and introduced them to industry players. Now, after multiple rounds of funding, it's D-Day, the date they make their initial public offering, and we've been holding our collective breath since the shares debuted. This is the part I love—where planning and investing in the long term marries a serendipitous, disruptive idea and revolutionizes the world. Instacart, Door-Dash, eBay, Snapchat, Facebook—they shook up our world and made their mark. This start-up will do the same. I know it.

The feeling of winning is addictive, and I wouldn't trade it for anything in the world. Hazel (the Coleman half of Coleman and Reed) knows exactly how I feel. Together we run one of the most successful venture capital funds in the world. What's VC? We're the Tooth Fairy and Santa Claus of the business world. If you've been very, very good and dotted all your *i*'s, crossed each *t*, we can make it rain cash and bring your dreams to life. It's a common misconception that VC guys are vultures, looking to swoop in and take over. I don't want to run your company or disassemble it. I want to take it public and sell it for a hundred—a thousand—times what it was valued at the day I walked in the door. Thank me and get out of my way.

We've been holed up in Hazel's office all day, monitoring the IPO while the rest of our team makes a valiant effort to pretend that today is just your average, ordinary workday, when it's all the holidays and a freaking pot of gold at the end of the Silicon Valley rainbow rolled into one. You see, Hazel and I did something different when we founded this particular VC fund. We insisted that everyone who worked here—from the guy who pushes a vacuum through our late-night sessions, to our Gal Friday receptionist, to the six analysts on our team—should have skin in the game. And to make that happen, we bumped their salaries up 20 percent and invested that extra in the fund.

As a result, Hazel and I have the richest janitor in Silicon Valley.

We also have the most loyal one.

Here in California, we've still got three hours of blazing hot sunshine until the close of the business day. Outside, BMWs and expensive luxury cars shoot up and down Sand Hill Road, a short stretch of asphalt that fronts the most expensive real estate in Silicon Valley. What used to be six sleepy miles cutting through western Silicon Valley is now the center of the VC universe. Hollywood has Rodeo

Drive and corporate big shots have Wall Street, but my tribe rules California. The biggest players have offices here and my heart still kicks into higher gear when I spot the green exit sign Sand Hill Rd above the sun-seared brown hills. That sign is the ultimate X-marks-the-spot and here-be-treasure. Sand Hill Road is where dreams come true or go bust, the epicenter of billions of dollars and power plays.

The closing bell rings, echoed by an audible happy sigh from the outer offices, like a sirocco ripping through the desert or a giant, man-eating raptor sighting prey. The stock popped and closed four times above ask.

You know that now-famous *Oprah* episode where she announces "You get a car. And *you* get a car. And you—yes, *everyone* gets a free car!" That's the prevailing mood in the offices of Coleman and Reed today. Our long-shot company just made its initial public offering and now we're all rolling in cash. You know what's even better than free money? Money that you earned because you were fucking *right*.

"Told you." I grab the champagne flutes from the shelf above her desk.

"Show-off," she grunts. Now that the market's closed, she pops out of her seat. Frankly, I'm surprised she's managed to sit still for so long. While our team celebrates, she grabs the edge of her desk, performing some kind of bendy, plié-squat thing. She claims it's important to get up and move every hour—otherwise your chances of stroking out escalate faster than a poorly capitalized start-up plummets during its debut.

I prefer to get my exercise on the beach. Surfing works, as does running. Standing in place and bending my knees? Where's the challenge?

"You know you can buy a new heart and a couple of kidneys with the twenty million dollars you just earned, right?"

Brown eyes narrow at me with laser focus. "Jealous, Reed?"

"Please. As if." I blow her a raspberry because that's what longtime friends do—they give each other shit.

"Mature." And then she sticks her tongue out at me, finishing her reps before grabbing her coffee mug and slurping down an obscene amount of room-temperature tap water.

Hazel's not a glass-half-full kind of person. She knows exactly how many ounces of liquid are in her oversize, llama-shaped coffee cup. Not part of the killer VC image, you say? Just wait until she looks at you. Brown eyes, long lashes, perfectly applied makeup (she did mine once on a drunken college night and I looked equally good) but you can tell right away that she's taking you in, performing a lightning-quick analysis that would make a NASA supercomputer jealous. Hazel lives for numbers. She's blunt and fact-oriented, and the shit that comes out of her mouth would be unbelievable except that it's also invariably true. She's smart and funny, and early on she nominated me to be the pretty face of the office.

Her reason? People *like* me.

She, on the other hand, never won Prom Queen, was never picked first for kickball and never received a dozen secret valentines. Hazel can rub people the wrong way, particularly when she's explaining why she's right and you're wrong. In the Hazel-verse, Hazel's always right and she's perfectly willing to explain at excruciating length why that's so. Still, Hazel's good people. If you'd told me ten years ago that she'd be my best friend and business partner, I'd have told you to lay off the pot brownies. She stormed a talk I was giving at UC Santa Cruz on statistical modeling and IPO valuation prediction, we argued about my methods (I still maintain I was right and Hazel was sadly deluded) and then we discovered unexpected common ground in a small tech company we'd both invested in. It had IPO'd while we'd been arguing, and we were both officially millionaires. She'd promptly offered to buy me a drink or a piece of cake because we were either the two smartest people in the world...or the craziest. And either way, we deserved cake.

The jury's still out on the crazy, by the way.

Ever since that celebratory slice of red velvet goodness, however, Hazel and I have been friends and business partners. We've conquered mountains together and my life doesn't work without her in it. She's always been one of the guys, a good sport, smart, driven. She's all the adjectives—and her amazing business abilities are the cherry on the sundae of awesomeness that is Hazel. Tact, however, is not one of her assets.

She sets down her llama mug on the coaster on her desk. "Are you taking Molly out to celebrate? Or are you just staying in and having wild monkey sex?"

They say married couples have sex ninety-eight times a year, while single people score only forty-nine times.

Jealous?

Hazel and I kept count last year. Let's just say that she's both single *and* a less-than-gracious loser.

"You bet, and you bet."

I grab my phone and text Molly. Home soon.

Soon is a relative term, of course—traffic sucks between Menlo Park and Santa Cruz. But I don't want to wait to share our good news. Plus, I have big, celebratory plans.

Just in case Mrs. Jack is otherwise occupied, I fire off another text:

Santa Jack has the following goodies in his bag of presents if you promise to be very, very bad:

A: Vacation home in Bora Bora.

B: Yacht.

C: Donate a building to your fave Ivy League school and then our kids are a shoo-in.

D: All of the above.

Hazel plants her butt on my desk and steals a glance at my phone. I'd like to tell you that we're working on her sense of boundaries, but she's a hopeless case. I've learned not to sext at the office, and she's learned not to read my texts out loud. Compromise is important.

She smacks my shoulder playfully. "You don't have kids."

"Not yet, but we're planning to get to work on that."

In fact, tonight seems like the perfect time to get started. Molly and I have discussed starting a family, and our plan calls for baby-making this year, with a pregnancy by next year if Mother Nature is on board.

"A plan." Hazel sounds dubious, although she should know just how well my plans work out. It's no accident that she and I are billionaires.

"Babies don't just happen." I mean, they obviously do, but Molly and I are going to have a planned pregnancy so that Mom and her Mini-Me are as happy and healthy as possible.

Hazel shakes her head. "Even ignoring the obvious issue with your logic, I feel the need to point out there are numerous ways your plan can derail. Male fertility decreases with age. As does semen volume. I can get you percentages on that—or book a honeymoon suite."

I gently lay a hand over her mouth. "Cease. Desist."

Hazel's response is to lick my palm.

I retract my hand because…gross. "Are you five?"

"Too much?" Hazel rolls her eyes. "You're such a baby."

"I feel the need to point out that my way's more fun, especially when it comes to babies."

"You need to plan less," she counters.

The only thing better than planning is winning, both of which I do very, very well.

"Do *you* have plans?"

"Big, celebratory, getting-naked plans?" Apparently, clarification is needed in the Hazel-verse, because she waits for my affirmatory grunt before shaking her head. "Don't tell my mom. She wants grandbabies and she wants them the 'natural' way."

"No turkey baster?"

Hazel shakes her head dramatically. "It's penis in the vagina or *nada* as far as she's concerned."

We both watch my phone. Is that weird? But Hazel's like an extension of me. Molly's read my text, and typing bubbles dance across the screen.

E.

Hazel frowns as she reads Molly's answer. "That wasn't one of the choices."

Hazel is often overly literal, but she's right. It wasn't. I text back: A mystery option? Awesome. I'll be home in an hour. You can pitch me then.

I can't help but notice that Molly's next text comes much faster. Much, *much* faster.

I won't be here.

Hazel groans. "So much for celebration sex."

Sometimes, it's as if Hazel can read my mind. I'm excellent with schedules, but… I look at Hazel.

"What's the over-under on me having forgotten Molly has a work trip?"

I'm texting before Hazel can respond. What's up?

Molly's response is a picture. It might be a moving van. It's like one of those impossible-to-make-sense-of security pictures where Yahoo invites you to pick out all the streetlights and you get the easy ones, but then you're squinting trying to figure out if poles count or wires or WTF because all you want to do is send an email, not play Pictionary.

"Words," Hazel mutters beside me. "Words are better."

Now there's a pounding in the office.

Stupid jackhammer construction. Who scheduled that for today? I should tell them to knock it off, to—

The pounding's almost drowned out by this strange whistling roar in my ears. Okay. That's my body making those sounds. Maybe I'm having a heart attack?

At thirty-two.

Sitting on my ass.

Hazel's right, although I'd never admit it to her. I work too much. I should have had more fun.

Hazel starts rubbing circles on my back. *Oh, no.* She's doing the sympathy gesture.

I'm moving out, Molly texts. I want a divorce.

Hazel's hand freezes. "Shit-fuck-damn."

Yes, all of those describe my situation quite nicely.

"I need to go home," I say. Or maybe I don't say anything and Hazel reads my mind, but somehow she gets me past the crowd of partying teammates and down the stairs to the parking lot. She bypasses my BMW and pops open the door to her Volvo. I bought Molly a Volvo. They have excellent safety features.

Normally, I avoid riding shotgun with Hazel because she's an *interesting* driver, but there's nothing normal about today. There's nothing normal about earning millions of dollars in one afternoon. Or arriving home to find your house meticulously half-empty. Or meeting the very nice process server in your driveway who hands over the stack of papers that signals the end.

Molly and I got married straight out of college. Graduation one week, big church date the next. We have a good marriage. We love each other, we have amazing sex on a regular basis, we laugh plenty and we routinely talk about both our future and our days. Sure, we also have rough patches and bad days and the odd fight, but those are balanced out by the memories, makeup sex and inside jokes. I know Molly. Her guilty pleasures are house-hunter shows, red dahlias and kitten memes. She's cried in my arms about shit that's gone wrong and we've killed more than one bottle of tequila celebrating her happy endings. We've been sick together, and lonely together, and I've shared the best and worst of me with her.

Except maybe I don't know her.

Maybe she's been pretending.

Or faking it.

Or—

"Jack?" That's Hazel's voice coming from far, far

away. I always have a plan, but I seem to be running on empty.

She pushes me back into her car, gets in on the other side and drives. She may talk. I don't know. I don't care. I just sit there and stare out the window at nothing. The sun's going down when we start the long, steep climb to her house. My place is on the beach, but as Hazel can't swim and prefers trees, she lives in a forest halfway up a mountain.

After Hazel marches into her house and I follow because she has the car keys and I have nowhere else to be, I discover that she has an enormous bottle of tequila from Mexican duty-free. Drinking it seems like an excellent plan. Although I haven't gotten drunk since college, I haven't forgotten how, which explains why at midnight I'm lying on Hazel's bed. It's sort of like sinking into an enormous cloud—if clouds were made from gray and purple fur. Or maybe that's the tequila. I squint, trying to make out one pillow from the next, but give up.

"Here." A bottle of water materializes in front of my face. Hazel's bed obviously has superpowers. "Take these."

Hazel unfolds a hand in front of my face, revealing two aspirin. As her one hand blurs into two, the room swims, but I manage to snag her offering. I swallow obediently and then take the trash can she holds out to me.

"Puke here," she says.

Hazel's always practical.

"Do you want to talk about it?" Hazel's not much

of a talker, not when it comes to feelings, so I appreciate the effort.

"I need to know why it happened," I mumble into the pillow. "What I did wrong. Why I wasn't enough."

"Failure analysis." I feel Hazel relax beside me. I'm asking for logic, not feelings. She's back on solid ground. "Something to think about—maybe this isn't about whether or not your marriage was good enough for Molly. Maybe this needs to be about whether or not your marriage was good enough for you."

"We were supposed to love each other," I whisper. "I was supposed to make her happy and keep her safe."

I turn my head so I can see Hazel's face. A little frown puckers her forehead as she thinks about what I've just said. She's not the best talker, or so she argues. She looks for connections, finds patterns, breaks things down until they make sense. So I need to hear what she has to say about my marriage. If she thinks it's over.

"Wrong," she says. "You have to ask, was the marriage good enough for *you*? Where are you going to set the bar on your happiness? What works for you? Were *you* happy?"

And that's the thing, isn't it? I've had a plan my whole life. I've hustled, I've executed, I've proven every single day that not only am I hungry, but I'm also willing to *work*.

And yet it wasn't enough.

Somehow my hand is tangled up in Hazel's and it feels perfectly normal to tug her down onto the bed beside me. "You're the best."

Right. We're almost-not-quite holding hands. I let go and try to pretend *that* didn't happen. Whatever it was. Instead, I reach around and attempt a friendly slap on the back, but I'm a drunken elephant and she's mouse-sized, so instead I face-plant her into the pillows.

Christ. Shoot me now.

"Fuck. Did I kill you?" I palm the back of her neck and tug her up. Brown eyes stare at me. Hazel has pretty eyes. Perhaps my new best friend, Tequila, has unearthed my inner poet?

Yeah. Unlikely.

Hazel's hand curls around the back of my neck. Her fingers squeeze gently and then she shoves me ruthlessly down. "Pass out, you nut. Wake up tomorrow."

CHAPTER TWO

Present day

MY NEIGHBOR IS hosting one hell of a party. The bass beat sets my bed to vibrating harder than the time I took a girlfriend to a Motel 6 and we tried out the Magic Fingers Vibrating Bed. Sadly, those beds don't seem to be standard hotel-room issue anymore. I open my to-do app and make a quick note to track one down—that would make an awesome wedding gift for Dev and Lola.

That party next door is their engagement party, although they're not actually hosting it at Dev's house. Dev, Max and I bought houses in a row on the same beach in Santa Cruz. It sounds weirder than it is. We've known each other since freshman year at UC Santa Cruz. As the first to move into our dorm, Devlin King and I had been standing in the three-bedroom oceanfront suite wondering how a bunch of broke freshmen guys had scored the best digs in a dorm full of seniors when Max blazed in and explained the secret. He'd hacked into the campus housing software, rigged the lottery in our favor and then picked out this place. High-handed? Sure. Borderline felonious? Maybe. But Max had good intentions and I'd decided we could housebreak him and teach him a few moral values along the way. Win-win. The three of us had become best friends, then billionaires. We're the kings of Silicon Valley, California. There's nothing we can't buy or hack.

Still.

Who would have thought Max, the king of kink, would be hosting a celebration of true love and happily-ever-after? Let's get real—he earned a fortune coding an app that hooks up horny people for hot, meaningless, no-strings sex. Quite frankly, milestone celebration planning is usually my bailiwick, but the fact that I'm still reorganizing my life after my divorce means I'm not in the fiesta mood. Ergo, Max stepped in when Dev proposed a personal kind of merger to his CEO girlfriend, the kind that comes with a diamond ring and a church date.

When the noise next door swells to deafening proportions, I plug in my headset and turn up the volume on my playlist. Coleman and Reed is scheduled to close an important round of funding for Silicon Valley's newest and hottest start-up later this week, making it all-hands-on-deck at the office. And even if things were slow at work or if I'd decided to do the FIRE thing, achieving financial independence and retiring early at thirty-two, I still wouldn't go over to the party next door. I'd rather have a root canal with no drugs. Hunt angry lions with my bare hands in Africa. Fight for a cheap TV at the Black Friday sales.

Why would I make those choices? For starters, going to the party means finding a clean shirt. It's currently me, my blue jeans and a bare chest, because why bother getting dressed? Plus, there are *people* at Max's. Happy, cheerful, celebrating people who will wonder—and then outright ask—how Molly is or if I'm dating. Everyone has a cousin Jo or Sue or Amy Beth that I should meet. But I'm okay by myself. Hopping back on the dating merry-go-round isn't part of my life plan…

Yeah. I need help.

My phone buzzes once, twice, and I eventually locate it underneath my pillow. I've missed a text from Hazel:

I'm stopping by. Scream now if you're naked or on the throne.

Should I respond?

Nope.

Sure enough, there's a brisk but brief application of knuckles to my bedroom door and the door flies open. Hazel marches in, one hand shielding her eyes, the other clutching two bottles of champagne to her chest. Brown hair, cut bluntly to stop in a perfect line between her jaw and her shoulder, swings about her face in a sleek, smooth curtain.

"Are you decent?"

She's practically hopping up and down. I watched

a video this morning of a labradoodle bouncing in place, wiggling its butt with canine glee as its owner arrived to collect it from doggy day care. That happy pooch has nothing on Hazel.

"I'm wearing pants," I say gravely. "But you should add counting to ten to your door-knocking routine. What if I were shy?"

"You're not shy. You surf half-naked all the time. I watch you from the beach." Hazel drops her hand, sets the champagne on the floor and takes me in. Brown eyes meet mine and then dip quickly to my bare chest. A mischievous grin tugs at the corners of her mouth as she crash-lands on the corner of the bed nearest the door and looks at me upside down.

She's a constant in my life, familiar and welcome. She has a strong face and bold eyebrows. Brown eyes. High cheekbones with three freckles she claims look just like Orion's Belt. There's another freckle in her ear, although she disavows all knowledge of it. She's of average height and curvy. She likes long walks on the beach—not because they're romantic, but to stay in shape. Hazel only needs people in small doses, so the running part happens when she spots a fellow walker (she claims it's a HIIT workout, but I know the truth).

Her gaze returns to my chest. I should probably figure out why. Whatever. It's a little weird, but it's also not as if I'm a virgin princess in a tower. My naked chest has been previously ogled. Still, I shove to my feet, pad into my walk-in closet and retrieve a

T-shirt from a hanger. The laundry service delivers them washed and pressed once a week.

"Why are you here, Hazel?"

The bed rustles and creaks, which is the most action it's seen in ages. Footsteps pad across the floor and stop in the doorway. When I finish pulling the shirt over my head and can see again, Hazel's standing in the doorway, watching me. We need to have another conversation about boundaries.

She's wearing her usual Saturday uniform of leggings and a tank top. A gold chain with an infinity loop nestles in the hollow of her throat and she's tied an oversize men's flannel shirt around her waist because she worries constantly that she'll be cold. It doesn't matter that we live in California or that the temperature will hit ninety this afternoon—she's prepared for arctic temperatures and the ice-cream aisle at the grocery store. Hazel herself isn't pretty or gorgeous. She's none of those adjectives you come up with when asked what your date looks like, but something about her makes you look at her and smile, even when she's driving you completely nuts. She's just so alive and full of energy that it lights up her eyes and the room. She's not particularly easy to be around, but she's never boring. In a world full of taupe and beige, Hazel's carmine and verdigris, framboise and vermilion. It's certainly made for an interesting business partnership.

"I'm here to stage an intervention." Hazel waves a hand at me just in case there's any doubt about who the intended recipient is. "You need to get back out there."

"To Max's party?"

I wander out of my closet and lean against the wall. I can't wait to hear this plan.

Hazel hands me one of the champagne bottles and plops down onto the bed. "Open sesame."

"I need the magic word."

"Please buy me a drink, Mr. Reed." She makes a hurry-up gesture. "I stole high-end champagne for you, so you should be thanking me."

I peel back the foil carefully. Given Hazel's vigorous delivery, odds are high I end up wearing champagne. I retrieve a towel from the bathroom and then grab my water glass. Hazel will have to share because I haven't gotten around to replacing the glasses Molly took with her. Hazel watches as I cover the cork and the cage with the towel.

"Why are you here?" I untwist the cage and then work the bottle clockwise until the cork pops free.

She throws her arms wide. "I'm hiding from the party. The big question is why *you're* here."

"It's my house." I pour a glass of champagne and hold it out to Hazel.

She swipes the bottle from me instead and takes a swig. "I call bullshit, Mr. Reed. You're hiding from life."

I take a sip from the glass. She's right about one thing. Max bought the good stuff for this party. "You don't want to celebrate Dev's engagement?"

Brown eyes widen dramatically. "Usually Max

has pool parties. Everyone over there today is wearing fancy clothes and there are no naked bodies in the pool."

"You don't even like swimming, so why do you care?"

Hazel can't swim. Her reasons include allergies to swimwear, bikini-line maintenance and chlorine. It's her loss. Pretty much all my nonwork time now is spent in the ocean.

She ignores me and instead inventories my desktop as she nudges the laptop screen closed. "You work too much."

Coming from Hazel, that's rich. She works all the time.

"Are you trying to tell me what to do?" I cross my arms over my chest and lean forward a little. Yes, it's wrong to use my larger size to intimidate, but these are desperate times. "Because you're my business partner, not my boss."

"Coleman and Reed," she points out, not a little smugly. She chugs champagne. "My name comes first."

I should *never* have discussed business with Hazel after doing tequila shots. She's entirely ruthless and far too convincing. "Because *you* insisted on alphabetical order."

"I'm first. You're second. If this was a wolf pack, that would make me the alpha and you the beta."

"You're still not the boss of me." My glass is empty, so I hold it out for Hazel to refill.

She grins the evilest of Hazel grins. "It's my month, so technically I am."

Right. Fuck. Hazel and I have control issues, which is a polite way of saying we both have a pathological need to be in charge. In our early days, we settled our differences with "rock paper scissors," but that looked weird once we started acquiring staff. So then we switched to taking turns. Every other month, Hazel gets to be the boss.

"We're not at the office." I feel compelled to point this out because not only are we both workaholics, but Hazel is also the kind of person who gleefully takes a mile when given an inch.

"You need to get out. No more working this weekend. That's an order."

"Since when do I take orders from you?"

She winks at me. "You should try it. I'm awesome at giving orders."

I'm not sure how to respond to that, but she doesn't wait for an answer, anyhow. She just nods as if she's finishing up an argument with herself and then tosses more words at me. "You need to get back out there."

That's alarmingly vague.

"To the party?"

There's a moment of silence, or as near silent as you can get when there are two hundred people crammed into the house next door. Somehow Max always gets away with the most over-the-top parties.

"Life." Hazel punches up a finger as she makes

each point. "Dating. Casual sex. When is the last time you had an orgasm?"

I choke on nothing at all. "Inappropriate, Hazel."

She grins at me unrepentantly as she sets the champagne bottle on the floor. "Make a dating plan. Go pick out someone fun on the Billionaire Bachelors app."

I don't have to think about it. "No."

"I've already set up your profile. Say thank you."

Jesus. I think I might pale.

Hazel beats me to my phone, probably because she's already on the bed thanks to her laptop-slamming move, while I'm an entire room away. She's such a cheater. She holds up my phone triumphantly as she punches in my passcode. She knows all my passwords, just like I know hers. And like any good friend, she lives to torture me. She starts scrolling and swiping, while I try half-heartedly to wrest the phone away from her. She's pointed out repeatedly that my gorilla size gives me an unfair advantage over her more petite frame, so I try to be careful. I go for a wrist hold, but she wriggles, my hands slip and we end up twisted together in a Jack-and-Hazel pretzel. Her boobs pop right onto my arm like I'm a shelf or something with way fewer nerve endings. Her tank top gapes and there's no way to avoid seeing that her bra's made out of a dark blue satin material. The fabric cups her boobs into sexy little mouthfuls. I shut my eyes, but it's too late.

Some things can't be unseen.

My brain's already assessing the new data points

and drawing conclusions. Hazel's got great boobs, two perfect handfuls from the look of things.

She's super flexible and I bet she'd look amazing naked, her face all lit up as she comes, her fingers digging into my wrists and holding on to me as she lets herself go while she—

Cease and desist.

You do not—not *ever*—think about your friend and business partner like that.

"What about this one?" Oblivious to my inappropriate sexual thoughts, she jams an elbow into my ribs as she turns the screen so I can see. I let her go because I need to put some safe space between us more than I need to win this argument.

Objectively speaking, Hazel's suggestion is pretty. She has two eyes and two ears, and a happy grin lights up her face. Blond hair spills over her bare, suntanned shoulders. Melanie likes water-skiing, scuba diving in tropical locations and designing jewelry. Wow. Is this what Hazel thinks is my type? I mean…maybe I prefer something less over-the-top. Or blue satin.

What is wrong with me? "No."

There. Two birds killed with one stone.

Undeterred, Hazel retrieves the champagne and flops back on my bed, swiping left like a madwoman. I can't remember if that's the dating equivalent of putting the girl in my shopping cart for later or not.

"How about this one? Tell me where she rates on the Jack-o-Meter. Better yet, tell me a story."

Ever since one drunken, amazing night in a college dive bar, Hazel and I have had a game. When we spot an interesting stranger, we make up stories about who he or she might be. There are no rules other than we use our inside voices—Hazel can get loud—and that we never, ever make up stories about someone we know. The redhead Hazel's pointing to could star in an ad for curl cream. Bright corkscrews frame her laughing face and a spray of freckles dusts her nose. She's impossibly cute and happy. I bet her favorite flower is the rose and her closet is full of Victoria's Secret Pink.

"Playmaker at a Mexican all-inclusive. Molly Ringwald body double. Georgia homecoming queen who runs an Etsy earring business. It doesn't matter, Hazel—I don't want a date."

She gives me the death glare. "You do."

I steal the champagne from her. Pretty much everyone who has ever worked with Hazel recognizes the mulish expression she gets and can tell a Hazel story. The tenacity that makes her such a brilliant investor and business coach sometimes backfires when she leaves the office. She's argued more than once that those backfires are an important contribution to the world because she shouldn't be right all the time (and Hazel absolutely believes she is), and this is just the universe's way of making sure things come out a little more even for the rest of us. She's stormed into court over a speeding ticket and out-argued the prosecutor. She's hauled all her clothes to Goodwill in trash bags and started over because she claimed that was easier than going through them and doing a Marie Kondo.

She shakes the phone at me like it's a Magic 8-Ball. "Yes or no."

"No."

"You don't like redheads who might or might not be homecoming queens and talented freelance artists? What's wrong with her?"

"Nothing, but I don't want to date her."

Hazel makes Hazel noises and swipes through a gallery of women. I can't tell if she's actually looking at the pictures or doing the adult equivalent of spinning a globe and pretending you'll travel wherever your finger lands when you're a grown-up and have money.

She puts down the phone—where I can't reach it, because Hazel's smart—and frowns at me. "You're weird."

"Pot." I swirl my finger in the air, turning an imaginary globe. I don't usually drink too much, but I suspect this evening is going to break any hopes I had of a sober streak. I know I should care, but the champagne wraps my brain in a delicious fog, so I decide to worry about it tomorrow. "Did you ever spin the globe when you were little and pretend that you'd have to go wherever your finger landed?"

"No one does that for real," Hazel says decisively.

I nod. "People do, too, do that. I was supposed to go to Antarctica because that was where my finger ended up."

"You fingered Antarctica." She sniggers.

"Mature." I tug on her hair as we lie side by side, staring companionably up at my ceiling.

Hazel transitions seamlessly from raunchy jokes back to my life. "You know I'm right. You need to get back out there."

Despite Hazel's insistence on always being right, I can't argue with her this time. I've turned into a cave-dwelling hermit.

"Why do you want me to date so badly?"

"You need to get laid. I suppose you could hire someone. Or just go to a bar and hook up. Or just use Max's app." She frowns at my ceiling. "What about the whole glory-hole thing? Don't they do that in San Francisco? Isn't that just sort of like having sex with a sheet with a hole in it?"

I have no idea how Hazel's brain works. I choke. "Google that later, okay? But, no. Thanks."

Maybe she's just having me on, because she starts laughing. Hazel's no giggler. She has a full-blown hyena laugh punctuated by weird, random snorts. It's impossible not to join in, even if I'm not entirely certain what we're laughing about. I knew, when I met her—when she took issue with every point in my slide deck, and then bought me cake and cackled with glee over the money we'd made—that Hazel did her own thing, but I respected the fact that she did it loud and proud. Hazel doesn't accept excuses—when she fails, she bounces back up like a punching bag and keeps going. It figures she'd see marriage the same way.

"Let me set you up," she replies when she's finally got the hyena snort-laugh under control. "I promise to pick someone you'll like."

"What are we? Girlfriends?" I ask. "Are we doing each other's nails next?"

She flicks my shoulder. "That's a stereotype—plus, I'm more of a sheet mask girl myself. I just want to know that my best business partner is okay. Happy also works for me."

She winks at me. Despite her well-earned reputation as one of Silicon Valley's most sharkish VC backers, Hazel's one of the most generous people I know. She's also—in a quiet, not-so-over-the-top way—one of the funniest. I'd lay even money that tomorrow or the day after, a Sephora box full of sheet masks will hit my desk.

"You're not exactly Ms. Happily-Ever-After."

"Are you challenging my dating credentials?"

"When was the last time you went on a date?" I turn my head so I can see her face. She's had the same shoulder-length bob for as long as I've known her, and her hair is always a well-trimmed, ruthlessly flat-ironed cap. The only thing more meticulous is her makeup. I can count on one hand the number of times I've seen Hazel look like a mess. Frat parties, college bars, beach trips, house moves—Hazel's hair and makeup is always on point.

"Three weeks ago." She stretches her arms over her head in some kind of yoga pose. I mimic the move. It's not bad at all for working the kinks out of my shoulder.

"And?"

She flops forward, stretching like a cat. "He wasn't second date material."

Her voice is muffled by the duvet.

"Did you introduce him to your family?"

She turns her face to look at me. "Do I look crazy?"

Three years younger than me, Hazel is twenty-nine, staring down the big three-zero. And while she's made it perfectly clear that she doesn't care about this milestone date, her mother, her aunties and her three sisters care. She's their baby, the maverick and the only one who wasn't either an English major or a liberal-studies major. The Coleman clan live crammed into a series of small cottages five blocks from the Santa Cruz beach on family land, and in every single one of my encounters with them, they've reiterated their desire for Hazel to move home, preferably with a husband and multiple mini-Hazels in tow.

Once a week like clockwork, someone emails her a link to a small house on Amazon or a caravan that "doesn't count as a house because it's on wheels"—think taco truck with curtains. Her mother is a poet, one sister teaches English at the local high school, and another is homeschooling her two kids and leading prison writing workshops. Hazel, on the other hand, doesn't get nuances, poetry or metaphors and her fridge-poetry-magnet set is used to make shapes. They're fun, they live life loud and even though Hazel's a bit of a cuckoo in the nest, they love her back even if they don't get her. They love me, too, which Hazel claims isn't at all unexpected as she's yet to meet anyone who doesn't like me.

"If I'd introduced him, they'd have had us engaged by the time we'd finished discussing the weather. If he didn't sprint for his car by that point, my mom would have booked a nice beach for the wedding. They don't get that I could just be using the guy for sex."

"For a bunch of free spirits, they do have some hard limits," I admit.

"There is *no* casual hookup sex." She waves a hand dramatically. "They just want me married and settled and that's the last thing I want."

"I miss marriage," I admit quietly.

"Molly?"

"No, not her specifically, not anymore. It's just…"

"Having someone?"

"That," I agree. "I miss the closeness, the intimacy, the *sex*."

This earns me another snort-chuckle. "You goof. You have two out of three with me. We just don't have sex."

Before I can stop myself, my brain gleefully goes *there*. To the land of Hazel-and-Jack-having-sex. I don't care if pundits claim all guys imagine having sex with their best friends if those friends are girls. This is the first time I've ever imagined naked Hazel and I don't like it. Not really. Or maybe I like it too much. I need to be able to work with her.

Hazel dangles my phone in front of my face. "Pick someone and get laid."

"Not a chance."

She laughs as I shove the phone under my pillow because I'm not taking chances. Hazel is fully capable of choosing a date for me.

"We both suck," she announces. "How can we make so much money but be so bad at meeting people?"

I don't budge from the pillow. Hazel plays dirty. "It's a gift."

Hazel, who's never still to begin with—unless she's reading, in which case she might be mistaken for dead except for the frantic *flick-flick* of the pages—bounces to her feet. The mattress shakes. I rescue the champagne just in time.

"List time!" she cries.

She produces a black Sharpie from somewhere and writes *Jack's List of Requirements* across my bedroom wall.

"Describe your dream girl. Five adjectives. Go."

I take a pull from the bottle. It's not as cold as it once was.

"No way."

"Don't make me pick for you, mister."

Fine. "Loyal. Trustworthy. Strong. Happy. Honest."

Hazel scrawls my words on the wall and then frowns. "Are you looking for a girlfriend or a pet?"

Holy fuck, I *am* boring.

From the way Hazel eyes my bedroom wall, she's done the same math.

"You should try something different," Hazel says. "But we can work on that later. Let's talk about what you bring to the table."

She sketches said table in bold, broad strokes. There's a Pro column and a Con column, plus my name, *JACK*, just in case there's any doubt who we're psychoanalyzing today.

Her teeth chew at her lower lip. "First candidate for the Pro column—wildly successful venture capitalist, so excellent baby daddy."

She writes *BIG* in the Pro column.

"Big?"

"Shorthand." She gives me a dramatic eyebrow waggle. "For your…assets."

Sharpie doesn't wash off, now that I think about it.

And I'm not entirely certain she's referring to my bank account.

"You're not supposed to say those things, Hazel."

She sticks her tongue out at me. "I'm too old to change."

"I don't think you need to change," I drunk-whisper.

"I like me, too." She nods her head vigorously. "But we're doing you here."

"All yours." I flop back on the bed. "But be gentle with me. Next point?"

She holds her hands up in front of her face and squints at me through the opening she's made. "Let's add big blond giant with bad-boy hair to the plus column."

"Okay. Wait, what's wrong with my hair?"

"Nothing." She scrawls *HUGE* on my bedroom wall. "But you do realize that you show up at the office looking like a poster child for sex, right? I guarantee half of our employees fantasize about running their fingers through it."

I roll onto my side. "Now I don't feel safe going to work on Monday."

Hazel is already busy adding another word to the list. *VERSATILE.* "You're equally at home on a surfboard and in a boardroom."

"Versatile? Since when is *versatile* sexy?"

"Fine." She scribbles out *VERSATILE* and adds *FIT* and *RICH* to the list. I'd like to argue with her, but both of those things are true.

"I'm feeling objectified here—these are all outside things. How would you feel if I summed you up as a great pair of boobs and a pretty mouth?"

"Should I say 'thank you'?"

"Not yet," I say darkly.

Laughter shakes Hazel's body. She has a nice butt, which her yoga pants put on display. Not that I'm noticing her butt. Even thinking about my business partner like that is a recipe for disaster.

SHARK.

I stare at the new word that Hazel's just scrawled on my wall. "What?"

She looks at me impatiently. "You have the killer instincts of a shark for a deal."

"I'm not sure that's a plus in the dating world."

Hazel taps the Sharpie against the *RICH* heading. "Hello. The leg bone's connected to the hip bone."

She shifts the Sharpie to the Con column. Great. Now we're moving on to my flaws. She may need more wall for that.

UPTIGHT.

"Hey," I protest. "I am not."

Hazel points the Sharpie at me. "You have the moral conscience of Michael the Archangel."

"That's a plus."

Hazel snorts. "Michael is judgy."

"You're just messing with me."

Her next words prove it.

TRUST ISSUES.

This one is in all caps and underlined. Wow. Hazel's not pulling her punches.

"You're wrong." I take a deep pull on the bottle. It's almost empty.

"You trusted Molly and she hurt you. Now you're hiding up here like the troll under the bridge so no one can trample on your feelings again. You need to find someone you can be one hundred percent you with."

"All this because I didn't go to a party?" I set the empty bottle on the floor.

"Why do you think your marriage to Molly ended?"

Max, Dev and me? We're equally relentless. We don't know how to lose because losing, quite simply, isn't an option, whether it's surfing, the boardroom or life. Wipeouts? Sure. Neck-breaking, skull-pounding slams into the ocean floor? Bring it on—I'll be back on my board in no time. Life isn't easy, but I've always been good at what I do. No. Scratch that. I've always been the *best*, so Molly's leaving doesn't compute. I went all out, I did everything by the book, I did everything I could for her.

And it wasn't enough.

Hazel makes a buzzer sound and chucks the Sharpie at me. "Wrong. You don't need to know whatever bullshit reason Molly had for ending things between you. That doesn't matter."

"Walk me through your marital credentials again, Ms. Single Gal. I'm pretty sure that caring about my wife's feelings was part of the marriage ceremony."

"That was then. This is now, so you need to rethink. Like, was the marriage acceptable to *you*?"

"Marriage is about two people."

"And you're one of them." She rolls her eyes. "Did you *like* your relationship?"

Fuck it. I've spent so much time lying. Lying to myself, to Molly, to the rest of the world. Was I happy? I wasn't *un*happy, but that wasn't really enough for a lifetime, was it? So I'll give Hazel the truth.

"No."

The word hangs in the air between us. Not so much a bomb as one of those stun grenades the FBI or the Marines use when they want to clear a room of hostiles. I shouldn't have said that, but it turns out that maybe I'm an even worse liar than I thought, because Hazel doesn't look at all surprised.

"So what do you want, Jack?"

Suddenly her face is near mine, so close that I can feel each word on my skin, my face, my mouth. Did she come closer? Did I move? I look around for answers, but the answer is standing right there in front of me. It's not *what* I want—it's *who*.

I think I fall on her and our mouths meet. Or she falls up. Down. The mechanics don't matter because there's definitely some kind of cosmic, completely-beyond-my-control accident that undoes all my plans.

I'm kissing Hazel.

Her lips are soft and plush. Her cheek brushes mine as she adjusts our fit and then glides her tongue over my lower lip. Wow. I did not see this coming. Or maybe it's not true. Maybe I've had a fantasy or two, but I certainly never planned on kissing her.

She opens her mouth and I take charge. Being the boss of Hazel is a limited-time offer and we both know it—she likes to be the one in control. Her hands are running over my body, pulling me here, touching me there. I sink my hands into her hair and hold her face still. She tastes like champagne and Hazel, sparkly and effervescent, wicked and deceptively sweet.

She presses her satin-covered boobs against me as our kiss deepens. She's an amazing kisser. Her mouth covers mine, her tongue exploring while her hands learn the shape of my jaw, my shoulders. I shouldn't want this kiss, but I do. She hooks a leg around my waist, shifting until I can feel… Oh yes…the soft, hot heat of her pressed against my thigh. Hazel's as hot for me as I am for her.

But.

She's my business partner.

My best friend.

My Hazel.

I pull back, staring at her face while my brain scrambles to catch up with what my mouth just did. My fingers cup her shoulders, tracing the strap of her tank top. Someone's slipped the silky material to the side, exposing the hollow of her collarbone. I imagine pressing my lips to that soft, secret spot of Hazel.

Kissing—

She opens her mouth and I can't even begin to imagine what she'll say. With Hazel, I never know. I just know that I can't.

I can't kiss her.

I can't do this.

Most of all, I can't lose her, so I shoot off the bed. She flops backward with a startled laugh as my hands turn her shoulders into a spring pad.

"I have to go," I blurt out.

"Baby." She gives me a face, but I'm not looking— I'm not. I'm definitely not listening to her or trying to decide if that one word is some weird kind of relationship-ish nickname or just a sweeping indictment of my social skills.

I'm out the door, flying down the stairs to the ground floor and then out the door toward the ocean.

There's no way this could work. Whatever *this* is. I zoom down the steps to the beach tucked away at the base of the cliff my house sits on. Halfway down I realize I'm taking stupid chances and slow to a hasty retreat. Sun-warmed wood creaks underneath my feet.

I kissed Hazel.

As soon as I hit the sand, I grab the surfboard I keep by the stairs. I keep going until I'm waist-deep in the chilly California ocean. Cold water sucks at my jeans, slapping the wet denim against my legs and dick. I deserve every second of the discomfort. I straddle my board and paddle hard for the outermost edge of the tiny cove, where the waves break. I think I know what happened back there, in my bedroom. I made a mistake. That's all. I was lonely and there's just something about Hazel. She doesn't so much light up a room as she makes it explode because she's always thinking, always questioning. She's just really alive and so totally unlike Molly that I was tempted. She's like the recipes I bookmark in *Bon Appétit*, flavors you'd never expect to work together, but then one taste and you want more because that one mouthful is an epiphany.

Except I don't get to have more.

Good guys don't kiss their business partners.

Smart guys definitely don't. I don't need an HR presentation to tell me what the right thing to do is here.

In the morning, I'll figure this out. I'll figure out how to erase the last hour, when I put my hands on

Hazel and I kissed her and she kissed me back. I'll figure out how to forget her hum of surprise and then the rougher, greedier sound she made as she opened for me. But tonight, it's me and the frigid ocean water, which slowly freezes my dick back into the state I need it in.

CHAPTER THREE

THIRTY-SIX HOURS AND two cold showers do not erase my memory of how Hazel's mouth felt beneath— and over—mine. The plush, slick warmth, the way she opened up for me and then the way she gave as good as she got, her mouth devouring mine as if she couldn't get enough of me. Hazel wants me. She wants all of me. So, of course, my brain freeze- frames, reliving each second of our kiss over and over.

And over.

I ran five miles this morning, swam and took an icy shower, but here I am: going to work with a hard-on for Hazel. I park my BMW in the first spot I find. Parking is tight for our building and I have a reserved spot by the door—the perks of being the boss—but Hazel's Volvo is already parked in her spot next to mine. She's crooked, I tell myself, so parking next to her would put my paint job at greater risk than normal. I'm safer with the length of the lot between us.

There must be something more awkward than

drunk-kissing your business partner, but right now I'm drawing a blank.

I need a plan. There has to be a way to get past making out with the wrong person. The important thing is to figure out the first step. Then I'll figure out the second step. And then the third. Numbers are a beautiful thing. One precedes two, two precedes three and there's no confusion about how things go. You can't screw up math.

Okay. Step one. I drum my fingers on the steering wheel. Do I acknowledge the kiss, or do I wait for Hazel to say something? She didn't call or text after I hightailed it out of my own house, so I'm voting for *ignore* as a strategy. I won't say anything.

Step two? No alone time. We need group hangouts only. Lots and lots of people around us. Unless Hazel has a well-hidden interest in group sex, this should safely move us past Saturday's kiss.

Step three.

Act normal.

That's all I have to do.

I run through the steps as I get out of my car. Fake it until you make it, right? I stride into the building as if I have nothing more on my mind than counting my billions.

Robert, our receptionist, greets me cheerfully. His weekend has clearly gone much better than mine. His face has that relaxed glow that no amount of sunshine or spa time can bestow. Nope. Robert's clearly gotten laid and is feeling good about it. I gamble that he's too distracted by his weekend memories to notice I'm ever so slightly off my game today.

"Is Hazel in?"

I think I sound suitably nonchalant, but Robert gives me a long look before deciding that my question is actually serious.

"She has a breakfast meeting," he says. "The two of you thumb-wrestled in the kitchen to decide who had to sit through it."

I'm sure he assumes I'm crazy or had a stroke in the parking lot. I don't forget details like this.

"Great." I think I'm smiling too widely. "I'll catch up with her later."

It turns out, however, that Hazel's badly parked Volvo is the most I see of her because she Ubered to her breakfast meeting and then hopscotched from there to four more. We try to not both be out of the office on the same day, and if I'd been less rattled after our kiss, I might have remembered that Hazel had called dibs on Monday.

Tuesday is my day to take off-site meetings, but I have to swing by the office to grab some files that no one can email to me for inexplicable reasons. Hazel is bent over her desk, typing away furiously on her laptop. Based on the staccato beat of her fingers on the keys, she's either pissed off at someone or has had what she refers to as "an evil-genius breakthrough."

She's dressed formally in a dark jacket, suit pants and a soft, silky blouse with a loopy bow that rests on top of the boobs I am absolutely not looking at. There's a gold necklace nestled in the hollow of her throat. I squint, but I can't quite make out what it says. All of Hazel's necklaces have messages, like mini billboards for her upcoming week. An elephant for good luck. A lightning bolt when she wants to "strike 'em dead." A cactus for exploring new frontiers and ideas. At least this one isn't an ax or a gun or some other murder weapon. Maybe she doesn't want to kill me dead.

She looks up as I saunter past her office because I'm going to pretend everything is normal up until she tells me that it's not. I can't tell if she's staring off into space or if she's ignoring me. I'll just have to fix this. Somehow.

This is the first time I've seen her since our kiss. Given we have an office full of people, I settle for muttering "hi" in the direction of her office door before burying myself in spreadsheets. I need to talk to her without the audience. Kissing her was the wrong thing to do, which makes apologizing the right thing. I'm just not sure that a handful of words can fix this. Does she think I'm a horndog? A player? A desperate ass?

Wednesday and Thursday pass much the same. Coleman and Reed has the bandwidth to take on one or two more projects, so we're actively shopping for candidates. Thursday, we bring in one of those candidates to pitch. The company founders look like their average age is fourteen. They're suited up, nervous and awash in cologne. If their pitch doesn't overwhelm me, the fumes will.

Since I'm first into the room, I do the meet and

greet. Hazel bursts in five minutes later. In the office, she wears her hair slicked back in this bun thing. There's no good way to describe it. A bun is something you buy at the bakery—a squashy, delicious treat—and it doesn't begin to describe Hazel's neat knot of hair. I compared it once to the black racer snake that Hazel found sun-basking on her doorstep. She didn't like that comparison, so I quit before she either killed me or sicced a snake on me. Plus, when she lets her hair down, that's really when you need to watch out. Hazel has crazy hair. It waves and curls and tries to be straight—all at the same time.

Despite the balmy California weather, she's wearing her favorite Theory suit, the one with slim blue velvet pants and a matching fitted jacket. I know from her previous complaints about the gymnastics required to pee that the shirt thing underneath her jacket is actually a bodysuit, that there are three snaps on the crotch, and that she'll be commando because she thinks it's silly to wear an extra layer underneath…

Danger.

Do not think about Hazel's panties.

She introduces herself to our visitors, reaching over the table to shake their hands. I try to reconcile put-together Hazel with the woman I kissed on Saturday night. I kissed *Hazel*. My partner. As kisses go, that one is definitely in my top ten. The way she ran her hand down my chest. Her teeth scraping gently at my upper lip. Her breath catching on my mouth.

The greedy pull of her mouth as if I was her favorite flavor and I made her feel just a little savage.

Hazel drops into the seat next to where I'm sprawled, still imagining her naked. She reaches beneath the table under the guise of adjusting her chair and smacks my thigh where it brushes hers.

She smirks at me. "Personal space, Reed."

Hazel is a relentless campaigner against man-spreading, but do her fingers linger and brush over my dress pants? She smells good and I fight the urge to turn toward her body and pull her closer, because the handful of inches between us is too much. I definitely want to kiss her again, press my lips against the vulnerable base of her throat. But maybe it's just me. Maybe Hazel's already forgotten our kiss even though she has the memory of an elephant.

I don't remember much about the meeting. I nod and pretend to take notes on my laptop, but the young, anxious baby executives could be pitching me luxury condos on Mars for all I know. It's irresponsible of me to be so distracted, because there is a lot of money on the line, not to mention the future of their company. I asked them here and I should be listening.

It doesn't surprise me that Hazel busts me as soon as we've walked our guests out and are headed back to our offices.

"Earth to Jack."

"Sorry." I scrub a hand over my head. I'm totally off my game, and we both know it.

"Do you even know what those guys pitched?"

I have the slide deck. I'll review later this afternoon. "Did you like it?"

Hazel shrugs and pauses in front of her office door. "What's not to like about a monthly sex-toy-box subscription service?"

Wait. What…?

"Gotcha." Hazel bounces into her office.

Later that afternoon the mailroom guy deposits a polka-dot cardboard box on my desk. When I unfold layers of tissue that stink like exotic flowers, I discover a small white cardboard card: *Merry Thursday. Love, Hazel.* She's sent me a dozen different kinds of sheet masks that smooth and plump. Lavender to hydrate, cherry blossom to brighten, tomatoes for turbo-charged radiance. There's also a bright pink pot for scrubbing my lips that makes me wonder about our kiss. Is that a hint?

I impulsively fire off a text: Was I too rough?

Shit.

This is why I don't do *impulsive*. Hazel's phone gives off a deafeningly loud ding in the office next to me. She claims she doesn't hear it unless the volume is set to stun.

Should I go over there and delete my text before she can read it? Plead temporary insanity? Fuck if I know, but I'll have to kick my own ass if I've offended her.

I clear my throat and pitch my voice loud enough to be heard through the wall. "Ignore that, 'kay?"

Hazel's response is a snort-laugh. That's a good sign, right? I'll fix this. I did kiss her, so I'll take the consequences. I haven't got to the next step in my baby plan, however, before a sharp rat-a-tat sounds on our shared wall. Right. Hazel claims she's a Morse code master, but I've yet to figure out what she's trying to convey.

Think. Figure this out.

My phone dings discreetly. Fuck it I'm coming over.

"Don't get your boxers in a wad, Reed," she bellows.

That's good advice, even if it does come from Hazel and I don't wear boxers. Which she doesn't know, although apparently I was willing to let her learn that fact for herself the other night. Play it cool. I can totally do that. I lean back in my chair and stretch my legs out beneath my desk. My tie's threatening to choke me, so I pull it free and toss it on the desk. My sleeves are already rolled up, putting my ink on display. My suit jacket is…somewhere. I'm about as stripped-down naked as I can legally get in a California office. I don't know why I think more clothes would help this situation, except that everything seemed to snowball this weekend when I was half-naked. Perhaps I should have worn a suit of armor to the office today.

Hazel barrels in at a speed that seems like it should be impossible given that she's wearing four-inch heels. She told me once that she likes to be eye level with her prey. I believed it then; I believe it now. The only difference is that right now *I'm* the prey in her sights. A laptop and a huge flip chart load down her arms and her hair brushes her jaw as she shuts my office door with her butt. Crap. It's going to be one of *those* conversations.

She dumps her stuff on my desk and rolls her eyes. "Stop being so weird."

"Is everything okay?" What I really mean is, *are we okay?*

Hazel flips up the lid of her laptop. "Was kissing me *that* bad?"

There is absolutely no good answer to that question. If I was a gentleman, I'd have acquired a very specific case of amnesia and wiped that handful of minutes from my brain. I definitely wouldn't be sporting wood beneath my desk because, yeah, kissing Hazel was every bit that good.

Her mouth twitches. "I thought we had chemistry."

"Uh." Nope. I've still got nothing.

She punches a button and PowerPoint springs to life on her screen. God bless a well-organized piece of software. "And while I'm annoyed you sprinted out of your own house as if I had some really nasty case of the cooties, I'm willing to work with you on this."

"What?" Hopefully my brain comes back online soon.

"You. Me." She gestures impatiently between us. "I think we could be the answer to each other's problem. I've made a deck with my plan."

Plans are good. I'd prefer us to execute a plan of my devising, but I'm happy to listen to Hazel's pitch. Plus, we both live and breathe slide decks, anyhow—it's an occupational hazard. She flips the laptop around so I can see the screen and then plants her ass on my desk. Still, the title of her presentation catches me by surprise:

Hazel and Jack:
Friends with Benefits

There's a fairly standard template for pitching. You hit the basics—company info, your concept, the problem—and then you start unpacking your proposed solution and why it's going to be a financial winner. The first slide has company info—Hazel's name and phone number. I already know this. I can't quibble with slide number two, either.

The Problem:
No sex

"Yes, no sex is quite the problem." I lean back in my chair and kick my feet up on my desk. Look at me, pretending to be all relaxed.

Hazel's gaze drifts over my crotch. "Exactly. You're not having it. I'm not having it. This means that we're missing out on a number of key health benefits. Sex has been known to lower blood pressure, reduce the risk of heart attacks, improve bladder control—"

I hold a hand up. "Sex is healthy. Got it. Move on before I have an aneurysm."

Hazel mock-glares at me and moves on to the next slide.

The Solution:
Jack and Hazel have sex!

I take a moment to make sure that no one innocently passing by in the hallway will get an eyeful of Hazel's presentation.

"Did you put this on the company server?"

Hazel taps an impatient finger on my desk. "No. I'm horny, not stupid. Next slide."

Market Size:
Two

She looks at the slide and then at me. "You should know that I'm not interested in sex with two guys. Or a guy and a girl. I find I have focus issues."

"Hazel—" The pain in my dick intensifies. Why is she so goddamn direct all the time? "You need to stop saying *sex*."

"I didn't think you were *this* uptight." She slaps her palms on my desk and leans forward. The problem with this is that the front of her bodysuit gapes and I can tell she's not wearing a bra.

"I'm not uptight at all. I'm desperate."

Very, very desperate.

"Why?"

"Because I haven't had sex in months," I growl. "Pretend it's Lent, you gave up chocolate and now

I'm devouring a box of Godiva in front of you, but you still have to act civilized."

She nods decisively. "I think the potential size of the opportunity is huge. I'm up for sex one to three times a week. I say this because I know you like to plan your week. Next slide."

The Competitive Advantage:
Hazel is easy

I can honestly say that I've never spent much—any—time thinking about how hard it would be to seduce Hazel. If I had, however, I'd have assumed that she'd make her date work for it. Hazel understands what she's worth and that kind of self-confidence is sexy. I try to imagine myself dating her, taking her out for dinner and doing couple things. We've been friends for years. We talk. We spend time together outside of the office. But the kind of nakedness that comes with sex and emotional intimacy? Not a chance.

But whether or not I could date Hazel, one thing is certain and I say it out loud because we both really, really need to be on the same page here. "Nothing about you is easy."

Hazel shrugs. "I'm a sure thing. You don't have to wonder whether or not I'm going to put out at the end of the night. I also don't require romantic dinners, compliments, presents or fancy dating scenarios, although foreplay and discretion are not optional. It would all be very simple."

"So you just want me to show up, bang you and go? How exactly would this *merger* work? Because this sounds like a merger and not a start-up."

Hazel decides to ignore me and instead clicks through to her next slide. It's optimistically entitled The Product: Features and Benefits. It's also a bullet point list of sex acts.

"Those are what I'm best at," Hazel announces. "Although I'm flexible."

I can't decide if her presentation is a train wreck or a porn manual. It's definitely the most unique pitch I've ever heard. I gesture for her to move on to the next slide because I suspect that if we don't, she'll either review the list out loud or propose a demonstration.

Hazel points to a new slide labeled *Traction*. "The Hazel-and-Jack product already has some traction. The Saturday-night kiss proves we have chemistry and that there's market interest, although you may want to conduct some A-B testing."

I blink. "Are you telling me to go kiss another girl?"

"I'd be the better kisser." She says this with the utmost confidence.

Which is still sexy.

Robert knocks on the door and I jump, then give serious consideration to throwing myself over the laptop. When I motion for him to come in, he cracks the door just wide enough to stick in his head. He nods at Hazel politely before focusing on me. It's suddenly 110 degrees in my office.

"You have the Salas Group in five minutes."

He withdraws, shutting the door behind him.

"I'll wrap up," Hazel says. I catch a glimpse of slides outlining the business model, financial forecast and potential other investors in our hookup. I don't want to know. She stops on the final slide. Usually, the people pitching us end with a thank-you slide. Sometimes they throw in quotes from other investors or industry experts about how fabulous they are. Hazel has included screen caps of texts from previous boyfriends.

Attesting to her abilities in bed.

Does she screenshot all her text messages?

"Well?" She beams at me as only Hazel can.

Am I supposed to clap? Whip out my dick? Call down to Legal and have them write up a contract? Because that feels a little too *Fifty Shades of Grey* to me.

"I've never been pitched quite like this," I say cautiously. She wants to be friends...with *benefits*.

"Knee-jerk reaction?"

This is familiar. I shoot to my feet because I do my best thinking on my feet. "Not a chance. This could never work."

Hazel promptly steals my chair. Her fingers tap out an impatient rhythm. "List the cons. One minute— go."

If she insists. I grab a dry-erase marker and stride over to the whiteboard. When I turn around, Hazel's stolen my chair.

Reasons Why Jack and Hazel Could Never Work
 1. Dirty little secrets suck
 2. We see each other every day
 3. We'll never leave work
 4. People will question our judgment
 5. Someone's gonna walk in on you bent over
 my desk and there will be questions

That last one doesn't quite fit and the words trail up the side of the whiteboard, but the point has to be made. Hazel cranks her head to the side, reading along.

"Do you only do it bent over the desk? I could be on top. We could do it cowgirl style in your desk chair."

She's completely, totally unrepentant. "This is our *office*."

Hazel looks me in the eye. "I won't make anyone here uncomfortable. No one will have to choose between Mom and Dad when we stop having sex. And I won't back your crap deals just because you have a pretty face."

I scrub a hand over my face. Robert knocks on the glass wall again and makes an urgent wind-it-up gesture. I'm behind schedule. "I don't even know what to say to that."

"We could not do it at work." Those are Hazel's eyes watching me. They look into mine before traveling over my face and down my chest. Pink flushes her cheeks. Maybe I'm not the only one who feels slightly off-balance here.

Or not.

She crosses one leg over the other. "There are no *legal* reasons why your penis and my vagina should be off-limits to each other. In fact, there's only one reason that matters. Do you or do you not find me attractive?"

This is not about whether or not I think Hazel is hot. All I want is to not screw up our working relationship. Considering how much is on the line here, she should be grateful I want to do the right thing.

I open my mouth to point this out to her—she can thank me later—but she's already off and talking.

"I find you attractive." She gives me the sort of look I imagine a surgeon gives a body on an operating table right before he dives in and starts slicing. "You have a nice set of abs, you're tall, you have big hands. The blond barbarian look works for me in general, but I can rank order or call out specifics if you want."

I debate sitting down before I fall down, but Hazel's in my chair and the only other spot to sit is my desk. I hate it when anyone sits on my desk, as it messes up my stuff. Plus, that would put me far too close to Hazel.

Who is looking at me as if she's sizing up a display of chocolates. Or chips. Or maybe the meat counter. When did she even notice all this about me?

"Now do me," she says. And then sticks out her tongue. "*Not* like sexy *do me*. I can't help it if your mind lives in the gutter."

"You're the one who brought up sex."

"Take a look." She gestures at her boobs…and lower. Her grin has my dick standing at attention in my pants. "Tell me what you like about me. If you need an icebreaker, I'll point out my favorite parts."

I tear my gaze away from her boobs. I do *not* need Hazel playing show-and-tell in my office. She watches while I try to pretend she hasn't knocked me for a loop.

Hazel thinks I'm hot.

"Look," she says impatiently. Her right foot is swinging like a metronome. "We've covered the fiasco that is my dating life. My sex life hasn't been any more successful, and you're clearly experiencing the orgasm drought, as well, so I thought we could help each other out. I like sex. I like you. We do everything else together, so why not have sex together until we're ready to be in real relationships again?"

"Are you messing with me?"

The laughter she suppresses lights up her eyes, making the corners crinkle and her mouth curve. We've always teased each other—it's what friends do—but everything feels different today, just that little bit off. It's not bad—at least, I don't think so. But it's different and I'm not sure things are supposed to be different between us. Hazel is my constant.

"Not really. There are walking groups, running groups, hiking groups…but the sex groups are really strange. So I'd rather just have sex with a good friend. Someone I trust."

I blurt out the next part without thinking. "Who is hot."

"Well, yeah." Her grin is incandescent. She has a lush mouth beneath the slick of bright red color. Usually, she's talking, lips moving, hands flying to emphasize whatever point she's making. It's as if Hazel's entire body is just punctuation for what she's thinking. Normally, it makes me smile because only an idiot would underestimate Hazel's intelligence. Today, however, it drives me crazy because now I'm looking at her mouth, her arms, her goddamn fingers...and I'm imagining exactly how she could touch me.

"I'm self-serving, not a saint," she continues, as if I'm not burning up over here. "I'm just suggesting that, when we're not in the office, we have sex until we don't want to."

She's staring at me expectantly. I sort of feel like I should start stripping like a Chippendale dancer. "So rule number one—not in the office?"

She nods.

"And then we'll just stop?"

"Rule number two," she says. "When we're done, we're done—but we promise to still be friends. In fact, we should be friends first."

I have no idea what that means.

"Think about it." She hops up from my chair as the alarm on her phone goes off, reminding her she needs to be across town for a lunch meeting. Plus, the Salas Group people must be growing impatient by now. "And while you think about it, give Max's hookup app a try. Find someone, go out for dinner."

"Now you want me to hook up with someone

else?" Somehow I'm moving across the room toward her, and not because I'm rushing to a business meeting. My voice is rough, as if I've been thinking really dirty thoughts.

She winks at me as she dances away. "I just want you to be sure I'm the best."

CHAPTER FOUR

I'VE KNOWN FOR years that Max is either a sexual deviant or extraordinarily creative in bed—and, no, I don't want to know which—but I've never actually used his apps before. It's not that I'm unfamiliar with the user experience they promise to deliver— sex in all its dirty, delicious, fun variants—but I was in a committed relationship with Molly when he launched. My involvement with his product was limited to financial advising.

Hazel loaded both of Max's apps onto my phone— the first is the now-infamous Billionaire Bachelors app that lonely boys and girls can use to find love, happiness and a relationship. As the name promises, it identifies billionaires in a twenty-mile radius, along with their likes, their dislikes and the spots where they can frequently be found. When I check my profile, I discover that I'm hot, filthy rich, pro-monogamy and most likely to be found on the beach. I'm not sure how I feel about having been reduced to a set of check boxes even if they're not inaccurate.

The second app is Kinkster and it promises

happily-ever-afters of a dirtier and much briefer duration. There are fifteen single ladies offering hookup sex, ten willing to go down on me in various exotic or public locations and an unspecified number who would like one or both of us to dress up and reenact some very specific fantasies. I actually consider it for a few minutes, but it's not what I want, so I close the app.

But even though I'm not ready for love, marriage and happily-ever-after, I do want sex. I ignore the little voice in the back of my head that's cackling gleefully. I mean, I really shouldn't think about hooking up with a stranger. I did that a few times in college—before I met Molly—and it was fun but not terribly satisfying. Kind of like having a Twinkie instead of a Thanksgiving meal. It tastes good for the few seconds it takes to consume, but then you're still hungry.

The minute Hazel put Max's stupid Billionaire Bachelors app on my phone, I knew I was in trouble. Still, I promised her I'd give it a shot, and I keep my word. I've already knocked the five-mile run and bathroom cleaning off today's to-do list, so that leaves find a date. Gingerly, I navigate away from my profile—Max is definitely going to pay for that—and tap the Find The One button. I guess that's how I know I'm using the Billionaire app rather than Kinkster—one lover at a time. I'm pretty sure everything comes in multiples in Max's dirtier app. I'm not a dirty-sex guy—I've never been a dirty guy—but it's not as if I don't have an adventurous side. I love sex and adventurous sex is awesome, but I'd prefer to trust the person I'm having it with.

My phone pings with an incoming text from Hazel. Do you have a date?

I text back: Working on it.

The more I scroll, the more I suspect there's a whole lot of Photoshop happening because there can't possibly be this many attractive single people in the San Francisco area. Hazel hasn't responded to my last text yet, but I hit her with another message anyhow: None of this is real, right?

This time I get a response. I need a subject there, hotshot.

I don't even have to think. Dating profile pics. Does Max screen this shit at all?

Hazel fires back, Max has people for that. Or an algorithm.

Whatever he has, it's not working. It's like picking a watermelon at the store.

I eye the picture on my screen. Okay. *Two* watermelons. Either nature has been exceedingly kind or this particular bachelorette paid a visit to the dermatological produce aisle.

As if she's reading my mind, Hazel texts, Don't thump your date, 'kay?

Duly noted.

I'm not a barbarian. All spanking is consensual.

In fact, I think I might be too civilized for this. I don't really know what to say or do because this feels remarkably like picking someone out of a lineup for sex. I swipe, tap and poke my way through a blur of pictures, feeling more awkward with each photo— each *woman*. There's a *person* behind each picture even if all I see is the outside. There's a hairstylist who does celebrity hair, a booker for a local TV station, a software engineer, a hand model and an organic-fruit farmer.

Holy shit, I could not be less interested. I squint at the picture currently filling up my screen. It belongs to someone named May and she seems fairly normal when I zoom in on her picture. She has shoulder-length blond hair, brown eyes, an impish smile. She's pretty. She looks happy.

> I'm a kindergarten teacher who loves yoga, apple-picking and the ocean. Weekends are for baking and watching movies or curling up with a book with my perfect someone. Right now he has four paws, a tail and a passionate love for his squeaky bone, but I'm taking applications for new friends, as well. If you want to join me, send me a message.

I dutifully try to imagine going out with her. The last non-Molly dinner date I had was with Hazel, naturally, and it was technically a business expense. We went to a casual seafood stall down on the San Francisco wharf, where we had a slightly smelly view of the water and a dozen sea lions. We worked our way through a mountain of crab on newspaper with lemon and butter because Hazel had made it clear that anything else would be a cardinal sin. I think we'd closed a big deal that day, but that memory is gone—that was just business. I remember the important stuff. The way the salt air had teased her hair into a Jackie Kennedy bouffant do. How she licked red lipstick and butter from her mouth.

I tap out a quick hello to May before I can overthink things. Max, Dev, Hazel—they're right. I need to try meeting people. May must agree with them because she messages me right back.

Five minutes later, I have a date.

The restaurant May suggests that we meet at is highly reviewed on Yelp and is on the edge of the Santa Cruz boardwalk, cantilevered far enough out above the water that falling overboard would necessitate an ER trip. I've tipped/bribed the host for a table by the windows, which are open to let in the sea breeze, and I spot May the second she arrives. People sometimes lie, posting pictures from ten years ago or borrowing from a J. Crew catalog, but May looks like her picture. Blond hair floats around her shoulders and she's wearing a lavender sundress with skinny straps. A cropped denim jacket with crystal buttons is slung over her arms and she's wearing a pair of wedge sandals. The polka-dot ribbons crisscross around her ankles. She looks fun and approachable and sexy.

She waves at me as the maître d' leads her to our table, so perhaps I look like my picture, too.

Or whatever she imagined a venture capitalist looks like. Possibly, she just googled the hell out of me because it's not as if my face isn't online. I stand up to greet her. I'm waffling between a handshake and a friendly hug when she takes the decision out of my hands and brushes a kiss over my cheek. She smells like summer flowers, the kind Hazel's sisters grow in their front yards.

I'd like to say we make awkward conversation, but we don't. There's mostly just silence. After we order drinks, she toys with her straw and I try to think of something to say. Work. Work is always safe. Everyone has work stories.

"So. How are the kindergartners?"

May shares a cute story about today's arts-and-crafts project, in which macaroni noodles and toilet-paper tubes feature prominently. She shows me pictures on her phone and I make the appropriate noises.

When May asks me about my own week, I share a couple of carefully curated stories with her because I don't quite trust that whatever I tell her will stay between the two of us. It's happened to acquaintances—you meet a girl or a guy, have a few cocktails, swap a few stories, but then your dinner conversation shows up on a gossip site or someone horns in on the deal you were making. It's a cutthroat world. We should talk about her instead. I rack my brain, trying to remember the details from her dating-app bio.

"Have you picked any good apples lately?"

May stares at me blankly.

I recognize that look. Usually it makes an appearance when I bust the person pitching me on something they added to their pitch deck because they thought it sounded good, but then they forgot that they put it in and that they know nothing about it.

"Apple-picking? A deep-seated love of? In your profile?"

She laughs. It's a happy, light, totally obnoxious sound. Does she make it in bed, too? "Busted. My friend wrote that for me."

She says this as if it's no big deal that I just caught her in a little white lie. And maybe I am overreacting. Dating profiles are just marketing, right? And we all know the creative license a marketing department takes—the CEO doesn't approve every single word.

I forge ahead. "Okay, so no apples. Bananas? Pears? Pecans?"

May stares at me as if I'm crazy.

When she excuses herself to go to the ladies' room—ten long minutes after she arrives—I seize the chance to text Hazel.

SOS.

Hazel's response is immediate: Don't be such a baby. What's wrong?
I have a long list, but I'll sum up. Sitting in an ocean of awkward silence. Also, the apples were a lie. I want my money back. My dreams of apple-picking-ever-after are dashed.

Hazel: Well, shit.

Me: Yes, this is shit, thank you for asking. Rescue me.

Hazel: Tell me the plan.

Me: What?

Hazel: I know you. You have a plan, a backup plan and a parachute. Hit me.

Me: Am I that predictable?

Hazel: You're a control freak.

Me: Pot, kettle.

Hazel: Penetration strategy. Go.

Me: Inappropriate, Coleman.

Hazel: Pfft. You've sold her on the billionaire bachelor fantasy—she's at your table. You took her somewhere nice, right? Not tacos on the beach?

Me: Technically she's in the ladies' room and you like tacos on the beach.

Hazel: But I'm the backup plan. Woo her. Ask yourself, what would Prince Harry say? You can't go wrong there.

Me: 10 out of 10. You're good at this.

Hazel: Pfft. I'm the best. You can thank me with lattes. If all else fails, do the billionaire bad-boy thing.

May bounces back and I feel like I've just plunged my head inside a greenhouse full of very exotic flowers. Taking a deep breath might actually incite dizziness.

"Let's get to know each other!" she chirps.

I decide the bright smile on her face is—mostly—

genuine. It occurs to me that she might be nervous about tonight, too. The only things she knows about me are what Max has programmed into his stupid dating app.

"I'd love to," I tell her, and I think she believes me, because her eyes light up.

May opens her purse and pulls out a stack of pink cards. "You go first. Pick one."

I take a card. There's a question written on the back in flowery script.

If you had all the money in the world, what would you do?

I go with Hazel's suggestion and play the royalty card. "I'd open an elephant sanctuary in Africa, where orphaned and injured children could come to work with the animals and recover."

"Wow." May possibly goes a little slack jawed. She definitely leans into me, which just proves Hazel's favorite point, namely that Hazel is always right. "That's so noble."

My fingers itch to text Hazel about my newfound nobility—she'd cut me down to size with a pointed insult.

Instead, I salute May with my wineglass. "Your turn."

She grabs a card, flipping it over.

What's the most expensive thing you've ever bought?

It's like freaking kindergarten but without the crayons. May launches into a lengthy description of a handbag and I zone out. I'm not a fan of games. I think I'd prefer a more direct approach. I try to remember how Molly and I met, but the details are gone. I know there was a college party and far too much cheap beer. We took a couple of classes together, including a required PE class, where we had to square dance. Molly was even worse than I was.

The food is good, the wine is better and there are worse ways to spend an evening, even if I do have to list the contents of my car trunk—emergency flares, first-aid kit, gym clothes. And list three words my closest friends would use to describe me—*organized, reliable, loyal*. And choose my favorite Christmas present ever—the Lego Death Star, hands down.

May's game turns out to have thirty questions—naturally—and we work through twenty during the main course, saving the last ten for dessert. After we finish our mains, we opt for a stroll around the restaurant's deck while the waitstaff clear our table and prepare a chocolate soufflé.

May loops her arm through mine, her boob brushing against my arm. I don't think it's an accident, although I shift away like a vestal virgin. Max would die laughing. May's pretty, I inform my dick. She's friendly, fit and probably a whole lot of fun in bed. When we pause to gaze out at the ocean, she leans back against me, as if we've known each other for weeks or months. I could slide my arms around her or rest my cheek against her hair or catch her hand with mine. I could kiss her.

The problem is that I don't want to do any of those things. May's lovely, but I'm not interested in getting to know her better. I don't want to find out if she's a morning or an afternoon or a midnight kind of person, or whether she starfishes in bed or sleeps straight and still like a vampire in a coffin. And as much as I want to have sex again before I reach Viagra territory, I don't want to have sex with *her*—May—who turns out to love yachts and pink nail polish, tequila cocktails and seafood, glue sticks and holiday crafts. Sleeping with her just because I'm lonely isn't fair, no matter how willing she is to be romanced by a billionaire bachelor.

While May makes a second call to the ladies' room, I hightail it back to the table and tap out another SOS to Hazel. I need an exit strategy. A nice one.

Hazel's response is almost instantaneous. Option A: Fake a food allergy.

My bad food experiences are thankfully limited. Only one particularly memorable encounter springs to mind, when I consumed bad something—tacos, tequila, you name it—south of the border.

You want me to lie to the poor girl?

Hazel fires right back: Get off your high horse, Archangel. Or just puke and skip the talking.

She follows this up with a GIF of a cartoon character spewing a green tsunami on a red-checkered tablecloth. My stomach lurches, preparing a sympathy hurl, but Hazel's still typing.

Option B: Spew embarrassing personal details until she runs screaming.

This one feels more honest, but hardly less unpleasant. I eye the ladies' room door, but there's no sign of May. The problem with being a billionaire bachelor is that I have to worry about internet gossip sites. TMZ would have a field day with the details of my divorce, for example.

Option C, Hazel texts, I'll crash and drag you away. Do you want me to be crazy ex-girlfriend, exwife, or ex-hookup?

I go for the honest answer.

Just come.

Hazel doesn't miss a beat.

That's what SHE said.

CHAPTER FIVE

RESCUE ARRIVES THIRTY very long minutes later. May and I have finished our dinner and shifted to the bar. The pink cards come with us, although I've given up hope for the night. The bar's great, though. It's classic: polished, wood countertop, tall stools and shelf after mirrored shelf of liquor bottles. I count ten different kinds of whiskey alone. In the mirror, May and I make a cute couple. The bartender winks at me and gives me a thumbs-up. I ignore his knowing smile and focus on my date, who is casting my astrological chart on a cocktail napkin and admiring my love line. It's bold. Or strong. Or something. I don't snort because that would be rude.

"What's my future hold, love?" Our bartender leans in, subtly cutting me out with his shoulder as he smiles at May. "I could use a good heads-up."

May asks when his birthday is and he winks at her. "Tomorrow."

He's probably lying, but May rolls with it and starts scratching on a new napkin. All around us, the bar is full of happy, drinking, chatting people who have plenty of things to say, but I feel like an observer. The bartender is promising May that he can guess what she'll like. I'm not sure he means a particular drink, but she accepts something pink and frozen with a happy smile. He makes her feel special.

I'm pretending an all-encompassing interest in the drinks menu when May's eyes widen almost comically. I follow her gaze instinctively, but then her face is obscured by the blonde who drops onto my lap. My brain promptly short-circuits because my new companion wiggles as she starts to slide down my thighs. She has a fabulous ass. Thighs. I mean, honestly, the whole package meets with my enthusiastic approval, even when she wraps her arms around my neck like ivy on an oak. For the first time tonight, anticipation buzzes through my veins. And other parts.

"You owe me," the blonde whispers against my ear.

Hazel.

Of course it's Hazel.

I do owe her, although I suspect we should have agreed on a less open-ended plan. I also had no idea that Hazel kept a stash of emergency wigs in her massive walk-in closet. She turns with another hard-on-inducing wiggle until she's facing May, who is still staring. I don't think she saw our date ending this way, either. Hazel is wearing a pair of skinny jeans, white Fendi boots that stop just below the knee and a fitted white T-shirt with a black-Sharpied *White Knight* scrawled across her boobs. Since we're separated by mere inches, I can tell her eyes are lit up with impish glee. She has that wicked, hot-biker-chick thing going on for her—the kind of woman who graced my teenage bedroom walls and who I jerked off to more than I care to admit in high school. How is this woman possibly single?

"Excuse me?" May crumples up the bartender's future, sounding rather proprietary. Yeah. She's definitely decided I'm her billionaire bachelor.

Hazel leans forward. Instinctively, my hands cup her ass because she's straddling my legs and my knees... Well, I'm pretty certain I'm not supposed to notice what they're pressing against. Let's just say it feels amazing.

Look, I know this is a bad idea. I should just tell May that I don't think we're a match and that we should get on with our separate lives.

But I might be a little too aware that May's been fantasizing about her billionaire date night. If I'd simply been looking for a hookup or sex, I might ask if I could take her home or sweep her away to a palatial hotel in San Francisco. It's not as if there's a billionaire code of conduct that gets passed out when your bank account hits ten digits, but I'm literate and Hazel keeps stacks of Harlequins on her bedside table. As a member of the billionaire-boys club, I'm supposed to wine, dine and charm, preferably in a Maserati, a Hugo Boss suit and a penthouse suite.

"Bonjour, mon chéri." Blonde Hazel throws her arms around my neck in an octopus hold and swoops in.

Holy *shit*.

Her hands cup the side of my head, angling it until

she has me exactly where she wants me, and then her mouth covers mine. It's the kind of aggressively hot kiss that goes from zero to sixty in under a second. Her tongue strokes along my upper lip, I open and she takes full advantage. Our kiss gets hungrier, *noisier*. There is nothing subtle about how she kisses me—it's balls-out, loud, messy and the hottest thing ever. I feel her arms tighten, her breasts pressing against my chest. She's practically giving me a lap dance and we're sitting in a bar.

In public.

In front of May.

This is not the plan I would have gone with, but nevertheless I find myself falling into our kiss, my tongue dueling with hers because Hazel tastes amazing and this is…fun.

Hazel comes up for air and I grab her hands because I'm not sure how far she'll take this. She looks over her shoulder and winks at May. *"C'est moi."*

I'm no French expert but I don't think that makes sense.

"I'm calling an Uber," May says with fierce dignity.

I nod because she's a grown woman and we both know this isn't going to work.

The bartender slips a new, folded-up cocktail napkin to May. I'm pretty certain that it's his number, but whatever it is—number, grocery list, scathing indictment of my social skills—she tucks it into her purse with exaggerated care.

I should say something to her. Instead, I lift Hazel

off my lap, set her down on the bar stool next to me and walk May outside. She doesn't say anything while we stand shoulder-to-shoulder on the sidewalk, staring at the car icon crawling across the screen of her phone.

When the Uber pulls up to the curb, I make sure she's shared her ride details with a friend and I give her my number so she can text me that she's arrived home safely. And then I open the door so she can slide inside, except that she pauses, the open door between us. From the corner of my eye, I spot the Uber driver grinning at me. Even he knows I was overly optimistic about how this night would turn out. I flick him a salute and decide that I'll date again. When hell freezes over.

I lean down—the advantage of being built like a Viking—and brush my mouth over her cheek. "Thanks for having dinner with me."

She bends toward me as if she's thinking of what to say. "You could—"

"Be safe." I take a step back, fingers curling around the door handle.

I'm not thrilled that she's going to be riding home in the dark with a total stranger, but if I offer her a ride, she's going to read things into it. Conceited? Not really. She's staring at me like I'm a piece of chocolate cake with extra frosting and she hasn't quite decided if I'm worth breaking her diet and the extra time in the gym.

When the car drives off and I turn around, I find Hazel grinning like a loon as she throws her arms wide. Her T-shirt stretches over her boobs in a way that's either alarming or fabulous.

"Congratulations—you're a free man."

My smile feels lopsided. "Thanks."

Hazel's gaze slides over my face. "You're terrible at dating. Why did we run May off?"

Even I know I should definitely not answer the question. Instead, I take the most direct course toward my car. You might think that living in California means I'm eco-friendly and carbon conscious and all the rest of those laudable things, but the truth is that I like knowing where my exit points are. Having a car close by means I'm not dependent on anyone—or anyone's app—for my getaway. Ergo, I'm valet parked.

Hazel clicks along at my side. I'm constantly amazed by her speed in those ridiculous boots she loves. She keeps up effortlessly for the two blocks it takes to reach the private parking lot where my BMW is being babied under the watchful eye of a seventeen-year-old part-time employee. I hand him my ticket and a twenty.

Hazel loops her arm through mine and leans into me. This is less a friendly gesture than it is a practical one. Her T-shirt is thin and her bra thinner still. She's visibly cold.

"Why French?"

Hazel shrugs. "Why not May? She'd date you. You could have sex tonight."

Valet Boy jerks to a brief halt at Hazel's words. The twenty in his teenage pocket works its magic, however, because he lurches back into motion. I pretend he's not imagining me and my dinner guest doing it in a penthouse suite.

"It didn't feel right," I say.

Hazel groans dramatically. "It was two hours. How did things go so *wrong*? You're a guy. You have a penis. This should be like basic math."

I try not to think about Hazel thinking about my penis. Or how she makes a popping sound on the letter *P*, the same kind of ripe, juicy sound her mouth would make coming off my dick.

"It was forever," I counter. "And easily."

"You just need more practice." Hazel's wrapped around my arm so tightly that she's starting to cut off my circulation. I'm honestly not sure if I'm allowed to think about Hazel's breasts, but they're hard to ignore. Her nipples are tight little twists that demand sucking.

No.

Cold Hazel is one problem that I can fix. I peel her off my arm, shuck my jacket and wrap her up in it.

When the valet finally returns with my car, I open the passenger-side door for Hazel and wait. She makes a face but slides in. I add a point to my mental score.

"Did you drive?"

Hazel laughs. It's part snort, part guffaw, all Hazel. I'm not sure she knows how to hold back. "Car service."

She pulls off the blond wig and tosses it into the

back seat. Her own hair is pulled back in a tight, sleek knot at the base of her neck.

"Prudent." Hazel's a late bloomer when it comes to driving, having only just gotten her driver's license a year ago—and only after three attempts at passing the road test. Max, Dev and I spent hours coaching her, but Hazel's still not convinced—she says—that God intended human beings to drive faster than twenty miles an hour. Max claims that she's a reincarnated Amish person in mourning for her buggy. Whatever the reason, however, the truth is that Hazel is the world's slowest driver. She still won't tell me how she actually passed her road test, but Dev believes bribery was involved.

It hasn't quite hit me that I've had my first date since Molly and I split. I stare at the road, concentrating on staying perfectly between the lines. The ocean spins away on our right, the dark water melting into the horizon. Just a few days ago, Hazel offered herself to me, suggesting that we sleep together until we both come up with better options. It's a strangely seductive thought, although not a plan that I should be entertaining. Hazel and I are business partners and best friends, and introducing naked activities to that relationship would be a mistake.

"Tell me about your date." Hazel manages to curl into me, despite the ample legroom in the BMW. She flicks on the seat warmer and groans. Is that the sound she makes when she's having sex?

"There's nothing to tell. We met, we had drinks, dinner was consumed and then a crazy woman landed in my lap and my date decided it was time to exit stage left."

Hazel's head against my arm makes shifting difficult, but I manage. "You need more practice. I'll help. I can be your practice date. Chat me up. Hit me with your best lines."

I slide a quick glance at her. "You want me to hit on you?"

"I'll start," she says. "You must be an angel because I'm in heaven!"

I mock-groan and one-up her. "Somewhere in heaven they're missing an angel."

"I can die happy now because I've seen heaven," Hazel shouts.

We trade corny lines back and forth, smirking as we try to top each other. I tuck an escaping strand of hair behind her ear. For a second, my finger traces the curve of her ear.

"Hazel?"

"Yeah?" She fiddles with the dashboard again, but I don't think she's still cold.

"What's the last pickup line that worked on you?"

She doesn't even have to think about it. "Guys don't try to pick me up, Jack. I'm too scary, too blunt, or too successful. Sometimes *D*—all of the above."

"They're stupid." It's not the most articulate assessment of my life, but it's accurate.

Hazel nods in agreement. "Absolutely. So I wouldn't want to have their babies, anyhow. Imagine the gene pool."

There's nothing I can say to that, so I lose myself

in the car. I love driving as much as Hazel hates it, and my BMW is fucking amazing. I downshift into a curve, slowing as we start up the mountain. The road to her place is a serpentine delight of curves and hairpin turns and steep, tree-covered drop-offs. The kind of person who lives here doesn't want to see or hear from neighbors, so even though the houses here come in all shapes, sizes and stages of dilapidation, the one thing they have in common is an enormous amount of tree-covered space. And since there are no streetlights, I have plenty of time to admire each and every branch as I ease forward.

"You should live on the beach like a civilized person," I tell her.

She sticks her tongue out at me. "And when the tsunami hits, you'll be begging to stay with me."

"The odds of a tsunami in California are low. It's the earthquakes you have to watch out for."

Hazel not only lives in the mountains, but she also has an honest-to-goodness log cabin for a house. Laura Ingalls would be jealous. Two stories of rough-cut goodness, a shit ton of windows and French doors, and closer proximity to the woods and its resident wildlife than I'm strictly comfortable with. While most of the snakes in Santa Cruz are either of the harmless or Silicon Valley variety, Hazel has spotted more than one rattlesnake swanning its way around her property. It is not a *feature* as far as I'm concerned.

"If you lived at the beach, you could have a moat,"

I point out. I pull into her driveway, easing to a stop. A barrage of security lights go on.

"True, but then I'd have to fend off all the surfers and riffraff. Nobody comes up here." She says that as if it's a selling point.

I put the car in Park as Hazel hops out at warp speed. I follow as quickly as I can just in case bears or other wild animals put in an appearance. Hazel makes a face. She's pointed out before that she has yet to get lost, mauled or otherwise injured on her way to her front door. As always, I ignore her because insurance never hurts.

"So. Hold this." She shoves her bag into my hand and proceeds to rummage inside for her keys. Hazel's bag is the disorganized disaster her life is not. "Next steps, Viking man. Invite a new girl out."

"I don't think I'm ready to date."

"Of course you are. You just need practice."

"We practiced. What do you think?"

She winks at me. "How's your kissing?"

"There's no safe answer to that."

"Dating's not low risk, either." Hazel's key disappears into the lock and there's a quiet snick as the tumblers turn over. "But if you can't charm the lady with your dinner-table wit, I'd suggest making her panties melt."

I shouldn't ask, but… "Is that really a thing?"

Hazel grins. "Do you really want me to explain it? Hint: it's directly related to your kissing skills."

I need to stop thinking about Hazel and panties.

"Do you want me to show you?" I brace an arm

over her head. If she opens the door now, I'll crash-land in her living room, but it's worth it for the comical look on her face. As if no guy in recent memory has gotten too close on her doorstep and gone in for a good-night kiss. Apparently I also can't stop thinking about her offer to be my friend with benefits. I need help. An intervention. Possibly a two-by-four to the head.

Because that's my voice still talking and digging a ginormous, dirty hole. "You're the one who said I needed practice. *Practice* with me?"

Hazel blinks, her eyes widening as her gaze moves over my face and then lower. Her tongue darts out to wet her lower lip and I'm lost. I've been lost for some time, if I'm honest. Every nerve in my body seems to be on fire, starting with where my fingers just brush her hair and our legs almost touch. I think I close that not-quite distance. Or she does. But somehow our bodies meet, erasing all the space I've worked so hard to keep between us.

I *feel* her.

Hazel.

"Tell me yes." I bend closer, so that my mouth brushes her neck. "Or tell me good night. But you have to choose for us, Zee."

I've stood next to her, beside her, behind her hundreds of times. Objectively, I know exactly how tall she is and when she changes her shampoo or tries a new scent. We're *friends* and yet I run my mouth up her throat, breathing this new, unfamiliar side of her in. The scent of her skin floods my lungs. I want to make her part of me, draw her deep inside my body so that she's always part of me and not this strange, exotic terra incognita that makes me wild to explore.

She reaches up, her arms sliding around my neck to pull me closer as her head tips back in invitation. "Yes, kiss me."

I can't bite back my smile. "You're the boss."

Her eyes narrow because she hates being teased, but now there's no way I don't kiss her. I cover her mouth with mine and I learn something new about my best friend. Her mouth is soft and warm. She tastes amazing. And she's an all-in kisser. Her lips part and she angles her head, trying to devour me. It's fucking hot. Her tongue strokes across my bottom lip and she groans something. A word. A plea. Knowing Hazel, it's probably a demand for more.

Her hands pull at my waist, tugging my shirt free and skimming up my back. Butterfly touches. Heat ignites in me. I pull back so that I can kiss her bottom lip and then the top. Her mouth is surprisingly, shockingly soft. She's hungry. I can hear her ragged breathing as if there's not enough air. Not enough touching. She's all warm female, sweet welcome and porn-star noises.

I could kiss her all night, but instead I ease my mouth away from hers. Her eyes meet mine as my thumb traces the curve of her lower lip. She's in a hurry, but me… I want to take this slow. I want to savor my first real taste of Hazel. A kiss is an audition. It's the magic moment when you judge me. Are we compatible? Do I want more? Do *you*? That cheek kiss with May? Not an accident. Bad kisses are the worst. They're hard to fix or to figure out why the hot ones rock our world so hard. Kisses are *personal*.

Christ, she's... These are the same lips that have barked at me, argued with me, laughed with me and told me more than once that Hazel's way is the best way. But I've never seen them this way before, not as belonging to someone I'd like to kiss. Not wet and slick from my mouth. Not kiss-bruised and greedy for me.

I find her hand with mine and thread our fingers together. It's silly, but I sort of want all the date things with her, and we haven't held hands yet. I cup her face with my other hand because I'm a greedy bastard. I'm a big guy and Hazel's petite, so my fingers curl around her neck and slip into her knot of hair. For one moment, I let myself imagine pulling her hair. Taking charge, taking over. I want to fuck her more than anything I've ever wanted.

"Again," she demands.

Anything. Everything, as long as it happens *now*.

Our mouths meet, clash, our hands running over each other, learning the outlines of our bodies. She's all warmth and lean strength, and I kiss her harder, deeper. She has a death grip on my neck now, her nails biting my skin as she makes a throaty, needy sound.

I rest my forehead against hers. "How am I doing?"

She beams at me and undoes my tie. "Nailed it."

CHAPTER SIX

YOU NEVER FORGET your first kiss.

Even when you want to. My *first* first kiss was a wet, enthusiastic middle-school attempt. Jenny Dormon cornered me behind the big oak tree on the far corner of the playground and I gave as good as I got. By high school, I'd learned why French kissing was the best, and by college I was a master. And, yes, this is technically our second kiss, but it's our first on-purpose kiss and it's fucking amazing.

I look down at Hazel. Her brown eyes are sparkling and she's got those happy crinkles she bemoans because she claims they'll lead to Grand Canyon–sized wrinkles when she's older. Her face is flushed, her lips still parted and damp. It should not surprise me that she's a champion kisser. Hazel doesn't like to be anything but the best, and she's competitive. I bet she's amazing in bed. She probably thumbs through her monthly *Cosmo* looking for sexy tricks to add to her bag even though she's totally awesome just being Hazel.

"I'm the king of good-night kisses," I whisper

against her hair because somehow we're touching again, her body melting into mine as if she's trying to imprint every second of our kiss. As if maybe she also wants so much more than just this.

"So," she says. "Answer a question for me?"

"You got it."

"As your practice date, will you respect me in the morning if I let you hit a home run?"

Considering how much time I've spent thinking about Hazel tonight, there's only one possible choice. "Open the door, Hazel."

She grabs my head with one hand and pulls my mouth down to hers. Our third kiss is rougher and hungrier than our first two. I break it off, scoop her up in my arms and tuck her against my chest as I open her front door.

"Viking man." It doesn't sound like an objection—plus, the way she's laughing and wriggling makes my dick harder still.

I tap her butt in mock warning, my palm sliding over the curve of her ass.

"I feel passionately about level playing fields and treating all participants equally," she warns. Laughter warms her voice, and fuck me if she doesn't reach around and pinch my butt.

"Are you a completely even-Steven kind of girl?" I head toward her bedroom. I've been in Hazel's house hundreds of times, so I know exactly where I'm going. Her bedroom's at the end of the hallway. "So if I go down on you for twenty minutes, you'll go down on me for twenty?"

"I'm the best partner ever," she says smugly as I toe-open her bedroom door. It looks almost the same. A mountain of decorative pillows devours the bed, and bookcases line the south-facing wall. The shelves are filled with her beloved paperbacks. The room is dark except for the night-light in the bathroom, which is more like a lighthouse or the Eye of Sauron, that cuts through the dark.

I shove the heap of furry, completely useless pillows off the bed with one hand, juggling my Hazel present as I yank back the duvet. Hazel's bought a new one since the last time I was here—it's pink and velvety soft. Strangely, it's not awkward, not like I thought it would be, not even when I drop her onto the space I've cleared and our eyes meet. Or when she laughs and throws herself backward, kicking her legs up for some reason known only to her.

I totally want to do this with her.

My fingers are reaching for her before I've finished replaying the steps of tonight's plan in my head. Thanks to yoga and designer jeans, bendy Hazel's got her ankles on my left shoulder now and my hands are reaching for the zippers on those merciless fuck-me boots. She has the best taste in footwear.

The air rasps out of me as I tug down the zipper on her left boot and slip her foot free. The boot goes… fuck if I know. Later—as in many, many orgasms later—I'd like to have Hazel wearing just the boots and nothing else, but right now I'm crazy for her and I can't wait. The right boot joins its mate on the floor and then my hands are reaching for the waistband of her jeans. She helps me shove them down, grinding her hips against the bed as if she's already skipped ahead in her beautiful, sexy head.

"Wait for me."

"Hurry up." The smirk on her face is awesome.

I run my hands up the silky skin of her inner thighs. She has a freckle above her right knee that merits much closer inspection. With my mouth. I kiss her there, drinking in the greedy sounds she makes. She jumps as I move higher, the muscles tensing and relaxing, tensing and relaxing. Her skin is so warm.

"Cute." Hazel's panties are black cotton boy shorts. I pause my upward quest to breathe her in.

"I was in a rush or I would have worn my date-night panties."

I grin and run my thumbs higher. She squeaks. "Are those like day-of-the-week panties? I'm going to need to check what you're wearing in the office."

"Don't make me put you in the naughty corner. The not-in-the-office rule stands." She wriggles, stretching, and her hand disappears between us. A second later, her fingers discover my dick. She squeezes gently and I make a rough noise. Hazel's take-charge. I'm not sure why I'm surprised. She loves to be in control…but so do I.

I cup her ass with my hands, drag her to the edge of the bed and press her legs wide with my shoulders. Bending my head, I consider my plan of attack. So many delicious options. I lean in and kiss her through the cotton of her panties. We'll take this slow. I'll make her scream. It's a great plan.

Step one—kiss her senseless. I press my mouth against Hazel, first softly, then harder. Higher. Her breath catches and her hands fist the sheets as I tease her with the lightest of pressure.

"Faster," she moans. "Don't be such a beast, Jack."

"Feedback is welcome." I suck lightly at her clit through the damp cotton. "But I think you'll like my plan."

Hazel curses, but she also angles her hips, pressing her clit against my tongue. I hold still so she can ride me, finding the angle she likes best, a small, tight circle. I try not to think about how she's going to feel wrapped around my dick, the hot, wet heat, the slick clench of her inner muscles letting me know exactly how much she's enjoying what I give her.

"Jack—" She moans my name like a porn star. Fuck, this woman is amazing.

She totally deserves a reward.

I move my thumbs, spreading her through the thin cotton. Slow is best, even though I want to lick her from head to toe right now. This is Christmas morning and I want to tear into all my presents right now, uncover all the secrets. I have all night, I remind myself.

I slide against her gently with my thumbs like I ache to do with my dick. Once. Twice. She arches, moaning more incomprehensible shit I decide I can ignore. If there's a problem, Hazel will tell me. Instead, I let my thumbs glide up and down the seam of her pussy while I trace her clit with my tongue.

She smells amazing, so I'm betting she'll taste even better. I need to do that next. I need—

And then she freezes. Bingo. Hazel's hips arch up as we find the spot she likes best. She's breathing hard, her fingers tearing at my hair.

"I've got you," I whisper against her. I won't leave her wanting.

"Cocky bastard," she groans. I think that's a compliment.

My hands drag her closer, gripping her sweet, toned ass, and I lift her higher so she can relax. And then I cover her clit with my mouth, sucking and stroking, scraping ever so lightly with the edge of my teeth. She shrieks and then, fuck me, she starts coming.

She talks the whole time, a litany of curses and my name and instructions of "don't move, don't you dare, like that, oh, *God*." I've been promoted to deity status and I don't even give her shit about it. I'll just have to do my best to live up to my newfound godhood.

A long time later she stops talking and collapses back on the bed as if someone just removed all her bones and replaced them with a puddle of happy. Yeah, that would be me. I hide my smirk from her because I'm not stupid. Her ass will be sore tomorrow from all the clenching—I make a mental note to offer her a butt massage.

I slide a finger beneath the edge of her panties, breathing harshly, trying to draw this out. She's so damn hot. And wet. My finger slips over her folds, finding nothing but sweet, sweet welcome.

"May I take these off?"

"Wait." Her fingers curl around mine, and it feels sexy and full of possibilities, but I pay attention to that one word. *Wait.* I ease back. *Please don't have changed your mind.* I'm not sure I wouldn't beg, and Hazel would never let me live it down.

I shift up the bed and pull her on top of me so that she's staring down at my face. "What's up?"

Her fingers squeeze my shoulder. "It'll be simpler if we just say what's off-limits at the beginning. I'm no good at guessing."

"Ladies first."

"I like it best if I sit on your lap facing you, but reverse cowgirl throws my back out. I can't kiss you and come at the same time because I have to focus. You can put one finger in my ass, but not three. Your fingers are huge. Fast is always better. Your turn."

I lean up and kiss her hard because laughing now would be a bad idea. "Face-off sex, no kissing at important moments, be aware of the size-volume ratio. Got it."

Hazel frowns suspiciously. "Are you making fun of me?"

God, she kills me.

"Never. I don't have a death wish." I pull her grumpy, beautiful face down to mine and kiss her because I can. She starts unbuttoning my shirt, shoving it open and pushing my white T-shirt up so she can run her hands over my abs and sides. My tie's gone, vanished, probably decorating her front doorstep.

"Off," she mutters against my mouth, tugging on the shirt.

I sit up, bringing her with me. Together we yank my T-shirt over my head and send it sailing across the room. Hazel's definitely impatient—her hands work the bottom of her own shirt, pulling it up. For a moment, the cotton catches on her hair and I'm staring at her bra-covered boobs.

Hazel's wearing lace. My brain short-circuits. It's not like I haven't seen a bra before, but this one hardly qualifies. It's more like a wet dream come true, like some dirty genie decided to grant the three wishes of my teenage self and started with the best-ever fantasy bra. Wicked little straps cross her suntanned shoulders and the cups barely skim her nipples. It's white, but that's the only demure thing about her. If I'd known she was hiding *this* underneath that ridiculous T-shirt, things would have gotten a whole lot raunchier at the bar.

"What is this?" I growl.

Hazel vanquishes the T-shirt, cups her boobs and smirks at me. "What I wore to the office today. I didn't have time to take it off before you cried for help. It's pretty awesome, isn't it?"

Apparently my dick can get harder.

"You're beautiful."

Hazel's smirk gets deeper. "I'm well-packaged. Unwrap me?"

Fuck. *Yes.*

She's laughing at me but I'm staring at her boobs, in heaven. Maybe those pickup lines weren't so cheesy after all. I rip off the bra, anyhow, then lower my head to explore this new piece of Hazel. My lips cover her skin in kisses and my slo-mo plan is rapidly flying out the window.

She feels so, so good.

I'll have to make her feel good. Better than good. Coming once isn't enough. It's not like I haven't had sex before, even if it hasn't happened in recent memory, but this feels different.

Because this is the first time for me and Hazel.

The panties come off now, I decide. I pull her up with me, dragging the cotton down her legs as I wrap my arms around her waist.

"You're still dressed." She sounds pissed off. "Fix it."

"Your wish." I shift her to the bed and toe off my shoes. "My command."

My socks follow and then we unbuckle, unzip, shove my dress pants down together. She's kissing down my chest before we finish getting me naked, licking and nipping like the stock market's closing in seconds. Her hand palms me, making me hers.

I suck in a breath. Naked Hazel is amazing. I run my hands down her arms, her back, her hips. Her skin is sweat-slicked and I lick her clean. More kisses, on her breasts, her shoulders, the sweet curve of her belly. I look at her, seeing her for the first time. Impatient, hot, funny Hazel.

Why haven't we done this sooner? She's magical— all lush curves, toned muscles, soft skin that begs for my touch. No, *demands*, because this is Hazel and she can't not be bossy. Her nipples are tight, dark points, her breasts the perfect size for me to cup. For such a petite woman she has surprisingly long, lean legs, the odd freckle dotting her skin. I'm going to learn them all. I'm going to make a map of Hazel and memorize her.

"You're beautiful." My voice is hoarse.

Hazel makes an impatient gesture. "Now."

It's a good plan. I reach down, fish for my wallet and come up with a condom.

"Somebody's prepared," she says.

It's true. I'd never put her at risk and I'm damn sure not going to make her ask awkward questions.

"I'll help." Hazel drops to her knees in front of me, her eyes on mine. Her palms wrap around my dick and there's no question that I'm ready for what comes next. She leans in and swipes her tongue over me. Let's be honest. There's no way to screw up a blow job. All it takes is one mouth and one dick and the results are going to be spectacular, but Hazel is unbelievable. She cups my balls gently and then sucks me in. It's slow and deep, wet and hot, and then her head's bobbing and I have no idea how the physics of this is working, and I don't care. She's working me until I'm pumping her mouth, fucking her hard and deep until I'm on the edge of the mother of all orgasms.

"Stop." I need to get inside her now.

She holds her palm out. "Condom."

I hand her the packet and she tears it open, rolling the condom down my dick.

"Now hurry up," she says.

"Compromise." My voice is a whiskey-rough growl. I lift her up, sink down on the edge of the bed and pull her slowly down onto my lap.

I'm in Hazel.

I'm pushing deep inside her body and she's stretching wide to take me.

I say her name out loud because there has to be a way to make this feel more real. "Hazel."

"Jack." Her eyes laugh at me, but then her mouth is on me and she's pressing little kisses against the hot skin of my throat.

Christ, she feels amazing. I shouldn't compare, shouldn't remember other nights, but nothing has ever felt this good. I pull her close to me, my arms guiding her hips as she rides me hard and fast, her arms thrown around me. She's not letting go, either. She buries her face in my throat, whispering, biting down, her whole body tightening on mine as she pants and groans.

Just riding my dick probably won't be enough. I reach between us and find her clit, drawing tiny, dirty circles around her. Hazel moves faster.

Her nails dig into my shoulders as she freezes, her body clenching hard. "Jack…yes."

I pound into her, my hips matching the rhythm of hers. I feel the heartbeat that springs to life between her legs, the tight pulsing of her body as she grips me, the hot, electric pleasure that has us both making rough, feral sounds. There's nothing pretty or planned about this and I'm so fucking triumphant, like her Viking man after he's pounded ashore and seized the castle.

I brace my feet against the floor and shove deeper. She slams down to meet me. "Harder," she growls. "Make me feel, Jack. Make me—"

She's amazing.

She shuts up, her body stiffening as she yanks me closer, and then she's coming and I'm not far behind her. We're not quite in sync, but this is even better. I feel every pulse of her orgasm before I follow her over the edge and empty myself into her.

"Tell me you came." If she didn't, I'll just start again and get it right.

"Yes." She nods enthusiastically.

I fall back onto the big, wonderful bed, taking her with me. My heart's trying to claw its way out of my chest and I can feel the answering beat from Hazel's. Her hair's all messed up, her face flushed. We're a hot, sticky mess and all I can think is

Yes

Let's do this again

Right now

Hazel exhales noisily into my chest. "Wow. That was…"

She flounders, looking for adjectives.

I know how she feels. "Everything. It was every-thing."

CHAPTER SEVEN

SUNDAY IS MY new favorite day. Hazel and I have a standing sleepover date on Saturday evening and then we hang out on Sunday. Sometimes we pile into bed and work next to each other on our laptops with cartons of takeout and champagne, or we lug everything down to the beach if we're at my place. Usually I can be productive no matter where I find myself. The train, stuck in traffic, a blanket on the sand near the ocean—it doesn't matter. I put my head down and focus because I have a lot to accomplish and time doesn't wait.

Being with Hazel, however, is its own challenge. Half of my brain looks at her and sees my business partner. That's the smart half, the half that thinks and plans. It suggests we should get to work. The other half of me, however, argues that working is the last thing I should do when I could be getting Hazel naked. Getting inside her. Unfortunately, that half is a really persuasive arguer and our beachy work sessions always seem to end with us naked.

This is why, when Hazel suggests we work outside at her house, I refuse. I don't care if there's an ancient Japanese-forest bathing ritual—I've seen what lurks in Hazel's trees and there's no way I'm lounging around on the ground. Even she has to agree that everything ends with sex. But I'm not complaining. After all, that's the whole purpose of this friendship with benefits. We hang, we do the business thing and then it's orgasms for all.

Four weekends after our first not-date, it's my turn to host. Saturday night we have a business dinner with some other Silicon Valley influencers. Not touching Hazel is torture. Afterward, I drive us to my place, but Hazel's brimming with ideas sparked by the dinner meeting and she can't not hunker down with her laptop and start working through them.

It's cute, plus she usually has great ideas. I'm not going to get in her way. I don't say anything as she climbs into my bed, arms wrapped around her laptop. I just grab my own laptop, fetch us both a cognac and prop the French doors open so we can hear the ocean. Turns out we do awesome bedroom brainstorming. Hazel's definitely on to something we'll chase next week at work. It almost makes waiting to touch her worth it.

I get up when Hazel waves her empty glass in my direction as she mutters at her screen. Since I can take a hint, I find the cognac, splash a few inches into her glass and decide it's too much effort to go downstairs for ice.

When I turn around, Hazel's made herself comfortable. She's sprawled on her stomach, the T-shirt she stole from my closet slipping down one bare shoulder. Kissing her seems way more fun than the twelve spreadsheets she has open on her desktop. I set the cognac on the floor a safe distance from the bed because we tend to send the pillows and blankets flying when we have sex.

Hazel's still distracted when I duck underneath the covers at the bottom of the bed and slide up. I run my hands over her legs and she shrieks. Hazel's super ticklish, which is both funny and fun. I press more firmly, the way she likes, then press her down into the mattress with my body and convince her to take a break.

Sunday sunshine pours through the floor-to-ceiling windows in my bedroom. The California king bed is loaded with crisp white cotton sheets, a white duvet and a small army of pillows, because—like orgasms—one is never enough for Hazel and she "hooked me up" with pillows after our first sleepover. Hazel is currently starfished in the center, taking full advantage of my absence. When I slid in beside her last night, she wrapped herself around me like a baby monkey.

She's sleeping hard, her hair ruffled around her face. After she showers, she'll flat-iron it and apply crap from a half-dozen mysterious tubes until her hair is once again a sleek, shining cap. Watching her put herself back together is almost as good as taking her apart.

Step one in my wake-up-Hazel plan involves a kiss. Step two is all about the mug of coffee I hand over when she cracks one eye and shoves blearily upright. I'd like for step three to involve morning sex, but I'm not sure if Hazel has other plans for us today or not.

"Do we have anything on for today?"

She clutches the coffee like a lifeline. "Noon brunch at the compound?"

"Got it." I peek at my phone and run the numbers in my head. It's almost eleven. We could probably still sneak in quickie sex before we're so late that we have to explain why.

Hazel's family owns an insanely large double lot in Santa Cruz mere blocks from the beach. It's crammed full of artsy bungalows, small houses and she sheds. I asked Hazel once if they were aware of the numerous zoning violations and she just shrugged and said that she'd taken care of it.

Unfortunately, Hazel figures out the time for herself and launches herself into my bathroom. She's high-maintenance in the morning, so I figure it's better to let her get started. She's been this way as long as we've been friends. Hazel's standing in the shower when I wander in—she gestures impatiently for me to join her.

"This will be quicker. Plus, we can save water and I'll fill you in on the brunch plan. We'll merit some kind of special California award." She slaps the soap into my hand.

I'm as much a fan of efficiency as the next guy,

but Hazel's mistaken if she thinks my being naked and wet in a shower with her will save time or water. We've already christened my shower, so she knows exactly what can happen in here.

"You'd better give me the details fast."

The look Hazel gives me says she's on to me. "We're having brunch at the compound. The usual suspects will be there, although I've been warned that George the Git is coming and that he wants to pitch you a business idea. What you do with that information is up to you, but any money you give him is a charitable donation to the Cause of George. You'll never see it again, but I guarantee he'll be back for more."

"Do we need gifts? Flowers? A restraining order?"

The monthly brunch is more of a birth-aversary-ation, a Frankenstein event that I should be used to. The Colemans celebrate every birthday, anniversary, graduation and date of note for the current month with one big breakfast meal. Hazel catches me up on who's been doing what and then shares the latest entirely unfounded speculations that have been making the family rounds. This consumes the rest of the shower despite my best efforts to distract her.

My family doesn't really factor into our weekend plans. They're across the country, in New England. I pitch them at least once a year about the benefits of California living, but so far they've refused to make the move. As a result, I own a farmhouse on the Maine coast. I travel back for all major holidays and work remotely in the fall. We didn't have much in the money department growing up, but we had each other and we made that be enough. I worked two jobs through high school and then I followed the money to college. Not gonna lie—I played for high stakes, banking on an Ivy League acceptance, but the best offer had come from UCSC and so that's where I went.

Good men look after the people in their lives. Bad men don't. I don't have to tell you which one I want to be, and a quarter-million-dollar education just didn't fit into that picture. From the time I was eight and my daddy dropped dead of a heart attack, it was me, Momma and my four sisters. The Reed rules are simple:

1. Take responsibility.
2. Family first.
3. No one you love should want or hurt.
4. Fix what's wrong. See rules 1, 2 and 3.

The Colemans play by a similar set of rules— they're just louder about it. Much, much louder. Their compound is like a hipster version of the Kennedy compound. It's surrounded by castle-worthy stucco walls and worth a small fortune. The first time I saw it, I asked Hazel if any of her high-school boyfriends yelled for Rapunzel to let her hair down.

Once Hazel and I are dressed and out the door, it doesn't take long to get to the compound. Unfortunately, since we don't arrive at the crack of dawn, I'm reminded firsthand that parking is a competitive sport in this neighborhood. I score the last open spot. Even better, I slide into it right before one of Hazel's sister's fiancés can do so. The Colemans respect ruthlessness—Hazel's ability to amass a billion-dollar fortune is entirely expected after you've met her family.

As soon as we go in, Hazel's mom greets us, George the Git firmly attached to her side. George is her boyfriend and a bad seed according to anyone not dating him. With the exception of Hazel, the Colemans are all terrified that Margie will finally agree to marry the guy. He's a flirty bastard who clearly adores Margie. Unfortunately, he's also a serial entrepreneur with zero business skills, and Margie spends far too much time picking up his messes.

"You've got the big three-oh coming up, darling. You should be doing something special." Margie stares meaningfully at Hazel.

George slaps me on the back and suggests, sotto voce, that we wander off for a craft beer and a catch-up because he has an idea he wants to run by me. I plant myself firmly by Hazel's side.

Hazel ignores her mom's subtext because she recognizes a losing battle. "It's a weekday. I'll be working, Mom."

"Ask your boss for the day off."

Hazel makes a noncommittal noise and steers me toward the table of food laid out underneath two enormous lemon trees. The food is amazing, as always. Two of Hazel's sisters cook and everyone else has mastered the concept of takeout. I hold two plates so Hazel can load them up. "Are you asking your boss for the day off? I've heard he's a strict one."

Hazel gives me a smug smile. "Pretty sure my *boss* isn't going to be a problem. I can give myself the day off anytime I want."

"You should check the calendar." Our fingers and arms brush as we navigate the length of the table. Something inside me aches a little that she knows what I want and don't want on my plate. "Because I'm certain that it's my month to be the boss."

Hazel frowns, clearly flipping through a mental calendar. "Nice try. Were you planning on being a hard-ass boss or just a hot boss?"

Heh. I lean closer because while I'm happy to share my fantasies with Hazel, I don't need to broadcast them to the entire Coleman clan. "I'm voting hot. I could also do bossy, bastard or bondage."

"Points for the alliteration." Hazel sounds a little breathless and I can't help but wonder which word she's thinking about.

"Should I elaborate, too?" I sound hoarse, but *hello*. Sexy banter at the Coleman brunch is a first for me.

The more important question is why *Hazel* sounds like she's doing some thinking of her own. I'm betting it's the word *bossy* that does it for her, or maybe I'm just being realistic about my ability to let Hazel take charge. The best I can manage is a fifty-fifty split, so it would be easiest if she had secret erotic fantasies about me giving her sexy bedroom commands in the boardroom, where anyone could walk in on us. The orange sundress she's wearing is definitely fantasy fuel. The skirt floats around her legs and I could flip it up, bend her over the table…

A voice from far too close has us springing apart. "You're holding up the line."

Katie, sister number one, taps me on the shoulder, indicating that I should move on. We do, taking our plates over to the crowd spread out beneath the big trees. There's California champagne with slightly squashy blackberries in Margie's mismatched—or totally unique—collection of glass flutes. Hazel sits cross-legged beside me, sundress carefully tucked beneath her knees, waving her glass as she makes some point to her sister. The rest of us are one big, boneless clump, sort of like a Roman banquet except we're reclining on Mexican blankets bought three for ten dollars in Tijuana.

I shovel my food in because I'm hungry and the Colemans like to Discuss Things. Not only do feelings get hurt and the volume level soar, but food fights also break out occasionally.

Sure enough, Em—sister number two—sets down her reusable plastic picnic plate and turns to Hazel. "Are you dating?"

"Nope." Hazel shoves a forkful of pasta salad into her mouth, as if good manners would keep her family from poking their noses into her business.

"Why not?"

Hazel makes mock googly eyes. "I'm here with Jack. I don't want to hurt his feelings by introducing another guy into our relationship."

There's a round of good-natured, mocking laughter. I'm not sure when the Colemans collectively got the idea that nothing romantic could ever be possible between Hazel and me. She's a girl and I'm a guy, which checks both of our boxes, so it's hypothetically possible.

Margie charges in. I suspect she's motivated by the possibility of new grandbabies. "Jack doesn't count. He won't mind. Would you?"

Brown eyes drill into me. It's easy to see where Hazel's good looks come from. I just hope that Margie's a shade less astute than her daughter, because explaining that I have carnal knowledge of said daughter would be awkward at best. I'm probably safe, though, since Hazel's family has me firmly in the doesn't-count camp.

Tread carefully. "I'm happy to cede my prior claim when Prince Charming comes along."

"You know lots of guys." Frankie, sister number three, joins the fray. "Can't you fix her up with one of those VC guys you know? Pick someone successful. Rich. Not too much of an asshole."

Frankie's opinion about Silicon Valley investment circles is clear, but George the Git perks up. He's willing to be supportive if it brings more business opportunities his way.

"You should settle down," Katie announces. I'm sure what she really means is *settle*, and that pisses me off. Why should Hazel pair off with someone who doesn't worship the ground she walks on?

"Hazel's having a hard time choosing," I tell the

crowd of faces turned my way. "She has a crap ton of options and you don't want her to make a mistake."

"Really?" Em sounds skeptical, but Margie just looks hopeful. I know that they only want what's best for Hazel, but their execution sucks.

"Scout's honor." I hold up two fingers. When Hazel elbows me, I add a third. "Hazel's awesome. She shouldn't settle for just anyone."

Hazel looks like she's trying to figure out how to turn invisible. When that fails, she pretends a sudden need for the restroom and scurries toward the main house. I'm sure everyone knows she's just removing herself from the temptation to commit murder, but no one says anything.

When I get up to follow her, Margie puts a hand on my arm. "My best friend, Julie, has a daughter who's a lawyer for an ocean-conservation group in San Francisco. I could introduce you."

"No thanks. I'm good." I give her a polite smile and stroll after Hazel. She's moving fast as always, charging down the hallway. I reach out and catch her swinging fingers with mine, tugging her to a halt.

For just a second, this feels like something more.

As if we're friends with possibilities.

As if I'm something—some*one*—more to her.

Hazel laughs up at me. "A character reference *and* sex. You're the best friend ever."

CHAPTER EIGHT

DOES IT BOTHER her that her family is so eager to hook her up with husband material? That none of them believe she can do this on her own? Part of me is starting to wonder why no one considers me to be Mr. Hazel material, when in some respects we're the most perfect of matches. We're both driven workaholics. We both love our families, prize loyalty above all and take care of our people. We're both *here* and all I can think is *why not?*

Why not see where we can go?

Why not stay together?

Why not go back down the stairs and introduce ourselves as a couple?

But that isn't what Hazel wants. It's not that she's antimarriage or anticommitment. Despite her mother's pressure-cooker expectations, she's still looking for her perfect one and only. It's just that she's most definitely not looking at me. We're each other's wingmen at the bar, sitting back-to-back on our bar stools and pointing out hot singles to each other. Buying consolation drinks when those singles hurt us. Offering to exact bestie vengeance.

Hazel's watching me, her eyes moving over my face, down my arm, to where our fingers are tangled together. "I needed some space."

"Do you want me to go?"

"This is good." She slants that secretive, catlike Hazel smile at me, the one that says she's happy and as relaxed as she gets, but that her brain is still moving a million miles a minute because Hazel never stops thinking. Even though we're standing in the hallway of her childhood home, I want to kiss her. I want to keep standing here beside her because I like it. I like *her*.

"I would apologize for my family, but someone will just say something else." She grins at me. "Then we'll be trapped in an endless loop of apologies and neither of us will be able to leave."

"We'd have to stand here forever." I make a face of mock horror.

"Champagne out of reach."

"Eternal sobriety."

Hazel laughs in agreement and then she pulls me toward her. Somehow we just fit together, side by side, arms around each other. Our arms know where to go.

"They shouldn't ask you to find me a date," she says. "But fair warning—they're not going to stop. They don't think I can find someone on my own and they see you as the mother lode of bachelor recommendations."

This is my cue to give her shit for her lack of accomplishments in the husband-finding-and-landing sweepstakes. I've done it dozens if not hundreds of times before, and then she would always tease me back about being a homebody and a one-trick pony who was monogamous and middle-aged at seventeen. It's a comfortable, familiar pattern…and it feels all wrong.

"Why doesn't it piss you off?"

Hazel makes a frowny face, forehead puckering. "Getting mad wouldn't be effective. I know I don't need a husband, but it would make them happy. I'm not a people person and my relationship skills need work, so they're just trying to be helpful. It doesn't matter."

"It does." I brush my mouth over hers. She's the perfect height for kissing. "You're not the problem, Hazel. You're fucking amazing and anyone who can't see that doesn't deserve you."

The frown melts into suspicion. "My self-esteem is perfectly healthy, thank you. I don't need compliments."

I nod even though I'm suddenly not so sure about that. "I'd demonstrate just how amazing you are, but we're in your mother's house."

"Oh." Hazel brushes against me, specifically against a very happy-to-be-supportive part of me in my jeans. "That's going to make an interesting brunch statement. How do you propose to fix this very large problem?"

She leans up and nips my bottom lip, which predictably just makes the problem bigger.

Conceding she has a point, I say, "Capital pricing models. Z test stats. Normal distributions." When she looks at me quizzically, I say, "That's what I'm going to be running in my head to make myself socially presentable."

"Nut," Hazel says affectionately. "Does that actually work?"

I'm fairly certain she's asking in all seriousness. "Let's run a test."

I pull her close to me, until my back's against the wall, her body pressing into mine, and this time *I* kiss *her*. My kiss is hot and wet, wild and urgent, like there's a mental countdown in my head of how many seconds we probably have before someone wanders down the hall and spots us. My hands cup her butt, lifting her up, and she reaches for me. Anyone could discover us, so it's risky to keep kissing her, but I can't stop.

"Lift," she groans against my mouth. And then before I can react, before I can do more than suck in a quick breath before she steals the air from me, she's wrapping her legs around my waist. I cup her harder, lift her higher.

I want this woman, I want all of her, so I kiss her like I mean it, trying to show her with my mouth, my tongue, how she makes me feel. She's not a consolation prize in the dating sweepstakes—she's the golden ticket, the brass ring on the merry-go-round, the first-place winner.

And then I hear the voices. A woman's voice, high and happy...and getting closer. I think it's one of Hazel's sisters, but either way it's a wake-up call. I'm really *not* going to get caught kissing Hazel in her mother's hallway. I pull back and let her slide down my body to her feet. We need a new plan—and an exit strategy.

Hazel looks up at me, eyes narrowed, grin in place. "Downstairs bathroom, upstairs bathroom, guest bedroom. Choose quickly."

Then she smacks my butt.

"Bossy." I narrow my eyes at her. I love Hazel, but she's never mastered boundaries. I have a moment of quiet panic; I didn't say those words out loud, not quite, and it's not as if I meant *love* love. *Love* is just one of those words you use, right? I mean, objectively, of course, I love Hazel. I love Max and Dev, too, although I have zero interest in getting either of them naked.

A door opens and closes somewhere. Sister averted, but Hazel has more than one and we're still in a very public spot.

"Action-oriented. Decisive." Hazel flaps her hands at me. "Stop waffling, Mr. Reed. This is a limited-time offer to get mostly naked with me, so shit or get off the pot."

God, the things she says. I laugh and capture her hand before it can land on my butt again.

I grab her, slinging her over my shoulder in a fireman carry. It's hardly dignified, but Hazel muffles a shriek of protest because we've both heard the new sounds coming from the other room—someone's Mini-Me, one of Hazel's many nieces and nephews, is rapidly approaching, belting out the words to a cartoon-show theme song. Now we *really* shouldn't get caught kissing.

That's my excuse, at any rate.

The truth? I haven't had this much fun in ages. I discard the idea of the downstairs bathroom—its dimensions are a miserly three feet by five feet and fitting two people in there would be challenge enough without the logistics of undressing my Hazel surprise. Plus, toilets are gross. Whatever you've done in there, a million other people have also done. Sorry to spoil your fantasies, but it's a fact—the unromantic 500,000 bacterial cells per square inch does not make for the hotness of potential discovery. The upstairs bathroom is larger but it's full of her mother's stuff—so that's also a hard no, leaving the guest bedroom as our sole viable option. Done. "Bedroom," I say.

I take the stairs two at a time before we can be ambushed by any more family members. Hazel works her hands down the back of my jeans, cupping and squeezing my butt. I can't see her face but I know the expression she'll be wearing—happy, mischievous, focused. Hazel doesn't believe in half measures.

"Left," she announces when I hit the top of the stairs and pause in the middle of the long hallway that stretches to the left and right of the stairs. "Third door down."

I walk-spring down the hallway, open the door and aim for the bed. Since the room's not that much bigger than the downstairs powder room or a closet, it's hard to miss. My knees bump the edge of the mattress as I tumble Hazel onto it and twist around to close and lock the door.

When I uncontort, Hazel's just setting her phone on the tiny table beside the bed. "Timer," she says.

"Is there a prize for who comes fastest?"

She looks interested for a second, but then shakes her head. "I project we have more than ten and less than twelve minutes before we're missed. Grab a towel."

She points to the stack of clean towels dwarfing the minuscule dresser—Margie's tiny house requires equally miniature furniture—and I do as ordered.

"Are we committing kinky acts on this towel?" I unroll it as Hazel shifts to make room for me.

"We can't get the coverlet dirty." Hazel reaches for me, tugging at my wrist. "Get naked and then get over here."

I'm surprised she doesn't decide we need to do it up against the wall or on the floor. Still, I strip off my jeans and boxer briefs and let her pull me down onto the bed. I definitely don't protest when she straddles me.

And I know we're in a hurry and that even if we weren't, this is only temporary, but I still kiss her slow, a leisurely exploration of her mouth, our lips pressed together, angling for surer, deeper possession. I cup the back of her neck, pulling her closer.

We're equally good at this—giving, taking, sharing the electric heat that builds between us. As if we were both cold before, but now I've found the right person to warm me up and so has she. Not the *one* person, but right—and that's more than good enough for me.

She presses harder against me, her thighs gripping my hips, her hands cupping my face as she moves me where she needs me to be. Her touch is determined and eager and so fucking amazing. Like she knows exactly what she wants and I'm perfect. Like I'm exactly right for her.

I kiss her harder, sliding my tongue over her bottom lip, tasting peaches and champagne, mint and something else that's entirely Hazel. Hazel opens up and we kiss like that for long, stolen moments, filling the bedroom with husky, rough sounds and naked need. If I could eat her up, I would. She feels... effervescent, like the bright fizz of the champagne we drank—sweet and sharp, a fleeting, impossible-to-capture pleasure.

"Hurry up," she whisper-orders. "Nine minutes."

I tug up her sundress, revealing a baby blue thong that deserves much more appreciation than I have time for. I drag my thumb up the hot, damp center of Hazel, but she's one step ahead of me. She slides her hands inside her panties and rubs her clit, her eyes on mine as she gives me the words I'll never forget.

"I want to come bad."

"Feels like you could use a hand." I slide her panties to the side and explore her slick, hot core with my fingers. She gasps and bites her lip, her forehead puckering as she concentrates, chasing the sensations. Sex is always amazing, and nothing feels better than sinking my fingers into my partner, but this, with Hazel—this is something else.

Before I can figure out what that *something* is or even pick up the rhythm I'm tracing on her body, she's moved on. She leans forward, wriggling out of her panties in a way that's truly miraculous, and places her hands on my shoulders, a look of intense concentration on her face as she sinks down onto my dick.

There's nothing between us.

Fuck.

"Condom," I groan.

"Problem solved." She rises up on her knees, sinks back down. "My test results came back clean and I'm on the Pill."

Hazel knows her facts, and we'd never hurt each other. I cup her knees, helping her rise and fall as we find the perfect rhythm together, faster and harder, our bodies slapping together in an earthy percussion. We need to be quiet, but we're both making sounds, groaning, gasping half words as I push inside her and she pushes down—taking me even as I take her— and it's so fucking awesome.

My mouth finds the spot between her neck and shoulder, the spot where I fit perfectly. I press kisses against her, whispering her name, whispering truths. She's beautiful like this. She's everything. I move steadily in and then out, controlling our bodies, keeping us together.

"Now," she demands.

"Yes." I shift to kiss her mouth, telling her everything I don't have words to say. *Yes, I want this. Yes, you. Yes, us.*

It's not enough. I reach between us and find her clit with my fingers. Petting and stroking, making sure she feels as good as I do. Her legs shake, her body stiffening as she gets closer. Her breathing gets rougher and then her fingers cover mine so we can make her come together.

"Jack... JackJackJack."

I groan right back at her. "Hazel."

I feel her tighten around me, her body grabbing hold of my dick, holding on as I drive into her, pushing us both faster and faster to our happy ending. I'm not sure who comes first or if it's one of those rare, photo-perfect ties where she comes in one breath and I in the next, but we're panting, our bodies collapsing together onto the bed as everything around us fades out.

The phone is buzzing an alarm when I float back to myself, Hazel's fingers brushing my hair back, her face burrowed into my chest. I'm still inside her. Moving? Not happening. The rest of the world will have to wait for us because I'm completely, one hundred percent undone.

CHAPTER NINE

NEXT FRIDAY, the whole gang gathers at T&T. T&T is a beachside restaurant with a *palapa* roof—it's our favorite stomping ground in Santa Cruz. Not only are the tacos awesome, but there are also margaritas, Coronas and a no-shoes policy. Lola's fat white pit bull snores audibly from under the table. I can sense from the looks that Dev and Lola exchange that they have news to share with the class. Their body language telegraphs intimacy, and not just because they've been glued together since they hit the beach. Any closer and they could be arrested for public indecency. Lola's engagement ring catches the light as she waves her hand, making a point. Maple, Max's girlfriend, grabs her hand, either to inspect the rock on her ring finger or to prevent any accidental blinding, as Dev bought the biggest diamond in Tiffany's and the stone is roughly the size of a small boulder.

I can't help but remember what it was like for me and Molly. We started with the dates and the wedding and then, at some point that I can't quite identify, things changed. *We* changed. The memories became less couple-y, less about us and more about each of us individually. The truth is, we grew apart.

Hazel's also noticed the suspicious closeness between Dev and Lola. She kicks me under the table and I cover my grunt with a cough.

Guesses? She mouths the word at me. The perfect slick of red painting her lips is the exclamation point for her dirty, wicked smiles. I want to kiss the color from her mouth.

"Not a clue," I breathe back.

The ocean breeze plays with her hair and she tucks it firmly behind her ear.

"So." Dev looks around the table. Lola bounces beside him in obvious anticipation. They definitely have good news to share. "Lola and I are eloping next weekend. We're getting hitched in Cabo and you're invited."

Lola flicks him on the head, a gesture of both exasperation and fondness. "Way to lead up to it."

Dev just shrugs and glances around the table at the rest of us. "Any objections?"

Max raises his hand. "Does that mean you're skipping the Pinterest porn and the bachelor party? Last chance, man."

Dev wraps his hand around Lola's ponytail and gently tugs her face toward him for a kiss.

"I'm good," he says when he comes up for air. "Got everything I need right here."

Dev's personal assistant must be on standby because all of our phones go off at once. Dev's like me. He doesn't leave things to chance—he always has a well-thought-out plan. I check my messages and find a first-class ticket to Cabo and a villa reservation at a five-star resort. Hazel leans over and peers at my phone. We're on the same flight, next to each other.

I say the only thing I can. "Can't wait."

We touch down in Cabo the following Friday night and are transferred seamlessly to a limousine. The resort Dev and Lola chose is on Chileno Bay, so we pass the thirty-minute drive from the airport exploring the miniature champagne bottles and beers on ice that the hotel has provided. Ocean waves pound the shoreline on our right, while the Mexican desert glides past the windows, the setting sun painting the sand orange and red. Cabo's a strange, beautiful beast, the Baja desert literally colliding with the Sea of Cortez at the tip of Mexico.

Our hotel is a mix of villas, casitas and luxury suites sprinkled across the creamy sand and tucked back into the rocky hills that frame Santa Maria Bay. Everything is tasteful, modern and beige. I've never seen so much brown in my life. Unfortunately, however, there's a hiccup in Dev's careful plans.

The manager almost strokes out on the spot as he explains the room shortage to us. Instead of four villas, he has three, so two of us will have to share. It doesn't take much imagination to figure out why putting Dev and Lola in the same villa as Max and Maple—or Hazel, or me—would be a bad idea. As for Max and Maple, there are things you can't un-hear and Max has no filter. I do *not* want to know what they do in bed.

I open my mouth to point out the obvious solution, but Hazel beats me to it.

"It's not a problem. Jack and I can share." She winks at the group. "My virtue is safe with him."

Our friends laugh, as if the idea of the two of us having sex is funny. Is that so inconceivable? I smile and laugh at all the right spots, however, before allowing the grateful manager to lead Hazel and me to our villa. I have no idea why it bothers me so much.

While Hazel wanders away, enthusiastically snapping pictures of the room with her phone, I tip the manager and the porter and send them on their way.

We'll be secret lovers.

Never in the office. Never in front of other people.

We'll never tell.

Would our friends really react that badly? Do I want them to know that we're a couple, too, even if we're only temporary and not forever? Dev and Max would worry like old biddies. They'd wonder if it was too soon, if I was really over Molly, if I was risking an amazing business partnership for sex because I was lonely.

The villa's so huge that I practically need a breadcrumb trail to track down Hazel. Wherever she is, it would be nice if she was naked. Or relaxed. It's been a rough week at the office and she's strung tight. Orgasms help with that, but I'm hoping some R & R works its magic.

She's not outside in the private infinity pool or

lounging on the massive deck that overlooks the ocean, so I work my way through the rooms. Lola called it Tuscan meets Santa Fe when she was describing it to Maple on the plane, which turns out to mean tall ceilings, wooden beams, terra-cotta walls and lots of stone. The living room offers a plush sofa that I can imagine spooning Hazel on and a coffee table made from a large slab of Mexican wood. There's also an enormous television, a bookcase stocked with books about the desert and local wildlife, and binoculars for whale-watching from the deck surrounding the pool.

I find Hazel on the little balcony just off the master bedroom that faces out onto the ocean. She's less tense than she has been. I hope. She stands in front of the wide-open French doors, face turned into the breeze. She doesn't turn around when I pad toward her, but she knows I'm here. I'm too big to move quietly.

Her pretty, beachy clothes flutter around her body. I check but I don't think anyone can see in, not unless they're suspended in midair above our balcony, so I prowl closer. Hazel's always so put-together and in control, but the ocean's making a mess of that perfect front. Little wisps of hair fly around her face, teasing her skin with butterfly kisses. I love messed-up, imperfect Zee.

I contemplate giving her some space, because things feel a little weird between us and I know she doesn't want the others finding out we're more than just friends. But I do want to have sex with her, the sooner the better, and I also miss holding her. Zee is addictive.

I'm overthinking... I think. I move behind her, bracing her body with mine. She relaxes against me, the fingers of her right hand tangling with mine. We stand there like that, staring out at the ocean. The sun set on our way here and now it's completely dark, although the moon spills a pale, silvery light across the bay. It's calm enough that there would be no point in taking out the boards.

"Are you meeting up with the guys?"

I raise her hand to my mouth. It's silly, the gesture of a white knight from centuries ago, but I do it, anyway, pressing my lips against her knuckles. I can feel the fine bones of her fingers.

I press my cheek against her hair and stare out at the ocean with her. The horseshoe-shaped bay cups the darker water of the Pacific Ocean, waves breaking on the rocky formations and licking at the golden sand.

"You should go swimming." She smirks at me. "If you promise to swim naked, I'll join you."

There's a beat and then a little frown puckers her forehead. "Unless there are sharks."

I grin into her hair. Thank God she can't see me smile or she'd kill me. Hazel doesn't believe in admitting fear. "You can take on a roomful of pissed-off investors and convince them you shit rainbows and fart glitter, but you're worried about fish?"

"I'm worried about really big fish with scary teeth. I need to check." She twists in my arms, patting her pockets. She seems more interested in googling Cabo predators than the romantic setup we have going on. Which is fine. We're not that kind of couple.

"They have giant squid here," I tell her. "They're particularly partial to divers."

Hazel hums, clearly trying to decide if I'm pulling her leg or not. I'm mostly not. There is a fifteen-foot squid here that's been making a bid for the apex predator spot as the shark population has declined. Cabo is rough and gorgeous, wild and dangerous, golden brown and never entirely safe. It's very much like life in that respect.

It's not that I don't know what Hazel expects from me: she wants my dick. She wants sex and closeness—but only up to a certain point. We're friends and business partners, but we're not lovers. Not really. We're just two people screwing each other while we wait for something more permanent to come along.

Still, part of me is angry that she's willing to settle. That she hasn't held out for what Dev and Lola have. They're getting married tomorrow, which means they'll stand up in front of us all and choose each other. They're making promises and plans. They're banking on forever. Of course, I, of all people, know that forever can end up being measured in years, months and days, but at least Molly and I had that long even if we didn't have forever. It's more than many people have.

And now Hazel eclipses all thoughts of Molly. She wriggles back against me, her ass finding my dick like a heat-seeking missile. Jesus, she makes me hot.

"So," she purrs, eyes still fixed on the ocean. "There aren't any predators I should be worried about?"

"Definitely not in the ocean." I nip her ear and she squeals. She needs to make that sound when she's riding my fingers. My face. Top of the list? My dick.

She tilts her head back, resting it against my shoulder. "Sea snake?"

"You know, there's a fish called the slippery dick."

Hazel snorts. "You know I'm not gullible, right?"

"Scout's honor. *Halichoeres bivittatus.*"

"Is it a *big* fish?"

Fuck, I love her sense of humor. "Less than half an inch. It's a fish with a permanent inferiority complex. There's probably hundreds of them swimming around out there in the bay."

"An entire bay of dick fish."

"One huge orgy," I say solemnly. "When it's mating season, all the boy fish get together and put on a show for the ladies, hoping to get lucky."

A smile tugs at Hazel's mouth. "Sounds like the San Francisco bar scene."

She shifts closer, her face turning up to mine, and I'm no saint. I thread the fingers of one hand through her hair and cover her mouth with mine. I taste tequila and chocolate, and underneath that, Hazel herself. She makes me wish I was a poet, that I had the words to describe the unique taste of her, but all I can do is kiss her.

Eventually she pulls away, her eyes moving over my face. "Let's go inside."

Part of me wants to do it right here, to take her against the balcony where we can see the ocean. Not because I'm romantic but because I'm impatient. I want Hazel right here. I imagine she's worried, though, that our friends can see. I suspect that they're already naked and trying out the beds, but I nod, anyhow.

There's a sudden swell of music coming from somewhere deeper inside the resort. Mariachis and trumpets, cheerful and bold. It's the kind of sound that makes you want to swim and maybe do a shot.

"We could take salsa lessons." I'm pretty sure I saw that listed on the schedule as one of the many activities we can sign up for.

Hazel tugs her fingers from mine. I don't want to let her go. "Is that what you want to do?"

"Only if you want to." I don't know how to salsa dance. Anything other than the white-boy shuffle and a bad wedding waltz is outside my bailiwick. "Just temper your expectations."

"Tell me something you've never done before," she says.

"Are we talking about dirty things? Or dancing things?"

I twirl her in an exaggerated circle just in case she needs a demonstration of my lack of dancing skills.

"I think it involves more—" She gestures at her hips and gives an exaggerated wiggle. "Name three favorite fantasies."

I'm equal opportunity when it comes to sex. I like it all, sweet or dirty. You need a complete stranger or a whole lot of trust to ask for your favorite dirty fantasy because the truth about fantasies is that they don't always make sense once you speak them out loud or try them. They're half-formed, sexy, dirty thoughts that you get off to when you're alone, but now you're inviting someone else in and it's risky. Especially if you're going to be looking your partner in the eye tomorrow, the next month, the next year. I realize that I'm more than willing to answer her question and that it's not because I won't be seeing plenty of Hazel in the future.

"First fantasy is sex in a cabana. We pull the curtains, but there are people walking by on the beach."

I give a hip thrust my best shot and she snorts.

"You know those nineteenth-century French dresses that scoop a woman's breasts up like ice cream in a cone? I want you in one. One deep breath and I'd have a handful. That's my second fantasy. I get turned on by all those secret layers underneath. Add the garter, and I'm a goner."

"You think we can order up historical dress from room service?"

I try to gauge if she's serious or merely joking. Her eyes are still closed, which doesn't help. Nor does the image of dressed-up Hazel that my brain promptly supplies. Could the hotel help me out with this? French maid, probably. Full-on Marie Antoinette dress? Not a chance. The concierges here are very, very good at their jobs, but they're not miracle workers.

"Number three, I fantasize about you letting me in." I drop my hand and tap her butt lightly.

About you giving me control.

About you.

"No Christian Grey spanking fantasy?" Hazel's voice sounds breathy and a little far away. She's running my fantasy playlist through her head, probably making a few adjustments and improvements because that's just how Hazel's wired.

I shrug. "I don't want to hurt you. Not even as part of a game. Is that making your top three?"

I don't know what I'll do if she's got a secret hard-on for bondage or spanking. I press the palm of my hand against her clit. Yeah. I know exactly what I'll do. I'll learn how to be the best dom ever because I don't want her to ever feel like she can't tell me something.

"Or we could just salsa dance. *Naked* salsa dance." I swirl her in a big, loopy circle around the balcony. It's safe to say there's no disco-ball trophy in our future. Even the lizard who's popped up on top of the balcony wall looks unimpressed with our moves.

Hazel squints out into the darkness at the shadowy shape of the nearby villas. "Is Maple watching?"

Since Maple danced professionally for the San Francisco Ballet, I assume Hazel's feeling competitive. Fortunately, both Dev and Max suck at dancing.

I point to the lizard. "You're a private dancer. You never wanted to be a ballerina as a little girl?"

Hazel makes a scoffing sound. "As if. I started a

lemonade stand and then franchised it to the neighborhood kids."

Yeah. That would be Hazel.

"I ran a crew of lawn mowers."

"And never mowed a lawn yourself."

My sisters have already pointed this flaw out to
me. "I ran the company. I brought in the business. I
was the brains."

Hazel's grin lights up her face, crinkling up the
corners of her eyes. I didn't bring up my middle-
school business empire on purpose, but I like swapping stories with her. It's true we've known each
other for years, but there's still a lot I don't know
about her.

"Dip," I warn her, bending her backward over
my arm.

We bumble around the balcony, arms wrapped
around each other. It's silly, but it's fun and there's
no one to see us. It's nice to not be serious and that's
the whole point of us, isn't it? To have fun? While
she hums to the music, I wrap my hands around her
waist.

"Leap."

"What?"

"Leap."

I lift her up even as she shrieks. "Jesus, Reed."

"Live a little. Let your inner princess ballerina
person out." I do it again.

"That makes absolutely no sense." Her hands
close around mine, but she doesn't push me away.

It's more like playing leapfrog, but we're both

laughing together as I bounce her across the length of the terrace. When we pass the bedroom door for the second time, I set her down.

I'm giving in to temptation but I'm meeting her halfway. I lower my head to hers and kiss her there in the open doorway, with the ocean behind us and the bedroom in front. She meets me, her hands sliding up over my shoulders as I cup her face. I need her so badly.

I need her and I'm going to take what I want from her. Her tongue licks over my lower lip, tasting. Fuck. She bites down and I automatically suck in a breath. She takes advantage, her tongue slipping into my mouth when I want to make us both wait because this is the best thing that will happen all day and I don't want to rush it. I don't want it to be over.

I pull away, but that's not what I want, either. Brown eyes watch me come closer…

Closer.

Closer.

My hands palm her ass, then I lift her up so she can wrap her legs around my waist. She kisses me as if she owns me, deeper, harder. I can hear the small, hungry sounds we're both making despite the mariachi band. Hazel swirls her tongue against mine, sweeping back inside my mouth as if we're doing this her way. She's the only woman I've ever known who even kisses bossy. I'm not letting her take charge. She doesn't get to rush this. I slow our kiss, moving my lips more slowly over hers, drinking her in. She angles her head, trying to kiss me deeper. *Not yet.*

We kiss-dance, moving in a lazy circle.

"My dance," I whisper roughly against her pretty mouth. Hazel hesitates and then she lets me take over.

Holy fuck, does she ever give me the wheel.

I won't disappoint her.

I keep right on kissing her as I walk her toward our bed. Her arms wrap around my neck, her heels dig into my ass, her hips rolling and grinding against my dick. The sounds she makes now are even better than the squeal she made earlier.

I set her down on the bed, but she pops right back up. Her hands drag my T-shirt upward.

"Strip," she demands. Okay, so the whole letting-me-take-over thing didn't last long. Hazel always goes for what she wants.

"Ladies first."

"Together."

Fair enough. I take a step back and strip off my shirt. For some reason, I don't want to make a game of it. I just want to be naked with Hazel, but she's in the mood to tease me—I slow down so I can give her the audience she deserves. She's wearing a tank top made out of some white material that poofs out around her chest, hiding her from view, and a pair of loose white linen pants. She's wearing leopard-print sandals and long gold earrings that brush her shoulders. Her toes are painted white with gold polka dots that match her jewelry. She looks elegant and put-together, so, of course, I want to mess her up, to make her look like sex.

The tank top goes first. She slides one strap down her sun-bronzed arm—she's been to the salon for one of those Mystic Tan spray jobs—and then she flicks the second off. When she shimmies, the whole thing slides over her hips and onto the floor.

I reach out a hand and trace the curve of her breast where it swells above the cups of the bra. The edge of her nipples peek out of their tiny, lacy nests. The bra is a miracle of white and lace, the fragile, gauzy fabric dotted with tiny, silvery polka dots. Apparently Lola is not the only one who went lingerie shopping. A smirk curves Hazel's lush, pink mouth. I'm staring.

"You like it?" She cups her boobs and arches her back just in case I missed anything. I'm accustomed to paying attention and I lean forward and show my appreciation with my tongue.

I taste her, licking and exploring, sucking the nipple that pops free into my mouth. It's important to be fair, so I make sure to pay equal attention to the other nipple. Hazel shoves her fingers into my hair, tugging so I know when I do something she particularly likes and to do it again.

She moans my name and pulls away so that she can stand up and slide her pants down her legs. Her hands reach for the buttons on my jeans. "You're slow."

Unlike Hazel, I didn't see the need to dress up for the plane. It's not as if the pilot cares. I shove both jeans and boxers down my legs and kick them away. "Hazel?"

"Yeah?" She sounds dazed.

"Did I tell you tonight that you're beautiful?" I don't always remember to tell her, and I'm not sure Hazel's heard it enough.

"Duly noted." Her hands pull me closer.

"You're beautiful here." I press a kiss against her mouth and work my way down her neck and over her throat, following the soft line down to her shoulder. "And here, too."

I keep going, down her arm, her fingertips, the palm of her hand and then back up again.

"Here for certain." I press a kiss against her collarbone and move down to the slope of her breast. "Here."

I try to show her with my mouth what I should be telling her with words, but kissing her is so much easier.

CHAPTER TEN

DOWNTOWN CABO SHIMMERS in the Mexican heat. Sticking my head in a pizza oven would be cooler. The driver dropped Max, Maple, Hazel and me at a flea market near the marina when Hazel announced she wanted to pick up some souvenirs. The colorful stalls are packed close together. Vendors call out to us, inviting Hazel to "come and look, senorita." She beams and chatters back in Spanish.

When did she learn Spanish?

And why does she want to buy this…crap?

I look around, trying to see the market through her eyes. There are art galleries in Cabo San Lucas, along with some seriously talented local artists and craftsmen. This stuff, however, looks less than authentic. I don't think a T-shirt announcing that "Somebody in Cabo loves me" is part of mainstream Mexican culture. In addition to stacks of cheap T-shirts, there are colorfully embroidered white dresses, serapes and these little bobble-headed animals—turkeys, dinosaurs, crocodiles and what looks like a mutant platypus. I set the tiny nodding heads into motion with a flick of my finger. Hopefully Hazel gets her shopping fix fast and we can head back to the hotel. We haven't christened every room in the villa yet and I have definite plans for the shower.

Max pokes at a pair of red-and-green maracas. He looks bored. "Why do they need us here?"

"Does it matter?" I ask.

"Do you think Maple would like this?" It's good that he's abandoned the maracas—the man has no rhythm, which makes his relationship with a professional ballet dancer miraculous—but the T-shirt he's holding is a little...obscene. I had no idea that you could walk around in public with that kind of suggestion on your chest.

"Put it back if you want to have sex tonight."

Max grins. He's fucking with me.

"So are you and Hazel a thing now?" Max drops the shirt back on top of the stack.

"Why would we be a *thing*?"

"Because you're getting it on?" Max's voice is light but the look in his eyes says I'd better not be messing with Hazel. She may have been my friend first, but she's one of us now and Max will totally throw down for her.

"Why would you think that?"

Max snorts. "You're not as subtle as you think you are."

"We're just friends," I say. "But with benefits."

Max nods slowly. "Right. But you and I are friends and we're not screwing."

"Because you're not my type. And it's none of your business."

Another hard look from Max. "I like her. I don't want to see her get hurt."

"I like her, too, dumbass. And it was her idea."

Max scrubs a hand over his head. "Fine. Then I don't want to see you get hurt."

"I won't," I scoff. "This is just fun. We're not in a relationship. Neither of us wants that."

"If you say so." Max shrugs. "But you're friends, right?"

"Of course." I turn to follow the girls up the aisle.

"So you're already in a relationship," he points out.

"It's not like that."

"So what is it like?" He frowns. "Because Maple and I are friends, but we're also in a relationship and we have sex. I'm not following."

"You go out together. You tell people that you're together. You plan on sticking together."

A smile curves Max's mouth. "Fuck, yeah. I'm not stupid."

"Hazel and I are just using each other for sex until we find someone else. It's not a real relationship." That doesn't sound good, now that I say it out loud. "I'm not her boyfriend. She doesn't want me like that."

"It's your business. I'm just trying to understand whether or not Maple and I have to keep pretending we don't know the two of you are having kinky sex every time you think the rest of us aren't looking.

And what's the plan when one of you decides to date someone else?"

"It's not dating. And it'll be fine." My brain conjures up a mental image of Hazel on a real date, the kind that involves a great restaurant, wine and roses. Hazel kissing Nameless Guy good-night on the doorstep and then inviting him in. Naked Hazel in bed with some nameless, faceless, spineless dick. "We'll work it out."

Do I want Hazel to end things between us? Not a chance. But that was the deal we had, right? We'd have sex temporarily until one of us found a better long-term bet. Even though she complains about her family giving her shit, Hazel wants that and I'm not capable of giving it to her. Plus, she's never indicated that she sees me as forever material, anyhow. She'd probably run screaming if I suggested it. Which I'm not going to do.

Maple and Hazel are haggling now with a guy in a pottery stall. They're surrounded by stacks of blue-and-white-print vases, sugar bowls and pitchers on the wooden shelves. A faintly musty smell fills the air, as if everything has gotten wet more than once despite us being surrounded by desert. Sunlight pours in the entrance and the heat bakes down on me. There's an entire toilet done in colorful tiles—tank, base, seat *and* lid. It's a miracle of either engineering or superglue.

Max eyes me. "So how does it work?"

"How does what work?" I ask impatiently.

"Looking for someone else when you're having

sex with your friend." Max frowns. "Is this one of those open relationships? Do you have three-ways?"

"No."

Hazel wraps up the purchase with a sharkish smile. The vendor looks halfway to being in love with her, even though he's practically paying her to haul away a sink made out of brightly colored tile. Apparently Hazel's decided to remodel her mountain cabin. I make a mental note to ask the concierge about shipping because there's no way that fits in the overhead compartment on the flight home.

"No?" Max isn't going to let it drop. "So you're both dating other people?"

"No," I repeat.

I mean, we don't really have any kind of a future together. I'm not making the same mistakes I made with Molly, and I don't know what Hazel wants, but I assume she hasn't changed her mind. So is it fair for me to keep sleeping with her and distracting her from the quest for a perfect man? Is awesome sex really enough? No matter how much she bitches about it, part of her wants that tiny house in the Coleman compound. She wants to fit in there all the way and sleeping with me in secret isn't really getting her any closer to that goal.

Maple dances back to Max, wrapping her arms around his neck and leaning into him for a kiss. He fists her ponytail, angling her head so he can kiss her deeper and harder. They don't care who's watching. She manages to make him look graceful as he lifts her up so he can devour her mouth. I look over at Hazel.

Hazel grins at me. "You don't want anything?"

I want you.

I want to kiss you like nothing matters more.

She waves a T-shirt at me—it's the same one Max showed me.

"Not from the market." I tuck her arm in mine. Max and Maple are practically climbing each other now, so odds are good we're headed back to the resort soon.

Which is good. Alone with Hazel is exactly where I want to be.

As soon as we get back to the resort, however, Hazel kicks me out of our casita, citing "girl maintenance." That means I'm not getting inside her anytime soon. I honestly don't care about her bikini line, but it clearly matters to her so I make a bar run because a pitcher of margaritas seems like a good investment.

When she flip-flops her way across our pool deck toward me, I try to spot what's different so I can compliment her, but there's no obvious difference. She just looks fabulous. Her hair is slicked up on top of her head in a braid-twist thing that I itch to take apart and she's wearing a pair of Marilyn Monroe–worthy sunglasses. She looks exotic and more than a little sexy. Plus, I'm a big fan of the caftan. It has little beads that clink as she walks and a neckline that plunges to her waist. It's been brought to my attention that I don't say what's going on in my head.

Apparently girls like to hear the spoken-word equivalent of the porn strip playing in there. It makes no sense to me, but I definitely like Hazel's blue dress thing. Plus, it's see-through. If she'd just lose the bikini she's rocking underneath it and hop in the pool for some wet T-shirt action, I could die a happy man.

She beams at me, dropping a ginormous tote bag onto a lounger. "This place is amazing!"

She pulls a tube of coconut-scented sunscreen from her bag, wiggles out of the caftan and starts rubbing lotion into her skin.

"I can't get my back."

But I absolutely can. I would very much like to rub lotion into her skin, but it's going to lead to other things very quickly and I'm not sure if she's ready for more vacation sex, or if she actually wants to do other vacation things.

"If I ask nicely, can I help with that?"

She holds the tube out to me. "I love a helpful guy."

I heave myself out of the pool, causing a small tidal wave. Hazel shrieks, and we wrestle for a minute—after even just a few minutes in the Cabo sun, she's warm. Her body bucks beneath mine and I pin her, using my forearm to capture her arms over her head. I throw a leg over hers. Based on the state of my dick and the not-sun-related heat spreading through my body, it's a good thing our villa has a private pool. We'd get kicked out of the main pool for public indecency.

We continue to half wrestle, half kiss, until Hazel

hops off me and jumps in the water. I follow her to the pool's edge. I'd like to be inside her, but apparently she's in the mood to look at the ocean—from the shallow end, naturally.

"It's really amazing," she says.

"Uh-huh." I kiss her ear. "I love this."

I trace a path down her stomach and over the front of her bikini bottom. She inhales softly as I run a finger over the lacy panel.

"You'll have to be quiet."

"A challenge."

I tug on the tie holding the side of her bikini together and the string comes free. Hazel's hands grip the edge of the pool. I'm sure that if anyone on the beach looks up, she'll just appear to be admiring the view. Only the two of us will know that my fingers are stroking between her legs.

I find her clit and circle it carefully, stroking the sides. Hazel loves it gentle, until she's desperate to come, and then she wants it harder, rougher, faster. So right now I tease her with the pad of my finger, circling, drawing little patterns over her.

After all these weeks, I know what she likes. She moans my name loud enough to be heard in San Francisco. She's close to coming, her body pushing down on mine, demanding more.

I kiss her ear. "Do you really want to sunbathe?"

She bites her lip. "What's on the menu?"

"I'll let you choose." I don't remove my hand— I have a very demanding boss to make happy. "Let me know if you need a hint."

She turns around, sliding her arms around my neck. Her legs wrap around my waist and I'm pretty sure we've just abandoned her swimsuit bottom somewhere in the pool. It's hard to kiss through laughter, but we manage, and I don't even pretend to drop her as I carry her inside to the bed.

We don't make it down to the beach for another hour. There's no such thing as too much sex. It's just not possible. Getting naked and inside Hazel is my happy place, and no beach or ocean can ever be better. But Hazel wants to go in the water, so here we are, sprinting over sand that's achieved nuclear temperatures while we've been heating up our bedroom.

Hazel informed me I could either be the pool boy or the pack mule and dumped an impressive armload of gear on me. I'm not sure if we're about to go snorkeling or launch a SEAL-style beach invasion. But when she gets that mischievous glint in her eyes, I'm putty—so here we are, me carrying the stuff, Hazel dancing on ahead. Which means I get to ogle her ass in a new bikini.

Winner, winner, chicken dinner.

The new bikini is pink and silky. The top ties around her neck in a big, loopy bow and there are more bows on her hips. I'd like to undo them, but she really wants to swim in the ocean. She leads the way, which means I can stare at her ass. I need to shave when we get back to the room, because I left a mark on the back of her thigh after I convinced her to go a little cowgirl on my face. Hazel's face still

turns the cutest shade of pink when I suggest something new, but she's game. She'll try anything once,
and if she likes it, she's back in line for seconds and
thirds. So far we haven't added anything new to her
off-limits list.

Actual, bona fide swimming is on her list to try
today. As soon as we hit the water, however, it becomes clear that Hazel has never been snorkeling
before. She's also not a natural. She sucks water in
through her snorkel, her mask fogs up worse than a
San Francisco morning and she has no clue what to
do with her fins, although she mutters loudly about
"misleading YouTube videos."

"You're enjoying this," she accuses.

Since it's true, I just wink at her. Hazel is fright-
eningly competent at most things, which makes her
inability to master snorkeling cute.

I'd like to tell you snorkeling's awesome because
everyone deserves the chance to come face-to-face
with something as pretty as coral and fish but that's
not the reason. Hazel's tits in a bikini top are fan-
tastic. They float along, threatening to swim out of
the tiny cups and make my day.

Since she's determined to check out the bay from
under the water, I spend some quality time instruct-
ing her. A mask and snorkel aren't the sexiest head-
gear ever, but Hazel makes it work. I suit her up in
a full-on life jacket rather than just a snorkel vest,
because even though I'm happy to be her personal
pool float, I don't want to take those kinds of chances
with her. Sharks, sea snakes, Mexican Mafia drug

runners, even a leg cramp—if I went down, she'd go down, too, and I'm not a fan.

We swim together, or rather I hold her hand, pulling her after me. The snorkeling in Santa Maria Bay isn't that great. The occasional blue-and-yellow fish darts through the big boulders that line the bay. There's also a small school of iridescent damselfish that dart around us. Hazel, however, makes excited, happy sounds through her snorkel, so that's good.

I want to ask her if she'd like to go to Bora Bora or the Maldives. Maybe one of the barrier reefs, in Belize or Australia. But it's not as if we're going to be together forever. No matter how much I don't want things to change between us, eventually they will.

Dev and Lola tie the knot at sunset. Lola didn't want anything over-the-top, so they've opted for a simple arch covered in white roses and velvety green succulents facing the bay. White candles in little glass pots twinkle from the sand. I typically don't pay attention to those kinds of details, but Hazel keeps up a running commentary, snapping a million pictures that she promptly texts to her family. Apparently the Coleman clan can never have too many wedding ideas. I inspect the flowers more closely just in case I've missed anything.

There's a green plant with white flowers just on the tip that looks like a dick coming. Hazel smacks my arm when I suggest this, so I shut up.

I've honestly never thought much about the actual ceremony. When Molly and I got married, it was about making her happy—and making her mine. It seems unlikely that Dev helped Lola pick out flowers, but what do I know? The two of them walk up the aisle together, hand in hand, barefoot and beaming. They look happy.

They get hitched as the sun goes down. To no one's surprise, the rings they give each other are custom-made, as are the vows they've written. Dev told me on the plane that he doesn't really care what the words are—he just wants to make Lola his. She'd leaned over him and told me that it worked both ways, but that he was still expected to put some effort into it and use his words.

Dev is an overachiever and, like all of us, he has a deep-seated need to be the best. He won't compromise or cut corners and I can't help but wonder how long it took him to write his vows. They're a little less action-oriented than I'd have expected: 10 Things I Love About You. From the look on Maple's face, however, Max should be taking notes. Or maybe he doesn't need to because his mouth is right there by her ear and he's whispering something that has her smiling.

Eventually, the officiant declares Dev and Lola husband and wife. We all clap enthusiastically and Max wolf whistles. Dev sweeps Lola backward over his arm for a dramatic kiss, and there's laughter. He's hers now, and while I'm happy for the two of them, I can't help feeling like I've just watched one of my best friends ride off into the sunset for the last time. Lola will always come first for him, as she should.

As we follow the happy couple down the aisle and toward the tables set up on the sand for a private dinner, I nudge Hazel. "Do you want to get married?"

She stares at me. There's one of those awkward pauses where you both realize that there's more than one way to interpret the words you just put out there. Does she think I'm proposing? What do I do if she says yes?

"Someday," I clarify. Fuck. I'm not making this better. "To somebody. I didn't mean—"

She pats my arm. "I know what you mean, Jack."

One of the great things about Hazel is that we're always on the same page about the big things. Sometimes it feels like we're married. Not the actual wedding part, but the stuff that comes after it. Like we're one of those old married couples who've put in fifty years together and who finish each other's sentences. I mean, it definitely couldn't work, but there are worse things than marrying your best friend and being partners for life. It seems to work all the time in Hazel's large collection of romance novels, although those are made up and no one I know is a duke in desperate need of a bride.

I'm definitely not a duke, and I swore I wouldn't get married again. No matter what Hazel says, I still feel as if I fucked things up with Molly, and that's not a great feeling. Plus, do I even know ten things about Hazel? I can't use the *L* word, not for us. I'm not too convinced about the math, that if you can just list ten things that make a person lovable, that equals loving them. I know exactly how I feel about

Hazel, and it's not romantic. There are no grand gestures in our future.

Right on cue, the night sky lights up with fireworks. Dev insisted that today had to be special for Lola, and he's overdelivered. She's gazing at him like he's Atlas, effortlessly shouldering the weight of the heavens. For all I know—and I most definitely do *not* want to think about it any more than I already have—he's a god in bed. I'm sure Hazel has all of the details.

While the night sky lights up with Lola's name and something that's probably supposed to be flowers or shooting stars, the girls pose for a few final photos while Max, Dev and I finish off the champagne. Waste not, want not.

"You're next." Dev flops down beside Max and me. Sand flies everywhere. When I slide him a glance, he's looking at Max and I breathe a sigh of relief.

Max reaches over and lazily punches me in the arm. "Unless Jack here decides to get back on the horse first."

I stare at him, not sure if he's serious or not. Apparently he's forgotten our conversation at the market.

Dev looks at me. "You're seeing someone?"

"I'm not looking for a relationship right now," I say carefully.

Max snorts. "Hazel and he are 'friends.'"

Dev gets a sort of arrested look on his face. Or maybe he's just constipated. Either way, this is not a conversation I want to have. "The two of you are together?"

Max nods, as if it's as simple as that.

"We're just friends." I'm pretty sure the tone of my voice makes it more than clear that I'm not in a sharing mood.

"With benefits," Max says.

Dev freaking gawks at me. This is one of the reasons why Hazel and I have kept our sleeping together a secret. I can practically see the thoughts marching through Dev's head. Hazel and I are business partners. We're part of the same friend group. What happens when I fuck this up? But it's actually nobody's business what Hazel and I do together. We're two consenting adults and nobody's getting hurt.

"So…does that mean you're ready to start dating again?" Dev asks.

"He's ready for something." Max sounds pissy, but you know what? It's still none of his business.

"I don't want to be in a relationship. Hazel is just Hazel." I shrug. "She's like one of us, one of the guys. She's not the kind of girl you feel romantic about."

Dev's face sort of freeze-frames. Right. I don't even need to turn around to know that Hazel's heard what I just said.

CHAPTER ELEVEN

It's Saturday, two weeks after Hazel and I watched our friends tie the knot on a Cabo beach and I made an ass of myself. We're both pretending everything is normal, even though it's not. We go to work, we go home alone on the weeknights, and on the weekends we have sex constantly. The only thing that changes is where, because Hazel still insists that we alternate houses. It seems to matter to her, so I give up trying to figure out why and just do it.

This weekend it's my turn to host, so we're hiding out in my beach house. I finally let Hazel pass out around one this morning, so we haven't gotten too much catch-up work done today, although we've both dutifully hauled our laptops into my home office. My office is a modern space with floor-to-ceiling windows. I can look out and see the ocean.

Today's one of those rare rainy California days where the ocean is shades of gray and it's cool enough that the heat is running. Hazel barely cracks her laptop before she passes out on the floor pillow she dragged next to the glass. She's definitely been working too hard these last two weeks, so I don't wake her up even though I was looking forward to lazy weekend sex.

After I clear my inbox, I open a new tab in my browser and look at Pinterest. There's only one desk in my home office, so it feels like I should get another one for Hazel. I pin a few ideas so I can run them by her when she wakes up. Somehow I end up migrating from my desk chair to the floor beside her. It felt weird sitting up there when she's down here—plus, I just like being next to her.

Hazel snores softly, making little sleep-whiffle sounds, and I pin. I have enough good ideas for thirty home offices, so we'll have to narrow it down. I reach over and rescue the laptop when she rolls over, stretching like a cat. She looks really good asleep. There's a smooth expanse of skin where her T-shirt pushes up, and I brush my fingers over it.

"You've been busy," she says, her voice thick with sleep. "I passed out. Sorry."

I close the laptop and set it to the side. "You were tired."

"It feels like getting busted by my boss," she grumbles.

She's not wrong. Before we hooked up, I'd have given her shit about sleeping on the job. Now I want to scoop her up and carry her to bed because she does work too much and sometimes that means she doesn't sleep enough.

"You know you don't have to work 24/7, right? There are health benefits to sleeping."

"I'm too old to sleep on the floor." Hazel makes a face and sits up, looking around for her laptop. I nudge it firmly out of reach and pull her onto my lap.

I reach for her shoulders, working my hands over the knots I find beneath her shoulder blades. She feels wound up and tense beneath my palms. "Problems?"

Hazel shakes her head. Now that I think about it, I can't remember the last time she opened up about something that was bugging her that wasn't work-related. Maybe when she first pitched me our arrangement and complained about the lack of orgasms in her life?

"We've found your backup career," she groans.

I smile into her hair. "If you'd sit in a proper chair at a proper desk, you wouldn't fall asleep on the floor and then you wouldn't have this problem."

"Nobody likes a smart-ass."

I distract her by setting my laptop in front of her and pointing to the browser bursting with Pinterest goodness. My top three choices are a hot pink lacquer desk, a white-and-gold number and another desk that's a rich dark blue. I'm betting she goes for the pink.

She scans the page, her eyes lingering on the pink desk. *Knew it.* "But picking out furniture together seems—"

"Like what? It's just some furniture, Hazel."

She groans, flopping forward. I can't tell if that's Despairing Hazel or another yoga pose.

"It feels like a couple thing. Like we're not just a temporary hookup."

I wrap my arms around her middle and rest my chin on her head. I can't see her face, which seems like a disadvantage for this conversation. "We didn't discuss a time limit."

"No," she agrees quietly. "We didn't. It's just that we both said we'd look for our forever people. Or, if not The One, at least a relationship."

"This works for me," I admit. "I've already had my One and Only. That's not happening again for me."

She pulls away, folding her body into what I've learned is a cat pose. She stretches, her ass shoving up in the air, her shoulders pushing down. It's sexy and hot as hell. "You really believe love only comes along once?"

I shrug. "I honestly don't know, but I also can't imagine looking to get married again. I don't think I have that in me, Zee. Once you've scaled Everest, you're done, right? Even if you fall down after you summit, you've still made the climb. It's expensive and dangerous and the view at the top is still the same, so why do it again?"

Hazel chews on her lip. "You're crazy."

"Pot. Kettle." I tug on the ends of her hair. It's a gesture I've made a thousand times in the office, but it feels different here. "But I'm not looking for a serious relationship, so if we could just keep doing us, that would be perfect."

"I like us." She folds back in some kind of pretzel shape. Wow. Could we do it like that?

"If it works for you and it works for me, we don't have to stop or change things. But if you decide you want someone different, then no hard feelings. You do what you need to do."

A Pinterest notification slides across my screen and I read it automatically. Molly Chase has pinned four new cowboy images. Since when has Molly had a thing for cowboys? I'm clicking before I realize it.

Wow.

I should be glad that Molly's getting on with her own life, but the cowboy thing is weird. There are tons of muscled, boot-wearing guys with cowboy hats. They stand legs apart, thumbs shoved into the pockets of their Wranglers, eyeing bucking horses and some seriously scary-looking cattle. Arms and legs—and entire bodies—fly as the same guys do their damnedest to hang on and ride the livestock, with more than one cowboy biting the sawdust. She's pinned one cowboy in particular.

The tags beneath the pin read: Real Cowboys. Sexy Cowboys. My Cowboy.

WTF?

"Do you think Molly's dating a cowboy?"

Hazel says something, but I'm already scrolling through Molly's Pinterest. Rodeos. Las Vegas. Image after image fills my screen. That's definitely my ex-wife on vacation in Las Vegas. Buffet shots. I pause on a close-up of a huge bathtub that looks like it could fit a dozen cowboys. Molly always did have a thing for bathrooms. I wish I hadn't looked. There's no way this ends well. And then I find the couple shots. Molly at an ice bar with her cowboy. Cuddled up to the cowboy in a helicopter as the sun sets over Las Vegas. Naked cowboy shoulders in the tub.

I get up off the floor, taking my laptop with me, and crash-land in my desk chair. I need to be sure before I make an idiot of myself. I mean, what kind of a name is Evan Wilson? And how the hell did she meet a professional bull rider? She teaches *English*—I don't think she's ever ridden a horse in her life. Walking away would be better, but now I have to know. It's like an itch that I shouldn't scratch but it feels so good at the moment that I don't care I'll be hurting later.

"You're a girl." I look at Hazel. She's retrieved her laptop, but the lid is still closed. She's watching me as I go down in flames over here and I don't care. "Do you think he's hot?"

I flip the laptop around so she can see Cowboy Bob in all his glory. I'm not thinking, and I can't even blame it on being drunk or tired. Once I saw those pictures, the logic train pulled out of the station and now I'm careening out of control. I don't care.

Hazel sets her laptop on the floor and comes around to stand behind me. "This is a really bad idea."

"Absolutely." Another cute couple shot. Click. Champagne on ice. Click. A selfie as Evan wraps one arm around my wife and another around an enormous trophy—compensating much?—and plants a celebratory kiss on her upturned face. Click. Click. Click. "She can't have known him for long, so what kind of feelings could she possibly have for him?"

"Fun ones," Hazel says dryly.

And now I'm realizing that I might have expected Molly to come back, to admit she was wrong.

I grab my phone and fire off a quick text. "I'm going to Vegas."

"Right now?"

"Yeah."

"You really think that's a good idea?"

"Yeah."

"Why? What's the objective?"

She looks baffled, so I point out the obvious reason to make an emergency trip to Vegas.

"Someone needs to vet Cowboy Bob. How much money can the guy make riding cows?"

"You think he's her boy toy?" Amusement colors Hazel's voice.

Objectively, however, Molly is probably the richest English teacher on the face of the planet. Definitely in the continental US. I was scrupulously fair in our divorce settlement and even Molly couldn't spend millions of dollars on books.

"Molly needs looking after."

"Jack—"

"You might as well say it." If it's physically possible for a grown woman to explode, Hazel's on the edge.

"Speaking as a grown woman myself, if you go charging in there to approve—or not approve—her choice in men, I can assure you things will end badly for you."

"Come with me."

"Are you nuts? One of us needs to not get arrested as a delusional stalker, because we have important business meetings next week."

"Come with me and make sure I don't get arrested."

"No."

"Please? It'll be fun. There are spas. We can have sex in a hotel room." I stab a finger at the naked cowboy shoulders. "I'll get you the biggest tub in Vegas."

I know I'm being irrational. It's not an incentive-rich offer. No sane woman would take it. My only hope is that Hazel is ever so slightly crazy. In the best possible way.

Hazel sighs, a big, gusty exhale. I know before she says anything that I've won.

"This is insane. I'm going with you because letting you get arrested or castrated in Vegas would be detrimental to our business."

My phone buzzes with a confirmation from the private plane people. "We take off in three hours."

CHAPTER TWELVE

THE PRIVATE JET terminal is posh. You never know who you're going to meet. I was about to board my jet for a European meeting once when I swear Prince Harry came strolling out of the men's room. I walk beside Hazel toward the plane.

She casts a quick glance down at my hand cupping her elbow, and a smile touches her mouth briefly as she shakes her head. "You don't change, do you?"

I don't know what she means, so I concentrate on getting us on board. The sooner we're seated and buckled in, the faster we can get to Vegas. Our luggage has already been stowed away by the ground crew. The cabin holds eight and looks like my uncle's living room. There are four cream-colored leather recliners with little red throw pillows and a big leather sofa grouped around a coffee table. Since the flight to Las Vegas is just over an hour, I passed on a stewardess. We can pour our own drinks.

It feels like it takes forever to get airborne, although it's really less than fifteen minutes. I debate hiring a PI to track down Molly and her Cowboy

Dick in Vegas, but since he's performing in the big national rodeo there, he can't be that hard to find. After the Pinterest fiasco, I texted her "to check in," but she ignored me. I tried giving her a call, but I rolled straight to voice mail. She's probably ignoring me.

One of the many advantages of flying private is that we'll go above the commercial traffic and take the most direct route to Vegas. This means no fighting for airspace and a shorter flight time. We can't get there fast enough for me. I bounce my knee up and down, considering next steps. Maybe I should have driven.

Hazel's hand covers my knee. "What's the plan?"

"I have tickets for the rodeo tonight. We'll go there, check out this Evan, and I'll see if I can have a couple of words with Molly."

"She's not going to want to talk about this," she murmurs.

"Then she shouldn't have a rebound cowboy."

"Mmm."

It's an excellent plan, but she's frowning at me.

"You think I overlooked something."

"I didn't say that."

"You're thinking it."

"What if Molly's genuinely happy?"

"With a cowboy? Molly doesn't like horses. Or cows. Or anything else you find on a ranch."

Except, apparently, for cowboys. Judging by her Pinterest, she definitely likes cowboys. I'm not sure what it is about a man in boots and a hat with a sweet spot for ladies that appeals. Huh. Put that way, why *wouldn't* Molly choose a cowboy for my replacement?

Hazel squeezes my knee, her thumb sweeping back and forth. It tickles, but it also feels good. She casts a glance at the closed door that separates us from the cockpit.

"How private is your jet?" she asks.

She makes *jet* sound downright dirty. I laugh and twist so I can see her face. "Not that private."

"You're not a member of the mile-high club?"

"Nope."

"Do you want to be?" Her hand slides up.

I capture her fingers with mine. "Do you really want to play naked sardines in an airline bathroom?"

Hazel makes a face. "Don't we get a bigger bathroom on this thing?"

"Not that big." I drop a kiss on top of her head. I doubt that she's really issuing an invitation to have a quickie at forty thousand feet.

Plus, Hazel is a nervous flyer. She usually takes a chill pill before boarding, which means that we never schedule same-day business meetings for her as she needs time to "turn her brain back on." I'm not sure what her doctor's prescribing, but she's definitely not anxious right now. In fact, she seems totally relaxed.

Maybe she's too comfortable.

"Plan B," she says. "You make me come."

Turns out she's not taking any chances. With a sharp grin, she grabs my hand and puts it exactly where she wants it. It's like I'm her very own magic rabbit toy.

I'm not quite sure if she's teasing me or not. I mean, she's *definitely* teasing, but does she want me to do something more? We're not exactly private here, even if we're alone. I also haven't made out on a plane in years and even then it was just kisses in first class. There's probably some kind of single-guy etiquette that covers this situation but I'm not sure what it is.

"Hold that thought," she announces.

Wait—what?

There's no thinking happening, at least not on my part. Even though our flight will be short, she's wearing clothing meant for relaxing on the plane—some kind of very clingy matching knit set. The fabric's soft beneath my fingertips, although that's not the reason I stroke gently back and forth. I love touching Hazel. The pants and leggings are a perfectly tame, muted gray, and I can't help but notice that there's no visible panty line. Is she commando? I'm immediately distracted from that avenue of inquiry, however, because when she leans down to rummage in her bag, the material hugs her boobs and does insane things to her ass. Plus, my hand's shoved against her crotch in the best ever Hazel sandwich.

A creamy strip of skin is visible above the waist of her leggings. *Naked.* She's most definitely naked underneath. I bite back a groan. My dick has been hard since we boarded the plane and this isn't helping the situation in my pants. Fortunately, I have about thirty-five minutes to make Mr. Happy less…happy.

Without missing a beat, she snags something from her purse by our feet—a cashmere throw I've seen dozens if not hundreds of times before. It's Hazel's constant companion on every flight because she's always cold, and on more than one occasion I've heard her vow undying love to it. With a flick of her wrist, she drapes it over us.

Hiding the evidence.

She's the smartest woman on the planet and my hand's still on her crotch.

I do my part and grab the remote, dimming the cabin lights. The pilots probably won't come out and I know for a fact that there are no security cameras in the cabin, but it never hurts to play things safe. Neither of us wants to read about horny billionaire business partners getting inducted into the mile-high club on one of the online gossip sites. The media sucks sometimes and this would be far too much click bait for them to pass up.

"Yes?" I run my thumb over the waistband of her leggings, asking permission to take things further.

"Absolutely." Hazel nods enthusiastically, shimmying in her seat. The throw slips and she catches it, her eyes laughing at me over the edge.

I slip my hand into Hazel's leggings. There's a moment of happy confirmation—she's not wearing panties—and then the scent and feel of Hazel becomes my entire world. She's slick and swollen, so wet that my fingers glide over her easily. She groans encouragement as I skim my fingertips down. The angle is awkward, my wrist bent in an uncomfortable bow. The dark, the blanket, the near pain in my wrist—it reminds me of high school and I tell her so.

She laughs. "Who was your first? Cheerleader? Best friend's older sister? Math teacher?"

I'm not sure why she wants to have a conversation *now*, but I want to make her happy, so I take a shot at forming a coherent sentence. "You have a dirty mind."

And it's fabulous.

Hazel makes that snort-laugh—mission accomplished on the happiness front—but then her breath catches. Oh, good. I've distracted her. "Yes, like that."

I skim her folds more lightly before sinking a little deeper. She's so wet and soft there. All the stupid comparisons come to mind—she feels like silk, a flower, rose petals. They're not enough. Even if she didn't blow my mind so completely, I'd never find enough words to describe Hazel. Somehow, she's simply more.

She presses harder against my hand and I find a faster rhythm with my fingers—teasing, circling, gliding my fingers around her clit. I can feel the little tremors starting in her sensitive flesh.

"I don't want to come yet," she groans.

"I could do this all night," I whisper roughly against her hair. "But there're two problems with that plan. First problem? Vegas is only a short flight."

I move faster until I'm getting her off with my fingers and she's chanting my name, her hands locked on my wrist as if I'd let go of her now. When she comes, it's fast and hard, and I savor each sweet pulse. I love making her lose control; I love catching her when she lets go and fall-flies over the edge.

We sort of collapse together in the sudden silence blanketing the cabin. Eventually, I trail my mouth over her cheek to her ear. "You're amazing."

She mutters something, but it's incomprehensible. I reach over and do up her seat belt before I pull her up against my side. The pilot announces that we're landing, and the Vegas lights rush up to greet us outside the windows.

We're on the tarmac at McCarran International Airport before she says, "You never shared the second problem with the class."

I smirk against her hair. "You're loud. No way we do it all night and the pilots don't hear you."

She folds up her blanket. "I'm just incentivizing you. Or giving you positive feedback on your performance."

"My boss is the best," I say mock-solemnly.

As we taxi toward the private jet terminal, she sits up and grabs her purse. I watch as she puts herself back together, brushing her hair, applying a red slick of lipstick to her mouth. This is Business Hazel—calm, in control, certain of herself.

She winks at me as the pilots bring us to a smooth halt. "I have the best plans."

CHAPTER THIRTEEN

THERE'S A DRIVER and car waiting for us when we get off the plane in Las Vegas. Hazel hums something under her breath that sounds suspiciously like a Christmas carol even though the holiday is months away still. I realize my palm is curled protectively around her elbow just in case she trips or there's a zombie attack, and I drop my hand. "Sorry."

"Let's try a compromise," Hazel suggests.

I slant a glance down at her as we start toward the terminal. Neither Hazel nor I compromise well. One or both of us always insists on being in charge.

On being right.

"Hit me," I say lightly, nudging her with my shoulder when she veers in the wrong direction. When I bring my fingers to my nose, I can smell Hazel. She wanted to show me some love but we ran out of time, so now I have an IOU that she scribbled on a twenty-dollar bill because neither of us had any paper.

"You're a dirty boy, Mr. Reed." Hazel leans into me, her arm brushing mine, and just that simple

touch sets me on fire. "But let's start with something that can be done in public."

She reaches for my hand, her fingers tangling
with mine, her thumb tracing a small, private circle
on mine. I look down at where we're now joined. It
feels good.

It feels like we're a couple.

"Is this okay?" she asks.

As if I could let her go now. I've missed this sense
of being half of a whole, of feeling connected to another person. "Yes."

She doesn't let go until I've handed her into the
waiting town car. Las Vegas is every bit as loud
and colorful as I remember. It's not a place I come
often—I prefer the ocean—but Max, Dev and I used
to drive over the mountains and through the desert
to spend long, decadent weekends drunk off our
asses to celebrate the end of another college quarter. Hazel's quiet as we drive up the Strip. Walking
might be faster thanks to the hordes of people crossing every corner and the never-ending streetlights,
but the casinos are all lit up and Hazel seems happy
to look out the window. I think about telling the
driver to turn off and take the back way, but Hazel
already has the window rolled down and is recording our slow crawl down the Strip for posterity.

When we reach the Bellagio, the fountains rocket
up into the air. Enormous jets of water rise and fall,
exploding across the surface of the lake in well-
choreographed bursts. Tourists crowd against the

wall that separates them from the lake, jockeying for the clearest point of view.

I booked a Bellagio pool villa. Typically the villas are available only to high rollers, but exceptions are always made for billionaires, and Hazel deserves nothing but the best for having my back. The living room of the villa is done in tasteful creams. Italianate villa but screams money. Two bedrooms, five bathrooms, a kitchen, dry sauna, massage room, fireplace, hot tub and our own private pool. The roar of the fountains almost but not quite drowns out the louder babel that is Vegas. While Hazel disappears, exploring, I tip the butler generously, willing him to disappear.

He doesn't catch my subliminal message. "Can I do anything else for you, sir?"

Before I can send him on his way with a polite "no thanks," Hazel bellows out her obscene admiration from another room for "the world's biggest fucking tub." I'm not sure if she's referring to the tub's proportions or to activities that could be performed within it, but it's Vegas. Anything is possible.

"Perhaps our romance package?" The butler makes the suggestion discreetly, but I can feel him fighting back a smile. I nod, because what the hell. I'm sure Hazel would enjoy rose petals in her bath or something.

We don't have much time before the rodeo starts, so I keep my plane IOU for later and we change and head out. I'm not going for the full-on Wranglers, boots and Stetson look, but jeans and boots seem like they would blend better than a suit. Hazel also gets into the spirit of things with a full skirt that stops just below her knees. She's wearing bright red cowboy boots and a Western shirt that she's tied up around her waist.

The rodeo is being held down the Strip, in the same venue where the resort usually hosts medieval jousts and dinner shows that serve enormous turkey drumsticks on platters so you can get your inner knight on. The cowboy hats are as outsize as their wearers, although nowhere near as large as the two-story posters of the top competitors lining the walls. This gives me an opportunity to check him out before confronting him face-to-face. Evan Wilson is not a bad-looking man. He's not as tall as me, which makes him a medium-sized Viking and a big man. Close-cropped brown hair, bad-boy stubble, brown eyes and—fuck me—a dimple in his left cheek.

I nod toward the picture of my replacement. "Do you think he's hot?"

Hazel's eyebrows pull together as she gazes up at larger-than-life Evan. If it takes longer than three seconds for her to decide, the answer is yes, though there's an unfamiliar, sort of hollow sensation somewhere near my stomach. Maybe I should work room service or dinner into tonight's plan. Maybe—

Hazel shakes her head. "Absolutely not."

Two seconds. I think she may be lying, but I appreciate it. Hazel's good people.

Our seats are the best money can buy, so it would be impossible to get closer to the arena without actually entering the competition. The rodeo one. Not the one for Molly. And not that I'm competing for her. Or want her.

Something twists inside me.

I'm not entirely sure why I'm here.

Evan's competing in the second event, bareback riding. Rider after rider explodes from the bright yellow chute, hanging on while the bronc does its best to knock them off. When Evan comes busting out, it's clear he's a big crowd favorite. He racks up an impressive score in eight seconds. It's not enough for the win, though. Second Choice Boy comes in *third*. I don't see Molly, though.

When we file out, Hazel nudges my arm. "There's an after-party."

"You think that's where they'll head?"

"I'm certain of it." She smiles at me, her fingers grabbing mine so she can lead me through the crowd. "I overheard Molly talking to another rider's girlfriend in the bathroom. Plus, he placed third. He'll have sponsors to talk to, people to schmooze."

The crowd's large and some of the cowboys have drunk their weight in beer. After the third time someone bumps into Hazel, I pull my hand free and wrap my arm around her shoulders instead. People think twice about bodychecking someone my size and it's a good excuse to touch her.

Naturally, the after-party isn't being held in the same place as the rodeo. We walk down the Strip for a quarter mile in companionable silence.

"Pit stop." Hazel yanks on my arm.

Obediently, I slow to a halt. "What's up?"

"We totally need to try those."

I follow her pointing finger. *Those* are Day-Glo margaritas in three-foot-high containers that look suspiciously like bongs and that can be obtained from a bar that's steps from the Strip, apparently serviced by a bevy of bikini-clad, boot-wearing, feathered mermaids. Hazel steers me past the neon statues of deep-sea ladies and five minutes later we're officially armed and dangerous. I take an exploratory sip of my pink to-go margarita as we walk. It's more mix than tequila, which bodes well for our ability to make it to the after-party.

Hazel slurps enthusiastically. Hers is green and she ordered triple shots. "Are you sure Evan's trouble? He's obviously good at his job and people seem to like him."

Sadly, she's right. Still, I go with the obvious counterpoint. "She hasn't known him long."

"Mmm-hmm." Hazel sucks an impressive amount of margarita through her straw.

"Words, Hazel."

She swallows a mouthful of lime-green slushy. "Well, assuming that she met Evan after she moved out and filed for divorce—"

"Of course she did," I growl. Molly's neither a cheater nor a liar.

Hazel pats my arm. "Then she's had a little over a year and a half to have met him."

"She could have met him last week."

"Or last year." Hazel salutes me with her margarita.

I force myself to nod. I'm aware that coming to Vegas is at best illogical. At worst, it's probably a misdemeanor. Clearly, Hazel is also aware of this because she goes right there.

"Why are you here?" She waves a hand around us. She's a lightweight when it comes to alcohol. Usually she avoids it at business dinners or I drink it for her. "If you want to reconcile with Molly, stalking isn't going to help your case."

Naturally, I double down on my stupidity. "I want to make sure she's okay."

"You're such a white knight! Always rushing to the rescue. Why can't she rescue herself? Why do you have to do everything?"

Hazel sucks fiercely on her margarita.

I try not to remember the way her mouth feels on my dick.

"I made promises." Wow. That sounds lame, even to me. "A judge can't just wipe those away with a stroke of his pen."

I'm not sure if actual pen and ink was involved in our divorce. The whole thing was handled by our lawyers and I never even had to go to court. The last time I saw Molly was at our mediation appointment. Hazel would have been horrified, because I agreed to everything Molly asked for. I try not to think too much about the fact that she asked for almost nothing. She didn't want money or our house or even most of our things. Just enough for a fresh start and a new life, one without me. It feels distant now and like a whole different life, as if somewhere out there is a happy Jack and Molly, married, making babies, carrying on toward happily-ever-after.

"Do you believe in parallel universes?"

"A multiverse?" Hazel pulls thoughtfully on her straw.

"Maybe there are multiple universes out there." I rest my palm against the small of her back, nudging her toward the crosswalk. The light's red, so we come to a halt, surrounded by a crowd of other pedestrians. "And there's a different version of reality in each one, right? One where Molly and I never met, one where we split up, one where we reconciled. Hundreds and hundreds of different endings."

"One where we never met or never had sex," Hazel says. "One where there's not this thing between us."

As usual, she takes me by surprise. Even after all our years working together, I'm constantly amazed by the directions that her brain goes. It's part of what makes her such a brilliant venture capitalist, though, because she sees connections and outcomes the rest of us don't or can't.

I try not to think about a universe where I never meet Hazel. Naked, warm, wide-open Hazel—her hands tugging me down until I'm at her favorite angle. God, she has so many preferences. Directions. Pointed suggestions. I never have to wonder if Hazel's enjoying herself in bed. The words just pour out of her, throaty moans, half-spoken commands, the bite of her nails underscoring the moment when I do something she really, *really* likes. She talks and talks and talks the whole time we're having sex, and I fucking love it.

"I think," she muses, clearly chasing down a thought, "that you need to decide which universe you'd choose to be in right now. If you had a choice or magic universe-hopping skills. Life's not a flip book, Jack. Eventually you have to pick one page. One place."

She shrugs and returns her attention to her margarita. The light changes and people flood the crosswalk. It's like a swarm of drunken salmon all battling to swim in opposite directions. I grunt and wrap an arm around Hazel when someone smashes his shoulder into her. I don't want her to get hurt, not ever.

"I know." I squeeze her shoulders gently, and not just because we've barely made it to the other side of the street unscathed. "But I just need to make sure that Molly's okay, that she's safe with this guy."

"White knight," Hazel says. "You're the guy who marches into battle glued to the back of his horse."

"So?"

There's nothing wrong with wanting to look out for the people in your life. It's good to care, to be loyal.

"So maybe it's not an accident Molly picked a guy who gets thrown off horses for a living."

"Sticking is better."

Hazel makes a noncommittal sound and applies herself to her margarita. It's pretty clear what her position is on white-knighting. I mean, I know we're not that kind of thing. We're friends and partners.

We're fun and we're each other's *benefit*. But we're not a couple, not for real. We're not in a relationship and I don't get to ride through her life, tilting at her monsters.

"Do you still love her?" Hazel laces her fingers through mine as she talks, tugging me toward the casino's entrance.

I don't know what to say. I don't *love* love Molly— not anymore and maybe not for a long time. Feelings aren't something I'm good at, if we're being honest. For all the effort I put in with Molly, I still didn't get it right. Rather than holding on like a cowboy, I went flying off and bit the ground.

"Jack?"

"No." I try it out and realize it's true. I have affection and regret, fondness and memories, but the bigger feelings are gone. Or more accurately, they've been redirected when I wasn't looking.

Maybe those parallel universes can overlap this one; maybe one small sidestep and *bam*, you're in unfamiliar familiar territory. Because there seems to be some alien place that I've just stumbled into, and it's a place where maybe I have feelings for Hazel. Not love, not that way, not yet, but there's more than a seed of something sprouting in my chest.

It turns out the rodeo after-party is open to anyone, so we don't have to sneak, bribe or buy our way in. Hazel's visibly disappointed. I'm not sure what her plan was. In addition to multiple cash bars, there's a country band performing up onstage.

And dancing.

Lots and lots of dancing. Hundreds of would-be cowboys and cowgirls strut their stuff, boots thumping in rhythm, hands clapping. It takes me less than a minute to spot Molly and Evan in the thick of the dancing. He twirls her in a circle, one arm wrapped around her waist, the other holding her hand. He's a cocky bastard, loose-limbed, confident. The asshole definitely knows what he's doing out there. You'd never guess he got tossed off a horse an hour ago.

"That's not a waltz," Hazel hisses. Her elbow digs into my side.

"Agreed." I'm not entirely sure what that particular dance number is called, although I'm clearly in the minority there. Everyone else on the dance floor is moving more or less together, heels tapping, hands clapping in bizarre synchronicity.

"I only know how to wedding waltz."

"We'll figure it out. Let's go."

Hazel has multiple sisters, all of whom I've watched get married. Honestly, I'm sort of a surrogate big brother for them. Not for Hazel, obviously— that would be gross—but I've pinch-hit as an usher, scooped up drunken bridesmaids and given my opinion on cakes, dresses and flowers. And, yes, waltzing was involved.

"Jack." She whips out her phone and starts googling. "That's not a waltz. So I. Don't. Know. How. To. Do. It."

Hazel's fingers fly across the screen and I tilt my head so I can see her search results. "We're going to learn to dance by watching YouTube? Before they shut this party down?"

"Yes! Maybe."

Hazel angry-glares at the screen, where a cowboy and cowgirl are dancing up a storm. She slows down the video. Rewinds. I don't think there's enough time to execute this particular plan.

I pluck the phone out of her hand and shove it in my back pocket. "We'll improvise. Or copy the people next to us. Come on."

"I'm going to suck, Jack," she growls. "You'll rock this. It's practically a sport. I, however, am going to look like an uncoordinated idiot and I don't want to. You always have a plan—make one up now. A good one," she adds.

I watch the dancers for a second. It doesn't look like rocket science. "Come on. Wing it with me."

"Jack. No."

"Trust me."

I grab her hand and tow her out onto the dance floor. Based on where we start and what seem to be the rules of this particular dance, we should intersect with Evan and Molly shortly.

I come to several conclusions in the next five minutes. First, Hazel is a bad two-stepper. Second, I'm even worse. Third, cowboys are really good sports. We bumble our way through the steps, careening around our line. We're still laughing when I twirl Hazel around and come face-to-face with Molly. Okay. Face-to-top-of-her-head. She's laughing, too, pulling Evan closer, and then she looks up and spies me.

Yeah. The laughter vanishes from her face.

"Can we talk?"

She leans up and says something to Evan that I don't catch. He nods, then he's holding his hand out to Hazel. Somehow I always thought partner swapping would be sexier. I lead Molly off the dance floor because I'm not having this conversation in front of an audience. The bar seems by far the better choice.

"Why are you here, Jack?"

"I love Vegas."

"You hate Vegas," she counters.

Not true, although it's not my favorite place.

"People change." I shrug. "You did, so why can't I?"

Of all the ways I've planned this meeting, line dancing wasn't one of the steps. I'd expected our reunion to be awkward, but surprisingly it isn't. It's more like running into someone from college that you used to spend time with. They're part of your past and you can't help but pick over the memories, reliving the fun ones, the parts that you enjoyed. But we've both moved on. And if I'm being honest, we'd both moved on long before we got around to filing for divorce. We're not the same people we were when we got married, and I'm not sure that's a bad thing.

I study Molly while I flag down a bartender and order drinks. She looks different. Gorgeous. Stunningly beautiful in a quiet Madonna way. But that's not new. It's something about the way she holds herself or maybe in how she watched the rest of us. As corny as it is, she knows who she is and what she wants. *Which is a cowboy*, my brain reminds me. *Your replacement.*

Out on the dance floor, Evan is valiantly trying to teach Hazel the two-step. She's game and laughing, but her results are subpar. It must be driving her crazy.

"So." I hand Molly her drink. "A cowboy?"

"So," she counters. "You and Hazel?"

"We're just friends."

She shrugs. "If you say so."

That's not what she means.

"I never cheated on you. And certainly not with Hazel."

"I know that." Molly takes a sip of her wine. "You were always fair."

Divorce has not granted me the super mind-reading powers that I lacked during our marriage. I still have no idea what Molly is thinking. It's beyond frustrating. I scrub my hand over my head, looking for the words I know I won't find.

"Why did we break up?"

"Because we were happy together until we weren't. Because we didn't work anymore. Because people change. Because we each made choices about what we'd do with our lives or who our friends would be or what we'd share."

Or not share, I think. But I don't say anything and Molly finishes her thought.

"And I couldn't fix *us* but I could fix me. I didn't handle the end well." She puts her glass down and meets my eyes. "I'm sorry."

"Are you happy?"

I'm talking about feelings. Shoot me.

"Yes." A smile curves her mouth.

"With a cowboy?"

She nods. Her eyes watch that cowboy. For a moment, I remember when she used to look at me that way, but then I let it go.

Evan's given up trying to teach Hazel the moves and is now attempting to limit the swathe of destruction she's carving through the neat, orderly line of dancers. He's grinning, though. My Zee has that effect on people.

I review what I've learned tonight, starting with the sad truth that apparently I'm an enormous jackass. Okay. I can live with that. I'm still running a full background check on *Evan* as if he's a candidate I'm thinking about bringing in and pitching to the board.

The management team makes or breaks a company. Sure, you need great people everywhere, and you should never overlook the guy or gal who's making the widgets or cleaning the kitchen. Those people count and shit doesn't get done without them. But you also need leaders, and sometimes people get so busy name-calling and screaming about the compensation package that they don't see what a CEO can bring to the table. Football games don't get won without a quarterback. You need everyone in that stadium—the people who buy the tickets, the guy hawking hot dogs, the engineer who makes the scoreboard run—but it's the quarterback who brings everyone together. The focus. The lightning rod. The guy reacting and putting years of training and practice into play. You can't cut corners on that guy—so I'm going to make sure Evan's everything he should be.

"There's nothing wrong with being friends," Molly says quietly as Zee and Evan abandon the dance floor and head toward us. "But there's nothing wrong with taking a chance on being more, Jack."

CHAPTER FOURTEEN

HAZEL'S UNCHARACTERISTICALLY QUIET after we leave Evan and Molly. It's not immediately obvious—even at three in the morning, the Strip is a loud place—but I know better than to expect silence from her. Hazel always has something to say. I take her hand, pulling her into my side. The sidewalks are still crowded despite the late hour. Couples stroll past us, arms around each other, but the annoying hawkers have disappeared for the night. No one offers girls or lap dances or a dozen other sexual services. Discarded nudie cards spill over the sidewalks and streets.

We're on the wrong side of Las Vegas Boulevard for our hotel, so I steer us toward the nearest crosswalk. The light's not in our favor, so we wait with dozens of other revelers. It's a noisy, half-drunk, cheerful crowd that jostles carelessly, everyone either judging their chances if they jaywalk, or jockeying for the best position to surge across the street when we get the green light. There's an older, blue-jeans-and-matching-shirt-wearing couple, somewhere in their midsixties, in the vanguard. The guy's rock solid, his feet planted. He throws an arm around his lady, anchoring her.

"Six o'clock," I say, nudging Hazel with my shoulder. "Tell me a story."

"Jack. Not tonight."

"Why not?" I brush a kiss over the top of her head. "Tired?"

"You're an idiot."

"What's wrong?" I run through the night searching for issues, but too much has happened. The likeliest candidate for her upset is the way I handled things with Molly and her cowboy, but I need specifics before I can come up with a plan to fix things. Hazel looks up at me, but I can't interpret the look on her face. Since nothing tonight has gone as planned, this shouldn't surprise me.

She pulls away from me, marching in silence by my side until we reach our villa. After I slide our card key over the lock and hold the door open so she can slip inside, she heads straight for the master bathroom, shedding things as she goes. Her jacket. Her purse. A cowboy boot. The housekeeper has been in and the bed is turned down. Chocolate mints decorate the pillows and a gold serving cart in front of the fireplace offers a choice of nightcaps. Cognac, calvados, scotch and soda—eeny, meeny, miny, moe. I wage a brief internal debate about the relative merits of adding more alcohol to the mess I've made of tonight and decide against it.

Instead, I strip down and slip into bed.

And wait.

The night may not have gone as planned, but I've realized something important. Something I should have figured out days and weeks ago.

The woman I want sleeping by my side tonight isn't Molly at all. It's Hazel. I feel like there should be some way to share this revelation with her, but I'm better at business than I am at poetry, so I'm still planning my explanation when she finally emerges from the bathroom.

She's wearing a UC Santa Cruz T-shirt, the silky skin of her bare legs lit up by the glow from the Strip. A moment later, she slides into bed, punching a button on the panel in the wall on her side and plunging the room into stygian darkness. The technology's amazing, but I'd rather see her face.

"Did tonight go as planned?" she asks. "Your conversation with Molly?"

I want to cup her shoulder with my hand. Want to pull her back against me, bury my face in her hair, her scent, her presence here with me. I suspect any one of those things would only make her angrier. So instead I give her the truth.

"Not at all."

I feel her nod. "Where did it go wrong?"

There are so many possible answers. For ten years, Molly was my center, my home, my heart. I thought we were going to be together forever, and then, when we weren't, I thought it was my fault. And maybe it was. And maybe it wasn't. What I realized tonight, however, is that it doesn't matter anymore. Molly is my past and I'm okay with that.

What I crave now is an entirely different future with Hazel. What I want with her is so much more than just the no-strings sex we promised each other. She's insanely smart and far too bossy, impossibly sexy and way too good for me. I'm just slow to realize it. And to realize that maybe I could have had a chance with her, but that after tonight she might not believe me.

"Everywhere," I whisper into the silence between us.

The sheets rustle and I wonder if Hazel's about to get up, to leave. I should reach out, but I don't know what more to say, so instead I say nothing as her breathing evens out and she falls asleep.

CHAPTER FIFTEEN

MORNINGS AFTER SUCK. There's the moment when you can no longer kid yourself that you're asleep or that the events of the previous night are some kind of nightmare. The mad flight to Vegas, the rodeo, the after-party and my stupid chasing after Molly march through my head in an endless loop. I was so stupid. At some point today—although I'm not certain what time it is right now—we have to head back to California. I also have to figure out how to apologize and fix what I screwed up last night. I don't really feel like getting up, though, so when my phone buzzes, I try unsuccessfully to telepathically silence it.

The second time it buzzes, Hazel fishes it out from beneath a pillow and silently hands it over. I can't tell if she reads the message preview or not, but I don't have secrets from Hazel, not anymore. She's seen me at my rawest, my most open, and it was okay. She didn't run screaming, and I count that as a win.

Molly's been angry-texting me for the last two hours. I get it. I drive her nuts and as soon as I walked away from her, she thought of all the things she should have said but didn't.

The latest text? Stay out of my business, Jack.

I ignore it.

I also have a voice mail from Evan that is far more profane than Molly's message. In his own words, I'm not to look at her, talk to her, talk to his manager, talk to his employer or otherwise stick my "goddamn nose" into their business. Executive summary? He's not happy about the background check I initiated. I'm guessing my PI was more of an eager beaver than I anticipated, because it sounds like he's already checked out an impressive amount of Evan. I just hope that doesn't include taking naked pictures of the man. I can live without ever seeing his dick.

Hazel sits up, tucking the sheet under her arms. "What did you do, Jack?"

I wish she hadn't heard that. "Nothing."

Hazel is staring at my phone. "You did something."

"A background check." I pulled the trigger on it at the after-party.

"On Evan?"

Well, duh. I already know all of Molly's secrets. Hazel's face, however, isn't happy. It's not her grumpy face, the one that can be fixed with cake or an apology. It's her let's-eviscerate-our-opponent face that I've only seen her wear when we lost a deal due to someone else's underhanded dealings. Usually I just help her take down whoever's earned The

Look, so I'm not sure what to say next because I don't feel like falling on my sword when I'm not wrong.

"I liked Evan," she says.

I blame the cowboy boots.

"Not you, too."

"Coming here was a mistake." Hazel drops the sheet. She's usually direct when she's mad, but she doesn't give me more words, just balls her fists by her sides, her eyebrows drawing together as she gets up. I might be misreading her since she's mostly naked and that doesn't help my concentration any. God, she's gorgeous.

She glares down at me from the side of the bed. "Are we done here? I think we are."

"Yeah." *Shit.* She's definitely mad. I should be better at not fighting after being married, but apparently I have a lot to learn.

Hazel marches across the room and bends over, rummaging in her suitcase. My dick definitely appreciates the view, but unfortunately, she promptly pulls on pants. More clothes follow, and not the kind you wear to bed or to lounge around your hotel room. Shoes, another shirt, a blazer. It seems too early in the morning—or late at night—for business casual.

"Are you going somewhere?" I sit up and look for my clothes. Chasing her naked will only get me arrested. Plus, it's creepy.

Hazel swipes her boots from the floor. "Jack—"

"Because I think we should go back to bed."

She yanks on a boot. "Do you remember the conversation we had when we first got together?"

"I'm sure you'll remind me." I'm feeling decidedly naked here. Her right boot and my jeans are tangled up together at the foot of the bed and she lobs the jeans at me. I force myself to pull them on. Why are we getting dressed when we could be naked? *Together?* Is she pranking me?

"We agreed that either of us could walk away at any time." She shrugs. "I've decided now is a good time for me to go."

Hazel's gaze dissects me and I suddenly have a very good idea how those frogs felt when we went after them with a scalpel in high-school biology. Except the frogs were dead and pickled, and I'm just confused.

"Where are you going?"

"It's really none of your business."

"I brought you here."

"This isn't a *date*, Jack. You don't have to walk me to my front door."

"The one time I walked you to your door, it turned out great."

Hazel stares at me for a minute. Then she turns around and slams the lid on the suitcase. "I had no idea you were such a dick."

My phone buzzes again. Fuck.

"You should answer that," Hazel says pleasantly. Way, way too pleasantly. I can almost hear her grinding her teeth. "Clearly it's important."

"I need you to tell me what's wrong."

Hazel grabs her own phone, swipes angrily and holds it up so I can see the screen. I'm not sure when she took that photo, although the obvious answer is last night. Molly and I lean into each other, talking. I'm sporting a fierce look on my face and I'm half-turned, putting my upper body between Molly and the rest of the world.

"Tell me a story. What do you imagine is happening here?"

"We're having a conversation, not sex."

"Mmm," she says. "That's not the story I see."

I turn off my phone and toss it on the nightstand. "Then explain it to me, Hazel. What do you see that I don't?"

I don't know what I expect her to say, mostly because there seems to a thousand hyperactive butter-flies roosting in my stomach. I don't get anxious, so it makes no sense that waiting for Hazel's answer is killing me. I shove off the bed and pace toward her.

She looks at me and then at her suitcase. "Fuck it. I'm rich. I'll buy new stuff."

"That doesn't sound good, Hazel."

"I see two people in that picture, Jack. You and Molly. I don't see us. You're smart—you figure it out." She taps the phone. "We said we'd be together until we both found someone for real, but I don't think you're looking."

"You think I still have a thing for Molly?"

She swipes up her purse. "I think you have your head up your ass, yes."

"Molly and I are over."

"You chased her to *Vegas*. Maybe you should think

about that." Hazel exhales. "But I won't do this anymore. No more benefits, Jack."

"She's part of my past. I only came here because I wanted to make sure she was taken care of. I promise I won't reach out to her anymore, but don't go."

The butterflies in my stomach achieve liftoff and rocket into outer space.

"Let me fix this," I whisper.

"I'll always be your friend," she says. "But I can't do this anymore."

CHAPTER SIXTEEN

THE DAYS TICK past and become weeks. Weeks become a month. I go to work and I close deals. I make a shit ton of money I don't need. Sometimes Hazel and I take meetings together and sometimes we fly solo. We meet and debrief, arguing the merits, or lack thereof, of the pitches we've heard. We fight just as much because we're both passionate about what we believe and that's what makes us good partners. We come at a problem from different angles and then we argue-listen to each other because we respect each other. Things between us are friendly. Polite. There's no extracurricular nudity or dirty talk. No kisses, no naked walks on the beach, no sex.

We're just friends.

My Santa Cruz beach house is three thousand square feet of empty. It's too big for a single guy unless he's a hoarder. When I float the idea of selling it, however, Dev and Max revolt. Dev points out that real estate is an awesome investment in California and that he doesn't want asshole neighbors so I have an obligation, as his best friend, to stay the fuck put. His words, not mine. Max suggests I rescue a dozen cats.

Animal lovers talk about how pets have their person, the one human they gravitate to, curl up in bed with, wait by the front door for, and whose stuff they pee on when the human's been away too long or otherwise misbehaving. Faithful companions. It sounds a lot like marriage, doesn't it? Been there, done that, got my half of the T-shirt.

Never again.

I had the rest of my life all planned out and it didn't involve inviting a woman to move into my house or my heart.

After I'd moved on from my divorce, I'd planned to grow my business. Make more money. Spend time with family and friends spending that money like that hobbit who threw the big-ass party for the Bagginses. I was going to become that favorite uncle who sweeps in at Christmas with the best presents and who helps you cover up when you've dinged the family car you borrowed/stole or got busted for underage drinking. I'd have a string of fun Friday nights, hook up when I wanted the company and keep on doing me. Just me.

And then Hazel pitched me the perfect sex project and all my beautiful plans went right out the window. In a matter of weeks I not only learned what she looked like naked—awesome—but what she was thinking about behind that beautiful, well-manicured, supersmart exterior she showed to the world. Hazel was more than just my best friend.

Somehow, over the course of those weeks, she was everything.

I miss her. I miss the way she snorts when she laughs, her fanatical insistence on hair-styling products and flat irons, her opinion that she's always, always right. She's smart and funny and loyal…and she's amazing in bed.

I miss the sex, too. Not gonna lie about that.

Stupid memories.

We had sex in this room and in that one. On that counter and that floor, up against that wall and on those stairs. That practically makes the house a piece of performance art. Perhaps I could donate it to a museum? It's something to think about.

It's not like the only sex shop in town is Hazel. I could find a partner using Max's Billionaire Bachelors app. If I want to get my kink on, I could pick someone from Kinkster. May's poked me, too. But while the idea of getting laid appeals, I don't want to fuck May or anyone else. It won't be enough because whoever she is, she won't be Hazel.

I miss loving her.

I love her.

And I drove her away. I told her that relationships and true love were like Everest—you only climb that mountain once and most people never get close to the summit. They don't visit the Himalayas. They don't even step foot on the right continent. I'm a lucky bastard. I've done it twice.

So, no, I don't want meaningless sex.

I want it to mean everything. I want to chase after

Hazel and beg until she takes me back. And then I want to have angry makeup sex with her. Awkward first-time-we've-tried-this sex, completely wild sex, sex that breaks the bed, morning sex that makes us both late for work. It would be amazing. There would be crazy hang-from-the-chandelier monkey sex and then those nights when we're too damn tired and I'll rub her back or her feet and then we'll both fall asleep without having sex. We could do a victory lap of all the places we've done it and rechristen them. Cabo, Vegas, my house, her house. The back seat of my car, her garden, the beach and that other beach just up the road from my house because we were in too much of a rush to wait.

All I need now is a plan.

Five weeks after I blew up my life, I put my new plan into action. I call it Operation Rescue Me. Monday nights are quiet. Everyone's recovering from the weekend and the week hasn't had a chance to pick up steam and roll over us all yet. Step one? Get Hazel alone, soften her up with food and prepare to grovel.

By Wednesday, there will be at least one person staying late to take care of something, but right now everyone has gone home. I'm pretty sure Hazel thinks I have, too, but I just ducked out to pick up Chinese from our favorite hole-in-the-wall place. They deliver, but I suspect she won't stick around if I do.

The distance between us has grown exponentially. Our team members are starting to give us uncomfortable looks—they realize Mom and Dad are fighting, even if they haven't decided which parent they'd choose in a divorce. And sure, I see Hazel daily. I sit next to her, and her desk is only one freaking office over…but it's like the Grand Canyon and the Mariana Trench had a ginormous baby. That kind of gap isn't something you can just step over.

Because I fucked up.

I stick my head into her office and wave the bag of Chinese at her. I'm counting on the kung pao bribe to get me in the door. "Can I talk to you? I have a pitch."

"Sure." She's head-down in her laptop—I barely merit a second glance.

I come in, set down the bag and shut the door just in case. Okay. I'm feeling a little vulnerable.

Hazel looks up at me and gives me a polite smile. That neat little grimace shows no teeth and no emotion. She doesn't give a shit that I'm here. It's a challenge. But I've won under more challenging conditions. She points to a chair across from her desk, but my usual spot is parked on the edge of her desk. We don't have a whole lot of personal boundaries, which helps explain—even if it doesn't excuse—my misunderstanding what I felt for Hazel.

I bypass the chair and park my ass on the edge of her desk. "I have a proposal for you."

It feels like the first—and last—time Hazel pitched me. She feels it, too.

"I've heard that before." The polite smile peels back for a moment—Hazel's furious. That's also an emotion I can work with.

"I'd like to revisit the Jack and Hazel project."

"Done. Dead. Buried." Her eyes narrow. "Next topic."

"Not done." I give her an easy smile because apparently I really want to pour oil on the Hazel fire. "We're revisiting."

"Pass." She turns up her pretty nose and dives right back into whatever it is she's doing on her laptop.

Two can play that game. I snag the laptop, unplug it and close the lid in one smooth move. Then I turn and toss it onto the chair she told me to sit in.

"What the hell, Jack?" Hazel surges upright—she *really* doesn't like it when she's parted forcibly from her hardware—but I'm ready for her. I pull her between my legs, my hands on her waist. I estimate I have less than thirty seconds before she realizes my balls are vulnerable.

"Why did you pitch me Jack and Hazel? Give me the reasons."

Hazel glares at me. "We are at the office, *Mr. Reed.* It is not professional to stand like this."

She sucks angry air in through her nose like an enraged bull. That's okay. I'm about to wave the red cape.

"I don't care about being professional. I don't care who sees us. I'm not going to be your dirty little secret anymore because I *want* the whole world to know we're together."

Detonation in three…two…

"You are an ass."

Succinct. Pithy. Sadly true.

"If people think we're having sex, they're going to think that's how I earned my place at Coleman and Reed. They'll assume I'm sleeping with the boss. I *am* the boss, Jack. I earned it and you don't just get to jeopardize it because you don't like something."

Coleman and Reed is a billion-dollar company. That would have to be some pretty phenomenal sex, but I'm smart enough not to point that out to Hazel. She's not entirely wrong, unfortunately. There aren't a ton of women in the VC world and some of the guys definitely are of quid pro quo mindset. Some assholes *will* think she screwed her way to the top. Her words hurt because this isn't something I can fix, not easily. It sucks to be a woman playing this game, and if you're a woman who's winning? Yeah. The other players are gonna go after you loaded for bear.

"Plus, we're not together. You're not my secret anything. If you need me to define the word *done*, I can do that. We had sex. I can write your penis a poem if you're feeling insecure."

"It was amazing."

"You've had amazing sex before, Jack." She smacks me on the chest. "So have I. It's not a big deal."

"It is to me."

"This is what I get for being selfish."

"Excuse me?"

Her eyes narrow. *Danger.*

"I wanted you, so I took you. I mean, have you

looked at yourself? You're a big, built Viking look-alike. How could I not want you? And then you and Molly split up and I saw my chance. I sat on your desk." She waves toward the wall separating our of-fices. "I suggested we have sex and you looked like the idea had never crossed your mind once."

There's no good answer to that.

Hazel shakes her head. "It doesn't matter. What's your pitch?"

It does matter. It matters more than anything. I resist the urge to punch my laptop or do something equally stupid. Hazel makes it sound as if we're com-pletely in the past, which is bad. I don't want to be her one-and-done before I can even ask her for a second chance. I turn, keeping my arm around her waist, and punch the key that starts my slide deck.

The start-up of Jack and Hazel.
Jack and Hazel 2.0

"I want a second chance. No. I want a *first* chance at us." I wish I knew what she was thinking as she studies my slide, but I'm pitching blind here. "I screwed up big-time. I thought I didn't want a re-lationship, that what I wanted was just sex with my best friend."

She pulls away and drops into her chair. I hate that she's putting that distance between us. "You made me feel like crap, Jack."

"I'm sorry."

"I wanted a chance at us. I knew you'd never make

a move, so I made it for you. And then you made it very clear—on multiple occasions—that you were perfectly happy sticking with the just-sex plan."

"I was a dick. I didn't mean it."

"But you said it."

She leans back in her chair, her expression pissed off and beautiful—and hurt. I hate so much that I've put that look on her face. I adjust my plan… and abandon it.

"Look. I have a slide deck. I have an Excel spreadsheet. I have a well-thought-out plan." I slam the lid on the laptop and lob it into Hazel's trash can. "I could give you numbers. Reasons. Plans. Hell, I'll do my best to give you romance, too, but there's only one reason I'm here and that's to fix us. Give me a chance."

Hazel stares at me for a long moment. I can't read my chances on her face. And then she stands up and sets her hands on my shoulder. Her mouth brushes over mine, once, twice. For the best moment, I think I've won.

Until she steps back. "You're fired, Jack."

And then she leaves.

CHAPTER SEVENTEEN

I ONCE TOLD Hazel that marriage was like Mount Everest. At most, you summit it once in a lifetime. It turns out I was wrong. Sure, it's not for the faint of heart or the out of shape. You do need to watch out for avalanches and bad weather and, yeah, most of the guys climbing that particular mountain plan to do it just once. But there are exceptions. It turns out that thousands of climbers have done it more than once—and done it successfully. Plus, the Sherpa guides climb up and down it all the time like it's a goddamn StairMaster. If they can do it, so can I.

Two weeks after Hazel shoots down my pitch, I have a new plan. I'm the king of plans. I'm going to climb and I'm not going to stop until I reach the top. Hazel's worth fighting for. So, new plan?

1. Design mountaineering training program. We have a shit ton of mountains in California—I can climb them all and write a bestselling book about whatever epiphany I achieve on their peaks.

2. Build my physical conditioning by schlepping enormous packs around at perfectly reasonable elevations so I survive high-altitude sickness when I finally reach Everest.

3. Strength train.

4. Run fucking everywhere.

5. Work on my flexibility. Yeah. There's a life lesson there.

6. Shell out a ton of cash and book my climb.

I can't wait to get started. To start my climb—to finally be doing something to fix the mess I've made of my life.

One advantage of living in Santa Cruz is that we have a ton of things to climb. Today I'm staring down a watershed full of granite crags. The baby crags are a mere fifteen feet, while the one I'm about to tackle stretches fifty feet into the air. There's a line up the steep face.

It's a pretty day, all sunshine and birds, and the only thing missing is a singing cartoon princess and maybe a baby fawn. Everest is going to be a whole lot colder and more crowded—have you seen the lines to summit? The top is more crowded than the BART train platform at rush hour. I start my climb, moving methodically up from one handhold to the next. Right now, I've got this, all my focus on the next step and then the next step after that one.

"Are you *insane*?"

I swing around, losing my grip.

Hazel glares up at me from the base of the crag.

* * *

In the brief second it takes me to fall ten feet, I get an eyeful of Hazel. Her hair's slicked back in that tight little knot she loves, emphasizing her cheekbones and the dramatic slash of her eyebrows. Her gray T-shirt emphasizes the sweet vee between her breasts and is tied up over a pair of black leggings. She's wearing hiking boots that seem far more practical than the little black leather backpack slung over her shoulder. I have just enough time to appreciate that she looks fucking amazing before I crash-land on the ground at her feet.

I suck in a breath. Ouch. My lungs still work, though the rest of my body is seriously unhappy. "Am I dead?"

"Jesus. I hope not." Hazel's face comes into focus above me. Bonus—there are three of her.

"Because I sure think I see an angel."

"What the fuck, Reed?" Hazel straddles me. I'm not sure that's an approved medical tactic, but parts of me perk right up. "What do you think you're doing?"

"I'm climbing." I'm disavowing all knowledge of how it happens, but my hands curl around Hazel's hips.

"You fell, you moron."

"You surprised me."

She slaps a hand on the ground next to my head. "What was the big plan?"

"I was thinking I'd climb to the top of Everest and then I'd send you a message."

"News flash. This is not the Himalayas." Hazel pats me with her hands. I'm not sure if she's checking for broken bones or frisking me for hidden weapons. It's a good thing I don't have a Florence Nightingale fantasy because Hazel's not much of a nurse.

"I know *that*." I reach up and pat the first part of her that I can reach. Fortunately for my health, it's her shoulder. "I'm practicing. You have to work up to these things, so I'm starting small *here*, and then I'll climb the really, really big stuff in the Himalayas."

Hazel rolls her eyes. "You're such an ocean boy. The whole message-in-a-bottle thing works best if you have water."

"It would make a great story. I could spell out 'I love Hazel' in the snow."

"*I love you?* You're going to hike five-plus miles in life-threatening conditions and that's the sum total of your message?"

"I was going to add ten reasons why," I say, "but yeah, that's the executive summary. There's not a whole lot of room on the top of Everest, so I may need to abridge."

I pull her down on top of me. Carefully.

"Mmm-hmm. And how would I know you'd done that, seeing as how you didn't invite me on this trip?"

I slide my arms around her. God, she feels amazing. "It turns out there's surprisingly good cell phone reception there for being on a 29,000-foot mountain. I could take a picture from the base camp."

I think she's trying not to laugh. "The base camp's not the top."

"I'm sorry." She freezes, but she doesn't leave, so I say it again. "I'm so sorry, Hazel."

"Say it again."

"Which part? That I'm sorry?" Because I am. I'm so, so sorry.

"I'll give you a hint," she says. "I say 'I love you, Jack.' What do you say?"

"That I'm the luckiest bastard in the world."

Someone erases the distance between us, and our mouths meet. *I missed you.* It's cautious at first, both of us waiting to see what the other does. *I'm sorry. I love you. Do you love me?* And then I palm the back of her neck and she works her fingers through my hair, and we yank each other closer. She tastes so fucking good, just like I remembered. Hot, wet, one thousand percent Hazel. How did I ever think I could walk away from this woman?

"I love you." My delivery isn't great. I'm hoarse, out of breath, pulling her so close to me that it's probably illegal in a half-dozen states. I'd much rather show her how I feel about her than use my words. Which is why I kiss her again.

And again.

At some point we have to come up for air. I can't stop touching her, holding her against me as I reacquaint myself with her bare skin. And her mouth, her smile, her heart.

She cups my face in her hands, making me look at her. "Were you really going to climb Everest?"

Remember that new plan? Whatever it takes?

I fish my phone out of my pocket—it's looking

a little the worse for wear thanks to my landing on it—and show her the tickets. Two first-class tickets. "I have a date and everything. You want to come with me?"

"To spend two months climbing a frozen ice mountain where people die?"

"It sounds really romantic, doesn't it?"

She leans down and kisses me. Is that a yes? Or a not-a-chance-in-hell? "I have a better idea. After we get you to a doctor, I have tickets to Paris. I could use a date—there's a Marie Antoinette exhibit at the Louvre and I might possibly have made a substantial donation so we can borrow a dress."

Hot. *Damn.*

There's one flaw in that plan.

"Marie Antoinette didn't have a happy ending."

Hazel grins at me. "Then we'll make up a new story. A hot, kinky love story about two best friends who get it on and fall in love."

"I love you." I pull her down onto my chest and wrap my arms around her tight. "This is going to be one of those indissoluble partnerships."

"I love you, too." Her mouth curls up in a smile. "I might love you most, Viking man. What do you have to say about that?"

"I love you so much. Challenge accepted."

* * * * *

WILD WEDDING HOOKUP

JAMIE K. SCHMIDT

MILLS & BOON

To the MTBs and the $7,000 coffee machine.
We'll always have Naples.

CHAPTER ONE

MIKELINA PRESLEY WALKED through the five-bedroom beach house, making sure everything was perfect for the bachelor party. Checking the list on her phone, she confirmed that the sheets were five-hundred-thread-count Italian percale. The fridge was stocked with steaks and seafood, and the freezer with several bottles of Russian Standard vodka. The bar was tricked out with top shelf liquor, and the bathrooms all had condoms.

The housecleaning team was putting the finishing touches on the toilet paper by folding the edges into neat triangles on the roll, and then spritzing the air with their signature lime and verbena room spray. Mikelina was confident that Bastien Ainsworth would find everything to his satisfaction for his two-week stay.

As she was locking up, she had the customary pang of fear that a group of selfish rich boys would trash the place for good this time.

She was more than just the concierge for this house. This had been her family's vacation home until her father's fraudulent stock market trades landed him in prison and her parents' assets were seized. Luckily, the beach house had been in Mikelina's name for several years. So when her parents lost their house, her mother stayed here for a while. When her mother needed more money to pay off her father's lawyer fees, Mikelina should have put the house on the market. It would have solved all their problems. They would have been millionaires.

But she hadn't been able to let it go. There had been a lot of happy vacations here. Growing up, her father had worked sixty-hour weeks while her mother concentrated on her charities and social events. But when they came to South Beach on vacation, they had been a family.

Mikelina's phone rang as she was entering the security code to lock up. It was her boss.

"The house is all set," she said by way of greeting. Kirk Diamonte didn't waste time with pleasantries like hello and goodbye, and if you let him start off the call, he'd never let you get in a word edgewise. He was the CEO of the global Five Diamond Resorts Vacation Club. You'd think he'd want to check in and get off the phone as soon as possible. But he gossiped worse than her mother. In fact, the only reason Mikelina had been able to convince her mother to move out so she could rent the house was because of the "nice" conversation she had with Kirk where he had spilled the tea about all their mutual friends.

"Good. The Ainsworth family has booked us for

the wedding and honeymoon, too, so we want to start them off with an excellent impression."

Mikelina had chosen to do a rental contract with the Five Diamond Resorts vacation club because her friend Selena worked as a chef for them. Selena got to travel all over the world cooking for the members of the club in whatever home they decided to rent for their vacation. Mikelina, stuck behind a desk in Manhattan, had thought that sounded glamorous and exotic.

When she contacted Kirk about the property, he had been impressed by the house's wraparound porch and its proximity to the beach, but even more so by Mikelina's hotel background. When she lost her New York job because she was spending too much time flying out here to keep her mother calm and centered, Kirk had overlooked her father's scandal and hired her to be the client liaison for his Florida properties. He also gave her a large percentage of the money that came from renting out her family's home and she gave that money to her mother to live on.

"I think they'll be satisfied," she said. "I was able to scrounge up tickets to Christian Dibiasi's jam session tomorrow night. Very exclusive. It's one of South Beach's best kept secrets."

Kirk whistled. "Nice score. That's what I'm talking about. Try to anticipate their needs. The Ainsworth family is one of our biggest clients."

"The bar is stocked, the fridge is packed, and the sound system is keyed up to *caliente*," she said. She only hoped they wouldn't puke in the pool or throw lamps at each other.

It had been hard enough to convince her mother that renting out the house was the best option. The fact that strangers would be touching their things and living in their space made her mother cringe. Mikelina wasn't too happy about it either, but her father hadn't left them much of a choice. Either they sold the house or rented it out. And in the long run, they'd still have their house once her father got out of prison in ten years. Reluctantly, her mother had moved in with her sister in Boca Raton, which was a far cry from Miami.

The worst was when her parents' antique four-poster bed had been broken by an enthusiastic couple. It hadn't mattered that they paid for the damages, as well as a hefty penalty fee. It hadn't mattered that Kirk allowed her to ban them from ever renting the house again. Mikelina had to tell her mother that her grandparents' bed was kindling.

"I've given Bastien Ainsworth your direct number," Kirk said.

Mikelina hated when he gave clients her cell.

"He'll be calling you shortly. He had a last-minute request, and you weren't answering your email."

"That's because I was at the house." Mikelina tried not to sound defensive. Bastien had been emailing daily her for the past six weeks. He wanted everything to be perfect for the bachelor party and was determined to micromanage every second. He didn't even have the decency to foist the responsibility off on a secretary. No, he had to handle this personally.

Mikelina had become accustomed to his 10:00 a.m. emails and even though he was anal-retentive about his schedule, they sometimes shared a joke or some meme. She supposed it was sweet that he wanted everything to be perfect for his brother-in-law, but she had a feeling that some of the activities wouldn't appeal to a younger groom. Of course, Bastien wouldn't take any of her suggestions, so what did she know? This was just her job.

"Whatever he wants, get it for him," Kirk said. "Money is no object. His credit is good."

Must be nice.

"They're spending a fortune with us for this wedding, so everything has to be perfect. I'm only stressing this because I need you to be available 24/7 for this party. No matter how outrageous, make it happen. Give them anything they ask for."

"I'm not providing them hookers or blow," she joked. Bastien hadn't even hinted at anything remotely wild. They were going to do day trips and hang out by the pool. And while that sounded great for a group of older businessmen, it wasn't what made Miami bachelor parties famous.

Although, she would kill to have Bastien's planned vacation. Mikelina missed lying out in a lounge chair with a good book. She missed this house. Patting the door affectionately, she turned to get into her car. She had been working killer hours this past year. She was determined that Kirk would never regret hiring her. She wanted to make sure no one thought she was a cheat and a con artist like her father was. It was exhausting, though.

Kirk snorted. "Trust me, these guys don't have to pay for it. And for the most part, they're gentlemen, so you don't have to worry about them getting handsy."

That was something. Although Mikelina had become rather adept at the step-and-avoid technique. "You've got nothing to worry about. I'll keep my phone on."

"I'm a little nervous. Rumor has it, the groom is getting cold feet. His name is Jace Benjamin, from the Reigning Benjamins clothing line. It's a good marriage between the two families. But from what I hear, he's still looking to sow some wild oats and his future bride, Kitty Ainsworth, has been keeping him on a short leash."

Mikelina couldn't care less. She had enough drama in her life. She didn't need any more. "I'm not sure what I can do about that."

"Just keep an eye on him. No groom, no wedding. And while Five Diamond would still get to keep the fat deposit, I'd rather have the wedding and the honeymoon at our properties."

"I think that's more his future brother-in-law's job." And Bastien Ainsworth was welcome to it.

"You know the area. Steer him away from trouble when you can."

Great. Now, she was a glorified babysitter to

spoiled rich boys. While she was trying not to sputter into the phone, Kirk hung up.

Her phone rang almost immediately afterward.

It was the client, and she answered it on the first ring. "Yes, Mr. Ainsworth?"

"Bastien," he corrected smoothly.

There was a smokiness to his voice that made Mikelina's toes curl. He didn't sound how she had expected him to. His emails sometimes had been curt and borderline rude. She couldn't wait to see what he really looked like when she met him to give him the tour of the house.

Over the past several weeks, she'd gone back and forth picturing him as a trust fund, Ivy League slacker with nothing better to do than make her job difficult, or as the son of a rock star with too much money and not enough people telling him no. She hadn't so much as found a picture of him on social media or gotten an idea on what he was really like, but she knew his type. She had gone to high school and college with men like him.

"I have a few more requests," he went on.

"Of course," she said brightly, even though her fingers tightened on her purse strap. He was arriving tomorrow morning and she could only hope he didn't ask for something ridiculous like a bowl full of M&M's—but only the green ones.

"I'd like to have enough beach towels to last us the week."

"You'll have two per person and the maids will launder them daily." *And if you had read the paper-*

work you were sent a month ago, you'd already know that. "Is that sufficient?"

"Make it three per person. What about bathing suits?" he barked.

"What about them?" she snapped, before she could stop herself. Mikelina recovered quickly, though. "Do you need me to have an assortment available?" She looked at her watch. She could just get to her friend Abbie's surf shop before it closed. It would be a good score for her. Five Diamond Resorts would buy them and add the cost to Bastien Ainsworth's bill—with a significant markup, of course.

"Yes. Ten male board shorts, size large."

"Not a problem. I'll have a selection put in each bedroom as well as the extra towels. Any female sizes?" Abbie had gorgeous hand-painted batik bikinis.

"No," he said curtly.

Right. Bachelor party. Who needed bikinis?

"Very well," Mikelina said smoothly. "Was there anything else?"

"Not at the moment."

Oh goody.

"Please don't hesitate to call me if something comes up," she added. "Otherwise, I'll meet you at the property tomorrow around eleven."

"Make it ten."

She rolled her eyes. The contract specified eleven. But whatever. "I'll see you then." After hanging up with him, she tossed her phone into her gigantic shoulder bag and headed over to South Beach Surf.

It was a quick walk down the quiet, residential area streets.

Mikelina kept her head up high as people looked the other way or glared at her as she passed. She had nothing to do with her father's schemes. She had been in New York, but Tanner Presley had hurt a lot of people in this neighborhood. Of course, he had hurt his family most of all.

Her phone rang again. Now what?

"Yes, Mr. Ainsworth?" She forced sweetness and light into her tone.

"I would like to review the schedule for the next two weeks with you."

"Of course," she said through her teeth. She had it memorized. "I have double-checked all your reservations and I emailed you the confirmation numbers yesterday. You're all set."

"Have lunch prepared for us on Friday."

Thanks for the short notice.

"What would you like?"

"Something light and healthy. We're going to want something substantial, but nothing heavy."

That was clear as mud. But she knew they were going parasailing in the late afternoon, so she'd probably have the catering company Selena recommended make them an assortment of deli salads. The shrimp and quinoa one was divine. Mikelina's stomach growled just thinking about it.

"I'll take care of it," she said.

"I was also considering changing Sunday's plans.

Can we switch the Segway tour to Monday? I think Sunday we should just hang around the house."

"That's a good idea." He had really overscheduled the bachelor party.

"I appreciate all your help. I couldn't have set this up by myself. You have made this very easy and I'll make sure Kirk knows how much you've put into this."

Mikelina blinked at the warmth in his voice. "I'm delighted to help." That was a stretch, but it was nice of him to acknowledge that she was on top of things. Maybe he wouldn't be such an entitled snot in person.

"And two of the groomsmen are lactose intolerant, so if you could replace half of the ice cream with nondairy, that should be sufficient."

And then he had to go and ruin it. She suppressed a sigh. "I'll make sure it's done." Of course, there had been a section in the paperwork on dietary restrictions and that hadn't been marked off. But at least he was telling her now. She didn't want anyone sick on her watch.

"See you tomorrow, Mikelina."

She got a shiver up her spine at the way he said her name. It tickled at her ear and she shook her head to get rid of the feeling. He had a sexy voice. Too bad he was a pain-in-the-ass perfectionist.

CHAPTER TWO

BASTIEN HUNG UP the phone and tried to work on his spreadsheets, but he couldn't concentrate. He wished the bachelor party was over and done with instead of just beginning. It brought back too many memories of his own wedding and what an idiot he had been.

Clicking over to his external drive, Bastien accessed Jace Benjamin's folder. Bastien checked the information that he had the private investigator gather for him. Jace was financially solvent. He was not marrying Kitty for her money. But Bastien strongly suspected Jace's father would reward him somehow for marrying into the Ainsworth family.

Unfortunately, Bastien didn't know how to prove that without breaking his sister's heart in the process.

"Knock knock."

Speak of the devil.

Kitty had short brown hair and green eyes. She looked like their mother's side of the family and had inherited the nose. Unlike her mother and her mother before her, Kitty refused to get plastic surgery to make it more "photogenic," as their mother put it.

Bastien thought Kitty was beautiful just the way she was. He only hoped Jace felt the same way.

"I was just thinking about you," he said.

"Is that why you were scowling at the computer?" Kitty flopped into the chair across from his desk. "I didn't do it. I swear it wasn't me. I wasn't even in the factory when it happened."

Bastien opened his mouth to ask, and then shook his head. "I don't want to know."

Kitty was a buyer for the company and had an eye for textiles and design. Their mother wanted her to be a model, but…the nose.

"I was hoping we could go out to lunch," she said.

Bastien checked his watch. It was barely 11:30 a.m., but he wasn't doing anything productive anyway. "I suppose I'm buying?"

"How kind of you to offer." She smirked.

They walked in companionable silence until they got to the elevator. "So, what's wrong?" he asked. "Is it Jace?"

"What? No." She shook her head. "I just wanted to spend some time with my favorite brother. Is that too much to ask?"

"I'm your only brother. How much?"

"How much time?"

"How much money do you want?"

"Well, if you've got your checkbook open, I wouldn't refuse if you wanted to give me an advance on next month's salary."

"What do you want to buy?"

"I want to elope to Tahiti."

Bastien grunted. "No way. You're not leaving me alone to deal with Mom and Dad getting stood up at the altar."

Crossing her arms over her chest, Kitty said, "I can't take it anymore. They're driving me crazy."

"Stop answering your phone. That's what I do."

"Then they come over unannounced. Last week, they caught me and Jace in the hot tub."

Bastien held up his hand. "I don't want to know what they caught you doing."

"We weren't playing pinochle."

"You've got three weeks and then it'll all be over," he said. "The wedding, not the marriage. I hope. Unless you're trying to beat my record."

"No, thanks," Kitty said as they walked out of the elevator and into the crowded lobby. "I'm all about the domestic bliss."

"And Jace is the one? You're sure, right? It's not too late to call it off."

"Yes, it is too late. Jace proposed. I accepted and I'm not letting him wiggle out of it." She stared lovingly at her diamond ring. It was practically the size of a golf ball.

"Is he trying to wiggle out of it?" Bastien growled, scaring the valet into dropping his keys.

"No. Of course not. Although, he doesn't answer his phone when he's avoiding conflict either. You two are so much alike in that area." She tugged on a knit hat and gloves that were in her coat pocket. At least it had stopped snowing. New York was getting snow early this year, and he wasn't a fan.

"Well, I guess that's something." The valet brought Bastien's car around and he and Kitty got inside. "Where do you want to go to lunch?"

"How about the Imperial Palace?" she asked.

Chinese sounded good. As they drove through the city, Bastien wanted to call Mikelina again. There was something about her that drew him in. He liked their email chats. She was bright and sexy, like he imagined South Beach would be.

"Reach into the glove compartment. I printed out the itinerary for the bachelor party."

"Who writes up a schedule for fun? Oh wait, you." Kitty unfolded the paper and read it. "You forgot to mark down the designated bathroom times. But I did see that you've allotted for eight hours of sleep each night." She rolled her eyes at him.

"I had some help with the schedule. The vacation resort assigns a concierge. Mikelina and I have been putting this together for almost two months."

"Mikelina, huh? Is she ready to throw you in the ocean?"

"No. She's very professional. I'm looking forward to meeting her."

"Is she pretty?"

"How would I know?"

"You've been chatting her up for two months and you haven't seen her Facebook profile?"

"I don't even know her last name," he said.

"I worry about you sometimes." Kitty shook her head. "Promise me that if you like this girl, you'll ask her out."

"She's my employee."

"No, she's not. She's an employee of the company who is renting you the house, and who you pretty much at least owe dinner to for putting up with this monster schedule. I hope you're not going to be too disappointed if you don't get to everything."

"We'll get to everything," he said. "Why? Do you see something on there that Jace wouldn't like?"

"No, it's perfect. I wish I was going instead of being stuck here," she grumbled.

"You're going skiing next week," he reminded her.

"I'm sick of winter. I want to lie on a beach, not toast marshmallows in front of a fire while I thaw out." Flipping down the sun visor, Kitty glared at her reflection.

Bastien didn't know why she was scowling. She looked the same to him, a pretty girl with wide green eyes who was too innocent for her own good.

"Do you want me to talk to your bridesmaids? Tell them to nix Vail and go for Tahiti instead?"

"If I go to Tahiti, I'm not coming back," she muttered.

He gripped the steering wheel hard. "It's not too late to change your mind."

"I wish I had your eyelashes. It's not fair that you have those thick and long lashes and I have to use half a bottle of mascara."

"You didn't answer the question," he said, giving a quick glance in the rearview mirror. Eyelashes? He blinked but didn't see anything out of the ordinary.

"Everything's booked."

"Not what I meant."

Kitty sighed. "What do you have against Jace?"

"He's not good enough for you," Bastien said.

"I get to decide that." She punched him in the arm. "Not you."

"I hope you hurt your hand."

Kitty stopped mid-shaking her hand out. "It was like hitting Jell-O."

Bastien didn't work out two hours a day for arms of Jell-O. He sniffed. "I don't trust him."

"You don't trust anyone since Gina."

That was true.

Kitty blew on her hands to keep them warm. Bastien put the heater on High.

"He's not like her," she said. "Sure, he can be a little immature and he avoids confrontation, but he loves me."

"Are you sure?"

She nodded. "I am. I wouldn't be putting myself through the wedding of the century planning if I didn't want to marry him. It would mean the world to me if you two could get along."

"I know. I'm trying. I organized the bachelor party, didn't I?"

"Yeah, you did good," she said. "You and Mikelina." Kitty singsonged her name. "I want you to send me a picture of her."

"Why?" Bastien said.

"I want to see if she's as pretty as her name."

"I'm not sure why that matters."

"It matters because this is the first time you've

shown an interest in someone since Gina, Queen of the Casinos."

Bastien sighed. "I'm not looking for romance. I'm looking to show your fiancé a good time in South Beach. You don't have to worry, though. I'll keep an eye on him. You saw the schedule. No strip clubs. No nonsense."

"Careful, it's not no fun." Kitty laughed. "Go easy on the rules. I'm going to have a stripper at my party."

"I do not need to know that." Bastien shook his head to clear that image away about his baby sister.

"Do you know the difference between male and female strippers?"

"I am aware of the differences, yes. I did pass biology in high school."

"That's not what I meant. Guys aren't allowed to touch the dancers, right?"

"So I've been told."

"Uh-huh, well, it's expected and encouraged for the women to fondle the dancers."

He was going to need brain bleach. "And Jace is all right with the fondling?"

"We didn't discuss it. But what happens in Vail is going to stay off of social media, that's for damned sure."

"If you want to touch other guys, why are you getting married to Jace?" This wasn't how the conversation to talk her out of getting married was supposed to go, but in for a penny…

"Bastien, it's not like I'm going to blow the stripper."

"Oh God." Bastien closed his eyes and then opened them quickly before he cracked up the car. He parked a few blocks from the restaurant. He'd trudge through the snowbanks and slush to get out of this conversation.

Kitty had to hurry to keep up with him.

"I think you and Jace got off on the wrong foot," she said. "It was wrong of me to come crying to you last year when he was being an asshole."

"No, I'm your brother. If some dude is being a dick to you, I want to know about it."

"He was a dick. And we broke up. But then we got back together, and he's no longer being a dick."

"Once an asshole, always an asshole," Bastien said darkly.

"He's not Gina," she said, exasperated.

Bastien stopped short and Kitty almost plowed into him. "I know he's not Gina. If he was like her, the wedding plans would have never gotten this far."

"People can change. Just because Gina couldn't—"

"She didn't want to," he corrected.

"But Jace did. We worked out our problems and our relationship is stronger than ever. Do I think that could have worked with you and Gina? No. But it worked for us."

Bastien took in a deep breath.

"I need you to be happy for us," she begged.

It was hard to look her in the eye. "I'm scared for you, Kit-Kat," he said, using the nickname he gave her when she was born.

"I'm not a little girl anymore. I know what I want

and I can take care of myself." She crossed her arms in front of her chest.

"I don't want you to be hurt."

"You can't stop that from happening, if it even does." She reached down and held his hand. "But you can be there for me. I'm always going to need my big brother." She stood on tiptoes and kissed his cheek. "I just know once you get to know Jace better, you'll be all right with everything."

That was the plan. Bastien couldn't shake the feeling of doom that was hanging over his head, though.

They sat down in their usual booth and ordered without looking at the menu.

"You had the right idea going somewhere warm," Kitty said. "I don't know what the hell I was thinking. If I wanted to ski so bad, I could have gone water-skiing. I see that's on the schedule. So, tell me more about this Mikelina. Is she smart, funny? Inquiring minds want to know."

"Yeah, I guess. She's easy to talk to. I liked her ideas."

"But you didn't get her last name?"

"I didn't ask. Why would I?"

"She just signs her emails off with Mikelina? Who is she? Madonna? Cher? Beyoncé?"

"Maybe it's a South Beach thing."

"Is she married?"

"I didn't ask," he said again.

"Well, why not?"

"It wasn't relevant."

"What do you know about her?"

"She likes science fiction and fantasy movies. We were talking about the new superhero movie. She's got a crush on Thor."

"Well, who doesn't really?"

Bastien shrugged. "He doesn't do anything for me."

"You're just jealous."

"Insanely," he deadpanned.

"You know who Jace reminds me of?"

"Please don't tell me."

"Bucky."

Bastien took a sip of her iced tea.

"Hey, get your own."

"I was just wondering if they spiked this because you're delusional."

"You know which superhero you remind me of?"

"Buzz Lightyear?"

"More like Buzzkill. No, you remind me of Iron Man."

"I'm not sure if I should be insulted or not."

"Play it up."

Bastien wished someone had spiked his drink. "Play what up?"

"If she likes superheroes, pretend that you're a billionaire playboy. You'll get laid in no time."

"I can't even believe we're having this conversation. Kitty, I'm not going to the bachelor party to get laid. No one is going to get laid at this bachelor party."

"It's a good thing you ordered a lot of booze, then."

"I need a drink right now." Bastien shook his head.

"Have one for me, too, because Mom just walked in."

Bastien craned his neck and sure enough his mother was heading right toward them. "Do you think it's too late to leave out the back door?"

"Welcome to my life ever since I announced my engagement."

"There you are! The office said you were out to lunch and I figured I'd find you here. Shove over, Bastien." His mother hip checked him against the side of the booth. She thunked a large binder on the table. "I need you to make a decision on the napkin design."

Kitty mouthed, "Kill me."

CHAPTER THREE

WHEN THE SIDEWALK ended at the beach, Mikelina kicked off her shoes and tucked them into her purse. As soon as her toes hit the warm sand, she felt the tension leave her body. She missed this. The sun and the salty ocean air. She couldn't remember the last time she sat her ass in the sand and watched the waves. There hadn't been a lot of time for that this year.

She was tense and tired and wished she was kicking up her heels at a decadent party for the next two weeks. Bastien's schedule was meticulous and planned down to the last minute, but it was going to be a fun vacation for the men—as long as they weren't expecting a wild time.

Maybe she'd ask Kirk for a few days off after the bachelor party left. She could sleep in her own bedroom again and pretend that her world hadn't fallen apart slowly after her father reported to prison last year.

The air perked her up some, taking her out of the funk that closed in every time she thought about her father. He still claimed to be innocent, even with the overwhelming proof against him. Breathing in deep, she centered herself. One day, she would enjoy all this from their wraparound porch. One day, they'd be a family again.

Her phone rang again.

"I swear to fucking god," she muttered, digging it out. But it was her mother.

She stared at the phone and for a moment considered letting it go to voice mail. But guilt had her answering at the last minute. "Hi, Mom."

"Hello, sweetheart. Any chance I could stay at the house this weekend?" Tawny Presley still liked to pretend that everything was normal and she could zip on down to the beach house for a quick getaway.

"No, I'm sorry. We're booked up for the next few weeks."

"Your aunt is driving me crazy."

Mikelina sighed. "I'm sorry."

"I want to get a condo or an apartment in South Beach."

Wincing, Mikelina rubbed her head. "It's expensive out here."

"I don't care. I can't take it anymore. All she wants to do is watch Fox News. It's blaring on and on, 24/7. I can't think." Tawny's voice rose up to an almost hysterical pitch.

"Okay, Mom," Mikelina soothed. "Why don't you shop around on Zillow or something and after the bachelor party leaves, we can see what you can afford."

"Bachelor party?" Tawny shrieked.

Mikelina groaned. She had not meant to say that.

"I don't want strippers and drugs in my house."

My house, Mikelina mentally corrected, but knew better than to say that aloud. Her parents had given her the beach house for her twenty-fifth birthday. It had been a tax write-off for them. She had been the owner in name only and had she realized what her father had been up to, she never would have signed the papers. "It's not that type of bachelor party. The best man has arranged for a tasteful getaway." If a little staid and overscheduled, but that was preferable to strippers and drugs.

"I can't do this anymore," Tawny repeated. "Why did your father have to ruin our lives?"

"He ruined more than our lives," Mikelina said sadly. People lost their retirement funds. One person had been dying in the hospital when he found out that Tanner Presley had bankrupted him, leaving his heirs next to nothing. One family had to sell their restaurant when their stocks he bought turned out to be junk.

"Why am I being punished?" Tawny lamented. "I did nothing wrong. I lost my home. My friends. My entire world turned upside down."

Tawny lived for the dramatic and while what she was saying was true, she had also been saying it for the past year. Almost on a daily basis. Mikelina's mother had never held down a job in her life.

Must be nice to live in that world. But back on earth, you had to hustle unless you had a husband or a daughter to hustle for you. Mikelina tried not to feel resentful, but when her mother complained about it, she wanted to scream.

"I'm doing the best that I can."

"I know that, sweetheart. I don't mean to keep bothering you with this, but you're all I have." Tawny sniffed and Mikelina could almost picture her eyes filling with tears. Her mother had been brought up to be a society wife, the perfect hostess. And now that she didn't have a husband or a party to plan, she didn't know what to do with herself.

"You need to get out more. Find new friends," Mikelina said. "You need to keep busy." *Maybe get a job?* But she knew better than to add in that last part. That was guaranteed to bring out the self-pity of how Tawny wasn't as smart as Mikelina. Which was bullshit—Tawny was plenty smart. She could set up a conference without breaking a sweat and handle a fund-raiser like nobody's business. Unfortunately, all the charities she used to work with wouldn't touch her now with a ten-foot pole.

"I'm so unhappy. But you're right. I need to do something about it, not just mope around." Tawny took a shaky breath. "I should let you go. I'm sorry to have bothered you."

"You're not bother—" But Tawny had already hung up. It was more dramatic that way.

"Damn it," Mikelina groaned. She'd pay for not comforting her more later.

The moment of beach zen was gone.

Abbie's South Beach Surf Shop was a cute little

boutique store, right off the beach. She made a mint selling boogie boards, surfboards, Sex Wax, snorkels and masks. And of course, racks and racks of bikinis and bathing suits.

"Hey, girl," Abbie said as Mikelina walked into the shop. The air-conditioning blew over her heated skin like a splash of cold water.

"Abbie, I'm about to make your afternoon. You can close up and go home." Mikelina leaned on the counter and petted the store cat, Jinx. Jinx flicked an ear at her.

"I'm about to close up and go home, anyway."

"I need ten board shorts."

"Ten, huh? Are you having a party without me?"

"I would never have a party without you. No, these are for the bachelor party that's rented my house, or should I say the jewel in the crown of the Five Diamond Resorts' South Beach properties?" Mikelina quoted the marketing literature, tongue in cheek.

Abbie gestured to a rack by the far wall. "Take your pick. Are you paying or is Five Diamond paying?"

Michelina slapped the corporate card on the counter with a grin. "What do you think?"

"I think we both deserve a treat. You're not going to believe this. I've got tickets to Flow."

"What's Flow? Sounds like something that happens once a month," Mikelina said, riffling through the suits, making sure to get an assortment of colors.

"Have you been living under a rock?" Abbie scoffed. "Flow happens to be *the* hottest new night-club in town."

"What happened to the hottest old nightclub in town?" Mikelina double-checked the sizes.

"It's still there, but it's not as exclusive as this place is."

"If it's so exclusive, how are we going to get in?" She grabbed five beach towels to supplement the house's stock.

Abbie flashed two gold tickets. "Because the bartender is trying to get in my pants, so I have these two get-out-of-jail-free passes."

Mikelina brought her purchases to the counter. "I can't go to jail, even if we get out free. I've got to open up the house for the bachelor party tomorrow at eleven." She closed her eyes. "No, wait. At ten because his lordship demands it."

"Who's his lordship?"

"Bastien Ainsworth. He's the best man who's in charge of the bachelor party. He's been on my ass all month asking for things." She sighed. "Actually, he hasn't been that bad. I've had worse. I'm just in a really nasty mood lately. I don't know why." She handed Abbie the suits to ring them up.

"I think it's because you're finally processing that Tanner is in prison and it's just you and your mom now."

"It's been a whole year. I'm over it." Mikelina swiped the corporate card, trying not to wince at the total. It wasn't her money. She loved her friends, but she wouldn't drop almost a grand on bathing suits for them.

"I think you've been in emergency mode for most

of that year and now that things are normalizing, it's your turn to be angry."

"I didn't know we were taking turns."

"That's because you've been Kirk's good little worker bee for the past year. When was the last time you went out on a date?"

"I went out to dinner with an investment banker in Cartagena last month."

"You didn't tell me about this." Abbie leaned her elbows on the counter. "Spill it."

Mikelina rubbed Jinx under the chin as she tried to keep the hurt feelings from entering her voice. "It was very romantic. He took me to this gorgeous seafood restaurant on the water. We had a few bottles of really expensive wine, and then…"

Abbie leaned forward eagerly.

"He put together my last name with my father's and ran out of there so fast, he stuck me with the check."

Wincing, Abbie folded the towels and added them to the large shopping bag with the bathing suits. "I won't even ask you the last time you got laid, then."

"I'll give you a hint. It was in New York."

"Oh, honey." Abbie waved the tickets again. "Let loose and come out for a little PJ Rosé. Find yourself a nice club boy and take him for a ride. Don't tell him your name."

"Those tickets come with champagne bottle service and a VIP booth?" Mikelina wasn't sure she was up for a one-night stand, but maybe it was what she needed. Some anonymity and orgasms. That way she wouldn't have to see the judgment on his face when he found out who her father was.

"At the very least, we can lord over the unwashed masses in our VIP booth and dance until the champagne runs out."

That sounded like a better plan. "All right. You talked me into it."

CHAPTER FOUR

BASTIEN AINSWORTH LOOKED around the bar and was bored. Flow might be the new "it" place, but to him, it was the same old shit. He did have to give the owners props for their idea of having several ice slopes set up as shot stations on tables around the bar. The server stood on a step stool to pour a shot of tequila or whiskey down a solid block of ice shaped like a ski slope and into a kneeling participant's mouth.

Maybe Bastien was just too old for this nonsense or maybe he wasn't drunk enough, but it didn't look appealing. Jace would love it, though. Bastien would ask his concierge to get them a VIP booth for one of the nights.

At least the bar had Wi-Fi, he thought as he thumbed down to his call history.

Mikelina.

Sexy name for such a prim and uptight voice. Bastien imagined she was this perfectly coiffed society princess who didn't care about anything beyond handbags and shoes. Still, she was polite and professional, and he shouldn't hold it against her that she should have been named something less enticing.

Mikelina. He liked the way her name sounded in his mouth.

Unfortunately, he got to say it into her voice mail. "Mikelina, call me."

It occurred to him that it was past midnight and the noise from the bar might have drowned out his voice. He wouldn't hold it against her if she didn't call him back before their meeting tomorrow. Then again, if she did call back right away, he could get her to let him into the house tonight rather than tomorrow morning.

He'd taken an earlier flight because he wanted to get some business done before the craziness of the next two weeks, and after lunch with his mother and sister, going back to the office hadn't appealed. So he dropped them both off at his parents' house and drove immediately back to his place to grab his bags. It threw off his itinerary a bit, but he could adapt.

He hadn't been looking forward to traveling with Jace and his groomsmen anyway. They got on his last nerve under normal situations. He didn't want to compound his aggravation by adding in Homeland Security and airports into the mix. Bastien was hoping that at the end of the two weeks, however, he and Jace would be friends. But he didn't think that was going to happen.

"Why are you marrying this douchebag?" was how he first phrased it to his sister.

"I love him. He's so exciting," Kitty had predictably replied, stars in her eyes.

Their father had looked at Bastien and inclined his head, telling him wordlessly to follow him into his study.

"It's a good match," he said when they were alone. "His father and I have an idea for merging a few of our clothing lines."

Again, Bastien had doubts. Ainsworth was an old and respected clothing brand. They paid fair labor costs and provided quality clothes that would last. All About the Benjamins's clothing line was more profitable and popular with the younger demographics, but rumor had it they cut a lot of corners that weren't socially ethical.

Not that it would matter to his father.

Bastien sighed and stared out around the glowing nightclub. When did all the women in Miami Beach start to look the same? He was about to turn around and leave when he caught sight of a beautiful woman dancing in a VIP booth all alone.

Well, that seemed like a shame.

She had her eyes closed and the neck of a bottle of Perrier-Jouët in her hand. He watched as she ground against an invisible partner, his body reacting as if he was there next to her. One of her hands scrunched a handful of curly black hair away from her face. Her soft pink lips mouthed the words to the song throbbing through the club.

I want you. I need you. Take me all night long.

Bastien's mouth went dry. He was moving toward her without realizing what he was doing.

The gorgeous dancer wore a white cotton halter dress that dipped into a deep V between her breasts. The tight fabric hugged her swaying hips and his fingers itched to touch her. Forcing himself to stop closing the distance, he made his way to the bar. He didn't want to be a drooling creeper staring at her from outside the rope when she opened her eyes.

He'd drool from a distance.

He caught the bartender's attention by holding up his Flow card, a shiny black badge that gave him VIP access and unlimited tab at the bar.

"Yes, sir?"

"Bottle of Perrier-Jouët Rosé," he said, basing his decision on the pink champagne bottle the women was dancing with.

He took the bottle from the bartender just as the song ended and his dancer reluctantly opened her eyes. She tipped the bottle up to her mouth but must have come up dry. She squinted into it, then put it back on the glass table.

When she looked up into the crowd, there was a hint of melancholy in her pale green eyes. Her gaze swept the bar, then stopped at him. She gave him a once-over that revved him up to the next level. He showed her the champagne bottle and raised his eyebrow.

Wriggling her finger for him to approach, she sank down on the couch and crossed her legs. The dress was split up to midthigh and showed off her long, sexy legs.

Bastien wove his way to the section separated by velvet ropes. He showed the Flow card again to a bouncer who scanned it as Bastien climbed the platform to the private VIP booths. Her skin was flushed, as if she was blushing.

"You've got good taste in champagne," she said, her voice breathless and sexy.

"I happened to notice you were dry." Bastien filled her glass. Their fingers brushed and he wanted more than the quick skim of her soft skin.

"Thank you for making me wet again."

The double entendre hit him low in his stomach. He hadn't been going that way with it, but he wasn't going to back away from it either. He caught a glimpse of her tongue as she licked her lips. It was all he could do not to groan aloud. After filling his glass, Bastien nestled the champagne bottle back into the ice. He hated champagne, but he'd choke it down for a chance to talk to her.

"Have a seat," she said, motioning next to her.

"I saw you dancing. Are you an actress?" He joined her on the couch.

She flashed him a smile. "We're all actors, aren't we?"

"Mysterious." Bastien clinked glasses with her. "All right, well, if you're not going to tell me, I'm going to have to guess. I think you're a choreographer for a local show."

"It's frightening how close you are to the truth. What do you do for a living?"

"As little as possible." He took a sip. It was god-awful. He forced himself not to grimace.

"I know a lot of guys like that." She rolled her eyes and slightly shifted away from him.

"Do I look like those guys?" he asked, leaning back.

"You don't." She appraised him again and the slight hungry look in her eyes made him forget the sickly taste of sweet champagne in his mouth. "You look like an MMA announcer."

"Announcer?"

Reaching out, she grabbed his hand and rubbed her thumb over his knuckles. "No calluses. So you must be a retired fighter."

"Retired? As in old?" He smirked.

"Seasoned, like a good steak."

"I'm salty all right."

"A good steak isn't salty." She looked down her cute nose at him.

"My apologies," he said with an incline of his head.

"Anyway, I'm guessing you're more like a lover than a fighter." She kept a hold of his hand, her thumb still gliding over it.

"It's astonishing how you were able to read me like that." Her light little touch shouldn't be as erotic as it was. "So what do you do for fun?"

"Truthfully, it's been so long I think I've forgotten how. I've been working nonstop this past year.

This is the first time I've taken the night off in a long time. Pathetic, huh?" She gave him a sad little smile.

"I'm the same way. I was just going to head out when I saw you. This really isn't my scene."

"What about it don't you like?" she asked.

"The music kinda sucks. But I liked your song. I'd probably like it better if I was dancing with someone. Do you want to try?"

"Yes, but first, a toast." She poured them both a glass of that nasty sickly sweet champagne.

"Okay." Bastien wondered if there was a potted plant he could dash the contents into without her noticing it.

"To Flow."

"Really? We're drinking to Flow?"

"Work with me," she said.

He clinked glasses and tried to swallow a mouthful without tasting it. He just barely resisted a shudder. "Now, we dance."

She led him out into the throng of people on the dance floor. The music was loud, but the song was familiar. He hoped he didn't look like someone was electrocuting him as he jumped and danced with her. She kept bouncing into him and that was all good. A slower song with a grinding beat came on and he got to hold her against him. That was even better.

"I need more champagne," she said after the song. Her face was flushed, and her nipples were clearly outlined against her dress.

If he stayed out here any longer, he'd have to dump the ice bucket down his pants. So he followed her back up to the table. She sat down in a graceful heap, while he grabbed a water from the fridge next to the booth.

"Where did that come from?" She craned her neck to see where he pulled it out of.

Bastien handed it to her and got another. "Perks of being a VIP."

"It's my first time," she admitted, tanking half the water bottle.

"A virgin, huh?"

"Touched for the very first time…today."

They finished their waters, but he didn't want to go back on the dance floor. He wanted to spend the rest of the night talking with her.

She gathered her thick hair up into a ponytail and twisted it up to the top of her head. Fanning her neck, she said, "I wish I was a delicate little flower that glistened when she perspired. Instead, I sweat like a warthog."

His bark of laughter surprised even him. When was the last time he'd laughed aloud? This was a great beginning to his first vacation in over two years. It was almost worth having Jace marry his little sister.

"I think you sweat divinely," he said.

"Very gallant of you to say so." She helped herself to more champagne and offered him a glass.

"I should stick with water for the time being."

"Are you the designated driver?"

"No, I'm here alone."

"What a shame. Me, too. I mean, I had my friend

here, but she ditched me to get laid. I can't really blame her."

"I blame her. It's bros before hoes. Or in your case, I guess it would be sisters before misters?"

"Chicks before dicks."

"Yeah, she shouldn't have left you all alone ripe for the picking of any urban predator."

"You make me sound like a gazelle. I thought I told you I was a warthog."

"A divine warthog."

"Exactly. Well, luckily I have a knight in shining armor to protect me from the club lions or club tigers."

"Or club bears," he said.

"Oh my," they said together.

"It's a little scary that we're right on the same page," he said.

She nodded. "You're weird, but you're my kind of weird." She took his hand and kissed the back of it.

"I think that's the nicest thing anyone has said to me in a long time. Do you want to get out of here?" he asked. "I'd love to take you somewhere a little more private."

She took a deep breath and he could see the indecision warring on her face.

"You don't have to answer right away. I just thought…"

She dropped his hand. "I guess I did just come on like a freight train. I'm not so good at this."

"I think you're doing great." Bastien wanted to ease the awkward moment. "I jumped the gun. I'm usually a little more slick than this. You're just so damned sexy, I lost my mind a little."

She gave him a shy smile. "You're kind. I like that about you."

"I don't think anyone has ever called me that. My sister thinks I'm a prick."

"Why? What did you do to her?"

"She has a hard time letting go of something we refer to as the Barbie-in-the-barbecue incident."

"You cooked her dolly?" She crossed her arms over her chest and glared at him.

Bastien held up his hands in surrender. "Okay, I was ten and she was annoying."

"Barbie or your sister?"

"Both, actually. But I saved her before she melted. Her hair never recovered, though. She was punk Barbie from then on. She rocked a Mohawk like nobody's business."

"You're funny." She smiled at him and he realized he liked being in this club next to this sexy woman instead of being bored and looking for an excuse to leave. "You've got expressive eyes, too. Maybe you're the actor?"

Bastien smirked. "No, I'm not all that exciting. I work in an office."

"Are you from around here?" she asked, taking a deep sip of her champagne and sighing contentedly.

How can she drink that stuff? "No. I'm only in town for the next two weeks."

Pushing her hair off her face, she said, "I'm not going to go home with you tonight."

Disappointment flickered through him, but she didn't seem to be rejecting him.

"I'm not that brave." She took his hand again. "But that doesn't mean we can't enjoy each other's company for a while. I want to kick up my heels and have some fun. But I don't want you to think I'm a tease. Can you handle a little flirting and a little kissing without it going any further?"

"I can do that." If he couldn't have her in his bed, having her in his arms was the next best thing. "Do you want to dance again? Although I have to admit, I could watch you dancing all night."

She blushed again. "You saw that, huh?"

"It's what made me come over here. Are you a local girl?"

"My job takes me all over. But I did get a tour of the VIP area before and this part is just the tip of the iceberg. I want to show you something." Standing up, she finished her champagne in one long swallow. "Come with me." She tugged his hand.

"I'll come after you," he said. Rising to his feet, he stepped in closer to her so their bodies brushed.

"I was hoping you'd say that," she said.

CHAPTER FIVE

MIKELINA'S HEART WAS thundering in her chest. She couldn't believe she was doing this. After Abbie had given her the tour of the VIP rooms, she and Cody the bartender took off never to be seen again.

It had been beyond awkward to sit on that cushy couch and drink expensive champagne all by herself. Like she had won the loser lottery or something. Everyone out there was dancing and having a good time. And she was all alone, the way she had been all year. It wasn't fair. So when her jam came on, she'd finished her champagne, closed her eyes and pretended she had Mr. Right in front of her.

And then after the song was over, it was like she had summoned him. He resembled Luke Macfarlane—the *Killjoys* version, not the Hallmark Christmas special one. Five o'clock shadow, dark hair and sexy eyes. She wasn't about to let this opportunity slide by.

So maybe she was a little bit forward. And maybe she was jumping into things without thinking it through. But it wasn't as if she was going home with a man whose name she didn't even know. There were places in the club where they could play around in relative privacy and safety.

Mikelina had the Flow card she had been given in her purse, if he turned out to be a creep. All the VIP cards had a plastic slide on the back. In an emergency, if she pushed the slide, security would come to her rescue. They could track her anywhere in the club. It made her a little more confident to push the envelope with her mystery man.

"Have you been here before?" she asked, pushing aside the velvet curtain.

"No, this is my first time."

Mikelina took his hand. "A virgin?"

He snorted. "Touched for the very first time... today." She liked that he repeated what she'd said to him earlier. She liked his voice and the easy way about him.

"What's your name?" he asked.

"Are names necessary?" she asked.

"That's usually how two people get to know each other."

"I think we know all we need to know about each other." The last thing she wanted was for him to recognize her last name. She didn't want to talk about Tanner Presley. She didn't even want to think about him and she was sick of being treated like a pariah because of his crimes. Swallowing her trepidation, she touched her handsome MMA announcer on the arm. He had nice biceps and she squeezed one as she rose up on her tiptoes. Brushing a kiss across his surprised lips, she put her hand on his shoulder. "Unless I'm reading this wrong."

"No, we're good." His arm snaked around her and held her tight. He returned her kiss with one that Mikelina felt straight to her toes. She wasn't going to go home with him, but fooling around seemed like a good idea.

His mouth was warm and enticing. She bit back a moan, leaned into his hard body. It felt good to be naughty. But if she didn't stop him now, they would be making out in the middle of the hallway.

Breaking away, she was breathless and giddy. She led him down the corridor to the first set of doors that Cody had shown her. "Do you want to go for a swim?"

"I didn't bring a suit. And if I'm going to skinny-dip, I'd prefer not to have an audience." His voice was gruff and sent shivers up her spine. She wanted to hear it in her ear as they danced.

"You've got to see the pool area, though. I'd be a bad tour host if I let you go back home without seeing this."

The pool room was set up to mimic the beach. And if Mikelina hadn't known this place used to be a warehouse club a few months ago, she could easily be convinced that they were outside. The lighting was brilliant and there was even a cool ocean breeze blowing through the space. They had to be piping it in from the air-conditioning because outside was muggy as hell.

The house DJ was playing Jimmy Buffett and

it was a more chill atmosphere than the part of the club they just left. Sturdy paper lanterns floated in the enormous pool along with about one hundred people in the water.

"Why don't they just go outside?" he asked.

"Because it's dark out. It's never-ending sunshine here."

Squinting up at the ceiling. "Heat lamps."

"You're such a spoil sport," she teased. "Enjoy the fantasy."

"Let's go back to the main area and dance."

"I've got something better in mind." She took him through another set of doors and the crisp air conditioner kicked on as they stepped into a 1920s-style speakeasy.

"It's like the Tardis in here," he said. "Bigger on the inside and lost in time."

"You're a Doctor Who fan?" Mikelina was thrilled to find a fellow nerd. As they walked past the jazz band to the bar hand in hand, they talked about the science fiction series.

"It's nice to have a conversation with someone in a bar that doesn't result in screaming over and over into their ear because the music is so loud," she said, handing him a gin rickey from the sampler of drinks.

Mikelina chose a sidecar and they clinked glasses.

"Oh man," she said, gasping after a sip. "That's strong."

"Let me taste," he said. But instead of trying her drink, he ducked his head and kissed her again. The hot sweep of his tongue on hers made her forget about the orange-flavored burn.

"Cognac," he said in satisfaction.

"Did you like it?"

"Oh yes." He took the drink from her nerveless fingers and pulled her onto the dance floor.

There were several couples slow dancing, but the world narrowed down to just the two of them. Held tight in his arms, Mikelina swayed to the sultry saxophone. Laying her cheek against the soft cotton of his shirt, her eyes drifted shut and the stress of the past year unlocked inside her.

She ran her hands over the hard muscles of his back and enjoyed his chest pressed against her breasts. She hoped this song would never end, just the two of them rubbing against each other in sweet friction. They swayed to the music. She could almost picture that they were back in time, during Prohibition, drinking illegal alcohol and sharing stolen, forbidden moments.

He kissed her again and she gave into it wholeheartedly. His mouth was sultry and the deep kiss left her trembling and wanting more. Maybe she would go home with him, after all. She didn't have to tell him her last name.

He stroked her hair back from her face. "What's a pretty girl like you doing all alone?"

"I'm not alone. I'm with you."

He pulled her in closer and his hardness pressed into her. She wanted to rub herself all over it, but even though she was feeling wanton, she was aware that they were attracting attention. She didn't want to put on a show. She wished there was a safe, private place they could explore their attraction in this part of the bar.

When the band picked up a livelier tune, the dance floor became more crowded as a crush of people pressed in.

Mikelina blinked up at him, still lost in the hazy desire that filled her with a sensual lethargy. Trailing his hand down to cup her ass, he danced her over to a smoky corner. Rubbing his thumb over her lower lip, he said, "Tell me your name."

She'd pretty much do whatever he wanted at this point, but he asked the one thing she didn't want to risk. She wanted more dances and sultry kisses. If she told him her name, the evening was over and Mikelina wasn't ready for that.

"It's our fantasy," she said. "Call me whatever you want."

He pressed his forehead against hers. "Tell me your name."

"Name me, and I'm yours," she purred, tugging his T-shirt out of his pants. She slid her hands up his stomach and his eyes closed in pleasure. "Say my name and kiss me."

"Mikelina," he groaned and caught her mouth in another deep kiss that had her clutching his shoulders to keep her knees from wobbling.

Unfortunately, her eyes flew wide open. Mikelina wasn't a common name. There was no way he could have pulled that out of his hat. He knew her. But how?

Was he one of her father's creditors? Or worse, one of his victims?

She pushed him at arm's length. "Who are you?"

"I thought you said no names?" He was breathing deeper and his hands were hot through the thin cotton of her dress.

Resisting the urge to rub against him some more, she tried to focus. "Tell me your name."

"Name me." He kissed her again and she enjoyed it so much, she dragged her nails lightly over his back. It was hard to think clearly when his tongue and mouth were making her not care that he could be an enemy. The Flow card was still in her purse, but she didn't want to call Security. She didn't get a danger vibe. In fact, when he kissed down her cheek to her neck, the only vibe she was getting was the pulsing one between her legs.

She'd never seen his face before. She'd have remembered. "Say something," she whispered.

"What do you want me to say? I'd kiss you all night if you let me. Let me take you back to my hotel."

There. If he was staying at a local hotel, maybe she could find out his name from one of her contacts. She'd have to excuse herself and go to the bathroom and make a few calls. Call in a couple of favors, but it would be worth it to see what this guy's deal was.

"Where are you staying?"

"Hilton," he said against her neck. "But just for tonight."

"You said you were staying two weeks."

His thumb skimmed over her nipple and she bit her lip to keep from moaning.

"Yeah, we've rented a house for a bachelor party."

Shock had her flinching out of his arms. Oh no, this was too coincidental. She hoped like hell this wasn't the groom. Did the groom even know her name? As far as she knew, the only one who knew her name was...

"What's the matter?" he asked, concern etched on his brow.

"Bastien?"

The sexy confusion on his handsome face narrowed into a sharper look. "What did you call me?"

She fumbled in her purse, ignoring the Flow card. Pulling out her phone, she saw she missed a call. From him. She pressed Call Back.

Bastien frowned when his phone vibrated and he pulled it out.

He brought it up to his ear. "Hello?"

"You called?" she said, slumping against the wall.

CHAPTER SIX

"AND THIS IS the security code. You and I are the only ones that have it, so if you leave while the maids are still working, please let them know to contact me and I can lock the doors remotely."

It was close to 3:00 a.m. and Mikelina was holding on to her dignity by a thread. She couldn't wait to finish up the orientation so she could go home and throw herself off the balcony. Only the cheap hotel room where she stayed when the beach house was booked was on the second floor and over a bunch of bushes, so she'd probably survive the jump. She wasn't sure she wanted to survive this night.

"Are we not going to talk about what happened in the bar?" Bastien asked.

It was very uncomfortable to have him seated at her family's dining room table while she nattered on about using the seven-thousand-dollar coffee machine.

"Can we forget all about it?" she asked weakly. "I need to be professional."

After the big reveal, she had to endure the painful ride back to the house with him because she had come with Abbie and didn't have her car. He had left a message on her phone that he had gotten in early and would rather check in tonight. However, she hadn't gotten it until after they met in the bar. Mikelina could have put her foot down and made him stay the night in a hotel, but they were both awake now and maybe by letting him check in early, he would forget that they were groping each other on the dance floor when he talked to her boss.

"Okay, let me know when you're finished being professional so we can talk about this. I'd rather do it tonight." Bastien looked at his watch and grimaced. "Or this morning. Before the groomsmen get here."

Mikelina sighed. "You're right. I don't want to be weird around them. I'm supposed to be working with you all closely to make the bachelor party go off seamlessly. I can't do that if I can't even look at you." She slumped into the chair next to him and held out her hand. "Hi, I'm Mikelina. I'll be your concierge for the next two weeks."

"Bastien Ainsworth. Do you want to dance?"

She gaped at him as he turned the sound system on the way she'd just walked him through it a few minutes ago. He put on a slow jazz number and took her outstretched hand and tugged her up and into his arms again.

This changed things.

He was no longer a stranger.

She was in her own home.

It was just the two of them.

The air seemed to leave her lungs when he kissed her slowly as they danced around her living room.

It was beyond unprofessional to sleep with the client. Kirk would fire her if he knew she was doing this. And yet... Bastien was still the sexy man from the bar that she had wanted to go much further with. They had the rest of the night, what was left of it.

It would cost a fortune to get an Uber at this hour. And she didn't want to go back to her crappy hotel room and face the stark white walls all alone.

What was done was done.

If she'd known who he was, she wouldn't have flirted with him in the bar. But she couldn't take it back now, so she might as well enjoy it.

The tension completely left her body and she kicked off her shoes. He groaned when she undid the tie on her halter dress and it pooled at her feet. Still dancing, she pulled his T-shirt over his head and kissed the curve of his abs and chest.

"Why did you call me Mikelina in the bar? Did you recognize me?"

"Mikelina," he sighed out, unhooking her strapless bra and tossing that to the ground as well. "I love your name. It's so sexy. You're so sexy. You told me to think of a name. You were on my mind."

She danced with him in her panties, grinding against his thick hardness. The tips of her nipples brushed over his chest hair and all thoughts about her boss and the bachelor party fled. They had tonight and Mikelina deserved to be cherished like this for at least one night. Fumbling with his belt, she drew it slowly through the loops.

"You are so beautiful," Bastien said, cupping her jaw.

"So are you," she whispered, unbuttoning his pants. Reaching in, she pulled out his cock and wrapped her fingers around it. As she stroked it slow, she stared into his eyes that were dark with heady desire and need.

"That feels good," he said, his head back as he enjoyed her caress.

His pants slid down his narrow hips and he kicked off his shoes and then stepped back. Mikelina swallowed hard, seeing his naked body in her living room. Bastien picked her up and seemed ready to carry her upstairs to the master bedroom.

"No," she said, pointing to the large bedroom off the kitchen. "That one." If she was going to have sex, it wouldn't be in her parents' bedroom. She was going to make love to her handsome stranger in her own bed.

Carrying her into the room, he laid her on the duvet and looked at her. "We're going to need to take these off," he said and peeled her panties down her legs.

Joining her on the bed, Bastien pulled her back into his arms. Mikelina entwined her legs with his and arched against his small thrusts. His kisses tasted like cognac without the burn. The burn was inside her, though, and she whimpered when Bastien began to kiss down her body.

He licked lazy circles around her nipples, sucking on them until her legs parted. Stroking his fingers through the wet folds between her legs, Bastien made her whimper in pleasure. Cupping his head to her breasts, Mikelina sighed. Warm waves of pleasure drifted over her and it felt like she was floating in the ocean. Turning her head, she looked out her window and watched the moonlight play over the pool.

She would have liked to spend the two weeks with him here. They could have drinks in the hot tub. He could grill up some steaks on the outdoor grill and then they could go for long romantic strolls on the beach before ending back here to make love again.

"Oh," she cried out, clamping her legs together, trapping his talented fingers.

Bastien chuckled low in his throat as she came against his fingers. "I told you that you'd come first." He brought his fingers up to his mouth and sucked on them. "Fuck, you taste good."

And while she was still quivering from her orgasm and his sexy words, his five o'clock shadow rasped on her inner thigh.

"Bastien," she cried.

"I liked that so much, I want to make you come again," he said and then dipped his tongue between her legs.

Fingers clenched in the bedspread, Mikelina's thighs shook against Bastien's face. Licking her fast, he held her hips tight. She ground herself against his mouth, taking in deep gulps of air. She no longer saw the moonlight on the pool or felt the sweet pang of nostalgia. No, she was on a runaway roller coaster and she craved the speed.

"Bastien," she cried out, her body shaking and trembling from the sweet pleasure his tongue was giving her. Incoherent with desire, she whipped her head back and forth. When the second orgasm exploded through her, she nearly blacked out.

"Condom?" he growled.

"Drawer." She pointed weakly to the bedside table.

He opened the drawer, tore open the box and shook a condom off. Mikelina could only watch his fingers shake as he smoothed it over his thick cock. Back on the bed, he grabbed her legs and pulled her toward him. Thrusting inside her, he gripped the pillow on either side of her head.

Arching into the wide heat of his intrusion, she kissed him. He wasn't slow or dreamy, but wild with the rhythmic pounding that she craved. Hooking her ankles together over his back, Mikelina encouraged him to go harder, deeper, more. More. As she held on, she sank back on her pillow and watched the slow turn of the ceiling fan. Everything was perfect and in place. She clenched around him again and again, feeling the deep need of pleasure. He groaned, a rough and guttural sound that sent her flying again.

Mikelina felt boneless, weightless. "Now, Bastien. Now. Let go. Come. Please."

Stiffening, his muscles locked and he threw back his head and shouted. His body twitched as his thrusts grew slower and slower until he stilled, panting above her.

He kissed her then as the fan slowly cooled their bodies. Rolling off her, he went into the bathroom.

It was second nature to climb under the covers and fall asleep in her own bed.

After Bastien had cleaned up, he went back out to offer Mikelina a coffee or something, but she was fast asleep. It was late. The other groomsmen's flight wasn't getting in until nine, but by the time they got their bags ready, it would be closer to eleven. So he and Mikelina had a little more time together. Bastien found he liked the idea of having quick shower sex before the others got here and he had to concentrate on Jace.

Sliding underneath the covers with her, he was surprised when she trustingly rolled over and cuddled into his chest.

Sleep wouldn't come. As much as his body was satiated and his mind sleepy, every time he closed his eyes, he saw the disaster of his own bachelor party and wedding. Mikelina shifted in her sleep and he soothed her by running his fingers through her luxurious hair.

Gina had wanted their bachelor and bachelorette parties and the wedding in Las Vegas and Bastien had been an idiot to agree. He and his groomsmen went to a few boxing matches, played some golf and went to a shooting range to fire a grenade launcher. The craziest thing he did was go up in a fighter jet.

The bachelorette party never got out of the casinos, and that should have been his first warning.

Gina had been a beautiful bride, an expensive one, but Bastien had money. What did he care? It had started turning to shit on the honeymoon when she spent more time in the casino than in their bed. Then the pit boss showed him the line of credit she had been running since they had announced their engagement. Suddenly, money was an issue.

After he cut her off, she cut him off.

Without his money, Gina suddenly didn't want to be married anymore. When Bastien wanted her to get counseling and work through things, she screwed a Greek billionaire. The prenup saved him in the quick divorce and Bastien counted himself lucky to get away when he did.

Last he heard, she was living in Monte Carlo with her aging husband and having more luck at baccarat than she used to. Bastien couldn't compete with the lure of the cards or the sounds of the slot machine. The ink on their wedding certificate hadn't even been dry when they started divorce proceedings.

He'd never let love blind him to a woman's faults again. And he'd never, ever get married again. If a big fairy-tale wedding wasn't what his sister had been dreaming of ever since she was a kid, he would have gladly written her the check for Tahiti.

And yet here he was for the next two weeks, try-ing to find some common ground with Jace Benja-min for Kitty's sake.

Kitty had been the only one in the family to give a damn about how he was doing when Gina left. His father thought it was good riddance. His mother had thought they should try to make it work. Kitty wanted to flush Gina's head down the toilet and give her a swirly. Bastien would move heaven and earth for his sister.

Mikelina threw her leg over his and his cock sprang to attention. She just might make this whole shitshow worthwhile. Two weeks of her sweetness would make this vacation tolerable.

He kissed her temple and fell asleep counting all the dirty things he wanted to do to her.

CHAPTER SEVEN

MIKELINA WOKE TO the smell of fresh ground coffee. She dug her toes into her sheet and stretched. In the moment between dream and being awake, she wondered who was making coffee. Her mother wouldn't be up until hours yet and her father was…in jail.

She bolted upright as it all came back to her. She squinted at the clock. It was just after nine. Well, at least she wouldn't have to rush to get to the house to open it up for Bastien.

She climbed out of bed and went to the closet, pulling one of the waffle-weave robes off the hanger and slipping it on.

Bastien was typing on his laptop at the dining room table in one of the bathing suits she had bought yesterday. Both their clothes were still strewn all over the floor. Straightening her shoulders, she decided to brazen it out.

"Can I get you a refill on your coffee?" she asked.

He looked up from the computer as if surprised she was there. "Yeah, thanks."

"Good morning," she said, kissing him.

"It is now." He pulled her on his lap and undid the tie of her robe.

Mikelina should put a stop to it, but it felt too damned good, especially when his fingers started teasing her nipples. They were in the middle of a really deep kiss when she heard her phone ring. Reluctantly, she pulled back. "I've got to get that."

Bastien let her go and she slid off his lap. She managed to get to her purse and answer it before it went to voice mail.

"Hello?" she said breathlessly.

"What time are you meeting Bastien Ainsworth?"

"Uh, ten. He wanted to check in early." She avoided Bastien's curious look while she gathered up her clothes from the floor.

"Whatever he wants. I'll be there soon."

"What?" She dropped her purse with a clunk.

"I'm on my way. I'll meet you at the house. Make me one of those special espressos, will you?"

"Shit," she screeched. Luckily, Kirk had already hung up.

"What's going on?" Bastien asked as she fled by him, back into the bedroom.

"My boss is on his way. He wants to greet you personally." She dumped her clothes into the hamper bin in her bedroom closet. She'd let the maids wash them with the daily loads and have them put them in the box of her things in the laundry room. Flicking on the light in the walk-in closet, she hit the button that lowered the stairs to the attic.

"You didn't see this," she said over her shoulder

to Bastien as she hurried up the stairs. "Where the hell did I put…" She muttered as she pulled a few bins down. She found underwear and a pair of dress slacks, but she had to borrow a pink shell blouse from her mother's bin and hoped the buttons would hold. She was bigger than her mother in the chest. It just had to pass Kirk's glance, and he never looked at her like that.

Hurrying down the ladder, she retracted it into the ceiling. Running into the master bathroom, she took the world's quickest shower. She wished she had time to do her hair, but that wasn't in the cards. She whipped it back into a fast ponytail and then twisted it into a bun and clipped it with a spare clip she found under the sink.

Before running back out into the kitchen, she closed the door to the bedroom. Kirk was pulling up in his red Maserati as she was fitting her club shoes from last night back on her feet. Her toes protested but she didn't care.

"I made you an espresso," Bastien said, handing her the cup.

"Bless you," she said. "Okay, the story is you came a little early and I've already given you the tour."

"Got it." Bastien hid his smile with his own coffee cup.

She hurried to the door and opened it just as Kirk reached it.

"Good morning, Mikelina," he said, taking the coffee cup from her. "Is that your mother's blouse?" he asked, walking in the house.

She gaped at him. Damn! "She has a similar one." She shut the door behind him.

"Where's your car?" he asked.

Double damn!

"I went for an early morning swim so I parked by the beach and walked back." That sounded lame even to her, but luckily Kirk didn't seem too interested.

"Bastien, good to see you again. How's the family?" Kirk shook his hand.

Mikelina wobbled into the kitchen to make herself an espresso. Damned shoes were killing her. Why couldn't cute shoes feel good the next day when your feet were swollen like balloons?

"I see you've made yourself at home." Kirk gestured to the swim trunks Bastien was wearing and his clothes still strewn all over the floor.

Mikelina stared at the two of them, hoping Bastien would cover for her.

"I couldn't wait to get into the pool. I'm just finishing up a few things here first." Bastien smoothly kicked his pants under the dining room table while he gestured to his laptop.

"You're on vacation. You shouldn't be working," Kirk chided.

"The bachelor party doesn't officially begin until Jace gets here in about an hour or so."

"Well, I think you'll be very happy here. This is my favorite property in this area. Mikelina is from South Beach and she's got quite an itinerary lined up for you. Have you told him about Christian Dibiasi yet?"

"I was just about to," Mikelina said, sagging

against the counter. The espresso hit her system like rocket fuel, and she needed it after the few hours of sleep she got. "I've reserved your group a table at the Water's Edge. It's a blues club. Christian will be playing songs that he's considering putting on his next album."

"Great," Bastien said, but he was frowning at his phone.

He'd better not complain that the gig wasn't on the original schedule. It had been a last-minute score and she was going to surprise them with it. Of course, she hadn't planned on last night being as intimate as it had been.

"Of course, if that doesn't appeal to you guys, Mikelina could arrange for something else," Kirk broke in nervously.

Was he kidding? Arrange for something else? Didn't he realize what she'd had to go through to get those tickets? Mikelina made herself another espresso. Okay. Whatever. Whatever the client wants. But Bastien still hadn't looked up from his phone.

"Is everything all right?" she asked.

"I'm not sure," he said. "I just got a text from Zack. He's one of the groomsmen. Jace took off with the limo. They've been trying to reach the driver, but his phone is off."

"Do the groomsmen need a ride?" Kirk snapped his fingers at Mikelina. "Get on that."

She raised her eyebrow at him. Just who did he think he was snapping at? She pressed her lips together and vowed that she'd speak to him later about that.

"No, don't worry about it," Bastien said. "Shane, another groomsman, already called in for a replacement. They'll be about an hour behind Jace."

"Why would he strand his groomsmen?" Mikelina asked.

"He's a douchebag," Bastien said, rolling his eyes.

"Oh well, he's young." Kirk grabbed Mikelina by the arm. "We'll let you enjoy some peace and quiet before the guests arrive. I'll give you a ride back to your car," Kirk said as he practically dragged her out.

She hoped that Bastien would ask her to stay so they could get a little closure on their one-night stand, but he was too involved with his phone. She had barely enough time to grab her purse before Kirk hurried her out the door.

Bastien walked out into the pool area, closing the sliding glass door behind him to shut out his conversation. "What do you mean he's missing?" he snarled into the phone.

Max, another groomsman and the only one with half a brain in his head, said, "I'm telling you, man. He's on the run."

"From what?"

"You. The whole bachelor party. I think he's got cold feet."

"How sure are you? Because I don't want to break my sister's heart by telling her that her fiancé is in the wind."

"No, don't call Kitty. I'm sure he'll be at the house soon. He's got the address. Maybe he just went out for a few drinks."

"We have a fully stocked bar here."

Max sighed. "Look, I didn't want to be the one to say this, but he was really bummed that we weren't going to a titty bar. I bet that's where he's headed to first."

I'm going to kill him.

"It's not even eleven o'clock in the morning," Bastien said between his teeth.

"From the flyers we saw in the airport, there's a lot of lunch shows going on."

"Where?"

"All over. Scarlett's looked good. So did Coco's. There's one right by the airport, too. Maybe that's where he is?"

"Go there. Find him. Drag him back here if you have to. I'll call the limo company to see if I could narrow it down."

"We already did that. The driver's not answering his phone."

"Leave that to me. I'll call you when I have something. Let me know if you find him first."

Bastien waited on hold for a half hour, but he finally got a supervisor to do a GPS trace on the limousine since the driver wasn't picking up. He downloaded their app and demanded the information be sent to him so he could track them down.

"I'm very sorry, Mr. Ainsworth. But the driver

was retained by Mr. Benjamin and Mr. Benjamin's orders were that he was not to be disturbed."

"If you ever want to do business with my family again, you will get me access to the tracker on that limo."

"There are certain legal issues we have to consider."

"You own the limo. I want to know where it is until my future brother-in-law is where he's supposed to be."

"Sir, if he doesn't want to be taken to you, we can't force him."

"I'm not asking you to. All I'm asking is for you to tell me where he is."

There was a long pause and Bastien was getting ready to go over his head to the next level supervisor when the supervisor said, "I understand you're concerned about your brother-in-law's safety. I can tell you that the limo is in Little Havana on the Calle Ocho strip. My guess is he's doing a little sightseeing before he goes to South Beach."

"Are there strip bars there?"

"Sir, I am not a travel guide. Please don't call back."

Bastien was about to snap back at the man, but he had been hung up on. This was ridiculous. He called Zack, Shane and Max but got their voice mails. He was ready to throw his phone against the wall, but

decided to put it in the pocket of his board shorts before he did something stupid.

"Mikelina," he called. But she and Kirk Diamonte
had already left. When had that happened?

CHAPTER EIGHT

LUCKILY, MIKELINA WAS able to ditch Kirk before he insisted on walking her to her car, which of course was nowhere near the beach. Unfortunately, now she was stuck in an uncomfortable outfit and really inappropriate shoes. Kicking them off, she went to Abbie's Surf Shop for some flip-flops.

"So?" Abbie said when she walked in. "Details."

Mikelina had shot the briefest of texts to her last night before going back to the house with Bastien. "I can't even," she said.

"Was the sex good?" Abbie played her fingers through the multi-colored beads in her long thin braids.

Sighing, Mikelina picked up a pair of flip-flops that were more comfort than style. "Oh yeah. That's not the problem."

Her phone rang. Bastien.

Abbie raised her eyebrow. "Is it him? That's a little clingy, isn't it?" She leaned her elbows on the counter and tried to see the phone number on Mikelina's phone.

"It would be, if he wasn't renting my house for two weeks."

Abbie clamped her hands over her mouth and scared Jinx who meowed in protest and slashed her tail.

"Where are you?" Bastien barked out when she answered.

"What do you need?" she answered.

"How well do you know Calle Ocho?"

"Fairly well," she said.

"Good. You're coming with me. We need to find Jace."

"He left his groomsmen stranded to go to Calle Ocho by himself?" Mikelina didn't have a good feeling about this.

"Yes. He and I need to have a conversation before I call my sister."

"All right," Mikelina sighed. "There are a few spots he could be at. Pick me up at the beach parking lot by the Coffee Hut down the street. Just turn left out of the driveway and you'll see it on your right." She'd grab some bagels because she was pretty sure Bastien hadn't had breakfast yet either.

"Sounds like an adventure," Abbie said, ringing her up.

Mikelina's feet immediately expanded into the soft foam support of the flip-flops and she sighed appreciatively. "I hadn't expected to chase a runaway groom today, but that's the glamorous life I lead."

"Have fun," Abbie called as Mikelina headed out the door.

Calle Ocho was fun. She wasn't sure how fun it would be with Bastien, though. He seemed really pissed that his future brother-in-law had made a pit stop. Bastien was already waiting for her in the parking lot when she came out with the bagels and coffee.

"I hope you're not the type of person who doesn't want people eating in their car," she said as she slid into the seat.

"It's a rental." He shrugged.

"I got your coffee black, but there's some cream and sugar in the bag. Hope you like lox and bagels."

"I'm from New York," he said, staring at the bag suspiciously.

"So's the owner." After buckling up, she unwrapped his bagel and handed it to him.

She doctored her coffee up with cream and sugar, but left his black when he shook his head at her questioning look.

"Thanks," he said after demolishing his bagel. "I needed that."

"You always need snacks if you're going on a road trip. Why are we trying to find Jace? You guys didn't have any solid plans for today." Mikelina dug out the schedule from her handbag. "I have unpacking and unwinding from the trip down for the afternoon. Maybe he just wanted some alone time before the party began."

"He could have called. He could have told someone." Bastien shook his head. "I don't like that he's not answering his phone."

"Do you think he's in trouble?" Mikelina wiped a bit of cream cheese off the side of her mouth.

"I'm trying to prevent that." Bastien wrung his hands on the steering wheel. "Is traffic always this bad?"

"No," Mikelina said. "Sometimes it's worse."

"Great."

"Did you give the groomsmen the code to get into the house?" she asked. She didn't like having so many people knowing the code, but she could always change it.

"They're not answering their phones either. But at least I know where they are and hopefully we'll have found Jace before they get back."

"Where are they?" she asked.

"Before I could get the limousine company to give me the GPS location, they thought Jace might have gone to a gentlemen's club or two."

"Ah," she said, nodding. "I noticed you didn't have any of that planned for the bachelor party."

"Of course not."

"That's kind of what happens at these kind of things," she said.

"Not if he's marrying my sister," Bastien said. "Besides, there wasn't time to fit that in."

"I could have fit it in."

He shook his head. "We have a full schedule."

"I noticed," Mikelina said with a smirk. "I guess you don't like winging it."

"I don't mind if it's just me. But when I have to wrangle idiots, it's easier to stick to a schedule. But to be honest, spontaneity gives me hives. I'd rather plan out my spontaneity."

"I think I know what you mean, and that's a little frightening."

"Don't be scared. I don't bite…much."

"I liked your bites." She put her hand on his knee. "I think last night was a nice spontaneous activity."

"I have to admit, it felt good to go with it. I didn't plan for you, but I would have had I known we'd hit it off."

"You're handling today's adventure pretty well all things considered."

"I'm not anal-retentive about the schedule. I just don't know how to relate to him and his friends without it."

"How old is Jace?"

"Ten years younger than me."

"And the groomsmen?"

"The same."

"It's possible that you guys have different ideas of fun," she pointed out.

"He could have said something. I asked him what he wanted to do and he left it all to me."

"That does seem a little inconsiderate," she said. "But maybe he just wanted a few hours to himself. I know after spending time in the airport and on a tight flight, I want to just decompress."

Bastien grunted. Mikelina stared at his profile. He hadn't shaved yet today and the slight stubble on his cheeks made him look like a pirate. He had changed out of his board shorts and into khakis and a polo shirt that showed off the curve of his biceps. He caught her looking at him and flexed them.

She grinned. Show-off.

"Busy morning, right?" he said.

"Crazy morning," she said, wondering why she was blushing.

"I had a great time last night."

"Me, too."

He reached over and held her hand. "You're beautiful and I wanted to thank you again for everything you did to help put this bachelor party together. I'm sorry Jace is ruining it."

"It's his party to ruin," she said. She wanted to lean her cheek against his arm and cuddle up next to him, but it would be awkward—even if the stick shift wasn't in the way. "Maybe I could arrange something especially tailored to his interests this week. What does he like to do?"

Bastien snorted. "I don't know. He and my sister go out clubbing all the time."

Mikelina remembered that on the intake form, Bastien had specifically said that they weren't interested in hitting any of Miami's famous clubs. "Do you think they'd like Flow?" she asked.

"Yeah. I certainly did." He smiled at her and her toes curled a bit in her flip-flops.

"That didn't really seem like your scene."

"It's not. I went because my buddy is part owner and wanted me to check it out. I was about to leave when I saw you."

"Dancing half-crocked." She pushed a lock of her hair behind her ear.

"I was enchanted."

She wished he wasn't a client and was just a nice guy she met at a bar. It would be a little less awkward and she wouldn't feel so guilty, like she was doing something wrong. Mikelina knew she wasn't. They were consenting adults, after all. But she still had to hide it from Kirk this morning and it made her feel that they were doing something dirty. And that wasn't the case at all. At least it shouldn't be.

Clearing her throat, she decided to steer the conversation back to business. "Well, you've got better connections there than I do. Maybe tomorrow night you can get a VIP spot."

"I think we'll be too tired from the fishing boat."

That's right. They'd had her charter them a boat. "Hoping for a marlin?" she asked.

"I'd be happy with a sailfish."

"Is Jace a big fisherman?"

Bastien's smile faltered. "I'm not sure. I think so."

Mikelina hoped Jace wasn't going to ghost Bastien on the fishing trip as well. "If you're lucky, you'll pull in a few dolphin fishes to put on the grill for dinner."

"What does dolphin fish taste like? All my fishing has been off Long Island Sound."

"It's also known as mahi-mahi. It's a light-tasting white fish."

He nodded in recognition. "Do you fish?"

"I used to, with my dad." Mikelina cleared her throat. "But that was a long time ago." A happier time.

"Do you bait your own hook?"

"Do *you*?" she snorted.

He chuckled.

After scanning the street for a limo and seeing too many of them, Bastien gave up and found a parking spot.

"Where do you think he could be?" Mikelina asked, stretching as she uncoiled herself out of the car.

He took a moment to admire her shapely legs and tanned midriff before she straightened her clothes. "I don't have the foggiest idea."

"Does he smoke?" she asked, putting a ridiculous set of heart-shaped sunglasses on her face. But on her, it worked. She looked adorable and he resisted the opportunity to kiss her. He held out his hand instead to help her step up to the curb and then decided not to let her hand go.

"You mean weed?"

"No." She laughed. "Cigars." She pointed to a few shops. "There are some master cigar makers in this area. If that's your sort of thing."

That was the problem. He had no idea what would interest Jace. Or what his sister saw in him. "Couldn't hurt to check it out."

Bastien didn't know much about cigars, but he was pleasantly surprised that the aroma wasn't as harsh as he had been expecting. When he mentioned it to Mikelina, she just nodded and said, "The good ones aren't stinky and acrid. I'm not a fan myself, but I've smelled a reeking stogie before and these aren't anything like them."

They went in and out of the shops, but there wasn't any sign of Jace.

Bastien peeked at a few limos but couldn't see through the tinted windows. He even tried dialing Jace's number on the off chance that he could hear his phone ring, but it went right to voice mail.

"I give up," he said. "I'm sorry to have dragged you all the way out here."

Mikelina shrugged. "It's a nice day. I got to spend it with a handsome man. Why don't we grab lunch? Maybe I can convince you to wander through a few museums before we head back."

"That sounds great. What do you recommend?"

"I've got the perfect spot." Tugging on his arm, she led him through the crowd to the Café Croqueta.

"What's a croqueta?" he asked after she negotiated a table on the street in rapid Spanish with the hostess.

"It's a fried ball of goodness. The ham and cheese ones will melt in your mouth. Just you wait." She grinned at him. "I also ordered us *dos Papa Dobles*. It's their Hemingway specialty drink. It's a rum punch to end all rum punches."

He whistled. "That's a heavy-duty cocktail in this heat."

"We'll go slow." Mikelina gave him a sultry look that made him wish they were back in the air-conditioned house with that big bed all to themselves. In fact, why was he wasting time here when he could be there with her? Jace and his idiot friends would show up sooner or later.

"It's all part of my nefarious plan to get you to spend some time cruising through the museums with me while we sober up a bit," she added.

"I can think of a few other ways to spend time." Museums? Just because he didn't want to go clubbing every night at strip joints didn't mean he was going to waste the sun, sand and surf.

"Too bad you didn't rent the limo then." She batted her eyes outrageously at him and he reached for his phone.

"I could have one here after lunch."

"But that's not in the schedule."

He loved that she flushed bright red and stammered a bit. Leaning in, he brushed her lips with a quick kiss. "It is now."

"I suppose we could pencil it in." She smiled shyly at him.

"I'll call your bluff every time."

"Maybe it wasn't a bluff," she said, taking a shaky breath.

He dialed the limo company. "Yes, I'd like a limousine to pick me up in an hour." Bastien glanced at the menu and read the restaurant's address off to them. "I'll need it for a few hours."

"Bastien, what about your car?"

He shrugged. "I can come back for it."

"This is crazy," she said.

"Hey, it's a bachelor party. It's supposed to get a little crazy. Spontaneous even."

CHAPTER NINE

MIKELINA WASN'T THE girl who had sex in the limo at a bachelor party. Until now. She ran her hand over the leather couch-like seats and watched the beautiful Miami skyline. She'd like to blame her breathlessness on the sweet rum punch, but it was all about the handsome man sitting across from her, waiting for her to make the first move.

Bastien sprawled against his seat, his dark brown eyes heated as he devoured her with his gaze. He made her feel daring and a little crazy and she wanted his attention more than she wanted her next breath. It was easier because this wasn't real. He would be leaving in a few weeks and she would go back to her boring life.

Kicking off her flip-flops, she made sure the privacy screen was down. "Should we stop for condoms?" she asked.

"Already took care of it. I picked some up in the restaurant's bathroom."

Some.

She shivered.

"We don't have to do anything you don't want to do," he said and that was even sexier than how he was looking at her.

"Take off your shirt," she said, feeling breathless and wicked.

Grabbing the hem, he slowly raised it over his rock-hard abs, teased it over his chest and finally pulled it over his head and tossed it on the bench seat next to him.

"Your turn," he said huskily.

Biting her lip, she untucked her pink blouse from her slacks and lifted it off. Instead of feeling self-conscious about being in the back of the stretch limo in her bra, she was excited. "Pants," she said, greed-ily watching as he kicked off his shoes and unbuck-led his khakis.

Easing them down his narrow hips, he got rid of them, too. He wore black boxers. "Stroke your nip-ples," he ordered.

"What?" she gasped, her eyes half closing in de-sire at his command.

"I want to see them through your bra."

Feeling naughty, Mikelina circled the tips with her fingers. The scrape against the silky fabric of her bra as well as the hungry look in Bastien's eyes made them hard. Her thighs were trembling. She had never been this wet, and they were both still partially dressed.

Bastien groaned. "You're so damned sexy."

"Get naked," she said, not recognizing her own voice.

Mikelina caught her breath when he tossed off his underwear. He was thick and hard. She licked her lips at the sight of his strong cock.

"You're killing me," he said softly. "Take off the damned bra."

Unsnapping it, she cupped her breasts and offered them to him.

He was next to her in a moment, kneeling in front of her. Bastien's hot mouth engulfed her nipple. When he swiped his tongue across the sensitive peak, she gasped and fumbled out of her bottoms. She wanted to be just as naked as he was. He wound up helping her as they frantically tried to free her from her clothes. Sitting next to her, Bastien pulled her into his lap and tangled his tongue with hers. She wrapped her arms around him as he parted her thighs.

Moaning around his tongue, Mikelina kissed him desperately. She didn't need to breathe. She just needed him to keep rubbing her just like that. Running her fingers through his short hair, she let her hips rock against him. He fingered her gently until she was ready to beg him to please just fuck her already.

She came shaking against him, her breaths coming in short gasps.

"I love watching you come," he said.

"Then you're going to love this." Mikelina shimmied off his lap to her knees in front of him. Guiding his cock into her mouth, she sucked him deep. Watching his head thunk back on the window, she felt a thrill of power. She was glad she wasn't the only one affected by this surge of decadent passion. Mikelina worked him up and down, dragging her tongue over the tip and then swirling around down his shaft.

Bastien gripped the seat and groaned deep. "So fucking good. Get up here. I need to be inside you."

Holding her hand out for the condom, she kept sucking on him as he unwrapped it and then handed it to her. She enjoyed him a bit longer until his breathing became harsh and unsteady. Letting him slide out of her mouth with an obscene pop, she rolled the condom down his thickness.

Bastien pulled her up and she straddled him. When she guided him in between her thighs and sank down on top of his cock, they both let out satisfied grunts.

Mikelina rose up, deliberately dragging her breasts over the stubble on his face. The harsh rasp of his beard over her sensitive peaks made her clench in pleasure around his cock. Bastien gripped her ass and moved her up and down when she just held herself still, enjoying the fullness of him. His lips and tongue were busy trapping her nipples as she undulated on him, the soft seat giving her extra bounce.

"Bastien," she gasped, holding on to his shoulders. The sweet friction as their bodies slid against each other made her crazed. She didn't recognize the sounds coming out of her mouth, but the primal noises he made resounded deep inside her. He let her keep the pace, all the while telling her how beautiful, how sexy she was. Every nerve ending was on fire. He wrapped his arms around her and she reveled in his tight muscles holding her close.

"Coming," she whispered.

Outside the window, Miami passed by them at sixty plus miles an hour. She caught a blur of palm trees and her head spun with the traffic. "Bastien," she choked out as her entire body quivered from the crashing wave of pleasure that stunned her. She was oblivious to everything but the spasms of her body on top of his. Still trembling, she climbed off him.

Off balance, she was boneless when he turned her so she gripped the seat across from them. Entering her from behind, it was her turn to hang on while he slammed deep into her. His grip on her hips yanked her to him as his thrusts went wild and deep.

"Fuck," she snarled as her body opened up to him, and each drive of his powerful body shook her. Her nipples dragged on the leather of the seat. Her hair was a colossal mess hanging around her face. She caught a glimpse of herself in the window and didn't recognize the slack-jawed pleasure on her face. Glancing back, she could see Bastien was nearly feral in his desire. It sent a quickening of passion through her. She wanted him to lose it, come so hard inside her that he was as crazy and needy as she was.

"So damn good," he groaned.

"Harder," she begged, and he swore. When he picked up the already lightning pace, Mikelina cried out, "Yes."

Bastien's entire body clenched and in one final

deep thrust, he shuddered against her and collapsed on her back.

"Fuck," he groaned. "I'm blind."

She giggled, feeling a little light-headed herself. "I needed that."

He pulled out of her and sagged back on the seat. "Come here, baby."

Mikelina didn't need to be asked twice. She climbed back into his lap and he stroked her back while they kissed gently this time.

"I want to make you come again," he whispered against her lips.

"Are you trying to kill me?" she gasped.

"Only with pleasure."

CHAPTER TEN

BASTIEN FROWNED AT the cheap hotel Mikelina had him drop her off in front of. Kirk Diamonte had said she was local. Did she live here? No wonder she kept a stash of clothes in the rental home. He wondered if she stayed there when it wasn't booked. The thought bothered him. She deserved to stay at a nicer place than this. Although maybe she didn't have a permanent place because her job had her hopping around.

Still, Diamonte should be paying her enough to stay in a decent hotel. Or if he was comping her lodging, he needed to step up the accommodations.

Making a mental note to find out from Diamonte what the deal was, Bastien slid open the privacy window of the limo. "Back to Calle Ocho."

"Yes, sir."

He had Mikelina two more times on the drive and Bastien's entire body felt wrung out. He could barely keep his eyes open. He was surprised Mikelina had the strength to get out of the car. But she had turned and blown him a kiss before entering the hotel. If he had anything left in him, he would have gone after her and followed her to her room.

His eyes drooped closed and he settled back against the wide bench seats and dozed off. When his phone rang, he almost didn't answer it. But habit had him checking the number and when he saw it was Jace, it was like a jolt of caffeine went through him.

"Where are you?" he snarled.

"Where are you?" Jace came back with. "Me and the guys are standing outside of the house." He whistled into the phone appreciatively—and right into Bastien's ear. "This place is off the hook."

Bastien looked out the window. They were almost back to where he'd parked his rental car. "I'm in Little Havana looking for you."

"Yeah, sorry about that. My phone was dead and I wanted a tour of Miami."

"Why didn't you take your friends with you?"

Jace laughed. "They wanted to see naked women dancing. I didn't want to tell them no. But I also didn't want to go with them. Kitty would kill me."

Bastien snorted. They could have been honest with him instead of letting him think that they were going into the clubs for altruistic reasons.

"So we parted ways for a few hours. But we're here now. How soon can you get back?"

"Depends on traffic."

"Well, no hurry. I just called the concierge to let us in. We're going to grill up some steaks and hang out by the pool."

For some reason Bastien felt a twinge of unease about Mikelina being there without him. Max, Shane and Zack were young, rich and loved to spend money—especially on beautiful women.

"I've already claimed the bedroom off the kitchen," he said, not wanting any of them to sleep there. What was wrong with him? He usually wasn't so possessive over a pleasurable fling. Except he wasn't sure that was all Mikelina was. He was almost disappointed that the bachelor party was back on schedule. He wanted more time with her. He didn't want this to be a one-night stand. He wanted to spend the entire two weeks with her. But this wasn't about him. It was about Kitty and her future happiness. "Do you want me to pick up anything while I'm out?" Bastien said, holding in his sigh of resignation.

"Yeah, can you pick up a box of Cohiba Behikes for us? I got two, but that's not going to last."

"Cigars?" Bastien hazarded a guess.

"Yeah, you should be able to get them anywhere down there."

"All right. Behave. Don't give Mikelina a hard time."

"Yes, Dad," Jace said and hung up.

Bastien grimaced. He didn't want to sound like his father. After tipping the chauffeur, he got out of the limo in front of a cigar store and found the thousand-dollar box of cigars. He got two. He wasn't going to smoke them, but if it brought him a little street cred with Jace and his friends, it was money well spent.

When he finally got back to the house, he was both relieved and disappointed that Mikelina wasn't there.

"Kitty says hi," Jace said from a pool lounger. He was on his cell.

"We didn't cook up your steak yet, but there's a lobster for you in the pot," Shane said.

Bastien tossed the boxes of cigars on the table. "Thanks." He helped himself to a lobster and a set of crackers and sat at the outside table while the others swam in the pool or rested on the chairs.

"Micky said she got us tickets to a blues concert tonight," Max said.

"Micky?" Bastien made a face at the nickname.

"Yeah, she's the concierge. What a babe."

Bastien glared at him but didn't say anything. Using the cracker to crush the lobster claw, he pried the meat out and dipped it into the butter sauce. Pure decadence. Now it was a bachelor party. "Toss me a beer."

Zack laughed and under-armed him a Corona. "Max had her show him how to work that coffee machine five times."

"To be fair," Max pointed out, "that thing is more complicated than my car."

"And now we're all high on espresso because of all the coffees he made practicing."

"I hope you were respectful," Bastien grumbled and then shook his head at himself. If he wanted to be treated like an equal instead of a father figure, he had to stop acting like one. Still, it didn't feel at all right to agree that yeah, Mikelina was a babe. He concentrated on decimating the lobster in front of him while he waited for the beer to settle down from the toss before opening it.

"I asked Micky if she could switch the tickets so we could go to Flow instead. She said we'd have to talk to you because you knew the owner," Jace said.

Irritation flashed through him. But he didn't show it. Friends. He wanted them to be friends. So he wasn't going to force them to go to an intimate blues show when all they really wanted to do was go clubbing. "Let me make a few calls," he said instead of asking them if they knew what an opportunity they were missing. Christian Dibiasi's new album would go platinum the first week it was out.

"Awesome. How do you like your steak, bro?" Zack asked.

"Medium rare." Bro? Well, Bastien supposed it was a start.

While the steak was cooking, he went into his bedroom and closed the drapes that looked out into the pool area. Before he called his friend who owned Flow, he dialed his sister's number now that Jace was off the phone and on a raft in the pool.

"Hey, squirt."

"If you're calling to rub it in, you can go drown yourself in the pool," Kitty said.

Bastien hadn't been, but now he felt that as an older brother he needed to. "I'm sorry, I can't hear you over the gorgeous sunshine down here in Florida."

"I hope it rains."

"It's Florida. It will. But then it will be sunny again. How's New York?" he asked innocently.

"It's a balmy go-fuck-yourself outside."

He loved his baby sister so much. Peeking out between the curtains, he could see that Jace hadn't moved from the raft except to light a cigar and accept a glass of whiskey. "Are you sure you want to marry this tool?"

"Bastien," she cried, drawing his name out four syllables.

"I'm just saying, it's not too late to call the whole thing off."

"Look, buster, I've had to sit through three—count 'em—three wedding dress fittings. Mom and Jace's mom almost had a fistfight over flowers."

"I can't even picture that." Both women were scions of society and prided themselves on being unfailingly polite.

"I swear to you. They almost threw down over stargazer lilies versus dahlias."

"Which do you want?"

Kitty gave a bitter laugh. "Why would that even matter?"

"Hey, Kit-Kat," he said. "Hang in there. Wedding is in a month. And then you're stuck with what's-his-name." Bastien looked between the drapes again.

Jace's groomsmen were now cannonballing him, which upset the raft and sent the drink, the hundred-dollar cigar and the groom ass over teakettle into the water.

"I've got to go," Kitty said. "Time to taste wedding cake. It's the highlight of the day. I think I'm going with chocolate with cannoli filling."

"Whatever you want, sweetheart."

She snorted. "That'll be the day."

Bastien got them a VIP booth at Flow and made sure the bottle service was put on his tab. He hung out for a few hours until he was sure Jace and his friends wouldn't miss him. The limo was outside ready to take them back to the house at last call, or when they got kicked out, whichever came first.

He couldn't be in that club without thinking of Mikelina and he didn't feel like dancing or drinking the night away. So he sneaked out when the groomsmen were doing shots and drove over to the intimate club where Christian Dibiasi was playing. Bastien hoped that his name was still on the list to get in so he'd at least be able to hear a few songs.

It was on the schedule after all.

The bouncer let him in and although the club was as crowded as Flow, it was more sedate with a chill vibe. An usher led him toward a curved booth with a high back. The air was hazy from the lights and it gave off a serene feel that immediately had him relaxing. This was exactly what he needed after a long day.

When he went to slide into the booth, he was surprised to see Mikelina sitting there. She was in a low-cut peach sundress that accentuated her curves. Her long black hair was held up by a shelled comb and it showed off her graceful neck. He wanted to nibble his way up it to whisper in her ear exactly what he wanted to do to her.

She blinked up at him. "I hope you don't mind. I didn't want the seats to go to waste."

"Is there room for me?" He sat next to her on the red velvet cushion. He didn't care if there was or not. His night just got one hundred percent better.

"It's just you and me."

"How did I get so lucky?"

He ordered a beer and had the waitress top off Mikelina's wine. Then he put his arm around her, and they listened to Christian Dibiasi play his heart out on the saxophone before switching to piano. It was bliss to sit there with his fingers lightly brushing her bare shoulder. He expected to feel sleepy after the day he had, but he was surprisingly energized.

And of course, he wanted her again.

"He's amazingly talented," Mikelina said after the final set. "My friend Selena has a huge crush on him."

"Why isn't she here tonight?"

"She's in Maui, the poor thing." Mikelina rolled her eyes. "She works for Five Diamond Resorts, too. She's a personal chef. So if you guys wanted gourmet meals, she would have come in and cooked them for you."

"I think these guys just want to throw meat on a fire and call it a day."

"That can be fun, too. They seemed like they were ready to have a good time."

Bastien rolled his eyes. "I'm not that much older than them, but they make me feel ancient."

"You have different tastes. That's not a bad thing."

"It is a bit." He took a swig of his beer. "I wanted to get to know him a little better. For my sister's sake. My father is only interested in this match because it will positively affect our business. I just want to make sure he's good enough for my little sister, you know?"

"That's so sweet. She's lucky she has someone like you looking after her."

"Do you have any brothers or sisters?"

Mikelina shook her head. "I'm an only child. My mother lives down in Boca Raton and my father is… out of the picture."

Bastien wondered at the painful pause, but figured it was probably a rough divorce that put Mikelina in the middle. He was lucky that his parents, while not adoringly in love with each other, at least never aired their differences in front of him and his sister.

"Jace will always have his best friends," she said. "But he'll come to appreciate having someone older, more experienced and more balanced to turn to as well."

"Balanced? You make me sound like a scale."

"I mean it as a compliment, trust me. I could use a little balance in my life."

Bastien grinned. "Here I am."

She blushed. "I meant that my life can be a little crazy."

"Your job?"

"Sometimes," she said. "I mostly stay in Florida. But if I'm needed, I can also manage properties all over the world. I was in Cartagena, Jamaica and Paris this year. It's great to travel, but all my contacts are here. I'm not as effective overseas yet."

"Contacts? What about friends?"

"I have friends all over, but if I need to book a bachelor party to a private jam session, I need contacts."

"I'm sorry the guys threw a monkey wrench into your plans," he said, not sorry at all that it allowed them this time together.

She waved a hand dismissively at him. "Oh, that's not a problem. As long as they didn't want to do something impossible like nighttime hot-air ballooning. When the clients get creative, I have to worry about disappointing them."

"Do they complain to your boss?"

"Sometimes." Mikelina shrugged. "For the most part, Kirk and I have seen it all, so there aren't a lot of surprises. But every now and then, you get a whack-a-doo and all you can do is damage control. And laugh."

"Tell me about one."

"I shouldn't," she said with a grin. "Client/concierge privilege and all that."

"I don't think it's a thing."

"Well, you wouldn't want me gossiping about your bachelor party, right?"

He liked that she didn't talk about her clients. "That's true. Forgive me for asking."

Reaching out, she squeezed his hand. "No forgiveness necessary. How about in your job? You work in retail, right?"

"At the corporate level, yes. It's all spreadsheets and number crunching. It's nonstop tracking trends and trying to anticipate the next big thing. Lately, though, I've been getting a little burned out. I feel like I'm a hamster on a wheel, scurrying fast but never getting anywhere."

"Then why do you do it?"

Bastien blew out a sigh. "That's a good question. It's a living. I know what I'm doing and it provides me a lifestyle that allows me to buy expensive cigars that I don't smoke and book a destination wedding for a bunch of strangers."

"You should have invited some of your friends, too," she said. "That way you'd have someone to commiserate with."

"I'd have better luck with some of my contacts. I don't have a lot of time or patience to make deeper relationships with anyone."

"Why? What else are you doing?"

"That's a good point. Lately, I've been wondering that myself."

"I noticed that you're not trying to micromanage the bachelor party as much."

"It's like herding cats." He shook his head.

"I think you're adjusting to going with the flow very well."

"I don't really have a choice."

"When was the last time you took some time off?"

Pulling her in, he kissed her sweet mouth. "Today."

She put her hand on his chest and caressed him. Even though they had just spent an incredibly carnal afternoon together, he wanted to tumble her into bed and not come up for air until morning.

"When was the last time you scheduled time off?" she amended.

He closed his eyes to better enjoy the soft stroke of her hand. "I can't even remember."

"How about you put me in your itinerary for the rest of the night?" she asked.

"I think I can squeeze in you. I mean, squeeze you in."

Her smile was wicked and he grabbed her back for another kiss. "Want to get out of here?" he asked after kissing her until they were both breathless.

"Oh yeah." She eased out of the booth. "Do you remember how to get back to my hotel?"

He nodded.

"I'm in room 304. Give me about ten minutes and come in. I have a surprise for you." Mikelina gave him a seductive smile.

He watched the sweet sway of her ass as she walked out of the bar.

CHAPTER ELEVEN

MIKELINA WAS GIDDY with excitement as she waited for Bastien to arrive. She had slipped into a red-and-black teddy and a pair of sexy heels that she wouldn't dare wear out of the bedroom for fear of breaking her neck.

"What are you doing?" she asked herself in the bathroom mirror. The woman who looked out at her didn't look like Mikelina, professional concierge. It was some newly sprung sex goddess. Mikelina the concierge didn't have hours-long sex fests with a guy she just met. And she certainly didn't bring him back to her hotel room for more.

"You deserve this," she told herself. Bastien was the perfect lover. He was sexy and sweet and knew exactly how to make her quiver and moan. Best of all, he'd be gone at the end of next week and she'd never have to worry about seeing him back away in revulsion when he found out her father was *the* Tanner Presley.

There was a quiet knock on her door. Now or never. She took a shaky breath, squared her shoulders and walked back into the bedroom. "Come in," she said, unsure of how to pose seductively. In the end, she just stood there. But it must have been good enough because Bastien's eyes darkened and he locked the door behind him.

"Take off your clothes," she said, giving him orders for a change.

He shrugged out of his T-shirt and kicked off his shoes. She loved watching the play of his muscles as he moved. He was erect and Mikelina couldn't wait to get her hands on him.

"I like how you look at me," he said when he was naked. "You look like a pretty present. Do I get to unwrap you?"

"If you're good," she said, licking her lips.

"I'll be very good, but I think you already know that."

She walked over to the night table and showed him the bottle of massage oil. "I thought you might like a rubdown after all that driving today."

His cock twitched.

"I'll do your back first," she said.

"Then do I get to do you?"

Mikelina nodded. "All night long if you like."

"I've got nowhere to be until 6:00 a.m. It's not like Jace and his friends will miss me."

Bastien lay on the bed with his arms crossed under his forehead. Straddling his ass, she poured the massage oil onto his back. He inhaled a quick breath.

"That's a little chilly."

"I'll warm it up," she said and started rubbing his back and shoulders with the heels of her palms. She moved in slow, wide circles, enjoying each curve of his muscled body.

"I can feel your wet pussy on my ass," he said, his voice muffled.

"What can I say? I like touching you." Mikelina stroked his neck and his arms before reluctantly getting off him to continue to rub her hands down his thigh and calves.

"That feels amazing," he said, sounding drugged and sleepy.

"You can roll over now," she whispered, her insides feeling shaky and needy.

She nearly came from the look in his eyes.

"Is it my turn next?" he asked in a smoky voice that made her even wetter.

Shaking her head, she straddled him again. Mikelina gasped at the touch of his hot, hard shaft between her legs. Pooling the massage oil on his chest, she continued her circular strokes. This time, she dragged her nails lightly over him and rocked against his cock.

"You're soaked."

She nodded, unable to speak. Her heart was thundering.

Bastien reached down and pulled the crotch of the teddy to the side. Now, there was nothing separating them, just skin on skin. He squirted some of the oil between them and Mikelina shuddered in pleasure when he arched and slid effortlessly inside her.

"Oh," she murmured as he poured oil into his

palms and then slid his hands under the frothy underwear to cup her breasts.

As she rocked on top of him, he glided his hands over her sensitive nipples. She was a little sore from their passionate lovemaking this afternoon, but she wouldn't stop this for anything. The decadent sensations of his tugging fingers and the friction of his hard cock inside her were awakening her out of a dream. She had been sleepwalking this last year, but now she felt present and alive.

"Are you going to come for me?" he crooned, rolling her nipples between his slippery fingers.

She nodded, unable to speak.

"I want to see you use my body to come."

Mikelina held on to his shoulders and rode him slow and deep. He half ripped, half pulled the teddy off her until just scraps of lace hung to her. He touched her everywhere with oil-slick fingers and as they glided together, every inch of her body was on fire for him.

She cried out over and over again as she neared completion. Bastien's eyes were half-closed and he was breathing hard. Mikelina called his name as her orgasm shattered over her and then let him flip her onto her back. Wrapping her arms and legs around him, she gave him everything as he took her fast and hard. He kissed her long and passionately until their breathing quieted down.

Rolling off her, he tucked her in close and fell immediately to sleep. It wasn't until she was stroking him and fighting off sleep herself that she realized they hadn't used a condom.

Bastien hated his alarm with the fiery rage of a thousand suns, especially since it was way the hell over there. Mikelina was a comfortable weight on him and fortunately his alarm hadn't wakened her yet. He peeled himself away and staggered to his phone which was still in his pants pocket.

5:00 a.m.

What asshole set his alarm for 5:00 a.m. when he was on vacation?

Oh right. It was him and he had a fishing trip booked for this morning at six. What asshole…?

Oh right. Him again. Groaning, he shut off the alarm and staggered to the bathroom. He closed the door and called Jace. Might as well get them going, too.

It went straight to voice mail. Son of a bitch. He tried the three stooges right in a row and their phones also went to voice mail. Fuck it. Bastien took a quick shower.

When he came out with the towel wrapped around his waist, Mikelina rolled over. "Is something wrong?" she said and yawned.

"No, sorry to wake you. I've got to get the boys up for the fishing trip."

"Have fun." She smiled and flipped back over.

He contemplated crawling back into bed with her, but that wouldn't help him get to know Jace any better. He wanted to say something to her, tell her what an amazing day yesterday was. But she was already snoring softly. Brushing a quick kiss over her temple, he pulled the covers up over her shoulder and quietly left the room.

He yawned the entire drive back to the house. At least he had a decent cup of espresso in his future.

After he let himself in, he started a pot of coffee and then went upstairs to get the guys up and moving. Except no one was in their rooms. It didn't even look like their beds had been slept in.

Another round of phone calls yielded the same result. They didn't know where to meet the boat. He hadn't thought he needed to tell them. He was sure they weren't already up and out. Were they still at Flow? Locked in? Doubtful.

Bastien got changed out of his club clothes from last night into shorts and a T-shirt. He wasn't about to spend the entire day waiting for Jace and his friends to stagger in. He made another phone call, hoping that Mikelina would pick up.

"Hi," she said huskily.

"Do you want to go out fishing with me today?"

CHAPTER TWELVE

MIKELINA BOOKED CHARTERS for her clients all the time, but aside from the first trip Captain Lila took her on to show her what she could offer her clients, this was the first time since her father was arrested that Mikelina had been on a fishing boat for more than a quick trip.

Tanner used to take her out on a boat called *Mermaid's Kiss*. Mikelina deliberately didn't use that boat for her clients because she couldn't take the memories. Maybe out here in the fresh ocean air and deep blue skies, she could make new ones.

It would be easy instead to think of Bastien with his shirt off and sunglasses on, perched on the side of the boat waiting for a fish to bite as the boat slowly trolled along. There were six poles in the water baited with squid. They were out for some sailfish, but anything could be biting today.

But she didn't think she could enjoy herself until she addressed what happened last night. Looking around the deck to make sure Captain Lila wasn't nearby, Mikelina stepped in close to Bastien. Her stomach fluttered when he snaked an arm around her and drew her in close. God, she loved the feel of his skin against hers.

"I wanted to ease your mind about something," she said in a lowered voice. "I'm on the pill and I've got a clean bill of health."

Bastien blinked. "That's good. I don't have any diseases either. Um. What brought this on?"

"We didn't use protection last night."

He gaped at her. "You're right. I hadn't even noticed." Rubbing his hand over his face, he groaned. "Of course, if anything comes of it, please let me know what you need."

"Nothing will come of it," she said. "Like I said, I'm on the pill."

"You have my number. Use it if you need to?"

She blinked her eyelashes at him. "New York to Florida is quite the booty call."

"But worth it." He slung his other arm around her waist and brought her in for a quick kiss.

"I think so, too." She grinned. "Do you want me to rub more suntan lotion on your back?"

"After last night, we'd be belowdecks before you know it."

"What would Captain Lila say?" Mikelina asked.

"I wouldn't care. I get paid whether you fish or fuck," Captain Lila said as she walked by, carrying a cooler.

Bastien barked out a laugh. Mikelina was used to her crusty ways and just shook her head.

"I got water, lemonade, iced tea and beer," Captain

Lila said. "Help yourself. We're going to drop anchor for about twenty minutes, but if nothing's biting, I'll take you to another spot."

Mikelina baited her hook and took the chair next to Bastien. She'd probably fall asleep, but that was all right. She was never any good at reeling the fish in. With any luck, they wouldn't get fish at the same time and Bastien could bring it aboard. She hoped they caught something so they could have fresh fish for lunch. Captain Lila cleaned the catches and cooked the fish to order right on the boat with her portable grill. Mikelina wanted hers dipped in egg and panko and fried up. Of course if they didn't catch anything, it would be cold-cut sandwiches.

She remembered one time she tried to use bologna as bait because she figured the fish would like that better instead of a crunchy old crab. Her father had let her and told her not to be disappointed if she lost her bait. Well, she lost her bait all right, but they hit a school of mahi-mahi and it went for her hook anyway. Tanner had been so excited, he almost dropped the pole and together they'd reeled it in.

It was a good thing her sunglasses were on. Turning away, Mikelina wiped the tears away before Bastien could see them.

She didn't want to think about Tanner. She also didn't want to hate her father either, but until he admitted what he'd done instead of staunchly proclaiming his innocence, she wouldn't speak with him. It was like her whole childhood was a lie.

Selena had asked her once if she was sure that he

was guilty. Tanner Presley could be very convincing when he wanted to be.

Mikelina had originally thought it was all one big mistake. But after the FBI seized all their computers, they found the evidence needed to convict. She wished it hadn't been true, but wishes were for children. Adult wishes never came true.

"Penny for your thoughts?" Bastien asked.

Snorting, Mikelina shook her head. He couldn't pay her enough to reveal those thoughts. "I was wondering where your groom and groomsmen are. Do you think they're in trouble?"

"If they were in a Miami jail cell, I'm pretty sure someone would have called me."

"The last time you saw them they were at Flow?"

"Yes."

Mikelina stared at her fishing pole for a second. "I know this is going to sound crazy, but it's possible they were still there."

"At five in the morning? Last call is at two."

She shook her head. "Nope. Flow's open until 5:00 a.m. for the VIPs. And they're not about to kick them out at five on the dot."

"I'm old," Bastien said sourly.

Laughing, she smiled at him. "Time flies when you're having fun and if they were still in the club, their phones would be dead by then."

"I don't think I can do this." He put his arm around her. "I don't want to dislike Jace. But we don't have a damned thing in common."

She liked when he played with her hair like that.

"It doesn't have to be friendship or mortal enemies. You can still have a pleasant acquaintance with him."

"I wanted my sister to marry someone better than him."

"What's wrong with Jace?"

"He's a spoiled little punk who has been given everything he's ever wanted. He's rude, inconsiderate—"

"Whoa!" Mikelina said, holding up a hand. "That's a lot of resentment. No wonder he's avoiding you."

"He's not avoiding me. Why? What did he say to you?"

"Nothing. But I'm sure he can sense all this hostility. Why do you have such a low opinion of him?"

Bastien sighed and angrily jerked on his pole, reeling it in to check his bait. "He and my sister have had a rocky relationship. Jace blows hot and cold. Sometimes he leaves on an adventure with his asshole friends for a week and doesn't think about telling Kitty until after the fact. One time, she had to find out about it on a friend's social media page. She thought he'd broken up with her and just didn't bother to tell her because he had an arm around another girl in the picture."

"That is gross," Mikelina said, scrunching up her nose.

"But it turned out it was just a friend's girlfriend and they all decided to go skiing in the Swiss Alps that week."

"He should have asked your sister to go."

"My sister has a job. She can't just up and leave. Jace knew that. His excuse was he didn't want her to feel bad that he was going away without her. It never occurred to him, though, not to go. YOLO, FOMO and all that crap."

Mikelina thought about it and her bullshit detector was buzzing slightly. "Does she trust him?"

"I don't."

"Yeah, I get that. But does she?"

"Yes, but she sees the best in people. I'm afraid this is just another lark for him and he's not settling down as much as he's doing what his father wants him to do."

"His family wants the marriage?"

"Both our families do. It's a good brand merger, but I want something more for Kitty."

"Does she love him?" Mikelina asked.

"Yes. She can't see what a complete schmuck he is."

"Does he love her?"

"He better."

"Do you think he loves her?" she asked.

Bastien clenched his jaw. "I think so. I was hoping to get a better insight these few weeks. I'm not sure what's an act and what's real when it comes to him. I'm afraid he's going to marry Kitty to shut his family up, and then continue on with his carefree ways. I'm afraid Kitty is going to get hurt."

"I think you're a good brother," she said.

"I think if he's having sex with hookers or strippers, I'm going to kill him." Bastien didn't sound like he was kidding.

"No need to go that far. If he is, I'm sure Kitty will call the wedding off."

"She's going to be hurt, though."

"If he's cheating, she'll be devastated. You going to jail for assault won't make that hurt any easier to bear."

"It would make me feel better."

"No, it would ruin your life," Mikelina said, feeling a pit of dread in her stomach. She was the expert in incarcerated relatives. "Look, if Jace is cheating on her, he's the jerk you say he is. But if he's not, you're getting upset over nothing. Until you have proof, you can't work yourself up into believing he's the devil. Maybe he's just an inconsiderate ass." She shrugged. "That's not a crime. If it was, there would be a lot more people in jail."

"True." Bastien got up and stretched, putting his pole in the rod holder. "I'm going to grab a beer. Do you want one?"

"I'll take a lemonade."

He rooted around in the ice chest until he found one and then brought it back to her.

"Your phone keeps beeping," she said, "but it's not Jace."

"It's the office. I haven't taken a vacation in over two years and I think the place is falling apart without me."

"Is it anything urgent?"

"We make shirts and pants. It's nothing that can't wait two weeks. And if it was, my father or my assistant VP can handle it. It's crazy that they feel the need to check in with me with every decision."

"That sounds like habit. Are you, Mr. Ainsworth, a micromanager?"

He snorted. "No. Who the hell has time for that?"

"Someone who hasn't taken a vacation in two years."

"You think they'd be glad to get rid of me for a few weeks. Hell, I'm surprised they're not throwing a party. It's Taco Tuesday and the prick is out of the office."

"I could go for tacos," Mikelina said. "I wonder if Captain Lila has some taco shells that are still fresh. A little bit of lettuce and chopped tomato would go nicely with some diced and fried mahi-mahi."

"You're making me hungry and we have to catch the damned fish first."

Just then her pole dipped low and almost jerked out of her hand. "Holy shit, I've got something."

Bastien saved the lemonade from going all over the deck as Mikelina hauled back on the rod and started reeling in the line. Once she was convinced the fish was truly hooked, she let out a little line to give herself a break.

"Careful it doesn't dart for the reef or rocks and tangle up the line."

"It's a big one, but it's not a sailfish." She turned the reel faster, her arms and wrists beginning to ache. "I hate being a wimp, but I think I'm going to need you to take over."

He eagerly stepped in. "Let me know when you're ready to hand off."

The rod jerked and she had to tighten her grip. "I'm afraid to let go."

Bastien put his arms around her and held the rod just above her hands. "I got you. You can keep reeling him in. Don't worry about the rod. You can do it."

"He's heavy," Mikelina grunted.

Captain Lila came out with a net. "Get it in close to the boat and I'll scoop it up and help you haul it in."

Grinning, Michelina concentrated on reeling in the line. With Bastien steadying the pole, she didn't have to worry about losing her grip on it. "My hands are killing me," she said, but even though she had to put in more effort, it was worth it to hear Bastien's hoot of delight.

"Look at the size of that thing."

Leaning over the railing, Captain Lila said, "Almost got it."

Then, she scooped the flailing and writhing fish into her net and the three of them brought it aboard.

"That's lunch," Captain Lila said proudly, setting the large dolphin fish in an ice chest while she unhooked it from the rig.

"We did it." Mikelina whirled to hug Bastien.

It was only natural to kiss him.

I really like him.

The thought surprised her and she broke away from him in dismay. She couldn't get too attached, but damn, she wished he was boyfriend material.

"That's a good-looking fish," he said.

Mikelina wrinkled her nose. "It's kinda ugly, but it's yummy. Now it's your turn to catch something."

They fished for the rest of the day. They caught a few amberjacks but tossed them back. Her father always said the big ones had worms in them. Bastien scored a couple of kingfish and was planning on smoking them for dinner. After a great lunch of battered fish sandwiches and fruit salad, Mikelina conked out on a deck chair. She didn't wake up until they pulled into the dock.

"I'm sorry," she said, stifling a yawn.

"Don't be. I was right there snoring with you. This has been a great day." Bastien smiled widely. "I can't remember a nicer time. I'm so glad I got to share this with you."

"Me, too."

She hugged him and his soft kisses made her clutch him close. She didn't want to get off this boat and step back into reality. But he was the client. She was the concierge. They had a full two weeks of scheduled activities.

And they were still missing the groom and his groomsmen.

CHAPTER THIRTEEN

BASTIEN DROPPED MIKELINA back at that awful hotel. "Is this where you stay when you're in South Beach?" he asked, trying to keep the disdain out of his voice.

Mikelina nodded. "Depends on which property, I'm representing. This one is the closest to the beach house."

"Where do you live when you're not working?"

"I'm always working," she said, getting out of the car.

"Don't you have a home base?"

"No, I pretty much live out of my suitcase."

"That must get old."

She came around to the driver's side and leaned down to give him a kiss goodbye. "Yeah, it does. But it's not forever. Give me a call if you need me. Or…" she looked away and blushed "…if you get stood up for snorkeling tomorrow. I know how important keeping to the schedule is to you. You're on your own for parasailing, though."

Mikelina kissed him again, seeming as reluctant to leave him as he was to leave her. After one last soft kiss, she pulled away and touched his cheek. "Enjoy the kingfish," she said, before turning around and going into the hotel.

He watched her walk across the lobby and disappear from his sight. Plugging in his phone to charge, he drove back to the beach house. He had a few missed messages, but he didn't bother checking them. He was still riding high from the day and he wanted to keep the feeling of peace and happiness he had with Mikelina a little while longer.

Unfortunately, he heard the music a block from the house. Jace and his friends were having a party with a bunch of strangers. Bastien tried to sneak in with the cooler of fish, but Jace caught sight of him.

"Where you been, bro?"

"Fishing." He held up the cooler. "Where were you guys?"

"That was today?" Jace slapped his forehead. "I totally forgot. Jet lag and late nights. Come on and meet everyone."

"Let me put this in the fridge." He was considering putting the schedule on the fridge, too, but he thought that might be too subtle. They should all have the itinerary in their phones by now. He'd texted it to them last night.

"What?" Jace said.

Bastien didn't try to shout over the music. He put the cooler in the refrigerator and joined Jace and twenty of his new best friends around the house. The groomsmen were making out with women in bikinis.

Bastien's jaw clenched, but it didn't look like there was a beach babe hovering around Jace.

"We met these guys last night at Flow." Jace then proceeded to introduce him to everyone who wasn't kissing and groping each other. Bastien didn't hear or remember a single name, and to be honest, he didn't care to.

He was getting a pounding headache. He wanted to go back to Mikelina's hotel. Actually, he wanted to bring her back here and kick the bachelor party out. But that wasn't why they were in South Beach, so he grabbed a beer and forced himself to mingle with the guests.

After about an hour, he had a splitting headache and his patience was fraying. It was impossible to hold a conversation because of the music and he was damned sure not going to be labeled as the old fart who told the party to lower it. Gritting his teeth, he forced his way through the crowd to Jace who was smoking cigars with a few guys in suits. They didn't look like the rest of the beach bum crowd so Bastien wanted to make sure Jace wasn't in trouble.

Jace looked over his shoulder and caught sight of him approaching and a flash of something went over his face.

Uh-oh.

He said something to the men and then intercepted Bastien before he could get closer.

"Rad party, right? I love this house. I wish I could live here forever. Do you think Kitty would like this place?"

Distracted by his sister's name, Bastien frowned. "Sure, but her job is in New York."

"Maybe as a vacation home then. I'll have to check with the hottie concierge and see if the owner is interested in selling. It would make a good wedding gift for Kitty, don't you think?"

Bastien nodded. "Who are those guys?"

"Just some guys we met at Flow. Hey, sorry about missing the boat. We wouldn't have been good company anyway, we just got up a few hours ago. But we're ready to dance and drink all night, right?"

He whooped the last few words, bringing a loud cheer among the guests. Then he proceeded to drag Bastien over to a group of giggling drunk girls, who surrounded him. Not one of them held a candle to Mikelina, but he didn't want to leave the group in case they turned their flirting onto Jace.

The neighbors put up with them until about midnight when they called the cops. Mikelina showed up shortly after the squad cars did.

She looked sun kissed and annoyed. She had thrown on a pale green wraparound dress that matched her eyes and the same flip-flops she had worn on the boat. Her hair was pulled back into a rough ponytail. He wanted to go over to her, but since Bastien was the only sober person, he had been delegated to talk with the police officers.

After turning off the music, most of the partygoers faded off before the police looked too closely at them. A few girls were looking for their bikini tops. Bastien pretended not to see the side-eye that Mikelina shot him.

"Just keep it down for the rest of the night," one of the cops said. "I get it's a bachelor party, but this is a residential area of older folks."

"Yeah," his partner said, with a hard stare at Mikelina.

Mikelina pretended not to notice and righted a vase that had tipped over.

Bastien hoped they weren't blaming her for this. "I apologize, officers. We'll be more considerate of our neighbors."

"Thanks." The first cop tapped his partner on the arm, who reluctantly turned away from Mikelina and then they left together.

"What was that about? You know that guy?"

Mikelina shrugged. "It's a small community here. I'm sure we've run into each other."

"He didn't seem to like you. Are you in trouble?"

"Me?" She laughed. "No. I don't even have a parking ticket."

Bastien couldn't help but wonder what roused the cop's suspicion. Maybe the owner of the beach house had reported her using it when it wasn't rented.

"I know we've only known each other a few days," he said, taking a deep breath. He wasn't sure how to broach the subject without embarrassing her. "But we have been conversing for a couple of months. And we've recently become more intimate friends."

"Friends?" A ghost of a smile traced over her face.

He rubbed his hand up her arm. "If you need something, I'd like to help."

"See, you are kind."

Bastien snorted. "I'm a prick. Just ask my sister."

"Thanks for offering, but I've got it covered."

"Okay, just keep it in the back of your mind that I'm here if you need me."

"I will." Mikelina hugged herself and looked out into the pool area. "I see you found them," she said, gesturing to Jace and his friends who hadn't left the pool to see their guests out. "Where were they?"

"You were right. They were still at Flow partying. I'm glad I missed it. Sorry you had to come all the way out here tonight," Bastien said, not sorry at all.

"The alarm company informed me of a dispatch call to the house and I was worried." Mikelina was walking around the house, frowning at the mess.

"Don't worry, we'll tip the maids extra."

Her smile looked forced. "I'm glad no one was hurt."

"They'll be hurting tomorrow. I wouldn't want their hangover."

She stepped over a pile of soaked towels. He saw her look at the closed bedroom door and caught a flash of relief that flickered in her eyes. Did she think he was sleeping with the girls at the party?

He caught a hold of her arm until she looked at him. "As crazy as it sounds, I wish you had come back here with me after fishing. Tonight would have been much more enjoyable if you were with me."

"It's not my place to be here," she said sadly.

"It is if I say so." He brushed a quick kiss on her lips and then moved away before anyone noticed. He could spend all night kissing her, but he didn't want Jace to know about Mikelina and him. Not yet. Bastien didn't trust the punk not to treat her like a sex worker instead of their concierge and Kitty would never forgive him if Bastien punched Jace out at his bachelor party.

"Micky," Jace said, staggering in.

Bastien took a step toward him. He didn't want Jace to get in her personal space. Not when he reeked of whiskey and cigars.

"I'm so glad you're here. I want to talk to you."

"You can talk to her tomorrow," Bastien said.

"No, that's all right," Mikelina said. "It's my job. What can I do for you, Mr. Benjamin?"

"Jace. Call me Jace. Mr. Benjamin is my father and he's no fun at all. I want to send my girl something cool from Florida. What do you recommend?"

"Does she like jewelry?"

Jace snorted. "She's a woman, isn't she?"

Mikelina exchanged an amused glance with Bastien. "There's a local artisan who does beautiful work with larimar and silver. Larimar is a light blue stone that some people say reminds them of the tropical waters. I could get an assortment and bring it to you. I think maybe a cuff bracelet or a necklace and earring set would be a nice gift."

Jace nodded and pointed. "All that. I trust you. You've got good taste. Wrap it up and send it to her."

"Don't you want to see it first?"

He shook his head. "I'm not feeling well." Then, his eyes rolled back in his head.

Bastien darted out and caught him before he hit the floor. "Douchebag," he muttered. "Zack! Max! Shane! Get in here and help me with this."

The three stooges staggered in.

"Why don't you guys take Jace up to his room?"

The three of them hauled Jace up and they took the stairs, weaving and cursing.

"We might have to postpone the snorkeling." Bastien looked over at her thoughtfully. "Unless you'd like to go with me?"

"I thought you were supposed to be spending time with your pending brother-in-law." Mikelina jerked a thumb at the four men who were banging into the walls and faltering on their upstairs climb.

Bastien leaned in to her so their lips were almost touching. She licked her lips and he almost groaned at the sight of it. He wanted to lift her up on the kitchen island, ease down her panties and slide his cock inside her.

Her breath caught and he wondered if he'd said that last part aloud.

"I did my time tonight. I deserve a break. I think they're going to sleep until after lunch. So that leaves the morning free for us. Are you interested?"

Mikelina bit her lip. "I am interested. If you're sure you're not doing this to avoid spending time with them."

"That's a perk. I have to admit it. But I'd rather be with you."

She caught her breath. "I'd like that, too."

"Let me walk you out to your car," he said, before he was tempted to fuck her in the kitchen while the four drunken idiots bumbled around upstairs.

It was blissfully quiet, although he could sense the neighbors' rage through their tightly closed windows.

"Was Jace serious about the jewelry for Kitty?" she asked.

"Yup, and I'll remind him of it when I see him. Put it on the bill. I'll text you the address to send it to." Sheltered by the darkness, he took her into his arms and covered her mouth with his.

"Bastien," she murmured, stepping away from him. "I don't want to give the neighbors something else to talk about. If you don't stop kissing me, I'll strip you naked and take you on the front lawn."

"Works for me." He bent to kiss her again, delighted that this crazy passion wasn't one-sided.

She gave him a playful shove. "Pick me up at nine so we can grab breakfast before we go out snorkeling. Unless…" she tugged on his shirt "…you want to come back home with me?"

Looking up at the second floor of the house, Bastien sighed. "I'd love to, but I should stick around and make sure they don't drown in their own puke. I couldn't care less, but Kitty would be heartbroken."

"You're a good brother." She put her hand on his cheek. "And like I said, kind."

He put her other hand on his cock. "I'm a prick."

Mikelina's eyes half closed as she stroked his hardness.

"You could stay here with me," he said, trying not to undo her jeans so he could play with her, too. "I'm pretty sure they're not going to know the difference."

"Tempting," she crooned. "So tempting, but I'm trying to be professional. And on the off chance that they catch me here, I don't want them to think I'm part of the service."

"The first one that does gets a bloody nose."

"You're so violent," she said against his mouth.

"I thought I was kind."

Then they were kissing again while she rubbed his cock. "You're going to make me come in my pants," he muttered.

"Take your pants off." She sighed.

The lights came on across the street, illuminating the driveway. Mikelina jumped away from him as if it was a searchlight. "I need to go. Sorry I couldn't finish what I started."

He opened the car door for her. "You can make it up to me tomorrow."

As she drove away, Bastien adjusted himself. Mikelina made him feel like a teenager again. And she made him want to throw his itinerary out the window and pleasure her all night long.

But this wasn't his vacation. It was Jace's bachelor party. He went upstairs to check on the idiots and found them all passed out in a puppy puddle on the common room floor between the bedrooms. Nobody was flat on their stomach and most of them were snoring away in drunken bliss. He snapped a picture and sent it to Kitty. Hopefully, he wouldn't wake her and she'd see it in the morning.

He picked up the soaking wet towels off the living room floor so they wouldn't damage it and tossed them into the laundry room for the maids to take care of in the morning.

As he was leaving, his eyes caught on a box marked Mikelina on the shelf. Curious, he reached up and brought it down. He supposed he should feel guilty for snooping, but it was right out there in the open.

There were cosmetic bags and other zippered bags that he didn't bother to open. Her clothes from the other night were folded neatly in there along with a purse and a few paperback books.

Confused, he put the box back where he found it. Why was it even here? Unless she was staying here when it was empty. He was sure that was against the rules and that the property owner would be pretty pissed if he knew about it. Walking into his bedroom, he opened up the walk-in closet and pressed the attic button.

He climbed the stairs that unfolded, sat down in the attic space and looked around. There were moving boxes and plastic bins filled with clothes and dishes. More boxes marked Mikelina, Tawny and Tanner. He wondered who they were and why their stuff was here.

Feeling guilty for snooping, he turned off the light and closed up the attic. It wasn't any of his business, but he wondered if Mikelina might have lost her apartment and was storing her things in the places she was a concierge for. He didn't want to get her in trouble or embarrass her by bringing it up.

Still, he couldn't stop that niggling feeling that he was missing something huge. It felt like it did when he found out Gina had been using him for his money. Was Mikelina playing him for a fool, too? Or was he just being paranoid?

She seemed too perfect to be real. It didn't stop him from having erotic dreams about her that night, though.

CHAPTER FOURTEEN

IN RETROSPECT, MIKELINA should have had them rent equipment and shuttled them down to South Pointe Park and had them snorkel close to shore at the Jose Cuervo Reef. And if Jace and his buddies had decided to snorkel this morning, she might have suggested it. Instead, Bastien insisted that she and he follow the schedule and they wound up at Biscayne National Park with a tour guide that didn't give them a moment's privacy, even underwater.

It was informative and while Mikelina had heard it all before, she could see that Bastien was enjoying himself. And she had to admit she got as excited as he did when they saw the pod of dolphins in the distance.

When it was time to get onto the paddleboards, they had a good time trying to knock each other off. When that got tiring, they lounged on them, floating in the water while the guide looked on from the boat.

"Having fun?" Mikelina asked.

"The guys would have hated this," he said. "Too much education. But I liked it. Kitty would have liked it, too. Maybe Jace will take her down here sometime. He loved the house. Do you know if the owner is willing to sell it?"

"No." As in hell no.

"Because I'm pretty sure they could name their price."

But it was tempting. Mikelina knew she could get a few million for the house and she wouldn't have to worry about her mother or have to work so hard. She could afford to buy her mother as well as herself a house.

But it wouldn't be in South Beach. And the new houses wouldn't have memories of when they were a family. The beach house was the only thing left of that time, after everything had been liquidated for the lawsuits and lawyer fees.

"It's a family house and it means a lot to them," she said.

"Would you do me a favor and just double-check with the owners? Jace has more money than he knows what to do with. It would be a quick sale."

"Okay." Mikelina might bring up the subject with her mother, but she already knew her mother would burst into tears over the thought of being "homeless"— even though she wouldn't be homeless for very long. She knew Tawny was waiting for Tanner to be acquitted and they could all live happily ever after again. But with each passing day Mikelina grew more certain that was never going to happen. Not when her father was still so unrepentant about what he had done.

Had he always been a crook or was it one mistake that snowballed into a life of crime? What had caused him to cheat people out of their money? She had asked her mother if they had been in trouble financially and Tawny had said no. Their bank accounts and credit hadn't taken a hit either. So why did he do it?

Tanner said he was innocent.

And if she hadn't read the files the FBI found on his computer, she would have believed him. She rolled off her board and swam down as far as she could to clear her head. She didn't want to think about her father the thief. She wanted to remember her father as the guy who smelled like English leather and took her to see the *Lord of the Rings* trilogy when it played back-to-back in the theater.

She kicked back to the surface just as she was about to run out of breath. She took in a deep lungful as she held on to her board.

"You okay?" Bastien asked sleepily.

"Yeah." She'd get there.

"I wanted to get some pictures of parrotfish on the reef down there. Kitty is a *Finding Nemo* fan."

"Nemo was a clown fish."

"How do you know that?"

"Everybody knows that, Bastien." She hauled herself up on the board and giggled when he tickled her butt. "You're not going to find Nemo in these waters."

"Oh well, I didn't want to get off my board anyway."

She smiled. "What are Jace and the boys doing today?"

"I don't care." Bastien's voice was muffled because his face was resting on his arms. She thought he might fall asleep on his board.

"That's a start. I'm proud of you. This is all very spontaneous."

He yawned. "No, it's not. I'm following the schedule, even if they're not."

"Do you think they're going to stick around the house all day?"

"I can't imagine they're going clubbing again, but who the hell knows? At my bachelor party, we were riding in airplanes and shooting automatic weapons. But we were in Vegas."

"Your bachelor party?" Mikelina tried to keep her voice down, but she heard the outrage in it. "You're married?"

"God, no." He lifted his head up to stare at her. He held out his left hand. No ring. "Not for five years, no. We're divorced. Happily divorced. I'm not even seeing anyone. In fact…" he frowned "…you're the first woman I've slept with in over a year. Damn, no wonder I'm all over you. Not that you're not irresistible, because you are."

"Nice recovery. It's been about that long for me, too."

"Why?" he asked, sounding aghast. "Are the men in South Beach idiots?"

"I travel a lot," she said. "I meet a lot of jerks."

"I'm sorry about that. You deserve to meet someone who treats you like a queen."

"You're doing all right."

"I'm a prick, remember?"

"I remember your prick." She tried to push him off the paddleboard, but he was too heavy. She wound up pushing herself away from him instead.

"I would hope you remember it. Although, I am regretting not going home with you last night. It would be fresher in both of our minds if I got to make love to you last night."

"No regrets," she said. "No matter what happens these next few days, I don't want you to have any regrets."

"Then I think I want you in my bed. Or in your bed. Up against the wall. I'm not picky. I was fantasizing fucking you on the kitchen island last night." He dragged her board back to his so they were touching. "Will you be my girlfriend for the next week and a half?"

Mikelina had to laugh. "I don't know if I can commit to that."

"Why not?" he growled.

"Because I might not want to let you go after the bachelor party is over."

Bastien was quiet for such a long time, she was afraid that she had made it weird and awkward. Just as she was about to make a joke to hopefully smooth things over, he said, "I'm willing to take that chance."

"Are you?" she said, her heart suddenly pounding loud in her ears.

"We've got something going on already. It's chemistry, sure. Pure unadulterated lust, that's for damned sure. But I really like you, Mikelina. It doesn't have to end when I go back to New York."

For a moment, she was elated. Once the bachelor party was gone, she wouldn't have to worry so much about her reputation.

But then she remembered who her father was. She'd have to tell Bastien about him if they were going to have a relationship beyond these two weeks.

"Let's get through the bachelor party first," she said breathlessly.

"You want to follow the schedule?" he asked. "Where's your spontaneity?"

"I think you're rubbing off on me."

He groaned. "I'd love to rub off on you."

After lunch on board the sailboat that had been giving them a tour of the bay, it was time to head back to the beach house. Bastien had a cookout scheduled with an ocean's worth of seafood that was sitting in the fridge. She only hoped that Jace, Zack, Shane and Max would be around to help eat it.

Back at the park, Mikelina grabbed her backpack from the lockers. "I'm going to get changed. I'll be right out."

Bastien was still talking with the guide, so he just nodded and waved.

She walked into the changing room. It was empty so she had her pick of the little stalls. Closing the bamboo shade, she stripped out of her wet suit and toweled herself off. She was having fun despite it being on borrowed time. For Bastien's sake, though, she hoped the guys would make it an early night so they could all go parasailing tomorrow. She sure as hell wasn't going to go up four hundred feet in the air.

The door of the changing room opened and she peeked out of the curtain. She was surprised to see that Bastien had followed her in.

"Shh," he said, coming inside the little cubicle with her.

Sliding the curtain back into place, he pushed her up against the wall. He kissed her like he couldn't wait a moment longer. He slid his fingers between her thighs as his tongue teased her. She was wet. Of course she was, and Bastien was tickling her into a quick orgasm. Mikelina didn't want to rush, but she was afraid they were going to get caught.

"What are you doing here?" she whispered when he came up for air. She moaned softly and went up on her tiptoes as he worked his fingers inside her.

"I couldn't wait until we got home. Hell, I couldn't wait to get into the car."

She reached down into his bathing suit and grabbed hold of his thick cock. "We've got to be quick. We can take our time later."

"I like the sound of that." He groaned quietly and pressed against her hand. He went back to flicking his fingers over her clit, and she moved her hips, wanting more.

"I need to taste you," he muttered and dropped to his knees. Casting her leg over his shoulder, he pulled her pussy in close to his face. "Damn." He licked her deep. "You taste amazing." Then he buried his face between her legs.

She had to cover her mouth to silence the cries that erupted from her. The rasp of his stubble and the cool wall of the cubicle added to the naughty feeling of doing this where anyone could walk in.

She came hard on his face and writhed when he didn't let her go. She was nearly wild with the need to have him inside her, when he tongued her to a second orgasm.

"I could do that all night," he said, breathing heavily.

"I'd let you," she said, quivering from head to toe. She dropped to her knees, taking his bathing suit with her, and moved her mouth over his cock.

Tangling his fingers through her hair, he rocked his hips into her eager mouth. She loved the thick, salty taste of him and hummed in pleasure.

Bastien cursed and held her there until she looked up at him. "I could watch you do that for hours." He let her go and she grabbed hold of his shaft and pumped it while sucking hard on the head of his cock.

He hissed between his teeth. "Baby, I'm going to either come in your mouth or your pussy. It's up to you."

After one last hard suck, she licked up his entire length and said, "Come in my pussy."

"Fuck," he groaned and sat down on the bench. "Get on my cock."

She straddled his lap, glad that they no longer

had to worry about condoms. Mikelina eased him inside her.

They stayed like that, foreheads touching. He was as deep as he could go inside her and she enjoyed feeling the entire length of him. "I needed this," she whispered against his mouth as she lifted herself up and down his shaft.

Grabbing her head, he pressed his mouth to her and moaned loudly. She couldn't stop to tell him to be quiet; it was too good to feel him slide in and out of her.

Bastien stood up, taking her with him and pressed her against the wall of the cubicle. Her arms and legs wrapped tight around him as he pounded into her. She was glad they were alone because the hard thumps on the wall made it pretty clear what they were doing. But she didn't care. She needed him this hard, this deep and completely out of his mind wanting her.

"Yes," she whispered. "Just like that."

"So wet. Can you hear how wet you are?" He glided in deep and fast. Her toes curled. The walls of her pussy clamped around him.

Bastien's teeth were bared in a pleasured grimace and he exploded inside her. He kept up the pace, slowing down only when her orgasm shuddered through them both. Then, he idly fucked her until she began to shake and her legs felt like Jell-O.

"Had enough?"

"For now," she said, wincing at the slight ache in her back.

"I didn't hurt you, did I?" He rubbed between her shoulders and at the base of her spine.

"I wouldn't say no to a massage."

"I know where we can find some oil." Bastien stroked her bottom lip with his thumb. "I want you again and I just had you."

The door opened to the changing room and they froze. Bastien smirked and reached between her thighs. She swatted his hand away and peeked through a curtain. A woman and her two children were getting undressed.

"Hurry up," the mother said as the two kids began to chatter and fidget.

"Now what?" Mikelina whispered in his ear.

"We be quiet." He rolled her nipple in between his thumb and forefinger. She bit his lower lip in retaliation.

"You want to play rough?" he growled in her ear and smacked her on the ass. It sounded loud in the dressing room. But it didn't seem like the mother or the two kids noticed.

"Clean up and get dressed," Mikelina said, throwing him one of the towels.

He wiped off and pulled up his bathing trunks and leaned up against the wall with his arms folded.

"It's like a reverse striptease," he said quietly.

She put her finger against her lips and glared at him to keep it down. She got dressed, her movements slow and jerky because she kept staring into Bastien's hungry eyes.

"I want you," he mouthed and she trembled because she could still feel him fucking her. Her entire body was on fire for him.

When she was completely dressed, she launched herself at him and they kissed until the mother and her two kids left.

"I can't believe we didn't get caught," she choked out, hanging on to him.

"Let's get out of here before I'm tempted to strip down again and go for round two."

They left the changing room together, arms slung around each other, and walked back to the car. Mikelina felt eyes on her and she tried to track down the source. Had someone seen them after all? Looking around, she saw a group of people about to take a snorkeling tour. Scanning the crowd, she recognized a few people she used to hang around the beach with during spring break.

She lifted her hand up to wave to them, but they glared at her and turned their backs.

It was too good to hope that Bastien hadn't noticed.

"Who's that?"

"No one. Someone I thought I knew."

CHAPTER FIFTEEN

BASTIEN WAS TRYING to figure out a way he could have Mikelina and the house all to himself tonight, but his brain was still mush from the excellent sex in the changing room. He glanced over and smiled at Mikelina fast asleep in her seat. She was beautiful and he was looking forward to finding out all her secrets and getting to know her better outside of the bedroom as well as inside.

He had a bunch of messages on his phone, but he didn't want to disturb Mikelina by listening to them while he was driving. He didn't want to take her to her crappy hotel. He wanted to hang out with her at the beach house. Maybe she could help him and Jace ease into a better relationship or something.

Mikelina woke up as they pulled into the beach house. "I'm sorry," she yawned. "I can't believe I fell asleep."

"I can. We've had a very busy schedule."

"We've had a very pleasurable schedule." She glanced out the window. "I shouldn't be here at the house."

"We'll make up a story. We'll say that you've come to check in on how things were doing and how they're feeling. Jace will want to know that you mailed off the larimar set to Kitty today."

She considered it for a moment. "All right, that works."

Good. He wasn't ready to say goodbye to her yet. Turned out that he didn't have to worry because the house was empty. Finally. Finally, something was going his way.

"I'm going to check my messages and find out where they are. Keep your fingers crossed that whatever they're up to will keep them out of the house long enough for us to skinny-dip in the pool and then barricade ourselves in the bedroom all night."

"I'm going to make some coffee," she said, smiling. "Do you want some?"

"Damned right I do. I need to keep up my energy."

"That's what I like to hear." Mikelina slapped his ass on the way by.

"Payback is a bitch," he warned her.

"That's okay," she said. "So am I."

"Feisty. I like that."

"Check your messages." Mikelina tossed off her shirt. He liked the sexy lace bra she wore, but he'd like it better on the floor. "We may not have much time. We may have to skip right to the barricading part."

He saw his father called once. He could wait. His office called twice. They could wait, too. Especially since Mikelina had just tossed her shorts into the room. Bastien had to stop himself from going into the kitchen and taking her on the island like he had been fantasizing about. Thankfully, Jace had texted him a few hours ago. Bastien scrolled down and nearly dropped the phone.

Gone to the casino. Don't wait up.

Fear shot through him. What if Jace was doing to Kitty what Gina had done to Bastien? He had to check it out. He wouldn't let Kitty go through the devastation of being married to a gambling addict. Been there. Done that. Burned the T-shirt.

"Mikelina," he shouted.

"What?" she said, coming back into the room in her sexy underwear, carrying two espressos.

Bastien was completely distracted at the sight. "Wow," he sighed. She took his breath away.

"Is everything all right?"

He closed his eyes and shook his head to clear it. "No. I've got a problem. Where are the nearest casinos?"

"Uh, the Gulfstream is the closet, but it only has slots, poker and horse racing. The Hard Rock casino has all the table games, but that's about an hour away with traffic. Why?"

"Jace and the boys went to a casino. I need to find him. Let's start at the Gulfstream and go from there."

"Why?" She put the coffees on the table. "Why can't you let them enjoy their night while we stay here and enjoy ours?"

Bastien rubbed his hand over his face. It was so very tempting to do just that. But he'd never forgive himself if he could have warned Kitty and he didn't. "I'll tell you on the way. Will you come with me?"

"Sure, but I'm not dressed for the casino." She indicated her underwear.

He could have groaned in frustration.

"But neither are you," she said.

"What's wrong with what I'm wearing?" He was in shorts and a T-shirt.

"Too casual," she said.

"Who cares? We need to hurry."

"The bouncers will care. If Jace and his friends are in the exclusive sections, we need to dress the part if we want to get in there, too."

Figured. He didn't want to waste the time to drive her back to her hotel. "Do you have anything that will work in your crates upstairs?" he asked.

She froze. "Did you go up there?"

Busted. He nodded.

"Why? That part of the house is off-limits."

"Is it off-limits to you?"

"Obviously not," she huffed.

"Does the owner know you use it for storage?"

"Not that it's any of your business, but yes. I told you I don't have a home base, so I keep the stuff that doesn't travel well here. Satisfied?" She raised an eyebrow at him.

"Yeah, I was just asking." Bastien had hoped that if she needed help, she would have used this opportunity to ask him, but maybe it was as she said and she and the owner had a deal going on. If Jace did buy the house, Mikelina would have to move her stuff. He wanted to ask her who Tanner and Tawny were, but maybe they were the owners.

"Well, now you know." Mikelina flounced off into his bedroom, presumably to get dressed.

Bastien drank his coffee and tried not to freak out. He looked up the casino on his phone. The Seminole Hard Rock was more Jace's speed, but he might have stayed local. The Gulfstream, on the other hand, was just across town. It was way tiny compared to the Native American casinos in Connecticut, but the lure of flashing slots and horse racing could have tempted Jace if he was truly addicted.

When Mikelina returned a few minutes later, she was in a short, black, sequined dress with sparkly, strappy shoes that he'd like her to leave on when she wrapped her legs around him.

"Wow," he said again.

But when he approached her, she crossed her arms over her chest and said, "You should wear a suit."

Mikelina wanted to stay mad at him for snooping around the attic, but it was difficult when he looked that good in a custom-tailored suit. Most men looked like *Men in Black*, but Bastien looked like a cross between a hot mobster and a fashion model. Besides, he hadn't made a big deal out of the attic and had dropped the subject, so it was a win. She'd rather be skinny-dipping in the pool and making love in her bed, but if he couldn't concentrate until he tracked down Jace, she'd be happy to help.

"What's so important about finding Jace?"

Bastien gripped the wheel. "My ex-wife Gina was an addict. She was addicted to gambling. She hid it from me until just a few days after we got married—in Vegas, which probably should have been my first clue. I'm just a little paranoid that Jace is hiding a similar addiction."

"Has he shown any similar behavior before this?" she asked. "Because it could just be a case of they wanted to play some slots or watch the horse racing."

"Or it could be that he's losing big and is hiding a gambling debt that my private eye didn't find."

Mikelina made a face. "You had him investigated?"

"Damn right."

"And the PI didn't find anything."

"Well, no."

"And you still don't trust Jace?"

Bastien didn't have anything to say about that, but Mikelina was beginning to feel sorry for Jace. She'd ditch Bastien if he treated her this way, too.

"You have issues. Don't you think you're being too rough on Jace? Maybe he's rebelling against the schedule and your disapproval?"

"I'm trying to give him the benefit of the doubt, but he makes it hard. He hasn't gone on one scheduled event. I could have done nothing and still had this week go off the same."

"Sometimes you have to throw the schedule to the wind, even if you worked really hard on it. Embrace the spontaneity."

"I'd like to embrace you," he said.

"There's still time for you to turn around and go skinny-dipping."

"You're killing me," he said.

"I think it's more self-inflicted."

"I wouldn't be able to relax and enjoy our time. Not until this question is out of my head."

"All right," she said. "I'll humor you. But if you think I'm not going to try my hand on a few slot machines, you're crazy. Mama needs a new pair of shoes."

He smirked and she was glad he was starting to lighten up a bit.

"I admit, I'm a little gun-shy when it comes to marriage, but I am worried for my sister. They broke up a year ago when he took her for granted. I told you about him leaving for trips and not telling her? They had a fight. I don't know even what it was about and he didn't call or text or return her messages for two weeks."

"So he has a history of disappearing," Mikelina said. "No wonder you're on his ass so much."

"I want to trust him, but he's done this before and it doesn't look like he's changed his ways."

"Do you know if he's ghosting your sister this week?"

"He talked to her the other day. I don't want to call her and get her worried in case he is. Until I have proof, I want her to think he's having too much fun with me to check in every day. She'd be all right with that."

"It's putting you in a tough spot."

"At this point, I'd be happy if I don't even see him for the next week and a half. But I want to make sure he's not screwing around or hurting my sister by doing shitty things."

"I can understand that. What are you going to do when you find him?" she asked.

"I'm going to peacefully observe."

"That's it?"

"That's it. If he is just out for a good time, more power to them. I'll buy them a few rounds of drinks and buy them a suite so they can stay the night. Then you and I are going to go home and spend some quality time together in that beautiful house."

"And if they're not?" she asked.

"I'll let Kitty handle it. After seeing what Gina put me through, she's not going to accept any bullshit from a gambling addict."

The Gulfstream had more shops than they did poker tables and the big draw was the off-track betting and the horses. Still, the lights and sounds were set up for maximum excitement and as she strolled around the casino looking for Jace and his friends, she couldn't resist the siren call of the slot machines.

"You mean to tell me you're not going to put a few quarters in these slots?" she asked as she won ten dollars.

"Do you want me to tell you the odds of winning?"

"Never tell me the odds," she grumbled in her best Han Solo impersonation.

"Three thousand seven hundred and twenty to one."

She blinked at him. "Did you just quote *Star Wars* back at me? That's like nerd foreplay. First Doctor Who and then this. I think there's a movie marathon in our future."

"There are a lot of things in our future." He brought her hand up to his mouth and kissed the back of it.

Mikelina sighed. She forgave him for snooping in her closet. Maybe she should come clean and tell him everything. She would. After the bachelor party. That way if he didn't want to associate with her because of her father, she could move on because he'd be going back to New York. If she did it while the party was still going on, she'd still have to face him in order to do her job.

As they continued to walk through the poker room, the thick smoke began to tickle the back of her throat. "I wish the casinos were smoke-free."

"Can you imagine the money they would lose having people step out for a cigarette break?"

"You're cynical."

"Damned straight. Hey, isn't that your boss?" Bastien nodded to the screens that showed the horse races.

Kirk Diamonte was placing a bet, but that wasn't what held her attention. Hanging on to his arm and looking up at him adoringly was her mother. Mikelina had to steady herself on Bastien as she craned her neck to keep them in sight while Bastien methodically went up and down the rows looking for Jace.

"Excuse me a minute," she said when they were about to get out of line of sight of her mother. "Keep looking. I'll be right back."

Kirk and Tawny were watching the screen intently. Mikelina approached them, unsure what she was going to say. She knew they were friends, but there was something in their body language that caused her to look twice. It was confirmed when Kirk's horse won and Tawny threw her arms around his neck and gave him a kiss that dropped Mikelina's jaw. It was similar to the kisses she and Bastien had shared.

"Mom?" she said, gawking at them.

Tawny broke away from Kirk and stared at her, equally shocked.

"What are you doing here?" they asked each other at the same time.

"I'm with a client." Mikelina turned to Kirk. "Bastien thinks Jace is here and I offered to show him around if he's not."

"Good work," Kirk said.

"Why were you kissing my mother?" she asked.

"I wanted to," he said.

"You know she's married," Mikelina said, crossing her arms.

Kirk waved his winning ticket. "I'm going to cash out. Tawny, why don't you address that with your daughter?"

After he walked away, Mikelina whirled to face her mother. "What is going on here?"

"I probably should have told you sooner, but there was never the right time."

"Tell me what?"

"I'm divorcing your father."

Mikelina couldn't hear anything over the roaring in her ears. "Does Dad know this?"

"He was served papers yesterday. I was going to tell you, but you rushed me off the phone so quickly last time."

"Divorce? Mom, are you sure?"

"Trust me. I've been thinking about divorcing Tanner ever since it happened. It's taken months for me to get up the courage to do it. But now that the papers have been served, I feel so free."

"I don't know what to say or how to feel," Mikelina said honestly.

"It'll take time. I know it did for me. But in the end, I feel it's for the best for my sanity. I can't go on living in limbo waiting for your father's appeal trial or after he's been granted parole in a few years. I don't want to waste my life or my time on someone who doesn't have my best interests at heart. I know Tanner is your father and you love him, but Tanner has always been about himself. I need more."

"Is that why you were kissing my boss?"

"Kirk and I go way back, you know that. He's an attractive man with a fat bank account and he doesn't mind spending it on me. You should find yourself a guy like that. Take him for a ride, enjoy yourself.

You're young. Enjoy it. And whatever you do, don't tie yourself down to a man who doesn't know how to have fun. Now, if you'll excuse me, I'm going to see if Kirk will buy me something pretty with his winnings. I'll call you later in the week." Tawny kissed her cheek and wandered off to find Kirk.

"Interesting advice," Bastien said from behind her. His hands were jammed into his pockets and he was glaring at her.

"I guess." Mikelina's head was whirling. Her parents were getting divorced.

"Who was that?"

Mikelina thought about lying, but she didn't want to start now. It was bad enough she was going all out to keep Bastien from finding out her last name. "That was my mom," she said faintly.

"Is Kirk your father?"

Mikelina barked out a laugh. "I wish. No. He's just a family friend."

"Looks like more than friends to me."

"I guess it's gotten a bit more serious." She looked into his eyes. He still looked on edge, but it was replaced with curiosity. "That was a bit of a shock."

"I take it you don't get along with your father?"

"That would be safe to say, and since my mother just told me she filed for divorce yesterday, my guess is it's over between them. I'm not sure how I feel about it."

"Was your dad surprised?"

"Wouldn't you be?" Mikelina was desperate to get off this subject. "I don't think Jace is here," she said. "Let's take the drive to Hard Rock and see if they're there."

"Are you okay?"

"I will be. I just need a distraction. Let's stop on the way for snacks and we can listen to the music or discuss geeky TV shows. I don't care. Anything. I need to get out of here. It's getting hard to breathe."

She hurried toward the exit, not even looking back to see if he was following her.

But Jace wasn't at the Hard Rock and he and his dipshit friends weren't answering their phones either. "I've about had enough of their shit," Mikelina said and then winced. They were paying her to put up with their shit.

"Is there another casino?"

"Yeah, but we went to the most popular ones." She rattled off a few, one of which she wouldn't be caught dead in.

The next casino they went to had a live racetrack and Mikelina schmoozed the desk to let them go down to the horse pens.

"Tell me again why I had to get dressed up like this to dodge horse shit?"

"Smile for the camera," she said to him, handing him a glass of champagne as they appeared on the big screen for the entire casino to see. "Tell me that if Jace and his friends are here, they wouldn't want to be down here with us. Enough of this running around. Let them come to us if they're here."

"You're smart and beautiful. I like that in a woman."

They made their way to the showing pen where

the jockey led around a horse with a red number five on his bard.

"He's a pretty one," Mikelina said as the jockey patted the horse and crooned to him. "We should bet on him. Do you know anything about horses?"

"My dad always said bet on the one that does his business before the race."

"That's profound."

"That's my dad. Did your dad have any nuggets of wisdom like that?"

Did he? Mikelina couldn't even remember. It was like her brain stalled on seeing him taken out of the courtroom in cuffs. "About horse racing?" she said, recalling an old joke. "Don't bet on a horse named Jetlag."

"Was it expected? The divorce?"

"No, I suppose I should have known it was coming. They've been separated for over a year. I guess I just thought they'd always be together. It's a bit of a shock to see my mom with another man. I mean, how would you feel?"

"Yeah, you're right. It would be uncomfortable. I'd feel twisted. Like I wouldn't know who to support."

"Caught in the middle?"

"Exactly. Is that how you feel?"

"I don't know. Still processing it, I guess."

"Was your father cheating on your mother?"

"No." Not on her mother but cheating everyone else. Mikelina needed to nip this conversation in the bud. "I want to bet on number five," she said, forcing her voice to sound bright and carefree. "I have a good feeling about him."

Bastien grumbled about it, but he went with her to make a bet. He even refrained from saying *I told you so* when poor old number five crossed the line in the middle of the pack.

"At least he wasn't last," she said.

"I don't think they're here," he said, squinting into the crowd as if he could pick them out. "Let's go to the next one on your list."

She'd rather play some more slots, but she diligently trailed along after Bastien as they went from casino to casino and still came up empty at the end of the night. She was down fifty bucks and her feet were killing her.

"It's possible they were casino hopping and we kept missing them," she said once they were back in his car and had given up for the night. Kicking off her shoes, she rubbed her aching feet. As they headed back toward South Beach, Mikelina was thoroughly not in the mood for any hanky-panky—especially if the groom showed up while they were fooling around.

"I'm exhausted," she said to Bastien when they were back in South Beach. "Can you just drop me off at my hotel?"

"You don't want to stay?" Bastien asked.

She shook her head. "I'm so tired I can't even think. Touch base with me tomorrow, though. Enjoy the parasailing." Her head was still whirling about her mother and Kirk kissing.

"All right," he said quietly. "Tomorrow can you contact the owner of the beach house? I'd like to know their asking price. I might buy it if Jace doesn't."

"I don't even know if it's for sale," she said, holding on to her temper. She needed to remember that this was business first and pleasure later. There shouldn't even be any pleasure, so she should get that out of her mind. But with him looking so sexy and confused sitting next to her, it was hard to remember that she had a job to do and that was to make sure all her guests had a good time, not just Bastien.

"If the owner does wind up selling," he went on, "and you need a place to store your things, let me know?"

"Thanks," she said. "I'm good. I could always drop it off at my aunt's house."

"Or maybe your mother can take some of it?"

"Yeah," she said. She wondered how serious it was between her and Kirk. Was her mother spending the night with him?

She squeezed her eyes shut. She did not want to think about that. With her father in jail and her mother in a new relationship, where did that leave her? She could live quite happily off the sale of the beach house. But then where would she go? Where would her home be if not that house?

The rest of the car ride was quiet and when he pulled up in front of her hotel, she thanked him absently and walked into the hotel as if she was sleepwalking. When she got to her room, she opened up her laptop and searched to see what the visiting hours were for the Federal Correctional Institution in Miami.

As much as she hated to visit him, she needed to see her father before she decided to do anything about the house.

CHAPTER SIXTEEN

BASTIEN HADN'T SLEPT well last night. He woke up surly and annoyed that Jace still hadn't bothered to touch base. This not calling or answering his phone was bullshit. It was childish and Bastien was done messing around.

He called the private investigator that had given him the dossier on Jace Benjamin.

"Mr. Ainsworth," Henry Jacobs said, picking up the phone on the first ring. "What can I do for you?"

"I need you to track down Jace Benjamin for me."

"I thought he was with you."

"He's supposed to be, but he keeps disappearing. His cell phone is conveniently out of battery. I'm worried he's screwing around on my sister."

"I can help you track him down. When was the last time you saw him?"

Bastien gave him the details as well as the cell phone numbers of all the groomsmen.

"I'll give you a report this afternoon. But it may take me a little longer to find him."

"When you do, I might have you fly out and tail him."

"I'll clear my schedule."

"While you're looking, can you do a property record search on this address?" Bastien rattled off the beach house's address. "I'd like to get some information on the owner. I'm planning on making him an offer and I'd like to see if there are any pressure points I could hit to get a better deal."

"Will do."

After Bastien rang off with the private investigator, he called Mikelina. From the background sounds, she was in the car.

"Are you sure I can't convince you to go parasailing with me?"

"Not for all the espressos in South Beach," she said. "Besides, I've got a meeting this morning. I'm going to be gone until late afternoon. Has Jace checked in yet?"

"Nope, but if he's staying true to form, he's probably sleeping somewhere. If I do hear from him, it probably won't be until after he wakes up around three this afternoon."

"Well, as soon as you hear from him, please let me know. Is there anything I can do for you in the meantime?"

Bastien wanted to make a sexy comment, but she sounded so distant he didn't feel comfortable with it. "You can go out to dinner with me tonight. If you're free. Maybe we can go to a movie afterward."

There was a long pause. "Like a date?"

"Yeah, you're my girlfriend for the next two weeks, right? That's what people do. Dinner and a movie?"

"More like Netflix and chill."

"I could do that, too. But I'd like to take you out on the town. You pick the place."

"I'd like that." Her voice warmed up a bit and he was glad. "How does seven o'clock reservations sound?"

"It sounds great."

"Oh, wait. You're scheduled to go to Casa Tua tonight with the bachelor party."

"Fuck the schedule."

"I think I just had an orgasm. What did you say?"

"I said, I want to be with you tonight. If the idiots want to go to Casa Tua, they can go without me."

"Well, what are the odds that they're going to show up?"

"I have no idea."

"Because we can take the reservation. There's a members-only lounge that I can get us into, and if they decide to join us, we could ditch them and go back home."

Home. He liked that. Home could be this beach house. This could be her home base in South Beach.

The thought hit him like a splash of cold water. He had just met her. He still didn't know her last name. And after having mind-altering sex with her for the past few days, he wasn't sure how to ask her for it now without sounding like an idiot. He needed to reel himself in fast before she hooked him like her mother had hooked Kirk Diamonte.

"I don't want Jace to ruin another night for us. I'm done babysitting them. At this point, I just want to protect my sister."

"I had an idea about that. Text me her number. I'll call her to see if she received the larimar jewelry that Jace sent. While I'm on the phone with her, I'll see if he's called her or if she knows what he's up to. Coming from me, it won't be suspicious. She won't expect me to know where Jace is, like she would if you asked."

"That's brilliant," he sighed. "I would really appreciate it."

"Good. I've got to get going. I'll be incommunicado for a few hours, but don't worry. I'm not pulling a Jace."

"I can't wait to see you tonight," he said.

"Enjoy flying through the air in a chair above shark-infested waters."

"Hey, at least I've got a parachute attached to it."

"See you soon."

Bastien grinned and realized he was as smitten as a high school girl with her first crush.

Mikelina waited for her father to be brought out to her. This was only the second time she had come to see him. It was hard for her to see him in the orange prison jumpsuit and even though he was in a minimum-security prison, he still had cuffs on his arms and shackles on his legs when they walked him through the door.

They weren't allowed to hug or touch, in case she slipped him contraband, so they sat awkwardly facing each other across the table.

Tanner Presley looked older and bitter. The laugh lines around his eyes weren't as prominent as the frowning ones across his brow. She tried to see him as the father she remembered and it was getting harder and harder to remember that man. That's why she needed the beach house. That's why she couldn't sell it.

"Do you need anything?" she asked to fill the silence.

"If you can swing a couple of hundred dollars more a month in my account, I'd appreciate it."

"I'll see what I can do." Mikelina couldn't stop wringing her hands.

"Why are you here? Have you changed your mind about my guilt?"

She looked around and saw that no one seemed to be paying much attention to them, but she lowered her voice anyway. "No. I saw the computer files. I found your backups, and before I turned them in to the FBI, I read them. I know exactly what you did and to whom."

His mouth twisted. "I can't believe my own daughter ratted me out."

"You were already busted. I handed over evidence."

"There would have been reasonable doubt if you hadn't."

She shook her head. "No. You made mistakes. The most important one being deciding to cheat people out of their hard-earned money."

He glanced around, too, and then leaned forward and spoke in a tone barely above a whisper. "I didn't take it from people who didn't have it to lose."

"Yeah, you did. Remember Mr. Edwards?"

Tanner looked away. "I had bad intel on that. There was a misprint of a couple of zeros."

"You denied a dying man peace that he had assets to leave to his heirs. But that was just one out of a dozen people you cheated."

"Everyone cheats. I got caught. My sentence is bullshit and you know it."

Crossing her arms over her chest, Mikelina said, "I'm not your judge or your jury. I'm not even your lawyer. I'm your daughter. And I'm trying to find a way to get back to a normal life."

"Cry me a river. I'm in a one-room cell with a roommate who picks his nose and snores."

"What is he in for?"

"Insider trading. He'll be out by Christmas."

"What's your lawyer say about parole?" she asked.

"Not a chance in hell for at least another five years. Maybe ten."

She closed her eyes and took a deep breath. She couldn't live in limbo for that long. She couldn't afford to live at the beach house either. She wanted a home base. She wanted to go back to New York where she had a life outside of her family.

"Your mother is divorcing me."

"I know," she said.

"That's loyalty for you. Who is she seeing?"

Mikelina opened her eyes. "What?"

"She wouldn't have done this on her own. She must have found a rich man to take care of her. Someone powerful enough to gloss over this scandal in society so she could go back to her friends."

"Well, why shouldn't she?" Mikelina said. "She didn't do anything wrong."

"Everything I did, I did for you and your mother." He jabbed a finger at her.

It caught the guard's attention, but he didn't approach them.

"Don't blame this on us. No one asked you to do anything illegal or dishonest."

"Did you think your college was free? Do you think your mother's spending account gets paid by the tooth fairy every month?"

"Dad, if you were having financial problems, why didn't you tell us?"

"Because I wasn't. I had everything under control until poor Mr. Edwards had his lawyer audit me."

"Because you were stealing from poor Mr. Edwards."

Tanner leaned back and crossed his arms over his chest. "Don't be naive. Broker fees are a cost of doing business."

"Yeah, if you're actually making the trades you said you were. Look." She held up a hand. "I didn't come here today to talk about this. What's done is done, right?"

Tanner grimly nodded.

"I have a couple of people interested in buying the house."

"Don't you fucking dare sell my house," he said in a low, ugly voice.

"It's my house. And you're not going to be using it for another five to ten years. I'm paying taxes on it, have been paying taxes on it since you signed it over to me."

"There's gratitude for you." He shook his head. "You're a real chip off the old block, you know that? You and your mother are bigger thieves than I could ever be."

"That's not fair," she said through numbed lips. "I was planning on splitting the sale money three ways. Me, you and Mom."

Glaring at her, he said, "You should ask for six million."

"I'm not sure if that's in the ballpark. I was thinking of half that." She wanted to get a glimpse of the father she remembered. She could use her father's advice. She leaned forward eagerly. Maybe by selling the house they could all get a fresh start, new life. New memories.

"It's worth at least five. Get a real estate agent. Put the money in my account. And don't come here again. Guards, we're done here." Tanner scraped back his chair and glared down at her until they escorted him back through the door of the prison.

Mikelina held it together as she walked back to her car. Taking short breaths through her nose, she blinked back tears that were threatening to burst out of her. With shaking fingers, she opened her car door and got in. As soon as she closed the door, she let herself mourn for the loss of her father.

CHAPTER SEVENTEEN

BASTIEN HELD MIKELINA'S hand as they waited for their dinner. She had picked a cozy Italian restaurant off the beaten path. It was quiet and the food and wine looked amazing. Everything would be a perfect romantic date, but she seemed sad and distant.

"Did I do something wrong?" he asked.

She focused on him instead of staring at the tablecloth. "No, I'm sorry. I'm just a little distracted."

The waiter poured them large glasses of ruby red wine from a decanter and then scraped the bread crumbs off the table before moving on. Mikelina reached for another roll and buttered it.

"Did your meeting not go so well today?"

She nodded. "That's the understatement of the year. I spoke with the owner of the beach house. He's not really looking to sell, but he threw out a figure of six million." She shrugged.

"Thanks for asking," he said. It seemed rather high, but he'd wait to see what Henry dug up. "Can you tell me what's bothering you?"

She sighed. "I saw my father today."

Stroking his thumb over her knuckles, he understood her melancholy. "He's not taking the divorce well?"

"He's bitter and angry and blaming everyone while refusing to take responsibility for his poor decisions."

"Sounds a lot like my ex."

"He said some hurtful things. I'm trying not to internalize them too much. I know it's got nothing to do with me, but…" She shook her head. "I'm having a hard time bouncing back from it." Mikelina took a deep sip of her wine. "Being with you here is helping, believe it or not."

"I'm glad. I want to be here for you. I want more than just the sex."

He liked that she blushed at that.

"Don't get me wrong," he said. "I love the sex. I'm hoping for some tonight."

That coaxed a smile out of her. "I think that can be arranged. Have you heard from Jace?"

"Nope. But I've got someone working on it." He glanced at his phone. "In fact, he should have touched base with me before now. So if I keep checking my messages, it's not you. I'm just looking to see if we have the house to ourselves tonight."

"I'm sorry. I forgot to call Kitty today. Like I said, I was distracted. I'll call first thing tomorrow. But if she hasn't heard from him, what's our next step? Do we go to the police?"

"He's not an official missing person until he's been gone forty-eight hours. The clock is ticking, but there's nothing the police can do until we have proof he's not just jacking off in a chicken ranch some-where."

"I think if he's jacking off in a chicken ranch, he's doing it wrong."

Bastien smiled. "I wouldn't know."

"Uh-huh. How was parasailing?"

"It was great. I saw a big nurse shark as I was floating around. But then I realized if it was big when I was looking at it four hundred feet in the air, then up close and personal it was probably the size of my car."

"It might have been a manatee."

"It was brown."

She twirled her fork at him. "I've seen brown manatees."

"That's more comforting. I wouldn't mind swim-ming in the same ocean as a manatee that size. The shark on the other hand, no way."

"Yeah, you guys are going water-skiing tomorrow."

"Allegedly."

As they were finishing up their dinner, Mike-lina visibly began to unwind. He encouraged her to drink some more wine and by the time they finished with dessert, she was a little bleary-eyed but back to her old self.

"Are you ready to get out of here?" he asked.

"I'm ready to make some new memories," she said, slurring her words a bit.

"I hope it involves a moonlight swim without suits."

Her smile was bright and happy. The tension inside him broke apart. She was okay. They were okay. Out of the corner of his eye, he saw a determined woman in a skin-hugging dress storming over to them.

Mikelina gasped. "Carmen," she said.

Carmen grabbed hold of Mikelina's water glass and dashed it in her face. "How dare you? How dare you come to this restaurant?"

"Hey!" Bastien lunged out of his seat and wedged himself between the two women. "Just who the hell do you think you are?"

"You stay out of this." Carmen drilled her finger into his chest.

He slapped it away.

"I thought your family sold it. I would have never," Mikelina babbled, wiping herself off with her napkin.

"This is between me and her. Move." Carmen tried to get around him.

Good luck with that. There was no way he was going to let her get another cheap shot in on Mikelina. "You need to back off, lady, or I'm going to call the cops."

"That's a laugh," Carmen said, trying to push him. He removed her hands from his chest, releasing her immediately.

"You want to make sure you keep your hands to yourself." A man sauntered up behind Carmen. He was trim and light on his feet and looked familiar. Bastien outweighed him by a good twenty pounds. He hoped the man wasn't looking for trouble because he was just in the mood to give him some.

"Is this horrible person with you?" he asked him.

"That's my sister," the man said between his teeth.

"Bastien," Mikelina shrieked. "That's Pedro Santanna. The former middleweight boxing champion."

Bastien nodded. "I saw you fight in the Garden. You've got a glass jaw."

"Oh. My. God," Mikelina said.

"Is he nuts?" Carmen asked.

"We could step outside and you could try to shatter it," Pedro said mildly, gesturing toward the door.

Bastien reached inside his jacket pocket.

Pedro tensed and went up on the balls of his feet. Bastien pulled out his billfold and smiled at him. Tossing three hundreds on the table, he tucked his wallet back inside his jacket and gave Pedro an *after you* wave.

"How did this become about them?" Carmen said.

Bastien had no illusions that he was about to get his butt kicked, but he needed to blow off steam. Otherwise, he might be punching Jace out later.

"You sure you want to do this, man?" Pedro asked.

"Your sister threw a drink at my date. I can't hit her, and since you butted into the argument, that makes you fair game."

"How well do you know that little *chica* you're with?"

"I know she's my girlfriend."

"Then you deserve this."

Mikelina held a cold compress over his eye and pressed an ice bag to his jaw. "You're an idiot. You know that, right?"

"Did you see the shot I got in on him? He was expecting a haymaker, not a gut punch."

"He's a professional boxer. He could have killed you."

"Nah, he wasn't wearing gloves. He'd never have risked his hands."

"He might have, if you pissed him off enough. Bastien, don't ever do that again." She made him hold the compress and the ice bag. Sinking down into the couch, she cradled her face in her hands. "I can't believe you did that. Who asks a boxer to step outside? What are you, sixteen?"

"You want to tell me what that was all about? Why did Carmen throw your water in your face? Did you steal her man or something?"

Mikelina snorted. "If I could steal him, he wasn't her man to begin with."

"Not a lot of people see things that way. Did you break Pedro's heart?"

"No. I only know Pedro professionally."

"Are you a boxing fan?"

"I'm a concierge. I get tickets to his fights from his agent."

Bastien waited, but she wasn't more forthcoming. "Do I have to play twenty questions or are you going to tell me?"

"It's complicated." She sighed. "I don't want to get into it right now."

"Are you in danger?"

"No."

"Would you tell me if you were?"

"Yes, it's old news. Carmen and Pedro are holding a grudge and I don't blame them. I'm sorry you got involved. But if you hadn't stepped in when you did, it wouldn't have escalated."

"I got hands on a middleweight champion. Best bachelor party ever."

"You're an asshole. Would you have let Jace get into a fight with the champ?"

"Pedro hasn't been a champ in a few years."

"Bastien! Not the point." She threw a pillow at him, but missed him by a mile.

"And no. Jace couldn't take a punch from a guy like that."

"Neither could you. You look like you went ten rounds with the man."

"I used to box in college. This is nothing."

"Fine," she said and removed the compress and ice bag.

"What are you doing?" he asked when she grabbed her phone.

"I'm going to take a picture and send it to your sister. See what she has to say."

Bastien held up his fists and mugged for the camera. "She'd say I probably deserved it. Hashtag prick."

"I don't know what to do with you." Mikelina took a few pictures and then tossed her phone on the table. "Put that compress back on your eye to keep the swelling down."

"Maybe you could kiss it and make it better?" he grabbed her around the waist and tugged her in close. She felt amazing against him. He knew he'd be feeling the bruises later, but right now he was flying high on adrenaline and freedom.

Ever since the scorched-earth debacle of his marriage, he had been playing it safe. Keeping to his schedules and working like a madman helped him get over the absolute failure of his relationship. He really thought Gina had been the one. But she never made him feel like Mikelina did.

Her lips were stiff and unyielding against his at first, but then she relaxed, and it was like her whole body opened up for him. Walking her back into the kitchen, he hoisted her up on the island.

"I've been thinking about doing this for two days," he muttered against her lips.

Mikelina demanded more kisses and he gave them to her. She made his head spin faster than Pedro's cross jab. Pushing up her skirt, he peeled her skimpy panties down her long, toned legs. He wanted to tell her she was beautiful and that she drove him crazy, but his tongue was too busy dancing with hers.

His cock was pounding with the need to sink inside her dripping wet pussy, and while he wanted to lick her until she drenched his face, he needed to be inside her more. Unbuttoning his pants, he slipped them down his hips. She immediately grabbed him and guided him inside her.

Greedy little thing. He loved that she wanted him just as much as he wanted her. He'd fight ten Pedro Santannas for her honor. She clamped around him and he moaned against her mouth. She was tight and sweet. When she squeezed him, he lost his mind. Somehow their clothes went flying in all directions as he eased in and out of her trembling body. Her legs wrapped around his hips and held him close.

His phone rang.

Fuck it.

"It could be Jace," she gasped, wresting her mouth away from his.

"Fuck him." Bastien took her mouth again. He didn't want to think about his brother-in-law. He wanted to concentrate on making Mikelina come all over him. Her earthy grunts told him she was so close. He thumbed her nipples and pumped into her faster and she kissed him with desperate, needy moans.

The wet slap of their bodies as they repeatedly came together was a mesmerizing wave of cresting pleasure. She screamed into his mouth and held on tight as she shook apart. His eyes rolled back in his head and his back arched as he followed a few seconds later.

He would never get enough of her. Slowing down, he lifted her off the island and carried her into the bedroom, still inside her. Easing them both down on the bed, he continued to fuck her, this time slow and easy.

The excitement built up again. Her fingers dug into the duvet cover and when he slid his mouth to attack her gorgeous throat, her husky cries encouraged him to pick up the pace.

Mikelina came screaming, wringing every last

drop of come from him. He shook with desire and was barely able to roll off her.

"Worth it," he panted. "Every punch."

"You idiot. I would have fucked you anyway."

CHAPTER EIGHTEEN

THE NEXT MORNING, Bastien was still conked out after she had taken her shower and gotten dressed. She let him sleep and closed the bedroom door on her way to the kitchen.

"Morning," Jace said from the kitchen table.

Every muscle in her body froze. "Hi," she said brightly and then, because she couldn't think of anything else to say, made her way to the espresso machine.

"So, you and Bastien, huh?" he asked. Jace had a huge bowl of cereal in front of him and was watching something on his phone.

"Yeah," she said. "Where have you been these past few days?"

"We did an overnight in Cuba."

"Cuba?" She blinked. "You are aware that travel to Cuba is prohibited, right?"

"That's why we didn't tell Bastien. He'd never agree to it and now he can't be held responsible if it comes back and bites us in the ass. It's also why I didn't ask you to arrange it for us."

"Out of curiosity, how did you do it?"

"Canadian registered boat. Paid cash. Max is a stringer for the *Washington Tribune*. Shane's a professional photographer. We went under the journalistic activity general license category."

"That was risky. Dangerous."

"Have you been to Havana?"

Mikelina shook her head sadly. "I missed my opportunity. I was waiting for the cruise ships to get out the kinks and the tourism to build up a bit."

"It's amazing. We took a vintage car tour around the city. Went to a rum museum. Snorkeled in the Bay of Pigs. Saw a cigar factory. It was great."

"I'm jealous," she said with a smile.

"And I'm bummed I can't share the pictures on Instagram."

"If it's not on social media, did it really happen?"

"Exactly. We want to keep it on the down low, though. So we're going to go old school photo albums. Do you think you can get us some?"

She nodded. "If you save the pictures to my Dropbox, I'll have them printed out for you."

"Sweet," he said. They exchanged information. "One for each of us."

"Even Bastien?"

"Maybe not for him."

"He probably would have liked to have gone." She didn't want to sound like she was scolding him, but she wanted Jace to know that he'd hurt Bastien's feelings by being so selfish.

Jace shrugged. "He wouldn't have lied to go to

Cuba. He's too much of a straight arrow. At least, I thought he was." He waggled his eyebrows at her.

Oh, was that how he wanted to play it? "I bet Kitty would have liked to have gone."

"I would have taken her if she had been here."

"If you asked her, would she have come?"

Jace stared at her, thinking about it. "Come to my bachelor party?"

"Shared a forbidden trip to Cuba with her fiancé?"

"She has to work."

"She wouldn't have called in sick to go on an adventure with you?"

He sighed. "Yeah, she would have."

"But you didn't want her there?"

"It's not that. I would have worried about her. She's beautiful, rich and American. What if I let her out of my sight for a second? I'd never forgive myself if something had happened to her."

"Don't you think she feels the same way about you?"

"I don't spend a lot of time in self-reflection," he said.

"I get it. It's your bachelor party and you get a lot of leeway for kicking loose. But going forward, don't leave Kitty out of the adventures. I think she'd be a great partner."

"You don't even know her." He smiled. "But she is."

"I know her through Bastien and if he adores her that much, she's got to be pretty special."

"Yes, I think so, too. And she loved the jewelry

you picked out for her. She thinks I'm a rock star. Thank you for that."

Mikelina shrugged. "It's my job. I'm glad she liked it." Her eyes caught sight of his travel humidor on the dining room table. "Please tell me you didn't bring back any Cuban cigars?"

"Smoked them all on the boat coming back."

"Good." She sighed.

"As far as you know."

She shook her head. It was better not to know. "Have you told Kitty where you were?"

"Not yet. She's in a tizzy over her brother."

Mikelina frowned. "Why?" She hadn't sent the picture last night.

Jace turned the phone over to her. There was a great YouTube video of Bastien's fight with Pedro.

"Oh shit," she said, covering her mouth with her hand.

"That's you in the corner, right?"

Mikelina nodded.

"Was he defending your honor or something?"

"Something like that. I didn't want him to."

"Doesn't matter. It's the bro code. I'm glad. He's such a tight-ass. He needs to get into more fights and have raucous sex on vacation."

She blushed. "Just when did you come back?" Mikelina was mortified that he might have heard them.

"A few hours ago."

"Are you going water-skiing today?"

"It's on the schedule, isn't it?"

"Are you done screwing around with him?"

Jace shrugged. "Probably not."

"Do me a favor," she said.

"I'll try."

"Go easy on him. He's trying his best to like you for Kitty's sake and you're not making it any easier."

"I am who I am, but I'll see what I can do."

"And if you could keep this…" she gestured to herself and the bedroom "…between us, I'd appreciate it. It's not very professional of me to be sleeping with my client and I'd rather it didn't get back to my boss."

"You got it." He leaned back in the chair. "What are your intentions for my soon-to-be brother-in-law?"

"I intend to have a good time."

"Is that all?"

"For now." She folded her arms over her chest. "Why?"

"I was curious about you. Why your business card only had your first name. I was also curious about who the owner of this property was because I'm looking to buy it for Kitty as a wedding present."

"You could have asked."

"Would you have told me?"

A cold chill passed over her. She schooled her face. "I don't like sharing my last name, and if you know the history of this house, then you know the reason why."

"I'm assuming Bastien doesn't know."

"Why are you assuming that?"

"Because he'd be more guarded with you if he did know. You wouldn't be in his bed, that's for damned sure."

My bed.

"He's been hurt before," Jace said.

"I know. He told me about his ex-wife."

"Gina was a user and a gold digger. You don't strike me as either. You should tell him, before he hears from someone else who your father is."

She grimaced. "Not yet. I don't want to ruin things. My father has nothing to do with this. I'm not asking Bastien to invest in stocks and I'm not a broker. What my father has done has no reflection on me."

"And yet, it does. With the money you would make on the house, you could change your name and start over somewhere people won't pick fights with you in local restaurants." He jiggled his phone at her again.

"You're not the slacker idiot everyone thinks you are, are you?"

"Everyone? Or just Bastien?"

"Good point." She sighed. "It's complicated."

"What do you want for the house?"

"If it was just the money, it would be an easy decision."

"If you do decide to sell it, can you give me the right of first refusal?"

"Bastien was interested in buying it, too."

"I have a deal for you."

"This should be good."

"I'll keep quiet about your relationship with Bastien, and I won't tell Bastien your last name. In return, before you put the property on the market—no pressure—*if you do*, please contact me first?"

"That sounds a little like blackmail," she said. Mikelina wouldn't underestimate Jace again. He was just as much of a businessman as her father had been. Maybe a little more honest. Maybe.

"You know how to make blackmail powerless, don't you? Just tell the truth."

She nodded. That wasn't so easy either. "I accept your terms. But I'm still not sure I want to sell this place."

"I get it. It's great."

"There are a lot of happy memories here," she said, surprising herself that she was opening up to him. "I don't have a lot of those to fall back on and it's hard to let go."

"It's just a house. You still have those memories."

"They're being replaced with new ones. Not necessarily better ones. Sometimes, I think this house is the only proof I have that at one point, my life wasn't a total shitshow."

She heard the shower click on from the bedroom. "I should go before he comes out and it gets even more awkward. Have fun water-skiing today. I'll deliver the photo albums before dinner tonight."

"You're welcome to join us for dinner," he said.

"No, I don't want to intrude."

"Thanks for everything you've done," Jace said. "But especially for getting Bastien to lighten up."

* * *

While the bachelor party was water-skiing, Mikelina decided to contact Kitty Ainsworth. Even though she knew Kitty loved the jewelry and that Jace was back where he belonged, she felt that she had to explain to Kitty why her brother went a few rounds with the middleweight champ. She sent her the picture of Bastien goofing off from last night with the caption, Got time to talk?

Her phone immediately started ringing.

"Hi," Mikelina said. "I just wanted to apologize for getting Bastien involved in the altercation last night."

"Please." Kitty snorted. "If I know my brother, he instigated that whole fight."

"Well, to be honest, yes," Mikelina said. "But he had reasons."

"Jace told me. It sounds like you guys are having so much fun. I'm obscenely jealous. I'm here in Colorado and I should be having a great time. Except I'm not. I miss Jace. My mother won't leave me alone about crudités platters and I'm just so done with this wedding-of-the-century bullshit."

Mikelina wasn't sure what to say to that. "I wish I could help."

"You know," Kitty said, her voice calculating, "I'm so glad you said that. Can you keep a secret? Even from my brother?"

Uh-oh. Considering Mikelina was already keeping a really big one from him, what was one more?

"Sure."

CHAPTER NINETEEN

MIKELINA SAT IN the beach chair inches from the water's edge and dug her toes in the sand. In about another twenty minutes, she'd be underwater if she didn't move, but she hoped Bastien would be here by then.

She had dropped the photo albums off with Jace like she was doing a drug deal. He wanted to surprise his groomsmen with them before showing the pictures to Bastien. She felt a little guilty sneaking around Bastien's back, but if Kitty pulled off what she was planning, that was the least of her secrets.

Jace had asked her to stay for dinner, but she wouldn't feel comfortable crashing the bachelor party. Even though it was her home and even though she was pretty sure the groomsmen all knew she was banging Bastien by now, Mikelina didn't want to face the awkwardness. So she had begged off and Bastien had walked her out to her car.

"Let's go for a walk on the beach tonight. Can you meet me there around sunset?" he had asked her.

"Sure." She had tangled her fingers through his and indulged in a quick kiss.

Abbie had already closed up shop by the time Mikelina got to the beach, so she got an order of conch fritters and fries and sat on a picnic bench and watched the ocean. She tried not to think about her parents, but it seemed lately whenever she had a spare moment they crept into her thoughts. Mikelina was happy for her mother and devastated by her father's rejection. But most of all, she wondered where did that leave her?

After she finished her dinner, she took the beach chair out of the back of her car and after a quick stop for an ice cream cone, plunked her butt in front of the encroaching waves and hoped to find some answers.

The ice cream was good, and the ocean didn't provide any insight, but she did realize that South Beach was not her home. It was a great place to visit, but it was time she got back to New York. A little part of her wondered if it was because Bastien was from there as well.

"I found a mermaid," a voice said behind her. Bastien. She turned with a smile and he helped her out of the chair.

"And I found a shark. Are you coming to eat me?"

"I've been thinking about nothing else since dinner. I plan to have you as dessert."

"Where do the guys think you are?"

"I didn't tell them. They're hanging out in the hot tub smoking cigars and doing vodka shots."

"As one does." She put the chair farther up on the beach and laced her fingers through Bastien's. They strolled hand in hand down the waterline, barefoot.

"Watch out for the wave," she said and then splashed him with her foot.

"Keep it up and I'll toss you in," he warned.

"Your sister's right. You are a prick."

"Did you talk to her today?"

"Yup. She loved the larimar set. She wants me to pick out larimar bracelets for her bridesmaids."

"On my dime." He snorted.

"Probably. Are you not authorizing the charge?"

"I'm smarter than that. She'll sic my mother on me if I don't. Yeah, get her whatever she wants. You only get married once."

"What if the first time wasn't so good?" Mikelina asked, thinking about her mother.

"Good point," he said. "Lord knows mine was a disaster."

"Have you ever thought about marrying again?" she asked.

"I haven't. Too much pain. Too much baggage."

"Oh."

"But lately?" He swung their arms. "Lately, I might be convinced to change my mind."

"I've been thinking about leaving South Beach."

"Why would you want to leave here?" Bastien said. "Sun, surf, sex. It's a trifecta of pleasure."

"Well, before you, I didn't have any sex and I was working too hard to enjoy the sun and surf."

"Where would you go?" he asked.

"Back to New York. I feel the pull of the city sometimes."

"Not in March you don't."

"True. I should wait until after the last snowfall to ease my way into things."

"I didn't know you used to live in New York."

"I went to NYU and then after college I didn't feel like going back home to Miami. I worked my way up a corporate hotel chain and then decided I didn't like the corporate bullshit."

"Preach," he said, crouching down to pick up a few shells. "Kitty wanted me to bring some home."

She pointed a small conch shell out with her toe. "Just make sure it's empty of critters before you take it home or it will stink to high heaven. Why didn't she ask Jace?"

"Because Jace will forget. What happened after you got sick of the corporate bullshit?"

"I worked at a few boutique hotels in midtown for a while."

"What made you come back here?"

"I got fired. Too many days off. I was lucky that Kirk hired me, and I've been here ever since."

"Would you try to go back to a boutique hotel?"

"I think so. It might be time to send out my résumé and see if anyone bites."

"Let me know if I can help. I might know a few people who can put a good word in for you."

"Thanks," she said.

"I'm being selfish. If you move to New York, I can see you more often than if you're down here." He put his shells in his pocket and turned to face her. Holding both her hands, he kissed her as the waves crashed into their ankles. "I don't want this to end next week," he said. "You know that, right?"

A lump appeared in her throat. "I don't want this to end either."

What would he say if she told him about her father?

"I'm hoping you'd be my date to my sister's wedding."

"You're kidding?" She smiled so hard her face hurt.

"No, you'll keep me sane. I'm going to bribe the priest to start out the vows by going 'Mawwiage. It's what bwings us together today' just like in *The Princess Bride*."

"You're a nerd. Your sister will kill you and no priest in the world is going to do that."

"Takes one to know one. She'd have to catch me first. And I plan on making a large donation to the widows and orphans fund if he does. Plus, you get to meet all parents and the whole family all at once. They're going to ask you a ton of questions, so be prepared for the third degree."

Like that didn't sound like her own personal version of hell.

"But don't worry," Bastien said. "You'll already know half of the bridal party. Unfortunately, they're going to make you do the chicken dance."

"Really?" She scrunched up her nose.

"And the Macarena."

"That's it. I'm not going."

"And the Electric Slide."

"Wait, are you going to do the Electric Slide?"

"You should see me. It's electric. Boogie, woogie woogie."

"Don't ever do that again," she said, laughing.

"I guess the Cupid Shuffle is out?"

"I'll do the Hustle with you," she said.

"Old school." He took her in his arms and did the Hustle down the beach. They got a few weird looks, but she didn't care. As long as no one was throwing water at her or boxers weren't throwing punches, it was all good.

They stopped to watch the sunset. The skyline looked like a water colorist's paradise with soft pastels of sweeping pinks and oranges. In the distance, a cruise ship floated by. Closer, a brown dorsal fin peeked out of the water.

"Is that a shark?" Bastien pointed.

"Dolphin," she said and as they watched, the dorsal fin dipped and a brown dolphin popped up.

The surf slid closer, leaving puffs of white foam by their toes.

Bastien let her go and crouched down. He drew a big heart in the sand. He wrote B.A. + M. "What's your last name?"

The words stuck in her throat. "Write the letter P," she forced out.

B.A. + M.P.

"That's the sappiest thing I've ever seen," she said, but tears pricked at the corner of her eyes and she stared at it until the waves deleted it.

"Alas, it was fleeting." He brought the back of her hand to his lips and kissed it.

"Did you just say alas?"

"I'm trying to be romantic. You know what? Fuck it. Let's go find someplace private." He bent down and threw her over his shoulder. She kicked her legs in mock protest.

"Don't forget the beach chair."

"As you wish." He grabbed it with the hand not on her ass.

Her breath caught. "Were you just quoting *The Princess Bride* again?"

Bastien didn't answer, which made her wonder if like in the movie when he said, "As you wish," he was really saying, "I love you."

She didn't get a chance to ask him again because she realized that instead of walking her back to her car, he was walking her down the pier. The sand made him stumble a bit.

"Don't you dare toss me in the water."

"Relax," he said.

"I don't think we're supposed to be down here. This is for boat owners only."

"Or people who have rented the boat for an evening." He set her down in front of a small yacht.

The ship had sleek lines and was gleaming in the fading sun. She could see her reflection in the chrome and windows. She looked awestruck and her cheeks were flushed.

"I mean, it's no limousine but I figured it would have to do."

"Can you drive this thing?" she asked.

"No, that's what the captain is going to do as soon as we're settled on board." He helped her step into the boat and then followed her in.

She saw two uniformed men untether the boat from the dock as the motor started up. Bastien took her up to the bridge and introduced her to the captain. "It's a nice night for a boat ride," the man said. "Enjoy yourselves."

Bastien put his arm around her waist and led her back to the main deck where champagne and chocolate-covered strawberries were set out.

"My favorite," she said. She took a sip of the champagne and sighed happily. "Why aren't you drinking?"

"I can't stand the stuff. Besides, it's much more fun to watch you." He guided her to a couch that was set up to face the side of the boat. Bastien held her against his chest and stroked her hair as she drank champagne and fed him strawberries. The breeze from sailing into the wind lifted strands of her hair into his face as the powerful boat glided through the waves. He tucked them behind her ear.

When the strawberries were gone, Mikelina turned to him. "Thank you for this. I love that you did this for me."

He pulled her back against him and kissed her forehead. "There's no place that I'd rather be. Except maybe belowdecks."

"There's a below deck?"

"Where do you think we're going to sleep tonight?"

"We're spending the night on the boat?"

"All night. Come on, let me show you."

He set her champagne glass down and led her down a short flight of stairs. There were three rooms. Opening up the main door revealed a bedroom that consisted mostly of a heart-shaped bed.

"Is it a waterbed?" she asked.

"Of course it is."

"Whee!" She kicked off her shoes and launched herself onto it. It didn't roll as much as she thought it would, but it was still a lot of fun to feel the mattress move underneath her. "Are you going to come here or not?"

Bastien locked the door behind him. "I was enjoying the view."

"Enjoy it naked. This is going to be so much fun." Mikelina shed her clothes and lay back on the pillow.

"I want to see you touch yourself," he said. Bastien quickly peeled off his clothes and soon had his cock in his hand.

Mikelina was mesmerized by the soft pulling action and she licked her lips.

"Show me how you pleasure yourself," he said. "I want to see you dip your fingers into your pussy and make yourself come."

Taking a shaky breath and unable to keep her eyes off him rubbing himself, Mikelina spread her legs wide and ran her finger over her clit.

"I like how your nipples react. Touch them, too.

Pull on them if you like, but please, please don't stop rubbing yourself."

The only sound in the cabin was their short, harsh breaths. Mikelina squirmed under his intense gaze. "I want you," she said.

"Come for me and I'll give you whatever you want."

His words teased her into moving her fingers faster.

"Yes," he breathed out, tugging himself in time with her fingers. She could see a glistening drop of come on the tip of his cock.

"Bring that here," she said, not recognizing her husky voice. "I want to lick that off."

Bastien moved around so that he stood next to her side of the bed. He cupped her breast as she leaned over to flick her tongue over the head.

"I like that," she said, doing it again.

Grabbing her hand that was between her legs, he brought it to his mouth and sucked hard on her fingers. Mikelina had to clamp her legs shut to keep from coming at the feel of his mouth licking her juices off her fingers.

"I like how you taste, too," he said.

She took all of him in her mouth and his fingers rubbed her clit. Arching up, Mikelina sucked hard on him as his quick touch brought her over the edge. He thrust two fingers inside her and fucked her with them as she bobbed her head up and down his cock.

He came without warning, gasping and swearing. "Holy shit."

Swallowing, she laughed and scooted over on the bed. "Now, that was a nice surprise."

"Here's another nice surprise." Bastien climbed on the bed and dipped down and rolled her around. He grabbed her legs and kissed her pussy like it was her mouth. His tongue licked at her clit and he sucked on her slick folds. "I love how you react when I do this."

She pulled his hair and guided his head back between her legs. Eyes closed, Mikelina writhed and moaned. Bastien gripped her hips as if she would ever want to get away. She was gleefully trapped as he made love to her with his tongue. Mikelina ground against his face until she came again and then sagged in a breathless heap.

"Holy shit," she gasped.

"I'll say. Roll over and grab the headboard. I want to go real deep."

Biting back a moan, Mikelina did as he commanded. He dragged his short nails down her back, and she raised her ass up toward him. He slammed inside her to the hilt and she tossed her head to look over her shoulder. The waterbed gave them a bit more bounce, and she felt all of him, every thick, hard inch. Bastien held her hips tight and rocked into her with quick, short strokes.

His eyes were intense, and he groaned in pleasure with each push of his body. Mikelina met him stroke for stroke, needing the rough friction in all of her sensitive places. He went deep and held her close to him as he nibbled on her neck.

She sagged and rolled onto her side as he continued to thrust into her. A low moan escaped her as he played with her clit while still moving inside her. She was coming and didn't want the feeling to ever stop. He continued to slide in and out of her with sloppy strokes that sounded erotic in the small cabin.

Bastien came, growling in her ear. The motion of the mattress took them further and when that slowed, the motion of the boat kept him hard inside her until they both drifted off to sleep.

CHAPTER TWENTY

THINGS HAD BEEN going so well. Bastien should have known it wouldn't last. Jace had spent the last three days partying and following the schedule. Bastien had let his guard down and started to actually like the idiot.

During breaks in the itinerary, Bastien had still managed to go out with Mikelina for breakfast while the morons were sleeping in and steal a few intimate moments back in her hotel room. But she had been busy these last few days, too.

Then Jace and the groomsmen took off again without telling him two days ago. No one had heard from them since.

At first, Bastien wasn't too upset because it gave him some quality time at the house with Mikelina. They had sex in every room but the master bedroom. For some reason, Mikelina wasn't interested in going into Jace's room. But Bastien didn't think twice about that, not when her favorite place seemed to be his bedroom.

The private investigator had told him that Jace

had been to Cuba the last time he disappeared and Bastien tried not to lose his mind. He hadn't brought up the subject, but now that Jace had pulled another disappearing act, Bastien was afraid Jace had gone back for more cigars or some other stupid thing. And now Bastien was worried about them causing an international incident. Where else could he have gone for two days?

Anywhere.

Today was Wednesday and there were only a few more days left of the bachelor party. Only a few more days to spend hours making love to Mikelina and then drinking and eating decadent food. Mikelina didn't want to stay in South Beach? Bastien didn't want to go home to New York.

He liked it here. He liked who he was when he was with Mikelina.

She was lounging by the pool and Bastien was getting hard just looking at her. But before he could act on his desire, Henry called.

"Please tell me you know where they are," Bastien said.

"I don't, but Jace has been calling a number other than Kitty's these past few days. I tracked it down and it's the owner of the beach house."

Apparently, Jace was still interested in buying it for Kitty. Wait until he found out the asking price. Six million. Jeez. If he could afford that, he was better off than Henry had found. "Anyone I know?"

"It's owned by Mikelina Presley."

M.P.

Even if he hadn't known her last name started with a *P*, how many other Mikelinas were there in South Beach?

"I don't understand. Are you sure Mikelina Presley is the owner?"

Why was she renting out her own house and living in crappy hotels then?

"Yes. She's the daughter of Tanner Presley. Do you remember the scandal a year or so ago? He's the stockbroker that rooked several clients out of their life savings. It seems just before he started doing that, he signed over the property to his daughter as a gift. It's the only thing that's left after his legal fees and paying restitution. The attorneys would have loved to get their hands on the house, but since it predates his illegal activities, it's untouchable."

Bastien leaned up against the glass and stared out at Mikelina.

"Are you there?"

"Yeah, I'm here. So she's renting it out?" Mikelina smiled and waved at him. He didn't even know who she was. "What's the daughter like?"

"Yeah, she's barely paying the taxes on the place. It's sixty grand a year. I couldn't find out a lot about her. She worked at a few high-end hotels in Manhattan, but after the shit hit the fan with her father, she moved to Florida to be with her mother."

"Her mother?"

"Tawny Presley, née Santiago. Her father worked in shipping. She married up with Tanner, and Mikelina is their only daughter. Tawny's coming back into the social scene. Lately, she's been cozying up to Kirk Diamonte. Who happens to be Mikelina's boss. Tawny just filed for divorce from Tanner. Convenient, right?"

"How many calls did Jace make to Mikelina?"

"In the past two days, about ten."

In the past two days? While she watched him get more and more pissed off about Jace's disappearing act.

"How many did he make to Kitty?"

"Two."

Jace spoke to Mikelina five times more than he spoke to his own fiancée. Bastien tried not to jump to conclusions, but he was getting an ugly feeling in the pit of his stomach. What the hell had they been talking about and why the hell hadn't she said anything to him about it?

"Do you think Mikelina is looking to sell?" he forced himself to ask. He didn't give a damn about the beach house right now. He was trying to figure out Mikelina's angle in all of this. "Or do you think Jace is fooling around with her?" Rage blinded him for a minute.

Mikelina had known Bastien was concerned about Jace, but instead of telling him she had been in contact with Jace, she had pretended she didn't know where he was. How could Bastien have been so stupid?

"I've got no proof that they are involved, but I'm not ruling it out either."

"Is that right?" Bastien gritted out. Jace had asked

Mikelina over for dinner the night she and Bastien went water-skiing. Had the affair started then? Had it been an affair? What else could they have been talking about? Now he wondered about all of Mikelina's business meetings this week. Had they been with Jace?

"The house, however, has never been on the market, but there have been a few altercations there. Irate victims have threatened the Presleys, as you can imagine."

"I don't have to imagine," he said, realizing that Carmen or Pedro had probably been hurt by Mikelina's father.

"Anyway, the taxes are paid for this year and what's left over from the rental of the house is supporting Tawny's lifestyle. Of course, now that she's found Diamonte, that might not be needed anymore. I think you could lowball an offer and it might get picked up. Especially if Mikelina is getting out of Five Diamond Resorts vacation club now that her mother has her hooks into the boss."

Was that why she was suddenly tired of South Beach? She had seemed so shocked to see Kirk with her mother that night in the casino. Had it all been an act? Bastien had so many questions and he was just getting angrier and angrier the more he thought of it.

"Or maybe Mikelina has found a sugar daddy of her own," Bastien said softly. Was it Jace or him? Or was she planning on playing both of them off against each other and ruining Kitty's wedding in the process? Was she going to follow them to New York?

She was just like Gina. And it broke his heart. She was using him for his money or Jace's money or for some other reason she was keeping secrets. She was hiding who she was. Just like Gina had done.

"Anything is possible," Henry said. "I'll see if I can track down Jace again. Are you sure he didn't head up to Vail to see Kitty? Or maybe he's shacking up with Mikelina?"

"Anything is possible," Bastien echoed. "But my gut says he's local somewhere. I don't want to leave here without knowing where he is."

"Leave there? I thought the bachelor party was going through the weekend."

"There's not much point in hanging around," Bastien said. "I've slacked off work long enough. There's nothing for me here now."

Not a damned thing.

"All right. Well, give me a call when you're back in town and we can go for lunch or something."

"You got it. Thanks, Henry."

Bastien pocketed his phone and glared out at Mikelina. At least he hadn't married this one.

Mikelina looked up when he slid open the sliding glass door and walked out to the pool. He'd give her one more chance to tell him the truth.

"Hey, sexy," she said, with a sweet grin.

He had to look away because he could feel his body respond to her. "Any news from the owner about selling? I'm willing to write a check for six million dollars today."

"What?" she said, sitting up.

He didn't have that kind of liquid cash, but he wanted to see what she would say.

"This is rather sudden," she said slowly, looking around. "I'm not sure they're ready to sell. I think it might come to that. But not right away."

"It's a gift. The house isn't worth more than four. Call them and tell them, take it or leave it. The offer is only good today."

Her face cleared in relief. "They're not going to go for it. But I'll pass along the offer."

What was her game? She couldn't possibly want more money. No one would give up six million dollars. Unless she was planning on running a scam out of the house. Her mother got her hooks into Diamonte. Was Mikelina hoping for a real estate mogul, too? Or was she hoping for Jace?

"What's your last name?" he asked her.

"What?" She blinked up at him.

"It just occurred to me that I don't know. Mikelina. It's like Cher or Prince. Or Elvis…Presley."

She flinched. "You don't have to be a dick about this."

"I'm being a dick? You lied to me."

"I never lied to you. I didn't share my past, that's all, and for this very reason."

"What? That I'd call you on your bullshit?"

"No, that you would judge me by my father's actions. Just like everybody else. I wanted to have a nice fling with someone who liked me for me. Everyone who has found out I'm Tanner Presley's daughter winds up acting like I was going to pick their pocket or do something illegal just because my father is a crook."

"This is just a fling to you?" he asked. It shouldn't hurt as much as it did.

"I thought we could be more. But you're just like all the rest. I didn't tell you my father is Tanner Presley because of this reaction right here." She pointed at him. "Can you tell me why you automatically painted me with the same brush? We've only known each other a week and a half, but I thought we were really connecting. I was going to tell you when the bachelor party was over because I was having too much fun to ruin it."

"You can't start a relationship out on a lie," he said.

"If you knew who I was, there wouldn't have been a relationship. If I signed my emails Mikelina Presley, you would have asked Kirk for another concierge. If I told you my name in the bar, you would have never gone back to the VIP sections in Flow with me. If I rolled over in bed the next morning and introduced myself, you would have never spoken with me again."

"That's not true," Bastien said.

"Yes, it is. Your reaction right now proves it."

"Do you know where Jace is?"

He caught her by surprise and if he hadn't been looking for it, he might have missed the flash of guilt that crossed her expression. "No," she said.

"You're a bad liar. Or maybe a very good one. I'm not sure which."

"Bastien, you need to back off. You don't know what you're talking about."

He advanced on her and then checked himself. "I'll tell you what I know. I know you lied to me about who you are." He held up his hand when she went to interrupt him. "A lie by omission is still a lie. I know that you've been keeping secrets from me about your family and about Jace."

She opened her mouth to speak but he cut her off.

"I know that you lied to my face just now and I know that you have spoken with Jace several times over the past few days."

"How do you know that?"

"Figure it out," he snarled. "You watched me worry about where he was and all the while you could have eased my mind. I can only wonder why? What game are you playing?"

"I'm not playing a game."

"I won't let you hurt my sister by playing around with her fiancé."

"I am not playing around with Jace."

"Why? Because it's unprofessional?" He opened up his arms.

"Go to hell," she said, getting up from the lounge chair. "I do not deserve to be treated like this."

"No? Then tell the truth. Where is Jace?"

Mikelina set her jaw and put her hands on her hips. "Why do you think the worst of him?"

"Experience."

"Why do you think the worst of me?"

"The same."

"You don't know me."

"And whose fault is that?"

"I am not Gina. I'm not an addict. I don't want your money. All I wanted was you." She looked away, blinking back tears.

Bastien's gut clenched. He wanted to believe her. "Why can't you tell me where he is?"

"Why can't you just let it go? Stop being such a control freak. He's not in danger. He's not hurting your sister. He did something spontaneous. It's a good thing." She went to touch him, but Bastien flinched away. He didn't want to feel her against him. Not when she was still keeping secrets.

"Where is he and why has he been calling you?"

"You think I'm having an affair with him?" Her eyes filled with tears. "Did you think that before your private investigator pulled his phone records? Which…" she hiccuped "…is illegal without a court order."

"I didn't say that's how I found out."

"I'm not an idiot. And it's that type of loose ethics that led to my father doing what he did. So be careful you don't slide off your high horse and find yourself on that path."

"Your father is not the victim here."

"I never said he was, but guess what? You're not the victim either." She pushed by him and slammed into his bedroom. He tried to follow, but she locked the door.

"I'm going out," he yelled. "I'll be back in a few

hours. I want you gone and I never want to see you again."

"Fine," she yelled through the door.

That was just fine with her. Mikelina threw herself on her bed and sobbed her heart out. It was worse than that asshole in Cartagena. It was even worse than her father telling her to get out of his life. She actually thought she and Bastien could have a future.

"It's not my fault," she whispered into her pillow. She could blame her father, or Kitty or Jace. But in the end, it was Bastien who chose how to react. It was Bastien who chose not to wait one more day to find out what happened to Jace. He thought the worst of her and wouldn't even give her a chance to explain.

She had been right not to trust him with who she was. He had not been worthy of her trust.

And it hurt so damned bad, because she had convinced herself that he was the one.

When Mikelina's sobs trailed off to a sporadic hitch, she forced herself to get up and splash cold water on her face. She had cried too much over men who didn't deserve her tears. Not her father. Not Bastien.

She listened at the door to make sure Bastien had really left. When she was convinced she was alone in the house, she left quickly, setting the alarm.

She didn't drive to her hotel. She headed down to Boca Raton. She didn't even know if that's where her mother was staying anymore. Mikelina just knew she didn't want to run into Bastien, and she wasn't ready to face Kirk with her failure to see the bachelor party through to the end.

CHAPTER TWENTY-ONE

BASTIEN TOSSED HIS keys on the dining room table of the beach house and slumped with his head in his hands. How did this go from the best week of his life to the worst? He'd lost his sister's fiancé. He'd lost the woman of his dreams. And now he was going to have to call Kitty before he called the police to report a missing person and let her know that Jace and his crew could be in Cuba right now for all he knew.

This was a disaster.

But what truly hurt was Mikelina. Pulling out his cell phone, he opened up the private investigator's report, hoping that the information would have changed. But it hadn't. The owner of the beach house was Mikelina Presley.

The reason why her stuff was in the attic was this was her house. It used to be her parents' place, but that was before Tanner Presley screwed a lot of people out of a lot of money and Tawny Presley decided to cut bait and screw around with real estate mogul Kirk Diamonte. It only stood to reason that Mikelina was in the market for a rich husband, too, to help pay the taxes on the beach house. Whether it was him or Jace, he wasn't sure.

He laughed without humor. He must be a magnet for gold diggers. The funny thing was, though, if she sold the damned house, she'd have more money than he did. And what really hurt was if he hadn't found out she'd been chatting up Jace, Bastien probably would have married her within the year. He was that head over heels in love with her.

He tried not to think of how her eyes filled with tears or how her lips trembled when they fought. He refused to feel guilty about it. She had lied to him. If she really wasn't like her father, she would have told him the truth about where that asshole Jace was and that Jace had been talking to her more than he'd been talking to Kitty these last few days.

A loud thump from upstairs caught his attention. Then seconds later, another thump came as if the other proverbial shoe had dropped.

"Jace?" he called.

It seemed too good to be true, but it was too quiet to be him and the groomsmen. The alarm had been set, so an intruder seemed unlikely. Maybe it was Mikelina? Maybe she hadn't left yet.

Bastien swallowed hard. Did he even want to see her? He crept up the stairs, still not sure of the answer, but he was leaning toward yes. He should have let her explain why she lied to him and kept Jace's location a secret. Not to mention, she let him think she was a homeless waif living from paycheck to paycheck in crappy hotels. He had been worried about her, damn it.

When he reached the common room, he heard creaking noises coming from Jace's bedroom. No. Hell no. It couldn't be. He wouldn't be dumb enough to bring a hooker or stripper back here. But Bastien recognized the rhythmic cadence of bedsprings and when Jace let out a low moan, Bastien saw red. What if he was with Mikelina?

Bastien kicked the door open.

"You son of a bitch. I'll kill you." It felt good to have a direction for the rage and sorrow he felt. He barely registered the two bodies diving for cover. Striding into the room, he reached for Jace.

"Bastien, you prick!"

He blinked as Kitty clutched the bedsheet to her naked body.

"Get out! You're ruining my honeymoon."

Bastien hurried out of the room and slammed the door. There was not enough brain bleach in the world to cleanse his eyes of that sight.

What the hell was Kitty doing here?

What the hell did she mean, honeymoon?

His phone buzzed. He looked down and saw a text message from his sister.

Get out. Don't come back until 8.

At eight o'clock on the dot, Bastien came back into the house to find that Zack, Shane and Max were also there. As well as all of Kitty's bridesmaids. Well, why not? Dance music was playing at a normal volume and everyone was sitting around the pool while

Jace grilled up what looked like all the food in the refrigerator.

Kitty was lounging in the chair with a drink in one hand and taking cell phone pictures with the other. "You need to learn to knock," she said, taking his picture.

He flipped her the bird.

He noticed she was wearing the larimar jewelry that Mikelina had sent her. A pang of hurt lanced through him and he flopped down into the chair next to her. Snagging her drink, he drained it in one long gulp.

"I never want to see his skinny ass like that again." Bastien pointed to Jace.

"Works for me, bro," Jace said and flipped a few burgers.

Max came over with the bottle of Gentlemen Jack and a bottle of Coke. He even brought over a glass for Bastien and filled it with the whiskey.

"Don't you dare," he said to Max when he went to pour the soda on top.

"I'll have some of that," Kitty said, having him top her whiskey off.

"I taught you better than that," Bastien said. "Use the regular Jack Daniels if you're going to do that."

"It's my honeymoon and I'll drink what I want," Kitty said primly.

"About that…" Bastien started and then took a deep pull of his drink. "What the absolute fuck is going on and why are you and the girls here?"

"Jace and I eloped." She showed him her wedding

ring. "I couldn't take all the bullshit from the wedding planner and the pressure to have everything perfect, so I said screw it and flew out here and kidnapped Jace."

"That's where he's been the last three days? You could have told me. I've just spent the past few days trying to hunt him down. I even hired a private detective." Who told Bastien more than he'd ever wanted to know about the woman he had been planning on getting serious with.

Bastien rubbed his hand over his face. "Does Mom know?"

"Not yet. I mean, she knows I flew out for my bachelorette party. She just doesn't know there was a change of plans. I know how much that makes you crazy." She patted his arm. "But it just seemed like the right thing to do."

"Mom and Dad paid a lot of money for your wedding."

"Yeah, it's the wedding of their dreams. I barely had a say in it. Don't worry. We'll still show up and go through the costume party. Now, I feel like I can relax because all the important stuff has been taken care of."

"Why didn't you tell me? I would have liked to have been there for the actual ceremony."

"It was a quick civil ceremony on the beach in Key West. It lasted all of five minutes and then we partied the night away before coming back here this morning. Mikelina arranged everything. I don't know what I would have done without her."

"What?" Bastien choked on his drink.

"Yeah, I invited her to come over tonight to help us celebrate."

"Here? Tonight?" Bastien couldn't suppress the happy leap his stupid heart took. He wanted to see her and talk about all of this. He had jumped to the wrong conclusions and he should have taken a step back and listened to her. He hoped she could forgive him.

"You can't get mad at her."

Too late.

"I asked her to keep all of this a secret from you. She didn't want to do it, but I begged her."

"Why?"

"I was afraid that you would tell Mom or Dad and that they would try to stop us."

"You're adults. They can't stop you."

"Yeah, well, I didn't want to hear it. I just wanted to let loose and have fun. Do you even remember what that's like?"

"I remember," he said hoarsely.

"But that's not the best part. She sold us this house." Kitty gestured all around her. "Can you believe it? This is our house." She got up and threw herself at Jace.

Holy shit. Why hadn't Mikelina told him? Why did she let him rant and rail at her without defending herself? She hadn't lied. She wasn't the owner anymore. It had been Kitty and Jace. The private investigator had old information, probably because the deal was going down as he was gathering information. Bastien had jumped to all the wrong conclusions. He had let what Gina had done to him color how he saw Mikelina and that wasn't right at all.

He needed to talk to her. But when he texted her, the message never delivered and when he dialed her number, it just kept ringing. She'd blocked his number. He couldn't blame her.

"Bastien, what's wrong?"

"I made a terrible mistake."

"Is it about Mikelina?" Kitty asked.

Bastien gave her a sharp look. "Why do you think it has anything to do with her?"

"Jace mentioned that you and Mikelina were getting pretty close these past few weeks."

"Jace should mind his own damn business," Bastien said.

"Says the man who burst into my bedroom." Jace brought them over a plate of grilled sausages and shrimp.

Bastien wasn't hungry, but Kitty dug in like she hadn't eaten in weeks.

While he had been waiting for eight o'clock to roll in, he had driven around South Beach hoping to catch sight of Mikelina. He had even parked outside her hotel, but he hadn't seen her car.

"It seems weird that she's not here. Unless she's avoiding you for some reason," Kitty said.

Bastien nodded. "She is. And she has good reason."

"What did you do now, you prick?"

"I messed up and I don't know how to fix it."

CHAPTER TWENTY-TWO

SURPRISINGLY ENOUGH, her mother was home when Mikelina got there. Tawny and Aunt Crystal were playing cards while Fox News blasted in the background. They dealt her in while she discreetly switched to the History Channel.

"Your mother tells me that you sold the beach house," Crystal said, putting down a set of threes. She was a shark at gin rummy.

"It was time."

"You're telling me. Now Tawny doesn't have to shack up with that Diamonte guy."

"What if I want to shack up with him?" Her mother laid down a straight.

"Ew," Mikelina said. She could only lay down a three. She wasn't really paying attention to the cards.

"Shouldn't you be at that bachelor party's beck and call?" Tawny asked, looking at her critically.

Mikelina was pretty sure her mother knew she had been crying. "I'm done. They're the new owners of the house. Their itineraries are set. It's over."

"It doesn't seem to be over," her mother said.

"Trust me. It is. Lots of doors closing for me lately. I told you what Dad said."

"Your father is a selfish jerk. Don't give him a second thought."

"Easy for you to say, Tawny," Crystal said. "You can get a new husband. It's not like she can get a new daddy."

"I don't need a new daddy, Aunt Crystal," Mikelina broke in before a brawl started. "I don't need a man in my life at all."

"Oh," her mother and her aunt said at the same time.

"What's that supposed to mean?" Mikelina asked suspiciously.

"Who is he?" Tawny asked. "Do we need to get involved?"

"No. It's over. He's going back to New York and I'm…" Well, that was the hell of it, wasn't it? She didn't know where she was going to go. New York had seemed like the right decision until Bastien turned out to be a bastard. With the house sold, she didn't need to be in South Beach as the concierge. Maybe she could find another city to become an expert in.

Somewhere the last name Presley made people think of The King instead of her father.

"You're what, dear?"

"I'm waiting for my next assignment."

"I'm sure Kirk will have something for you soon. Gin!" Her mother laid down all her cards in glee.

Aunt Crystal threw hers on the table in disgust. "You guys distracted me. And who changed the channel? I was watching the news."

Mikelina rolled her suitcase into the condo in Maui that she was sharing with Selena. Selena was busy at the client's house, cooking a romantic dinner for two.
Must be nice.

After stowing her clothes in the spare bedroom, Mikelina powered up her laptop and brought up the email Kirk had sent her about what the couple wanted to do this week. It wasn't like him not to dish about who they were and what potential scandals to avoid. It was a last-minute arrangement and Kirk couldn't get his usual Hawaii concierges to step up. She was a little nervous because Maui wasn't her area of expertise, but she did know a few people and Selena said she would hook her up with some of her contacts, too.

Mikelina was grateful because she just had to get out of Florida. The pain of Bastien's condemnation of her hit harder than she wanted to admit. She fell in love with the big jerk and that was on her. But he judged her for her father's actions and that was on him.
Focus.

She stared back at the wish list and saw that the couple wanted the usual Hawaiian things. She booked them a snorkeling tour of Molokini. Of course, her mind went straight back to Bastien making love to her in the dressing room after they went snorkeling.

Groaning, she got up and took a bottle of POG from the fridge. The papaya, orange and guava juice was sweet and refreshing and helped her get back on task. The happy couple also wanted a fishing trip and she booked them on a party boat, forcing the image of her and Bastien catching fish together.

Finally, she booked them an authentic Hawaiian luau and that didn't bring up any memories for her at all. Her text message alert sounded and her heart jumped in her chest, but of course it wasn't Bastien. It was her mother.

The divorce was going to be final in six months.

Tawny was going to marry Kirk in a civil ceremony and she wanted Mikelina as the maid of honor and to plan the bachelorette party.

Mikelina closed her eyes. It shouldn't be this hard. She decided to hold off on texting her mother until she could agree to do it with a clear conscience. Her father chose his path in life and made his decisions and was now living with the consequences of his actions. There would never be a beach house reunion. That house was slated for happy memories with another family.

Her father would never again toss a quarter in the pool so she could dive for it, while her mother blended up piña coladas and Celia Cruz played over the speakers. Those people didn't exist anymore.

It was time that they all got on with their lives. Maybe once her mother did, other people who weren't affected by Tanner's crimes would be able to as well. Tawny would become Tawny Diamonte and her new life would begin.

Mikelina would still be Mikelina Presley—no relation to Elvis, but daughter of Tanner Presley, the crook.

Maybe she'd ask Kirk to adopt her. Mikelina Diamonte sounded pretty flashy.

She closed her laptop with a snap and checked her watch. The couple should be arriving at the client's house in another hour and she wanted to be there to greet them and show them around the house. Mikelina had only represented this house once and she wanted to familiarize herself with it so she sounded confident. Besides, she could help Selena in the kitchen and maybe sample some of the dinner she was making.

She was looking forward to spending some quality time with Selena and a lot of mai tais. They could take in a luau, too. Mikelina had never been to one, but it sounded like fun.

The house wasn't on the ocean. It was more up-country, but the views were incredible, and it was only a short drive to the beach. It was attached to a coffee plantation, very private and secluded. As she pulled into the driveway, Mikelina felt a pang of envy. It was the perfect escape from civilization, with all the comforts of home.

"Smells good in here," Mikelina called out, her stomach growling. Whatever was simmering in the kitchen beat the hell out of airplane food and the bag of chips she had grabbed for lunch.

The small dining room table was set with shining silverware and porcelain china on a lace tablecloth.

"Fancy," she murmured, admiring the plumeria pattern on the china.

A bottle of Perrier-Jouët Rosé was wedged in among the ice in the bucket. Mikelina swallowed hard. When would everything stop reminding her of Bastien?

The kitchen was empty and she couldn't resist peeking into the slow cooker on the counter.

"It's kalua pork," a deep voice said behind her. "Selena wanted me to apologize that she used a Crock-Pot instead of an underground oven, but we did kind of throw this together at the last minute."

Not believing her ears, she whirled around. "Bastien?"

He handed her a plumeria blossom. She couldn't resist sticking her nose inside it while she recovered. The smell was light and beautiful and for some reason she wanted to run away and cry.

"What are you doing here?" she whispered.

"Apologizing. I told you I was a prick."

This couldn't be happening. Mikelina turned her back on him and wiped her eyes with the back of her hand. She didn't want him to see her crying. She trembled when his warm hands touched her shoulders.

"I was a jerk. My head was so far up my own ass, I couldn't see clearly. I was pissed off about Jace. I thought I was over Gina's betrayal. And I really fell hard for you. None of which I was expecting or dealing with like a rational adult."

Mikelina gasped. She couldn't have heard that correctly. Fell hard? They were great in bed and enjoyed each other, but she could have sworn that the falling-in-love part had been one-sided.

"Can you forgive me for being an asshole?"

"It's all right," she said, her voice catching as she tried to get a hold of herself.

"It's not all right." He gently turned her to face him. "But I'm hoping it will be. I'm sorry I hurt you. I was wrong to jump to conclusions. Believe me when I say, Kitty has already read me the riot act about that. I was an idiot to think you were like Gina. I know in my heart you're not and could never be like her or your father."

Mikelina blew out a shaky breath. "What makes you so sure now?"

He brushed away a stray tear with his thumb. "I was sure then, I just was too blinded by hurt and rage to see it. And I took it out on you."

"You really hurt me," she said. "I let my guard down around you. I thought I was safe and then it was my worst nightmare."

"I'm so sorry. Will you give me a chance to regain that trust?"

Mikelina hugged herself. She wanted to. Every fiber in her being wanted to. But she knew if he hurt her again, she might not recover from it. "I don't know."

"Give me these two weeks?"

Her head came up. "What?"

"You and I are the couple Kirk sent you here to be a concierge for."

Blinking, she realized that should have been obvious the moment Bastien had stepped in the kitchen. "Give me a minute. My brain is trying to catch up here."

"All I could think of during the bachelor party was how I would much rather spend the time with you, getting to know you better than spending it with Jace and his groomsmen. I'm not the type to believe in love at first sight, but damn, Mikelina, I've never felt this way about anyone. Ever. Will you stay with me? Here, for the next two weeks and see if we want to take this to the next level?"

"Bastien, I can't just leave my job for two weeks."

"Yes, you can. I cleared it with Kirk. Two weeks paid vacation."

She gaped at him. "What about you? You'll be away from your job for over a month?"

"My dad owns the company. And I'm owed a lot of vacation time. Besides, we had scheduled a light month because of Kitty's wedding anyway. Bottom line, though? You are more important than any of that. What we have? This connection? This explosive passion? It's worth exploring. Please say you agree."

"Bastien, I'm overwhelmed."

"Well, let's start with lunch then. It would be a shame to let the pork go to waste. There's even some jasmine rice in the rice cooker already made. We can save the champagne for later, when there's something to celebrate."

"Selena's pork is something to celebrate," Mikelina said, her insides shaky and raw. She slid her hand into Bastien's and gripped it.

"Let me make it up to you. I want to be in your life. We can work out the details as they come up. But right now, I need to kiss you more than I need to breathe. Is that—"

Mikelina didn't want to talk right now. She wanted to be in his arms and feel his mouth on her again. She wanted to make love in every room in this house and then, and only then, indulge in Selena's romantic dinner.

She was dimly aware of Bastien carrying her into the bedroom. But once they were there, they tore off each other's clothing until they pressed against each other skin to skin.

"Missed this. Missed you," he moaned, kissing down her neck to her nipples. "I'm not sure if I can go slow this time."

"Feel how wet I am," Mikelina said, grabbing his cock and guiding it through the folds of her pussy.

"Works for me." And with a quick thrust, he was deep inside her.

"Yes," she groaned, her toes digging into the bedspread.

Bastien fucked her with long, sweet strokes that seemed to go deeper every time he rocked against her.

She laughed in delight as she wrapped her legs around his waist. Mikelina was afraid this wasn't real, that she was still sleeping on the overnight flight to Maui. But the hard pounding of his body against hers was too thrilling to sleep through. She grabbed his ass, probably leaving half moons from her fingernails.

Yes, he had been a dick and jumped to conclusions. And yes, he hurt her with his careless words and attitude. But he was here, and he had been spontaneous to arrange all of this last minute. It had to mean that he cared for her, that he was as head over heels in love with her as she was with him.

Rolling over, she pushed him on his back so she could take over the pace. Bastien tugged on her bouncing nipples as she rode him hard. His hands clamped down hard on her ass and she arched in pleasure.

She could see out the sliding glass doors into the vast plains of Upcountry Maui and off in the distance, a sliver of blue and then the great looming of the volcanos. It was exotic and erotic and this felt like both a vacation and coming home.

"Bastien," she whispered.

"Come for me, my love. I want to feel you shake apart."

Her nipples pebbled harder at his deep, husky voice and the look of adoration in his eyes. She could forgive him quite a lot if he kept making her feel like she was the only woman in the world.

Pleasure sparked through her at his guttural moan. "Better hurry, because I'm going to go off any second," he said.

"Yes," she breathed, shivering in excitement. "I want to feel you. Every inch."

He sat up, but his arms forced her to stay where she was, riding on top of him with him deep inside her. She came as he was tongue kissing her, and she rocked herself into oblivion. He jerked and moaned and shuddered, but he never stopped kissing her.

EPILOGUE

Six months later

MIKELINA WAS STILL recovering from the bachelorette party, having flown in on a red-eye from New Orleans to make sure all the arrangements at the church and reception hall were perfect for her mother's special day.

Originally, Tawny and Kirk wanted to get married by a justice of the peace in City Hall, but somehow over the last six months her mother's pretty beige suit had warped into an epic lace wedding dress with a cathedral-length train, and the wedding had become *the* event to go to in South Beach.

Mikelina couldn't wait until it was all over and Kirk and Tawny were settled in at the beach house for their honeymoon. It was the last rental that the place would have before it turned over to the new owners, Jace and Kitty Benjamin.

The good news was that Mikelina wouldn't have to say goodbye forever to the house and all its wonderful memories. She was still dating Bastien and she imagined that they would be able to convince Jace and Kitty to let them borrow it from time to time. The bedroom off the kitchen was no longer her bedroom in her mind, but her and Bastien's. And that was a memory that she would treasure forever.

"Is my veil on straight?" Tawny asked her.

"You look beautiful, Mom."

"I'm doing the right thing, aren't I?" Tawny gripped her arms and looked frantic.

"I think it's a little late to be asking this now, but…" Mikelina took in a deep breath. "Yeah, I think you chose a good one." Kirk adored Tawny and he was an honest businessman who cared about his family and his community.

Tanner Presley was going to be in jail for at least another five years before he was eligible for parole. It was time for all of them to realize that their lives had been forever changed. Mikelina only hoped her father would learn something and work toward absolution in his new future.

"Okay, they're playing our song," Mikelina said as the "Wedding March" started. Tawny had wanted her to walk her down the aisle.

Kirk had the aisle strewn with purple rose petals because they were her mother's favorite. Blinking back tears, Tawny smiled at all their friends and family. Mikelina's gaze snagged on Bastien who was looking delicious in another custom-tailored suit. She felt herself blush at the carnal, possessive look he gave her.

The passion between them hadn't faded yet and

Mikelina thought she would always want him as desperately as she did the first night in the club. It was nice not to hide who she was anymore, but it was even better to realize that she wasn't defined by her father's crimes, and anyone who wanted to paint her with the same brush didn't deserve her time or attention.

The ceremony was short and sweet and after Kirk kissed his bride, the entire congregation got a surprise when Christian Dibiasi came out and played his latest hit for the bride and groom to dance back down the aisle to.

Selena gripped her arm when they were leaving the church. "Please tell me you can introduce me to him," she said.

"I think I can arrange that." Mikelina knew Selena had a huge crush on the musician. After everything Selena had done for her, it was the least she could do to make Selena's dream come true.

Speaking of dreams coming true, waiting outside the church was Bastien. He picked her up and whirled her around.

"What was that for?" she laughed, hanging on for dear life.

"I love you, that's what it's for."

Mikelina hugged him tight. "I love you, too."

"I got something for you," he said, but he was interrupted by the loud beeping of Kirk's Cadillac as it pulled away from the church trailing tin cans and scrawled with happy messages.

She reached down and, as discreetly as she could, palmed Bastien's cock. "Does it involve a limo?"

"It could," he said, taking her hand away. He pressed a kiss to her knuckles and then got down on one knee.

"Bastien," she gasped.

"Wait! Shit! Wait!" Kitty came running over to them. "Damn these stupid heels. Hold up." She had her phone out and was taking pictures. "Mom and Dad wanted me to film this, but I can't figure out the camera."

"Buzz off, squirt," Bastien said.

"Come on," Jace said, guiding his wife away. "We can stage a proposal for the parents later. Let Bastien have his moment."

"Maybe he's not such a douchebag after all," Bastien said when they were out of earshot. "Anyway, back to us." He cleared his throat. "Mikelina Presley, would you do me the honor of becoming my wife?"

Mikelina forgot to breathe. She had just moved to New York to be closer to him. She was working in a boutique hotel in Manhattan and was considering moving in with Bastien. She'd never even suspected he was going to propose. Of course, they had been spending every waking minute together and most of the sleeping ones, too.

"Are you sure?" she squeaked. "Won't my father damage your reputation?"

"I don't care if he does. I want you as my wife. I didn't think I would ever remarry. I didn't think I would want anyone to be as close to me as you are.

But I've liked you from the moment I first read your emails. When I heard your voice for the first time, I wanted you in my bed. And once I had that, I never wanted to let you go. Be my wife?"

"Yes. Yes, of course."

He got up and whirled her around again. "I hope you don't mind being late for the reception."

Waving his hand, Bastien gave her a smoldering look as a limousine pulled up to the curb.

"No one will notice if we're a few minutes late," she said as he slipped a diamond engagement ring on her finger. It was a marquise cut that reflected the sunshine and she was momentarily dazzled by it and by the handsome man beside her.

"It's going to be more than a few minutes," he growled in her ear. "I want you wearing nothing but that ring."

"Sounds like a plan I can definitely get behind." She bumped him with her hip as she climbed into the limo.

* * * * *

COMING SOON!

We really hope you enjoyed reading this book.
If you're looking for more romance, be sure to
head to the shops when new books are
available on

Thursday 23rd
July

To see which titles are coming soon, please visit

millsandboon.co.uk/nextmonth

MILLS & BOON

LET'S TALK

Romance

For exclusive extracts, competitions and special offers, find us online:

f facebook.com/millsandboon

🐦 @MillsandBoon

📷 @MillsandBoonUK

Get in touch on 01413 063232

For all the latest titles coming soon, visit
millsandboon.co.uk/nextmonth